KH

LINDSAY McKENNA

NEVER SURRENDER

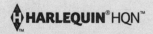

ISBN-13: 978-0-373-77882-9

NEVER SURRENDER

Copyright © 2014 by Nauman Living Trust

This edition published by arrangement with Harlequin Books S.A.

For questions and comments about the quality of this book, please contact us at CustomerService@Harlequin.com.

Printed in U.S.A.

Dear Reader,

Never Surrender is one of the most powerful books I've written. The last one in this vein was *Morgan's Wife,* a Morgan's Mercenaries saga novel about Laura Trayhern.

With our women having been in combat for well over ten years, on a shifting "front line" that no longer exists in today's wars, we have lost 150 of our military women. Most people don't know that, but as a veteran myself, I stay up on our women who volunteer and sacrifice for their country right alongside the men. All of them are heroes and heroines in my eyes and heart.

This is the sequel to *Breaking Point* (Harlequin HQN, May 2014), and part of the Shadow Warriors series, where men and women are in combat side by side. You met Gabe Griffin, U.S. Navy SEAL, and Baylee Ann Thorn, U.S. Navy corpsman.

You followed their progress within Gabe's SEAL platoon, stationed at Camp Bravo in Afghanistan. I wanted to explore some of the possible issues that would automatically occur when a lone woman is ushered into an all-male SEAL team. To say the least, Bay was not welcomed, but she was assigned a mentor, Gabe Griffin, and he helped her seed into the platoon over time.

The love that blossomed between Gabe and Bay was powerful. *Breaking Point* has that title for good reason. These characters impacted me more than most I've written about. I rarely write sequels and do it only when they grab me by the heart and I just simply cannot part with them. I want to know the "rest of their story" and end up penning a second book about their ongoing lives and love with one another.

Never Surrender is gritty, edgy and an intensely powerful story about love transcending trauma. And it is love that gets us through everything in our lives, whether the issue facing us is large or small. I don't know how many times, while at the computer keyboard, that I cried while writing this book. I'm a sop anyway, and it's not unusual, because in order to write at the emotional depth that I do, I have to feel the same emotions my characters do.

In the end, this book is about the incredible power of love to meet any adversity, the love between a man and a woman. And love is the greatest healing emotion we have in our world.

Warmly,

Lindsay McKenna
www.LindsayMcKenna.com

To our military women who are in combat around the world. Thank you for your service, courage, honor and your sacrifice for all of us. Being a warrior is in the heart and spirit of the person. Love of our country, wanting to fight for it, being a patriot has no gender. Hooyah.

CHAPTER ONE

WAS HE TOO LATE? Navy SEAL Chief Gabe Griffin jogged through Lindbergh International Airport in San Diego, California. He was hurrying to meet his fiancée, Baylee-Ann Thorn, who was supposed to have just landed. Dressed in his desert cammies, dirty and sweaty, he'd just barely made it onto a Black Hawk helicopter to catch a lift directly to the airport. His platoon, part of SEAL Team 3, had been up in the scrub brush of southern California mountains undergoing compass and map training. Lucky for him, Chief Doug Hampton had given him the next seven days off.

Focused and weaving through the crowds, he took the escalator two steps at a time, barely breathing hard. He knew people, civilians, were looking at him, startled as he swiftly and silently moved past them. As a SEAL, he prided himself on the fact that no one, especially not his enemy, would ever hear him coming until it was too late.

His green eyes narrowed as he hit the top of the escalator. He knew which security area Bay would be coming out of, and he slowed his pace, circling to the left of the security departure exit. This was the same one he'd met her at six months earlier when she was coming out of Afghanistan. Bay had been in a firefight three days earlier, taken a bullet to her Kevlar vest and had been injured. As he thought back to last Christmas, he remembered how the airport had been flooded with holiday travelers. Gabe had found an empty wall near the outlet where all departing passengers would walk past. He chose the same spot once again.

Today, June first, the crowds were a lot lighter, less noisy, with less bumping and jostling. Glancing down at his Rolex, he saw her plane should have already landed. It was five in the evening. He took off his black baseball cap and distractedly ran his long fingers though his short, dark hair. His gaze never left the opening.

There were floor to ceiling windows through which he could easily spot Bay. God, had it been three months since he'd seen her. Their last time together, he'd managed a three-day weekend break from his platoon training, hopped a flight out of NAS Coronado to Washington, D.C., where Bay had been anxiously waiting for him.

Now, swallowing hard, Gabe leaned against the wall, his hands resting on his hips, waiting. Just waiting. He was anxious to see Bay, hold her, kiss her, love her until they were both senselessly wrapped in euphoria. It would be heaven and hell. Heaven that she'd be once more in his arms and he could love her. Hell because in ten days he would be saying goodbye to her as she deployed one last time to Afghanistan for six long, dangerous months. There, she'd get ordered into one of the black ops groups.

Gabe was praying it would be a SEAL team, which is where he had met her almost sixteen months earlier. SEALs always took the fight to the enemy. They weren't like the Army Special Forces guys, who had a very different strategy agenda. Bay would be safer with the SEAL teams. Plus, Gabe would make their engagement known to the platoon over at Camp Bravo, an FOB, forward operating base, so brother SEALs would watch and protect her.

Sweat dribbled down his temples, and he wiped it away with his long, large-knuckled fingers. Where was Bay? Damn, he ached to see her. There was no question their love was strong and steady. It had only gotten better with time.

Gabe anxiously watched the security area. People were starting to filter out from another flight that had just arrived. He felt his cell phone vibrate. His heart leaped as he dug into his cammie pocket for it. Lifting up his iPhone, he saw a text message from Bay. His heart galloped in his chest, and his fingers trembled as he read the words:

I'm home.

God, did Bay realize she *was* his home? Gabe couldn't conceive of life without her being in it.

In the thirty years of his life, she was the best thing that had ever happened to him. And in the dark recesses of his mind, Gabe pushed away his fear. After all, Bay was a vaunted 18 Delta medic, the only woman in the military to be given access to that world-class course and who had passed it with flying colors. Bay would give her life for another in a heartbeat. And that worried Gabe.

Wiping his sweaty hands down the sides of his dusty cammies, Gabe felt as if he was going to burst with impatience. The joke was, he was a respected SEAL sniper, who had patience to burn. *Not today. Not now.*

Where was Bay? He loved her so damned much, it hurt. Gabe had never known what real love was until he'd met Bay. She was so damned unassuming and down-to-earth humble. She never spoke about herself or her many accomplishments. All she wanted to do was serve and stop people from suffering. In the four months she'd been with his SEAL team at Camp Bravo, he'd seen her unselfishly devote herself sixteen hours a day to helping others at the medical dispensary. If she wasn't with the SEALs on a patrol or a mission, she was at the dispensary at Bravo, helping the beleaguered doctors and nurses with shot-up Special Forces, Marines or Rangers being choppered in to be stabilized by them. At Shinwari Afghan villages, Bay worked from dawn to dusk, holding medical clinics for girls and women. How many lives had she saved? Improved? Gabe knew it was a high, unaccounted number.

Where was Bay?

Even his sniper patience was failing him as he searched for the woman he loved with a quiet desperation.

Bay!

Gabe instantly straightened, hands dropping to his sides, his heart a staccato beat. He watched her coming up the slight incline, her medical rucksack, probably weighing close to sixty-five pounds, on her back. Bay was tall, five feet ten inches, with a sturdy frame. Lean and moving gracefully, she had her softly curled light brown hair pulled back into a ponytail. She wore Navy cammies of blue, gray and brown. He took the precious seconds to simply absorb her into his wildly beating heart. This woman loved him. She couldn't wait to see him.

A crowd began to gather around the opening to security that spilled out into the escalator area. Gabe hung back, not wishing to push and shove to meet her. He instantly became worried as he saw purple shadows beneath Bay's large, beautiful blue eyes. There was strain at the corners of her full lips, too. The final test on her medical training had been a son of a bitch. You didn't get to become an 18 Delta medic unless you could save lives out in the middle of combat. Had she passed? Gabe was sure she had. But the look of exhaustion was clearly etched in Bay's face. Even her cheeks, which usually had a soft pink color to them, were pale. *Damn*.

Moving to the side of the plastic window, near the security opening, Gabe watched her turn and look straight at him, as if she sensed his presence. His mouth pulled into a wide grin of hello. Bay's face lit up, as if suddenly consumed by sunshine. Every cell in his tense body clamored for her. His arms ached to hold this courageous and very brave woman once again. The tiredness disappeared, and a flush appeared across her high cheekbones. She picked up her stride.

Within seconds, Bay was beyond the security area, and he opened his arms to her.

"Gabe!"

In seconds, Bay dropped her ruck and threw herself into his welcoming arms. She fell against him, her arms sliding around his broad shoulders, her face pressed against his. Gabe took her full weight. At six foot tall, lean and toughened by continued training, he laughed, his face tickled by her curly hair. "God, it's good to see you again, baby." He felt her turn her head toward him, her lips hungrily seeking his.

All sounds disappeared around Gabe as he curved his mouth hotly over Bay's smiling lips. He tasted coffee and chocolate on them, inhaled her feminine, womanly scent along with the jasmine soap that she loved to wash her body with. He felt her breasts pressed solidly against his chest, felt her sharp, shallow breath as they clung to one another. Their kiss so deep, so needy, that he didn't care if he ever came up for air.

"I love you," she whispered in a trembling voice, her throat tight with unshed tears of joy.

Seeing tears glistening in her eyes, Gabe cupped Bay's face, staring down at her, inhaling her, absorbing her as if he was the thirstiest sponge in the world. "Now, you're not going to cry on me, are you, baby?" Gabe couldn't stand to see a woman or child cry. It tore him up, and he felt so damned helpless to fix it or stop it. A woman's weeping actually cut his heart in two. Gabe didn't know why, but it had always been that way with him. Maybe the day his alcoholic father had swung at his mother, her terror-filled scream hurting his ears, had triggered that reaction in him.

Bay gulped several times, trying not to cry. But dammit, he felt his own eyes grow hot with tears, too.

Laughing through the tears streaming down her face, Bay shook her head. "Fool. You think I can't cry because I missed you so darned much? And look at you! What's that I see in your eyes, Griffin?"

It wasn't good to see a SEAL crying. Gabe couldn't help himself as he fought against the tears. He took a couple of deep breaths, using the sniper control he had over his body to push them down deep inside himself. "Mine are gone," he noted, a slow grin crawling across his mouth. "Yours aren't."

"I'll darn well cry if I want to, Griffin. I missed you so much!" Bay leaned up, taking his mouth, tasting him fully, her tongue moving boldly, teasingly against his.

Groaning, Gabe pulled her away, feeling himself going hard. This wasn't the time or place for this kind of obvious affectionate display. Not in the middle of a civilian airport, of all things. "Let's get your duffel bag down at Baggage?" he suggested, helping her pull the ruck off the deck and slinging it over his shoulder. Gabe saw the gleam in her eyes, knowing how happy and relieved Bay was to see him.

"Okay, let's rock it out, Frogman." She flashed him a wickedly playful look, her arm curving around his waist.

He grinned and slid his arm around her shoulders,

holding her close, and he teased, "Is that my new pet nickname you've given me?" All SEALs were frogmen. Gabe loved it when she was playful. He didn't see that side of Bay very often because of the deadly business they were in.

"It is when you've clearly got teenage hormones out of control down below." She gave a significant but quick look down toward his crotch. Luckily, cammies were bulky and hid everything about a person's body. No one could actually see he had an erection. But she knew his body intimately. No doubt, she could feel it when he'd kissed her earlier.

Her smile widened as she saw his cheeks grow a dusky red. "Why, you're blushing, Gabe. First time I've ever seen you do that. What a bad boy you are. Good thing your team isn't here. They'd railroad you into the ground on this one." She laughed heartily. SEALs took no prisoners when they teased one another. It was a merciless blood sport.

"Woman, you need to be tamed down a little," he growled, taking the escalator with her at his side.

"Mmm, I'm more than ready, Frogman. I like swimming with the sharks."

She was testy, flippant and God he loved her. Those lips of hers could crack rocks open, they were so lush and hot. They sure as hell cracked him wide open down to his soul in the best of ways. "Well, we'll do a little swimming all right," he challenged her, a warning glint in his eyes. "We'll see who comes up for air first." SEALs could easily hold their breath under water for three minutes or longer.

As he tipped her head back, giving her a swift kiss, Bay's husky laughter filled his heart. Still, those purple shadows beneath her eyes bothered him. She had to be exhausted. Tonight, he'd be gentle and tender with her, hugging her, loving her, welcoming her home. And then, he'd hold her in his arms throughout the night. There was nothing better than that in his world.

He became somber as they made their way into the baggage area on the first floor of the airport. "Have you gotten your orders yet?"

"Yes." Bay shrugged and frowned. "I'm being assigned to an Army Special Forces team out of Camp Bravo."

"Shit."

"I tried to change it, Gabe. I even put in a personal call to General Maya Stevenson who runs Operation Shadow Warriors at the Pentagon. I told her I'd really like to continue working with the SEAL team at Bravo." She noticed how his green eyes were filled with worry. For her. His mouth was thinned, telling her he was holding back his emotions. They halted at the carousel, waiting for her duffel bag to be spit out by the system.

"Why couldn't she change them? Is it politics?"

"Not this time around. The SF team just lost their 18 Delta medic. He was badly injured in a firefight outside the village a week ago. You know every SF team needs two medics, and they're down to one. I'll fill in for a while." Bay looked up at him, feeling his powerful sense of protection surrounding her. He was definitely fighting his anger and frustration over her assignment. She lowered her voice, and it was filled with regret. "I'm sorry, Gabe. I really am. I tried..."

He leaned down and pressed a kiss to her temple. "It's all right. You'll be okay with them." He didn't believe it himself, but he wasn't going to make her worry over something she couldn't control. SF was black ops, but not on the same level as SEALs. Their priorities and objectives were very different.

Bay could tell Gabe was lying through his teeth to her, saw it in his eyes. No SEAL in his right mind would ever think someone was okay in any other black ops team except theirs. Even though Gabe was a SEAL and they were experts at hiding how they felt, he couldn't hide his emotional reactions from her. Maybe their love opened doors between them that gave them deep, private access to one another. Bay was intuitive enough to feel his controlled anger and worry.

But Gabe wasn't angry at her. He was angry at the system. In his eyes, no one was better than Navy SEALs when it came to a gunfight. They always took the fight to the enemy, no holds barred.

"Well," he growled, "I'll contact the chief who's with that SEAL team at Bravo, then. I'll make sure they know you're my fiancée, and they will have your back." He looked down at her, his eyes hard. "They will help you, Bay. If you need anything, I want you to go to that chief of the SEAL platoon. I'll find out his name and call him myself. We won't leave you hanging out to dry if it comes down to a gunfight."

She smiled patiently, letting him blow off excess steam. She'd worked with SF teams before. If she truly believed Gabe, she'd have asked General Stevenson to retract the orders. Her experience in Iraq and Afghanistan with SF made her confident to work with them again. Bay wasn't going to try and argue the point with Gabe. It would be a useless waste of time and energy. Besides, they didn't have much time together, anyway, and she didn't want to spend it on a no-win discussion.

Bay had only six months to go before her enlistment was completed with Operation Shadow Warriors. Her time in the military would come to an end. She'd been one of the forty women volunteers for the seven-year top secret Pentagon project to see if women could handle combat. They each spent half a year with a black ops group, the reports on them being funneled back into the Pentagon and to General Stevenson. It was the general's contention women could handle combat, and so far, the stats were proving her right. Bay was proud to take part in this top secret experiment.

"Six months. It will be okay, Gabe." Bay squeezed his hand to reassure him. He didn't look reassured at all, his eyes blazing with discontent. She could feel him thinking, feel him trying to find a way to fix this. To get her out of the assignment. But it couldn't be fixed as much as he wanted.

The duffel bag fell out onto the carousel. Gabe released her and went over and hefted it across his broad shoulder. The thing weighed nearly ninety pounds, and he handled it as if it were nothing. He walked over, cupped her elbow and said, "The SUV is parked out front. Let's blow this joint."

On the way to his condo on Coronado, Bay asked, "Did you just come out of the field?"

He snorted. "Don't I look like it? Hell, I must smell pretty bad, huh?" And then he chuckled. "Yeah, we were doing nav course training up in the rocks, cactus and that damn manzanita that tears holes out of your skin the size of craters up in east San Diego County."

"Did you win the navigation course contest?"

Gabe turned and met her sparkling eyes. "It always pays to be a winner, baby."

"You did." She reached over and slid her hand across his dusty shoulder. "Congratulations."

"Thanks. I was paired with Hammer for the contest. Chief Hampton told me if the two of us won the course competition, he'd grant me my seven-day leave request to be with you." His lips drew away from his teeth. "And I sure as hell wasn't going to lose that one. Hammer hauled ass with me, and we made it through the course in record time."

Pride for him, for his being a warrior, rose in her chest. Gabe was a supremely confident man. Nothing rocked his world except her, she had discovered. He was a vaunted sniper and had killed too many Taliban to count. He'd had four rotations into Iraq and Afghanistan. Out on a patrol he was steady and reliable.

Bay had found that out several times when she was teamed with him on different missions last year. Nothing affected Gabe. Except love. Their love. And it was a miracle to Bay. She had been privileged to meet the man who was a SEAL warrior. His military demeanor took a backseat when they were alone. When she was around him, the man in all of his facets became available to her. She looked at his large, spare hands on the wheel as he drove. There were so many old and new scars all over them, she winced inwardly.

"Is that dried blood on your fingers? Did you cut yourself on that awful manzanita?"

He frowned and looked at his right hand. "Yeah, guess I did. No big deal." Hell, SEALs worked hurt all the time. They were always in pain. It was just part of their profession.

"I'll look at them when we get home."

He picked up her hand she had in her lap. "It's nothing, Bay." He squeezed her fingers. "How did the final exam go at medical training?"

"It was a mean mother," she admitted, her hand tingling with his roughened fingers around it. Touching Gabe was like touching the sun. She could feel his powerful male warmth infusing her hand, sliding up through her arm and encircling her heart and then teasingly embracing her womb. The man was so damn sexy. All he had to do was give her that smoldering look, and she began to tremble in anticipation. And when he touched her, she melted and went hot, starving for him in every possible way.

"You passed?"

"Yes."

"How many didn't?"

"Fifty percent of the class, unfortunately. It was a tough course, Gabe. Really tough. It involved women's issues, pregnancy, birthing, labor and health issues with newborns."

He smiled a little. "Right down your alley. You're a woman. You know a woman's body. Bet those guys in the class were sweating bullets."

"Some were," she admitted. "I loved the course. Every second of it. I knew how to birth a baby, but this five-month course went into just about every aspect of prenatal, natal and postnatal care, plus health issues with the baby."

"Bet you aced the test?"

It was her turn to chuckle. "I got a ninety-eight percent."

"And if I hadn't asked you about your score, you'd never have said a word about it, would you?" Bay was one of the most modest people Gabe had ever met in his life. She never bragged or spoke about what she knew or how good she was as a combat medic. The only way Gabe could drag intel out of her was to ask her many questions and then piece the answers together to get the larger picture.

Shrugging, Bay sighed. "It doesn't matter in my world, Gabe. You know that. What matters is that I'm good out in the field. I want to stop suffering. I want to ease pain."

"You are such an R.N. at heart," he teased gently.

When Bay was finished with her military duties, she wanted to go to school and become an R.N. God knew, she'd have a huge jump on the courses with her being the consummate combat medic trained by the military—18 Delta medics were the best in the world. They were the people you wanted around if you got gut shot. They were the "golden hour" to the military in harm's way. Their ability to save lives was legendary. He was so damned proud of her but, at the same time, scared to death. Bay would not hesitate a split second to put herself into the cross fire to save a man's life during a firefight. And being exposed meant she could be killed. Just like that. His hand tightened around the steering wheel, his knuckles whitening.

"Some of the guys in the course and I would go out and get pizza and a beer off base after classes. I usually ended up drilling them on techniques and quizzing them to help them pass the course." She smiled a little. "And all of them did pass."

"And that's why you have dark circles under your eyes. You burned the candle at both ends, Bay. Again."

A wry look crossed her face, and she squeezed his hand. "Now, now. You know I like to help others. It's who I am, Gabe. You love me for who I am. Not what you want me to be. Right?"

His mouth curved faintly, and he risked a glance at her in the heavy traffic heading toward the Coronado bridge. "I fell hopelessly in love with you just the way you are."

"That's what I thought. So stop gigging me about the dark circles under my eyes."

"But that doesn't mean I don't worry about you."

"One good night's sleep will take care of that."

He gave her a feral look. "Who said we're getting any sleep tonight?

CHAPTER TWO

HOME. BAY STOOD inside the door of Gabe's condo, feeling exhaustion sweep through her. He walked past her with her ruck and duffel bag, going down the hall to put them into the guest bedroom. She looked around, appreciating the quiet instrumental music in the background.

Gabe's condo was one of six in the building and he owned them all. His individual condo reflected him: spare, understated and peaceful. The blond bamboo floor shone. Furniture made of the same wood and jade cushions gave Bay a sense of infinite calm. This was where someone who wanted peace and quiet came to live.

She lifted her head as Gabe wandered back down the hall toward her. He had gotten rid of his dirty, sweaty shirt already, pulling off the tan T-shirt that stuck to him like a second skin, revealing his dark-haired chest, powerful shoulders and lean torso. Her body automatically went to burn as she followed the dark-haired line down across his belly, disappearing beneath the waistband of his trousers.

"Welcome home," he said, pulling the door closed

and then placing a light kiss on her lips. "Want to take a shower with me?"

She smiled and felt the heat coming off his body. The sweat was like an aphrodisiac to her. "That's the best offer I've had all day."

He dropped the T-shirt on the couch and grabbed her hand. "Come on, then…"

She loved his large tiled bathroom. It was huge with a glass-enclosed shower for two, plus a Jacuzzi tub in another corner. She sat down on the small chair and took off her desert combat boots, setting them aside. After yanking off her socks, she sighed and rubbed her sore, tired feet. Hot water was going to feel good on them.

She glanced up and watched Gabe lean over to remove his dusty boots. His every motion was spare and clean. As his arm muscles flexed, the corded strength of his back was highlighted, and she sighed with pleasure. The man was beautiful in every way.

Gabe straightened and opened his pants, pushing them to his ankles. Heat curled in her lower body as he shoved the cotton boxers downward, revealing his erection fully. Her throat tightened with need. Though tired, she felt a wave of lust. Want of Gabe, his hands on her, loving her, him inside her, taking her to an unknown destination together.

When he turned and walked toward her, she met his eyes and clearly saw arousal in them. "Do I get a running start?" she teased, standing and unbuttoning her blouse.

"Maybe," Gabe growled, going to the shower to

turn on the two large, round raindrop nozzles. "Do you want a head start?" he teased, closing the door and picking up two towels and setting them nearby.

"I don't think so," Bay answered, setting her blouse on the caramel-colored granite counter. She wore a silky white camisole because she hated bras. Never wore one unless she really had to. She felt his masculine warmth and looked up to see him inches away from her. He lifted his hands and tugged at her waistband, opening it.

"How tired are you, baby?"

Bay trembled beneath his gritty voice heavy with passion. "I was tired. I'm not now." He slid his hands down and around, bringing her cammie trousers across her hips and thighs. Her skin flamed wherever he grazed her as he pulled the material down and helped her step out of it. She wore silky boxer shorts, and he slowly slid his hands up the outside of her legs while he rose to his full height.

"Good," he crooned, giving her a boyish smile. He eased his fingers beneath the soft, silky material around her waist.

"Ummm." Bay sighed, her knees already growing weak. He must have sensed her instability because one hand left her silky boxers and curved gently around the small of her back to hold her steady.

He sighed. "Good having you here, having you standing so close to me, almost naked…"

His dark voice fell over her, and Bay closed her eyes, easily seduced by his hands, the soft shorts falling away from her thighs. She leaned against Gabe's powerful chest. She could smell his sweat, the scent of sagebrush and hot sunlight on his sun-darkened flesh. She wanted to move closer, but he held her away from him.

"Not yet, baby… Your camisole has to go…" And he lifted it up and over her head. As it dropped to her feet, white-hot heat plunged through his entire body. Bay was five foot ten and a large-boned woman. Her breasts were perfect and her hips wide, the kind a man could hold on to. She was in top shape, her body taut and firm.

Gabe slowly slid his hands from her proud shoulders, skimming her strong arms and finally grasping her fingers. She opened her eyes, and he smiled down at her. "You're so damned beautiful. I don't know what I did to deserve you, baby, but I'm glad you're mine. Ready to shower?"

She drowned beneath his hooded eyes that glinted with desire for her alone. Her fingers curved around his. "Let's go, Frogman…"

He chuckled and opened the door, the steam escaping momentarily from the enclosure. "You have such a way with words, woman."

The gentle water rained down upon Bay. She groaned as Gabe led her to a small seat, her hair becoming wet. In moments, he'd applied jasmine-scented shampoo throughout her hair, the fragrance swirling around in the steam surrounding them.

"Tip your head back a little," he coaxed, standing near her left shoulder, kneading the soap gently across her scalp. He saw her lips part, her eyes closed, a look of utter pleasure on her face. Gabe always wanted to see that look. He loved Bay so much. There wasn't anything he wouldn't do for her to always keep her happy.

"Ohhhh, Gabe…" Bay uttered with a sigh. "That feels so delicious…what you're doing.…" She trembled as his strong fingers wreaked relaxing magic across her scalp, the water softly drizzling warmly around her. The way he massaged her scalp, she was putty in his hands. The soreness in her shoulders disappeared. The tension she'd been carrying dissolved beneath his slow, sensual ministrations. As he took a large cup, catching the water from the showerhead and rinsing the shampoo out of her hair, Bay made a soft sound in her throat.

"I think your hair's clean now," Gabe said later, setting the cup on the shelf. When she opened her eyes, her long lashes framing those incredible blue irises, he felt himself grow even harder. It was always a balance and a matter of control on his part. He loved her, wanted to pleasure her, hear her soft, husky sounds, watch her expression melt into utter joy.

"You always come first, baby." Gabe leaned over, brushing his mouth against her wet, parted lips. A moan vibrated in the slender column of her throat, and he absorbed the happy sound into his body, his soul.

In one smooth motion, he lifted her and brought her into his arms, the raindrops surrounding them. Gabe didn't want to leave her lush mouth, meeting her tongue as it shyly danced with his. Her breasts pressed against his chest. He felt her belly taut against his erection. Easing his hand down her spine, his fingers splayed outward, cupping her hips, pulling her more tightly against him. Now, he groaned. He had to have the control and wait. But her sleek, wet body sliding against his was undoing him.

Bay eased from his mouth, stepped back and picked up a bar of soap. "My turn…" She lathered the soap between her hands and skimmed her fingers across his scalp. Next, came his hard, weathered face. Gabe rested his hands lightly on her hips, and he closed his eyes. There was such trust between them as Bay gently began to remove the dirt and sweat encrusted in his short, gleaming hair. The dirt dissolved, and she lathered more soap, tracing his deeply lined brow. A brow of a man who thought a lot, said little, but had a mind like a steel trap. Her fingertips moved lightly across his straight, black brows and feathered across his closed eyelids. She felt his hands grip her hips a little more firmly, and she smiled, wanting to give him equal pleasure.

Gabe gratefully absorbed her healer hands as they washed his face, neck, arms and chest. Every touch was building a fire within him, stoking his need for her until he wasn't sure he could last beneath her tender foray. As her soapy fingers glided toward his narrow hips, he drew in a sharp breath, clenching his teeth. Her fingers wrapped gently around him, and his entire body locked up on him. Gripping Bay, he hauled her against him. He drowned in her wide blue eyes that were filled with love for him. Her lips were parted, and she licked her lower lip. It was damned near his undoing.

"Just a little longer," she pleaded huskily. "You want to be clean, don't you?"

He sucked in a ragged breath of air, feeling her clean him slowly, thoroughly. Gabe thought he was going to lose it. Her hands skimmed his hard thighs, sliding down to his knotted calves and finally, his large feet. Every stroking touch of her fingers was healing. At every scar, Bay stopped, kissed it gently and then moved on. Gabe didn't know whether to cry or scream. No woman had ever loved him with her hands like Bay did.

The first day Gabe had met Bay, he'd noticed her long narrow hands. Her fingers were tapered and beautiful, nails blunt cut. He remembered thinking how much he'd wanted to feel her touch on him. And when he learned she was a medic, it had made even more sense to him. Healing hands. Loving hands. Compassionate hands that knew…they just knew…and Bay knew he needed this…needed her touch like this. But by every name in his book of life, Gabe couldn't stop loving her for who she simply was: a very kind, sensitive and caring woman. Who loved him.

What the hell had he done to deserve Bay? Gabe hadn't led a stellar life. It had been ugly and dysfunctional throughout his childhood. He knew abuse. He knew a man's fist, his belt lashing his flesh until it welted and bruised. He'd never known the tender touch, the loving touch that she now shared with him alone.

Bay watched all the tension drain out of Gabe's face, out of his hard body. The sexual tension that replaced it was as it should be. She washed herself as he stood beneath the streams of water, soap sloughing off him, his flesh clean and glistening. Gabe looked at her beneath hooded, burning eyes, not making a move toward her. Simply watching her.

The dark desire was evident in his eyes. And he loved her. She gave him an impish look as she approached him, placing her hands lightly on his powerful shoulders. Leaning up, she whispered in his ear, "I'm ready to swim with the sharks, Frogman…."

Her smile dazzled his senses as she eased away to see his reaction. "You're mine," he rasped, and he began a slow, sensuous path, starting with her mouth.

Bay leaned into him, the water nestling in nooks and crannies between them, liquid flowing heatedly down her body as he took possession of her mouth. At the same time, he brought her hard against him. His other hand moved toward her breast, cupping it, moving his thumb languidly across the hardened peak. She uttered a small, fierce cry into his mouth as an electric shock bolted from her nipple straight down to her womb. Her entire body convulsed.

"Easy, baby, easy," he coaxed, moving his hand even farther downward, exploring her waist, her hip.

She felt his lips leave her breast and then kiss the area between them. Gripping her hips, Gabe held her as he continued the trail of kisses down her stomach, across her abdomen. Giving a whimper, she gripped his thick shoulders as his mouth followed the crease where her thigh met her torso. Her knees shook with anticipation; she wasn't sure she could remain standing, his tongue slowly following the crease down, down, down....

"Oh, Gabe," Bay whispered, nearly crumpling if not for his steel strength holding her. Tightly shutting her eyes, her breath became ragged and shallow. He parted her, leaving her open and available.

"I can't...stand...Gabe..."

He rose swiftly. "I've got you, baby. Just let me do the heavy lifting." He gave her a heated look. "Ready to swim?"

Her heart fluttered wildly. The warm water only increased the heat already scalding her aching lower body. "Y-yes..." she whispered brokenly, her knees beginning to give way. In the next moment, she felt Gabe's arm slide beneath her thigh, and she lifted upward. He guided her legs around his waist and then gently pressed her back against the warm, wet tiles, holding her in place.

"Open your eyes," he rasped. "I want to see the look on your face when I enter you...."

Water sluiced across Bay's face in rivulets. Her body was cramping, almost painfully, wanting him inside her. She was more than ready as she barely opened her eyes, her breath uneven. His eyes were narrowed, focused solely on her. Gabe was a sniper. No one had more focus than a sniper. They sighted their quarry, and they never let it go. She was his quarry. Gulping, she whispered, "Hurry...oh, please, Gabe...."

As Gabe gently entered her, he watched her eyes

widen. It wasn't from fear but from raw, welcoming pleasure of their bodies meeting like fiery, melting flesh into one another. Slowly, so slowly, he brought her down upon him, watching the wildness come to her eyes, the yearning and then the feverish heat enter them as they fused completely into oneness. He captured the hard nipple, suckling her. It made him feel so damn good to give Bay this kind of pleasure. Her fingers spasmodically gripped his shoulders, her head moving side to side. He increased the pressure, feeling her tighten and so near climax. That was what he wanted for Bay, utter, wild sensations that only he could give her.

Thrusting quickly, he established a fiery rhythm. Gabe felt her tensing, so close to orgasm. Bay cried out, gripping him, arching into him, spinning into the heat and light as she came, a cry tearing out of her. He prolonged the rippling sensations, urging her to let go, to fully give him the gift of herself, her love. And she did. Bay leaned forward, arms around Gabe's tense shoulders, gasping for breath, sobbing.

And then, his entire body stiffened. His breath hissed between his clenched teeth, his hands tightened around hers as he released deeply into her. Bay rested her cheek against his wet shoulder, the raindrops sliding gently across her face and soaking into her hair.

Gabe dragged in air, his body quivering beneath the onslaught of his release. He steadied himself, using Bay and the wall to remain standing. Feeling her lips against his taut neck, her breath mingling with the water, he gently removed himself, holding her, easing Bay away from the wall. The water made it easy for her to slide down the length of his hard, quivering body and through his arms. Her feet touched the floor. Their brows rested against each other, noses touching, lips millimeters away from one another as they leaned against one another for support. Breathing shallow and fast, Gabe held Bay tightly in his arms, loving her fiercely. Loving her forever.

"Are you okay?" he rasped unsteadily. They hadn't made love in months. That was a hell of a long time. He was worried about her.

Bay managed a strangled laugh. She slowly raised her head, caught and held his sated gaze. "I've decided to call you Shark Man. You've graduated from being just a frogman." She gave him a drowsy, sweet smile radiant with love only for him. "Helluva swim, Shark Man..."

CHAPTER THREE

"COME HERE, BABY." Gabe hauled her into his arms as he settled into the bed. They were clean, dried off and so damned weak it had taken them leaning on one another to make it to the master bedroom together. Bay had fallen asleep immediately. Gabe felt Bay's softened breath, the warm moisture flowing across his chest as she slept deeply, her head resting in the crook of his shoulder. Her hand across his pounding heart. God, did life get any better than this? *Hell, no.*

Gabe closed his eyes, his woman in his arms, her body pressed wantonly against his, their legs entangled. Her hair was still damp, although he'd done his best to dry it off with a towel afterward. He'd seen the exhaustion in Bay's half-closed eyes and knew she had to sleep off five months of brutal training. The darkness was complete in their bedroom. Gabe felt himself begin to utterly surrender against her warmth and curves.

He lay awake for a long time, his body still vibrating with simmering heat after having made love with her. Bay's background was as a Hill person from the Allegheny Mountains of West Virginia. She was a woman of the earth, wild and completely natural. Her spontaneity was unfettered, freeing him from his dark and miserable past, infusing him with hope of a bright future. Love did incredible things for a human being, Gabe was discovering.

Closing his eyes, his arm wrapped firmly around Bay's shoulders as she slept, Gabe couldn't shut off his mind. Bay had come from a happy family, deep in the mountains, away from most of civilization. She'd lived and hunted in those mountains. Not only was she a crack shot, but her mother, Poppy, was a Hill doctor. Bay obviously got that healing gene from her. Her father, Floyd, had been a Marine Corps sniper and had started teaching her at a young age how to hunt and shoot. When her father died of Black Lung, she'd entered the Navy afterward to make money for her economically struggling family.

Moving his fingers slowly across her firm, warm flesh, he felt her inborn strength, her Hill backbone. Lowlanders, people who weren't Hill-born, would say she was backward and uneducated. Nothing could be further from the truth. Bay was simple, homespun, and had a strong sense of right and wrong. When her father had become ill, she'd picked up the family mantle of responsibility, being the oldest, to feed and care for her mother, father and her mentally challenged younger sister, Eva-Jo.

A sigh slipped between his lips as he savored the darkness embracing them. He felt Bay's hand twitch and move slightly on his chest. She was moving more deeply into a healing sleep, and that was good. His mind revolved back to her, back to her simple way of living.

When he'd met Bay last year in Afghanistan, he'd instantly felt attracted to her. It was her humbleness, the idealism she saw in others, her compassion, that called powerfully to him. In those four months of combat, they'd known they had something good between them, but they could never act upon it. Not in a combat team. Fraternization could tear a team apart. And it could get people killed. They'd cooled their heels, looked, but hadn't touched one another. And only after Bay had come home after her six-month rotation out of the combat zone, did they realize the beauty of what they held in one another. *Real love.*

Frowning, Gabe thought about how at twenty-nine he'd thought he'd known what love was. He'd married Lily after five days of sex and heat. It was the stupidest choice he'd ever made in his entire life. He was divorced before he'd met Bay, hurting and wounded by the experience. He'd thought he'd known what love was, but he hadn't.

Meeting Bay changed his life, but Gabe had been afraid to act on it for any number of reasons. And only in those thirty incredible days after she'd returned home to his arms, did he understand what real love was about. She'd given him her heart without games, manipulations or lies. That was the only way Bay knew how to be. And she had healed his heart in the process, taught him how to laugh once again, to love another once more.

A ghostlike smile curved the corners of Gabe's

mouth as Bay's shallow breath continued to calm him, anchor him to the here and now. At Camp Bravo as soon as they'd made eye contact, something magical, something beautiful, had occurred between them. He ran his fingers slowly up and down her arm. Her heart thudded slowly against his rib cage, and Gabe absorbed every beat of it into his soul. Bay was alive, so sensitive and kind to everyone.

He continued to be amazed that she'd spent three years, half of them in combat with black ops teams, and still retained that sweet, simple disposition of a woman who held hope out for the hopeless. Bay had the inborn ability to pick someone like him up and, literally, change his life for the better. What kind of titanium steel backbone did she possess? A damned strong one, for sure. Combat changed people, and yet, Gabe had watched her handle it. Bay was…remarkable. A stunning example of a strong, passionate woman who knew what she wanted out of her life.

Gabe felt the corners of sleep tugging at him, dragging him downward as his heart started to beat in rhythm with Bay's. She had chosen him as her partner. How lucky could he get? Of all the men on earth, Bay chose him. His last feelings were a deluge of love smothering him, dissolving his mind and taking him to that place of peace and tranquility, his woman in his arms, at his side. As it should be.

BAY AWAKENED SLOWLY, wrapped in a sense of protection and love. Dragging her eyes open, she lay on her left side. Gabe's slow, deep breathing brought a soft smile to her lips. She was home. She was at his side once more. Easing up on her elbow, she watched the morning light peeking around the dark drapes at the window that faced the Pacific Ocean, which surrounded Coronado Island.

Her gaze moved lovingly across his sleeping features. Gabe's hair was military short, mussed, softening the hard look and lines in his weathered, darkly tanned face. In sleep was the only time he looked vulnerable to Bay. Awake, he was a SEAL warrior, alert, always watchful, on guard. And how sweetly he bristled over his need to protect her. He was like a knight from King Arthur's Round Table that she'd read about so often when growing up as a child. She remembered her mama reading about Sir Galahad, Sir Lancelot and beautiful Guinevere. At times she would lay out in a field of wildflowers, hands behind her head, watching puffy white clouds slowly move by. Sometimes, she imagined shapes within them of these powerful knights on mighty chargers who saved others.

The corners of her mouth tugged upward as she absorbed Gabe's sleeping face. She took in his rugged features, trying to imagine his childhood, how horrible it had been on him. His drunken father had used him as a punching bag. He'd made sure to conceal the damage and bruises done by his fists and leather belt. And his father had made sure it was hidden from his mother, Grace. All he'd known as a kid was that fatherly love packed a fist and a punch. His father had sworn he'd kill his mother if Gabe ever breathed a word of his punishment to Grace. Bay couldn't imagine how it would have affected her emotionally.

Tears gathered in her eyes momentarily as she imagined his past. A few dark strands lay across Gabe's broad, lined brow. She wanted to reach out and gently tame them back into place. Bay knew if she did, he'd instantly awaken and become fully alert. On guard. Looking for an enemy. That's what SEALs did; they took the fight to the enemy and they were always in harm's way. They learned in BUD/S that five-minute combat naps could carry them for days without real sleep. Resisting the urge because she knew Gabe had just come out of intense training himself, Bay didn't move. She wanted him to sleep.

Her fingers itched to touch his darkly haired chest, run her index finger across his full lower lip that knew how to bring her world into a fiery cauldron of hungry need for him alone. No one could love her to the depth and breadth that Gabe could love her. It was simply a part of his being able to touch not only her willing body, but gently hold her heart in his large, scarred hands and twine her soul with his own.

Drawing in a ragged breath, her body responded, knowing Gabe loved her on every possible level. How had she drawn such an incredible man like this to her? He was Sir Lancelot, and she was his Guinevere. He was a warrior. She was a healer. He knew combat, and so did she. And all they wanted was to find peace and sanctuary from a crazed world in the arms of one another.

Gabe shifted, his breathing changing.

Bay watched, mesmerized. SEALs had an almost telepathic and clairvoyant sense about them. They were such finely honed warriors in combat that their sixth sense was operational, much like an invisible radar moving three-hundred-and-sixty degrees around them all the time.

Gabe slowly emerged from sleep. He sensed her watching him, and although it wasn't threatening, Gabe still felt her eyes—and her love—upon him.

His lashes fluttered. A soft smile played across her lips as Bay observed the slow opening of those drowsy forest-green eyes, now looking in her direction.

"I love waking up with you," she whispered, leaning across Gabe, her breasts skimming his chest, her mouth grazing his. Bay kissed him chastely, with love, not with sex on her mind.

Gabe's mouth gently took hers, his arms wrapping around her. He groaned and pulled her more tightly against him. She reveled in the strength and yet, the utter tenderness of his mouth cherishing hers. Bay drank in Gabe's breath, like life feeding her, opening her heart even more. His hard, lean muscles flexed against hers, drowning in the splendor of his mouth, making her feel hunger for him all over again.

Easing back, Bay broke the kiss, drowning in his expression. He watched her, his hands framing her face, holding her prisoner. His pupils were large and black, a thin crescent of green surrounding them. Bay could feel Gabe coming awake on every level, absorbing his intensity, his powerful, consuming love for her.

"Can we do this every morning for the rest of our

lives?" he rasped, smiling up into her sleepy features. Bay's warmth, her womanly curves fit perfectly against his body. Her full mouth drew into a wry smile, her blue eyes sparkling.

"Soon," she promised huskily.

Grunting, he released her for a moment, pushed himself into an upright position, the covers falling away to his hips. "Not soon enough," Gabe growled, dragging Bay into his arms, guiding her head against his shoulder. Bay slid her arm around his waist. Nostrils flaring, he hungrily inhaled her sweet scent. Bay had a special fragrance, a natural one that sent him into a powerful sexual response.

Gabe knew she had to be sore from their lovemaking last night. He needed to hold off and let her relax. Today was for Bay. He'd been planning it in his mind for months since they'd been separated. Love, she had taught him, had so many aspects. Love wasn't always about sex, although, God knew, Gabe always wanted to be in her, love her, make her smile and sigh and watch her eyes grow sleepy and sated because he'd love her so thoroughly and completely.

"Want a hot bath?" he asked, his lips pressed against her hair, the curls tickling him.

"Mmm, that sounds wonderful. Are you joining me?"

God, how he wanted to, but Gabe knew better. "No, you need some down time, baby. We went at it pretty hard last night." And then he smiled. "Pardon my pun." Gabe traded a boyish grin with her.

She sighed, closed her eyes and squeezed him. "I've never made love in a shower before."

"You said you wanted to swim with the sharks."

Laughing softly, Bay nodded. "So I did. It was my fault, but I'm not sorry. Are you?"

"Sorry for loving you?" Gabe pressed a kiss to her brow, the curls soft and silky around her temple. "Never. I'll have to be dead and gone before that would happen." A chuckle rumbled up through his broad chest.

"That's true," Bay whispered, turning her cheek to kiss the strong column of his neck. "A bath sounds perfect...."

"Then let me get it ready for you. Stay here and just rest. All right?"

Bay didn't want to leave the circle of Gabe's arms. His unselfish protection surrounded her and made her feel utterly loved. Pouting, Bay tipped her head back just enough to catch his lambent gaze. His green eyes glittered with lust for her. Instantly her body reacted, a slow heat spreading throughout her lower body once again.

In truth, she was sore. Gabe was a careful lover, and she knew he would live in a special agony if somehow he accidentally hurt her. He knew what pain was all about and was always concerned he'd hurt her. It had never happened, and Bay knew it never would, but Gabe didn't. Childhood pain patterns, she knew, bled over into an adult's life like a stain they could rarely erase from their being. The care burning in his eyes touched her deeply.

"Okay, call me when it's ready?" His secrets were safe with her. Sometimes, Gabe was that scared little ten-year-old where she was concerned. She saw Gabe struggle every day with that unconscious knowledge that he'd never been good enough to really have been loved by his abusive father. To know he deserved to be hugged. To be told by his father that he was proud of him. To know that he didn't carry his father's sickness or need to hurt others. It was up to her to fill that void. Heal that deep wound within him.

As Gabe kissed her brow and then left their bed, Bay closed her eyes. She was afraid he'd see or sense her sadness for him, and she in no way wanted him to see her unhappy. He could easily misinterpret it, blame himself instead of blaming his father who imprisoned him in that terrible, lonely, loveless space no child should ever experience. Bay had promised herself long ago that she would love Gabe with all she had, replace that darkness with her light, heal that soul-stealing wound within him and make him whole once more. She knew she could do it with time. She'd seen her mother heal her father's war wounds, so she knew it could be done with her patience and love for Gabe.

As she lay there, head nestled on the pillow, Bay stretched out her hand, slowly running her palm over the warm sheet where he'd lain moments before. Maybe that was why Gabe had been powerfully drawn to the SEALs. They were an intense, small family in their own right. The men called one another brothers. They were fierce warriors who always protected one another. Gabe needed a positive male environment, and Bay thought the SEALs had provided him with that. The SEALs had, in effect, become like a surrogate father for him to grow into the man he was with her today.

God, how she loved him. She would work hard to ensure that he healed from his past and that their love was enough to make them whole.

CHAPTER FOUR

BAY TRIED HER best to hide her sadness over their inevitable separation, but it was a losing battle. Today was their last day together. She wanted to cry, feeling as if she were being wrenched away from Gabe. Her heart wept with sorrow.

She saw him sitting out on the jetty where massive rocks had been laid a hundred years before to stop the erosion from occurring to the island of Coronado. The evening was upon them, the sun near setting. High clouds hanging on the western horizon were turning a gold-pink color, infusing everything, even the flat, mirror-like bay. The salty water was calm, and she noticed Gabe carving something between his long, spare hands. Hands that had loved her so well that she still felt wrapped in euphoria from their afternoon in bed together.

Bay moved quietly, never believing for a moment Gabe didn't sense and hear her approach. The first morning at his condo, after getting a delicious bath, she'd told him the story about the Incan jaguar warriors and their powerful clairvoyant abilities. He'd grinned and ruffled her hair, teasing her about it. Yes, SEALs did have heightened awareness. But to be able to invisibly travel to their loved one? Impossible, and Gabe had laughed, shaking his head over her flights of fancy.

Hurt had flowed through her, and she'd tried to hide her reaction from him. Gabe had sensed it immediately, awkwardly trying to make amends. Grudgingly, Bay had allowed him his belief, but there was something inexplicable going on between them. Maybe telepathy? She didn't know.

Her mother, Poppy, had raised her to believe in the invisible realms that surrounded humans on this planet. She believed in fairies, gnomes and elves, too. And Bay had seen her mama at work with the invisible realms. Why were her herbal tinctures, her homeopathic remedies she made by hand in her medicine room, so potent? So healing and life-changing in the best of ways for others?

She wished with all her heart Gabe could believe in her world, but his childhood had been taken away from him. No one had set him upon their knee to read wonderful tales of fantasy to him. No one had infused his mind with the possibility of magic and creativity actually existing side by side in their everyday world. He was a no-nonsense SEAL. She released her longing for him to share her world. He loved her fiercely; Gabe was doing the best he could, and it was enough for her.

"Hey," Bay called to him softly, moving from the lawn to the big black rock where he sat. "What are you doing?"

Gabe barely turned his head, catching her curious gaze. He'd heard her approach, knew her footstep and the sound of it. No matter what Bay wore or didn't wear, she was breathtakingly beautiful in his eyes. She had on a soft pink tee and body-hugging jeans that outlined her lower body to perfection. Her curly brown hair was loose and free about her shoulders, a perfect frame for her oval face.

"Just whittling," he murmured, gesturing for her to come over and join him. Gabe sensed her sadness, the parting coming tomorrow morning.

She took his proffered hand, felt his strong fingers wrap securely around her own. She'd chosen a rock next to him, but instead, Gabe gently guided her across his long, hard thigh to sit upon his lap. Gabe wore a desert-tan T-shirt and a pair of dark blue swim trunks. He'd just run five miles a little earlier. Every day he ran down the beach of Coronado where the SEAL BUD/S trainees were trying to make the cut. He called it The Strand. Some small beads of sweat still clung to the short, fine hairs along his temple.

"What are you carving?" she asked, settling on his lap, curving her arm around his broad shoulders. There was such stability and rocklike steadiness to Gabe. Bay could feel it, inhaled it and absorbed it. He was a rock of the best sort in her world. Sometimes, she was overemotional, and he could reel her in with a word, a tender look or by simply holding her.

"Something for you," Gabe murmured, working on a small figurine he'd been shaping for her all week. He closed his Buck knife and handed the carving to her. "Keep this in your Kevlar pocket. Another kind of guard dog to keep you safe while you're downrange."

Gasping as he placed it in her opened palm, Bay's eyes grew wide. "I-it's a jaguar!" She stared in disbelief at the finely detailed jungle cat. He'd even stippled tiny patterns across the jaguar to symbolize the black spots on its golden fur. Bay didn't know what kind of wood it was, but Gabe had chosen it carefully because of its golden color, the same color as a jaguar's coat.

The figurine wasn't more than two inches long, delicately carved and with painstaking care and attention to detail put into it. She'd seen many of Gabe's carvings he kept in a locker. He was an artist few could rival when it came to wood being gently shaped between his large hands.

"This—this is so beautiful, Gabe." She leaned down, sought and found his mouth. For long moments, the wooden carving sat curled safely in her palm as Bay felt his mouth gently taking hers. Sorrow tore through her as Gabe's mouth moved strongly against her lips, reminding her once again, she was his woman. This was their last night together.

Oh, Lord, give me strength to be strong for him. Don't let me cry. Don't let me show him how sad I am about leaving him. Please...

Gabe reluctantly left her warm, wet lips. He saw love shining in her eyes for him alone, saw her sexual desire for him, as well. He had a night planned for her, a surprise, he hoped in keeping with the magical world she lived within. Somehow, Gabe wanted to atone for hurting her that morning when she'd talked about the jaguar warriors. He'd laughed at her silliness.

Desperately casting around for some way to make

it up to her, Gabe recalled something Bay had told him last year that he'd never forgotten. Tonight, he was going to surprise her with it and prayed it would touch her heart and she'd forgive him for hurting her. Bay loved surprises, more child than adult when it came to Christmas gifts, as Gabe had discovered. By her being able to be childlike, it had helped him to discover his own inner child. Gabe never thought he had one, always the adult who had matured very early in his life. His heart warmed as he watched the awe in her face as she delicately picked up the jaguar and closely studied it.

"When I told you about the jaguar warriors," she said, breathing softly, holding his dark gaze, "you made fun of me." Holding up the delicately wrought cat, she shook her head. "You believed me, didn't you?"

Sliding his arm around her waist, drawing her against him, Gabe felt a sense of peace descend over him. To the west of where they sat, the sun was almost touching the Pacific Ocean. The high clouds lying horizontal to the ocean looked like cake layers above it. The clouds were suffused with pink-and-orange tiers of color, as if celebrating their joy with one another. "I should never have teased you about it." Why had he? Gabe didn't know, and it had bothered him all week. He loved Bay. He never wanted to intentionally hurt her. And he had.

"I'm not one of your SEAL buddies," she said, her voice low with feeling. She closed her hand, tucking the carving in her palm and holding it against her beating heart. "I know SEALs play mean and rough with one another. But I'm going to be your wife in six months. I know you guys are unmerciful, but I'm not from your world, Gabe. We have to create a world that is only for us. You can't drag your SEAL teasing into it."

Gabe felt his heart rush open with incredible love as she slid her arms around his shoulders and rested her head against his. "Sometimes," he admitted quietly, "I think you're nothing more than my lonely imagination, Bay. As a kid, I used to dream…but I stopped dreaming when I was about five. I felt lost. Like I'd lost something precious that I should have had, but no longer had. And then you dropped into my life. All my lost dreams had suddenly come true right in front of me." He lifted his chin, catching her gaze. There was moisture in her eyes. He gave her a gentle shake. "Hey, no tears. Not for me. Okay?"

Nodding, Bay compressed her lips, swallowing several times. "Tears scrub your soul clean of the dirt we collect from life, Gabe."

"Something your mama taught you?"

"Yes," she sighed, content to sit on his lap, her head resting against his. The gentle lap of water on the rocks was soothing and calming. "I've always believed in magic, Gabe. I believe in the unseen world that's all around us. I've seen my mama talk to flowers, to trees and bees. I once saw her ask a honeybee to come over to a flower in her herb garden, and ask it to pollinate it. I watched that bee follow her to that flower. And when she pointed out which flower, the bee went right to it and pollinated it for her." Bay gently squeezed his shoulders. "There's more to our world than you see, Gabe. I know that, but you don't." *At least not yet.* Bay silently promised him when she got off her last deployment downrange, she'd help Gabe discover her world. He had high curiosity. And she would use it as a show-and-tell, in real time, so he could experience the magic firsthand that was all around them.

"I'm sorry I didn't believe your story about jaguar warriors. I got to thinking about it later, and they sounded like early SEALs to me." He laughed quietly. "They were badasses, no question." Gabe sobered and held her melting, warm gaze. "Can you forgive me, Bay? Honest to God, I never meant to hurt you. I didn't realize what I'd done...." His voice turned hoarse.

Gently, she touched his cheek. "Of course I forgive you. We love one another, Gabe. Things like this are going to happen. You did the important thing. After you thought about it, you came back and apologized. That's as good as it gets, don't you think?"

Relief surged through him, and he violently quashed his emotional response. "You deserve better, baby. I'm not good enough for you. I'm really not." But he was so grateful that she loved him unabashedly. Gabe honestly didn't know what Bay saw in him.

She kissed his temple, tasting the salt of the sweat beads still clinging to the strands of his hair. "Thank you. It means a lot to me, Gabe. And you're more than good enough for me. I know you're with me whether you realize it or not. And I feel the same way about you. I don't know what I did to deserve you, but I'm so grateful you're a part of my life."

She eased back just enough to hold his gaze. "I've felt you too many nights come to my side after I went to bed while I was away at medical training. As exhausted as I was, I could feel your weight depress the mattress on the bed when you sat down next to me. I could feel you move your fingers through my hair, soothing me after a rough day. And then I'd feel you move, stretch out and curve me against your body." Bay swallowed and looked down at him. "You were there, whether you knew it or not. You have no idea how much it fed me, helped me. Almost every night, you came and you held me. It was—wonderful... It was a comfort, really because I was missing you so much...."

The shimmer in her eyes, those tears that threatened to fall, ripped his aching heart. "Baby, I believe you. Okay?" Gabe squeezed her gently as if to persuade her. "Why do you think I carved that cat for you?"

She closed her eyes, knowing he was apologizing the only way he knew how. And it was more than enough for Bay. Trying to keep the tears out of her voice, she whispered unsteadily, "I know you had a horrible childhood. I know so much was taken away from you, darling. I—I just wish with my heart and soul, I could somehow transfer my world to yours." Bay opened her eyes and gave him a sweet smile. "I know you would love it, believe in it as I do. But I can't. It's not transferable. It can only be experienced..."

"In my own way," Gabe told her, sliding his hand

and cupping her chin, "I believe in magic. I see it out on patrols. There's times when I swear the SEALs I'm with have shared telepathy between us. We never have to talk to one another or even use hand signals. We'll somehow sense a trap that's been set for us in the middle of the night, even if we can't see it. We sense it. Maybe, when you're lonely for me, your magic happens for you in the same sort of way? And you draw me into your fairy-tale world?"

"That's magic, too," she agreed, her voice hoarse because she fought against crying for him, for what he'd endured. Bay didn't want discord or upset on their last night together. All she wanted was for good memories to come out of it, instead. For both of them. She could cry later. Alone. No one would see her tears or hear her sobs. She was very good at hiding her emotions in the world of combat, because tears always bothered the men. For her, they were a release, enabling her to return once more to her core center where she needed to live in order to survive to help others.

"You're more magic to me than real, baby. You always have been." Gabe held her gaze, feeling her boundless love encircling them. "Yeah, you're magic for sure." He patted her hip. "Come on, I need to fire up the grill and cook those hamburgers for our dinner. You want to get the cold beer out of the fridge?"

As he rose, he kept his hand around her waist and guided her toward the condo. Gabe often thought of her as an otherworldly, beautiful being. And she was his.

"Yes, I can set the table and get out the beer for

us," she said, content to lean against his tall, strong body. The wooden jaguar in her palm felt as if it were burning a hole straight through her flesh. The sensation was real to Bay. The love she felt radiating out of it like a powerful beacon was just as real, feeding her heart and soul. It was Gabe's way of loving her, of acknowledging her world of magic and possibility. Of apologizing. Bay sighed softly and closed her eyes, allowing him to guide her. She trusted Gabe with her life, and he'd never failed her. Ever.

"ARE YOU READY?" Gabe whispered near her ear, his hands lightly across Bay's closed eyes. They stood in front of the master bedroom. He could feel her excitement.

"I am. What have you done, Gabe?" Bay heard a rumbling chuckle in his chest. He'd hinted after dinner that he had a surprise for her. Gabe knew she was such a kid when it came to surprises. Bay felt his rough hands resting lightly across her closed eyes. Felt his heated body inches from her own.

"Well," he teased her huskily, "let's open the door and find out, shall we?" He nudged the door with his toe, and it slowly yawned opened. "Okay," he said, "now you can open your eyes...."

Bay gasped as he removed his hands and settled them on her shoulders, standing quietly behind her. The room had been transformed by soft candlelight. She loved candles! And she remembered telling Gabe last year how candles created magic and transported her to the other worlds. She loved the dancing, flickering light and shadows because she could close her eyes and, in her wild imagination, see such incredible, mythical beings.

"Ohhhh," was all she could manage, her throat tightening with tears of joy. "This is so beautiful, Gabe!" Bay gave a cry, turned and threw her arms around him. "I love you so much! Thank you! It's such a beautiful gift! It really is!"

His arms encircled her, holding her gently against him. She felt his mouth against her temple, placing small kisses down to her cheek, and finally, as she raised and turned her head, she met and melded against his waiting lips.

He kissed her tenderly, and she couldn't stop the sweet trembling. She was so easily touched. So easily moved. Pulling away from her mouth, he smiled down at her.

"You like it, baby?" he asked.

"Like it?" Bay whispered incredulously. "I love it, Gabe." She loved purples, lavender and soft green-and-blue colors. He'd seriously thought about all she'd told him because on the dresser were four candles of varying heights, in the purple to lavender range. On the nightstand were four more candles ranging from pale blue to a cobalt color. And in the master bathroom, a group of them flickered, sending out muted, soft tones of gold flames.

They'd already showered, and although he'd kissed her, touched her, Bay wanted to love him here, in their bedroom. But this was their last night together. They didn't need to rush. She would carry the memories of these last moments deep in her heart. It had to last her for six months until she returned home, to his arms.

Gabe leaned down, resting his cheek against hers, drawing her back more tightly against him. "The music? Do you hear it?"

Gulping back her tears, Bay heard soft unobtrusive classical music in the background. She immediately recognized one of her favorite classical songs, "Ode to Joy." "Everything is so perfect, Gabe. Thank you." She was profoundly impacted that he'd go to this much trouble for her.

His mouth curved faintly, relieved. "I had one hell of a time finding all those pieces of classical music you like." He laughed a little shyly, holding her close, her head tipped back against his right shoulder, eyes studying him warmly. "The guys at HQ teased the living hell out of me when I sat down to use the computer at the office. Hammer, damn him, found out I was tearing my hair out trying to find those classics on iTunes. He was ragging on me, accusing me of turning into some kind of damned sissy." Shaking his head, he grumbled, "I'll never live it down. Classics aren't what SEALs listen to."

"You're such a hero in my eyes, Gabe," Bay whispered, meaning it. Bay was sure the word "sissy" had struck him like a dagger into his heart. She was sure Hammer didn't know his father had called him that name, either. SEALs were a pack of male alpha wolves. Each was a consummate, confident warrior. And they mercilessly, ruthlessly teased and taunted one another, a constant unspoken game of one-upsmanship. "I grew up on the classics. My pa taught me all the Greek myths from Robert Graves's books. I read voraciously as a child. My mama read me fairy tales every night before me and Eva-Jo went to sleep. I had so many dreams about the gods, goddesses and mythical beings. My dreams were in color and crammed full of excitement. I could hardly wait to go to sleep at night so that I could dream. Classical music inspires me," Bay said, meeting and holding his gaze. She felt his heavy desire for her, felt it settle in her womb, between her thighs, so sweet with promise.

"I'd do it all over again for you, baby," Gabe rasped, leaning over and lifting her into his arms. "I'll take any kind of ribbing those guys want to dish out and hand it back to them in spades. They don't love you. I do. Come on, let's go to bed...."

CHAPTER FIVE

THE FLICKERING CANDLELIGHT danced around the darkened room, making movements on the walls, shadowing Gabe's intent-looking features as he untied her blue silk robe. It had been a Christmas gift from him last year. The silky robe clearly outlined her breasts, the nipples already firm peaks beneath the superfluous material. Gabe eased the robe off her shoulders, allowing it to whisper and crumple to the floor.

He leaned down to capture one of the nipples. It hardened in his mouth. She moaned, arching tautly into him, tensing, her fingers digging into his shoulders.

Gabe heard a faint rush of air from between her lips. There was a fine line between pain and pleasure, and he gauged her response to keep it in the pleasure zone.

As her hands tightened on his shoulders, Gabe felt her strain to lift her hips and press hungrily against his thick erection. It made him feel powerful to hear the sounds caught in her throat. Bay trusted him fully. In every possible way. And as he moved his lips to the other nipple, tasting her, he heard her shallow breathing accelerate.

She was a strong woman, and her hands, in particular, were fierce. Her tight grip on his shoulders showed him that he was pleasing her.

As he gazed at Bay, the candlelight softened her beautiful face, made her look almost angelic. She stood naked before him, and he could feel her knees weaken beneath his onslaught. Bay was slowly opening him up to another kinder, gentler possibility, the magic between them, the magic of her affecting and changing him in good ways.

Gabe eased his fingers slowly up her warm rib cage, felt her soft, smooth skin against his roughened fingertips. He couldn't help smiling into her slumberous-looking blue eyes that burned with arousal. The candlelight made her flesh glow an unearthly but breath-stealing color. Golden, radiant skin beneath his exploring hands.

Magic.

He picked her up and carried her to the bed and then bracketed her thighs with his own.

Gabe ran his index finger from the lobe of her ear down the length of her neck and across her proud shoulder. He devoured Bay with his eyes and his heart. He could see the faint beat of her heart near her left, curved breast. She meant the world to him. Gabe could not conceive life without Bay in it. Her flesh was radiant beneath the flickering candles. He monitored her expression, listened closely to her breath, watched the sharp rise and fall of her rib cage. He slowly curved his hands around each of her breasts. Bay's expression tensed as she anticipated the touch of his thumbs wreaking pleasure across her taut nipples.

Anticipation was one of Gabe's favorite ways of bringing her to the edge, increasing Bay's hunger for him, for craving his touch, getting her keyed and so damned close to an orgasm until she started coming apart in his hands.

Her lips parted with a hitched breath, and she gripped his arms, waiting, wanting.... Gabe held her pleading gaze and smiled a very male smile. Leaning down, he exhaled his warm breath across the first nipple without ever touching it. Bay moaned with anticipation. He slowly circled it with his tongue, never touching the hardened center, tasting her salty flesh, drinking it into his body, drinking her into his heart. Her skin was firm, trembling and incredibly velvet beneath his exploring tongue. Feeling her frustration, her need of him, he finally gave her what she wanted: he drew the peak into his mouth, suckled her strongly, listening to her give a sharp cry of relief.

Gabe practiced the same tactical strategy with her other nipple, listening to her sigh and then a catch in her breath, craving his touch. He'd planned this for days, how he would tease her until she was mindless, achy and wet with the promise. But he never wanted to see tears, just the pleading in her eyes, her husky cries, as he turned her inside out with his hands, fingers and mouth. And then, he'd enter her, take her with him, his final objective to have her orgasm as many times as she wanted before he unleashed his power within her that final time. He brought his knees inside her thighs, opening her.

Gabe stroked the inside of her thighs, feeling how

damp, how ready she was for him already. Her entire lower body cramped and convulsed as he slowly traced her wet feminine entrance. He knew how much she needed him inside her.

His thick, heavy erection lay across her belly as he captured one of her nipples in his mouth, suckling her. He sensed her need, that feeling of urgency. But he only gave her that patient, heated grin and eased her gently back down on the bed, making her wait.

Leaning down, he rasped near her ear, "Now...how do you want me, baby? Just tell me. I'm yours...."

Moaning, Bay gripped his hips urgently, crying out, "I need you...please, Gabe, I ache so much I hurt... please..."

He nodded, spreading her thighs, his erection at her wet entrance, barely brushing her, seeing her eyes shutter close. Her hips bucked upward to capture him. She sucked him deep into her. A groan ripped through Gabe as he arched forward, his body straining as she pulled him even deeper into her core. He kept steel control over himself, swam into that shocking, heated pleasure of sheathing into her. Bay was first. *Always. Forever.*

Gabe watched her eyes go wild with yearning, her hands grasping his hips, pushing herself against him in a begging gesture. He smiled and captured her lips. Her ragged breath exploded into his mouth, and he drank it down, drank from her lips, drunk with the heat streaking through his body, hardening him even more, wanting to thrust so deeply they'd never be able to untangle themselves from one another when it was all over.

Bay gasped wildly, then moved her tongue into his mouth at the same time he'd thrust forward deeply into hers. As she shut her eyes, he could feel her orgasm building, empowering her even more. He thrust his hips at just the right angle to give her intense, jolting pleasure.

Suddenly, a serrated cry spilled from her lips, and Bay threw back her head, spine arching upward. Gabe's large hand slipped beneath her hips, holding her just the right way, increasing the pressure times ten. Her cries grew stronger with each powerful rippling orgasm as it tore through her. The tide surged through her in invisible, violent waves. She couldn't breathe, couldn't gasp, captured in the storm of her body releasing fully and completely. And then, she collapsed, breathing hard against the bed, her body shuddering and her limbs suddenly going weak, barely able to move.

Then and only then did Gabe release the steel control over himself. He swam in the heat and slickness of her gift to him. He could do no less for Bay, surging into her soft, accommodating body that so tightly surrounded him. The heat seized him, and he could feel the glovelike tightening pushing his hungry body into overdrive. His lips lifted away from his teeth as he pumped relentlessly, hungrily, into her. His release exploded out of him. Beads of sweat popped out across his brow, his eyes tightly shut as he rode that hot, fiery explosion hurtling down through him. He had no idea how long it lasted, but it was a damn long time. Finally, Gabe collapsed on top of Bay, fighting to keep his full weight off her.

"Come here," he said, his voice rough. He didn't want to leave her body just yet, and he pulled Bay against him, his one leg between hers so they could remain coupled. "I love you, baby. God, I love you," Gabe whispered against her lips, taking her gently this time, with all the tenderness he possessed as a man. Tonight was her night. Tonight, he wanted to love Bay with every cell he had in his body, make her his.

THEY REMAINED TOGETHER in every way, Bay's head resting tiredly on Gabe's massive chest, her arm limp across his torso. She dozed with him. The clock read three in the morning when Bay drowsily awoke, still in Gabe's arms. He stirred, sensing her coming awake. Taking her to his side, he nestled her against him, tucking her in, his arm sliding around her shoulders. He kissed her brow. Her hands grazed his chest, her fingers tangling in his soft hair. His skin grew taut, muscles reacting to her gliding touch.

"Mmm," Bay said, pulling back just enough to catch his sleepy gaze. "That was world-class, Griffin. You continually surprise the pants off me."

He chuckled darkly and raised his hands, tunneling his fingers through that soft, curled mass of hair across her shoulder. "I like surprising any pair of pants off you. You look damn good naked."

"That was a Hill expression," she said archly, leaning up on her elbow and placing a kiss on his smiling mouth. A mouth that knew how to take her to the rim of the universe and back. Bay absorbed the tenderness burning in his eyes and rested her brow against his. "I just don't want this night to end, Gabe."

He sighed and moved his hand across her shoulder. "It will, baby, but you can always take it with you. Remember it and us in the quiet moments over there in Afghanistan." Not that there would be many.

Bay didn't want to discuss leaving. "I want to talk to you about our wedding."

Gabe woke up a little more. The seriousness in Bay's softened expression forced him awake. "Sure."

She traced invisible patterns across his upper chest with her finger. "Our wedding is something positive. And right now, that's all I want in my life, Gabe."

Nodding, he understood. "Is this about your Grandma's dress you want to wear?" A UPS box sent by her mother, Poppy, had arrived the third day she'd been with him. Inside the box was a long, cream-colored lacy wedding dress her grandmother had worn. Bay fiercely loved her Grandmother Lilac. He remembered watching tears come to Bay's eyes as she'd gently removed the old but beautiful dress from the box. The sadness in her eyes over the loss of her grandmother had touched him. Lilac had died when she was seventeen years old. Bay had wanted to wear her grandmother's dress for their wedding. Gabe wished his family had had that same closeness.

Bay stirred, kissed the damp column of his neck. "Mmm, yes. Do you mind?"

"Of course not," he whispered, moving his fingers

through the soft strands of her curly hair. "I want you happy, baby. I want you to plan that wedding at your mother's cabin."

She smiled a little, nuzzling his jaw and placing a slow kiss to his sandpapery flesh. Her body glowed hot, and her womb felt as if it contained deep, simmering coals. Pleasurable, subtle heat was still radiating throughout her. Bay couldn't get enough of Gabe. She moved her hips, watching his length already hardening once more. He was so incredibly masculine, so incredibly tender with her, making her body sing. Her mouth was dry, and she swallowed. "I already promised Grace and Mama that we'd work out all the details in emails. Mama has Skype, so I can talk to her directly sometimes, when I can."

"Good," he murmured, inhaling her womanly scent, the fragrance that was only her. Bay fed his soul. Gabe knew she wanted to take part in the wedding plans, no matter if she was in Afghanistan or not. He cupped her shoulder and looked deeply into her eyes. "Listen, you can't give yourself away over there this time, Bay. When you were with our team, I finally realized you were burning the candle at both ends, working seventeen hours a day helping others medically. It was taking a toll on you, baby."

Bay felt so utterly satisfied. Closing her eyes, she sensed sleep stalking her again. A good kind of lethargy after a great lovemaking session. "I know…"

"Promise me that you will give yourself the time you need?"

"Yes, I promise, Gabe…."

His dark brows moved downward. "Bay, this is important. You can't give yourself away over there this time. You're a damned good combat medic, but you're human and you need downtime, rest and plenty of sleep. Please?"

Hearing the urgency, the concern in his deep voice washing across her, she whispered, "I want to come home to you, Gabe. I'm not going to do anything stupid like I did when we were at Camp Bravo the last year. I learned my lesson, my beloved."

My beloved. Every time she whispered that endearment to him, Gabe felt it go straight to his wounded heart. And every time, it healed another piece of him. Kissing her damp brow, her hair utterly mussed and beautiful around her face, he said, "Okay. I'm taking you at your word."

"You worry too much," Bay slurred, feeling sleep enfold her. "I want to come home to you. You're my life, Gabe. Believe that if you don't believe anything else."

"I'VE GOT TO LEAVE," Bay whispered, choking on the words, holding on to Gabe's strong, scarred fingers. She stood near Security at the airport, her ruck over her shoulder, dressed in her Navy blue cammies. It hurt to look in his eyes, his SEAL mask well in place, no hint of emotion anywhere in his expression. Bay knew better. Her body radiated hotly beneath his stormy look, felt it in the tenderness of his fingers as he rubbed them against her own.

They had slept in one another's arms, woken up,

loved one another again with a desperation that chased reality away for just a few hours longer. And this morning, at dawn, the sun barely edging the Pacific Ocean, he'd made hard, swift passionate love with her one last time. Feeling exhausted in a good kind of way, Bay managed a sweet smile as she tugged at Gabe's fingers, silently asking him to release her. For an instant, she saw the fear, the anxiety in his expression, no matter how hard he tried to hide it from her.

As she turned, Bay raised her hand and placed it against his jaw, sought the hard line of his mouth, kissed him with everything she had. She felt consumed within the powerful curve of his descending mouth, his strong arms coming around her this one, last time. Heart pounding, tears in her eyes, Bay could barely control her wildly fluctuating emotions. She didn't want to leave Gabe. But she had to.

Gabe reluctantly released her mouth, both of them breathing hard. God, he had to let her go. He had to release Bay from his grip. Gabe was peripherally aware of people turning, watching them. He could give a damn about them. Was their loved one going into combat where a bullet could sever her life in a heartbeat? *Hell, no!* He swallowed hard, anger warring with his love for Bay, the lump large and painful in his throat. He couldn't stop looking at her, for fear she'd disappear too soon. He loved her silently in those few seconds between them. Her smile for him was so loving and innocent that it staggered Gabe. Her smile filled him with love, and it pumped hope through his heart that ached with real fear for her safety. And then...

Gabe released her soft, long fingers from his...one last touch...one last time....

Oh, God...

Bay turned away. If she didn't, Gabe would see her tears. And she knew with great certainty, it would tear him apart. No, she couldn't let Gabe see her like this. Fighting herself, Bay gulped and moved into the Security line, quickly swallowed up by other passengers crowding in behind her. She could feel his eyes on her back, feel his love encircling her. It was crazy, but she could feel it as easily as she felt her breath raggedly drawing in and out of her lungs.

Only when she'd passed through Security, did Bay get a hold of herself enough to turn and look back at him. Gabe stood alone now, his hands at his sides. He wore a dark blue T-shirt that showed off his powerfully lean upper body, his jeans barely hiding how sexual and sensual he was to her. His face... Oh, Lord, his face was so hard. She understood he had to be that way or he'd break down, too. Lifting her hand, she touched her fingers to her lips and blew him a kiss. It was all she could do, now separated and unable to run back into one another's arms.

Bay saw Gabe lift his hand in acknowledgement and then gave her a hand signal they'd created between themselves. He lifted his hand, placed it over his heart and then extended his hand outward toward her. A deep love welled up through her, giving her strength at the last minute. She repeated that silent hand signal back to him and then watched as his hard expression dissolved into a slow, male smile filled with so much heat and love for her. She was his. Gabe owned her heart and soul, and he knew it. And so did she.

Turning on her boot, Bay walked down the long corridor that would take her by commercial flight to Seattle Sea-Tac International Airport. From there, she'd hop an Air Force C-5 going across The Pond, the Pacific. They'd stop in Hawaii, refuel and then fly to Bagram Air Base near Kabul, Afghanistan. And then, she'd find a medevac or Black Hawk heading out to Camp Bravo, hitch a ride and find her Special Forces team that she'd join.

As she forced herself to walk away, put space between Gabe and herself, Bay touched a leather thong around her neck, hidden beneath her cammie blouse. Gabe had fashioned a small sterling silver ring on the top of the jaguar's back. He'd strung a fine, thin piece of sturdy leather so she could wear it around her neck while in Afghanistan. The jaguar lay over her heart.

A fist of serrating grief shoved up through her, and her throat tightened painfully. Head down, Bay tried to hide the tears that fell out of her eyes and down her taut, pale cheeks. At least, Gabe had not seen her cry this time…

CHAPTER SIX

"REZA!"

Reza turned. His eyes widened enormously where he stood within the Shinwari village. "Is that you, Baylee?" His mouth dropped opened as she waved enthusiastically at him, jogging toward him in Special Forces cammies, her medical rucksack on her back. His smile increased as she drew near. Happiness danced in her blue eyes as she halted, taking off her soft cover and grinning at him.

"It's so good to see you again!" Bay said in Pashto to her old friend. She said to hell with Muslim protocol because she'd worked with this man two times before. He accompanied U.S. black ops as a tracker and interpreter. "Can I hug you?"

Reza, who was in his middle thirties, giggled. He opened his arms. "I know how to be an American! Come here!" He laughed, striding up to her and throwing his arms around her.

Bay hugged her Afghan friend tightly. Tears came to her eyes as she stepped back from him. "It's so good to see you. I didn't know you were here. Are you staying long?"

He wiped tears from his eyes, too. Reza had worked

with Special Forces near the border with Pakistan with
her two years earlier. He knew the Hindu Kush mountains, their thousands of caves and the goat paths so
instrumental in tracking down Taliban, better than
anyone else. His family had been slaughtered by Sangar Khogani, a Hill tribal warlord, several years earlier. His wife and five children had been cut down
before the guns and curved knives of the brutal Taliban. Since then, Reza had pledged his life to helping
the Americans eradicate the Taliban from his beloved
country.

"I will be here for a while, yes." He shook his head.
"You look beautiful in my eyes, Baylee. Something
must have happened since I last saw you. You are better filled out, not so starved-looking as last time. And
I see happiness in your eyes. Tell me, what has happened?"

Bay looked around the village where she was to remain for the next six months. "I'm engaged to a very
good man, Reza. We're going to be married when I
get off this rotation." She sighed. "He's wonderful,
Reza. Gabe is…well…I just never thought I'd ever
meet someone like him." She smiled softly, missing
Gabe so badly. "I've just gotten off a helo from Camp
Bravo and have to go see Captain Drew Anderson.
He's the head of the SF team here. After that, let's
have tea and catch up."

"Of course, of course," he murmured. "Come, I'll
show you where the team is staying. So, you are replacing the medic they lost?"

Nodding, Bay shortened her stride for Reza. He

was only five feet four inches tall. "Yes, I have to give him my orders. And then I'm sure he'll give me his orders." She laughed.

Originally, Reza had made a living as a cobbler, making shoes for his and other villages. He was greatly loved in the valley near the border. Not the leader of the village, but his kindness toward all earned him a special place in the hearts of everyone. And when she'd met him two years ago and worked six months with him, they'd become fast forever friends.

Bay's heart lifted with joy because Reza was some-one she could honestly talk to. He was a trusted ad-viser, worked as a terp, interpreter, and was often asked to lead black ops teams into the Hindu Kush to hunt down HVTs, high value targets. The Taliban had a high price on Reza's head. They wanted him badly because he knew the Hindu Kush like the back of his hand, better than anyone else and certainly better than any American did. He'd been born in them, grown up there and was intimately familiar with the tall moun-tains and thousands of caves where the Taliban hid. The black ops Marine Force Recons, Army Special Forces, CAG/Delta Force and Navy SEAL teams all wanted his help and knowledge. Since Reza had begun working to avenge his family's death with the Ameri-cans, Taliban deaths had increased two hundred per-cent. Bay thought that was one helluva way to get even.

"Captain Drew is a very nice man, Baylee. You will find him even-headed."

She smiled and clapped his shoulder. "Levelheaded, Reza, but I know what you mean."

He flashed her a shy grin, his face sun darkened, bearded, his black hair long across his shoulders and receding in the front. He dressed like all Afghan males, but she had always seen him as cosmopolitan and worldly. He was one of the few Afghans to get the macrocosm view on his country and his people. He was a fierce fighter in a firefight, and she was so darned glad he was here, with her. Bay knew Gabe would be happy to hear about it. Maybe he wouldn't worry so much, she hoped.

ARMY CAPTAIN DREW ANDERSON was bent over his planning board with his warrant officer and four sergeants when Bay entered the one-story mud house in the center of the village. They all looked up in unison. No doubt, they recognized her immediately. On the left side of her cammies was the black medical symbol. Relief came to the blond-haired commanding officer's face. The man straightened up, his gray gaze quickly assessing her.

"Petty Officer First Class Baylee-Ann Thorn reporting as ordered, sir. I think you were expecting me, sir?" She pulled out her orders from her pocket and handed them to him.

"We're damned glad to see you, Thorn," Anderson muttered, swiftly perusing her transfer orders. He nodded and introduced his second-in-command, a young man of about twenty-four, Warrant Officer Jerry Bannister. Bay shook his hand. The four sergeants were older, and she knew they were the backbone of any SF team. They all eagerly shook her hand, knowing she was an 18 Delta medic. Anderson dismissed the group, wanting to talk to her privately.

"Have a seat, Doc. You ready for some black coffee that'll curl your toes?"

Bay liked the officer's laid-back humor. He was about thirty-five years old, and she saw he wore a wedding ring on his left hand. She thought about her own engagement ring Gabe had given her that was tucked away in the top pocket of her Kevlar vest. A warm feeling of sadness and missing him moved through her. "Uh, yes, sir, coffee doesn't scare me, but the Taliban sure does."

He chuckled darkly and poured two mugs. Both white pottery cups were chipped but salvageable. Anderson handed one to her as he sat down at the planning board across from Bay. "I've got to tell you, I'm damned relieved you're here, Doc. Losing our other Doc…Sergeant Brokelman, well…it's been a hard loss on all of us."

"Yes, sir, I'm sure it's been rough on everyone. I know how tight SF teams are. You're like family."

"Well said. I'll have my team sign those top secret papers your general needs shortly, so no worries. I'll send them on to General Stevenson."

Bay felt him probing her a little. "You ever worked with any Operation Shadow Warrior women before?" she asked.

Shaking his head, he said, "No, but frankly, I don't care what your gender is. You're an 18 Delta medic, the best we have in any branch of the military. You've already earned your stripes with me, Doc."

"Do you think I'll have any blowback from the rest of your team because I'm a woman?"

"No, these men have been with me for four to five years, and we've been through plenty together. Most of them are married. Only two who aren't, but they're engaged. How about you?"

"Engaged, sir."

"To who?"

"A SEAL, sir. Chief Gabe Griffin."

He nodded, assimilating the intel. "Yeah, I ran into his team just before they left to rotate out of Camp Bravo last year. Good man. He's lucky to get you. Congratulations."

Bay felt his sincerity. "Thank you, sir."

"Well," he said, a slight grin on his face, "SEALs are known to be damned protective of their women. I don't suppose he's any different?"

She chuckled a little. "No, sir, he's the same."

"I guess I'd better treat you right then, or he'll be climbing my ass. SEALs don't really see officers any different than enlisted people."

"That's true, the rank and ratings blur in the SEAL community, sir."

He sighed. "Let me give you the lowdown, Doc. My sergeants have gotten you a small, abandoned mud home about two blocks down from our HQ. The Taliban is trying to put new rat lines through this valley. For the last year, the Shinwari tribe people have been absolutely terrorized by the Taliban. They don't want them going through here, and neither do we. But, as you know, the Taliban doesn't take no for an answer.

Our medi, Brokelman, was seriously wounded in a hot firefight three weeks ago. The enemy keeps probing us. They hide in the mountains, strike at night and then disappear before dawn. We've put an SF team in all three villages, and we're trying to stabilize the area and help the people, who are frantic with fear, to give them some security. They hate the Taliban as much as we do.

"A number of them have gotten night letters. And you know when a family finds one tacked on their door, it's a death card. The Taliban utilize hit-and-run raids, and they've got some damned good snipers among them. They shoot mostly children as a way to warn the villages that if they continue to support Americans, they'll continue killing them." His mouth grew grim.

"That's terrible," Bay whispered, her heart breaking over the thought of children arbitrarily being murdered. She knew the Taliban was ruthless and used stone-age tactics against anyone who was their enemy. And in Afghanistan, it usually worked. Few villages had the weaponry and manpower to fight them off. They had to rely entirely on American support and help.

"It's sickening," he growled, shaking his head. "You're going to have to watch your step, Doc. I'm not going to take you out on patrols. I want you here, in this village. I know you're combat trained, but I cannot afford to lose another medic. This village is far from safe. You're going to have to watch yourself all the time. Don't get distracted. The Taliban have sent men in, and they've kidnapped some of the elders, demanding money or they decapitate them. Just stay alert, okay?"

"Yes, sir," Bay murmured, actually happy she wasn't going to be patrolling. She wanted to get home safe and sound to Gabe, to get on with the rest of their life. Maybe she had a short-timer's attitude, but she didn't care. Fewer bullets would be thrown at her, less chance of being killed or injured.

"You're going to be a genuine asset. You know Pashto and you're a female medic, so you can start tomorrow morning by finding a place to set up a clinic to help the women and children. I'm sure some of the men will drop by, too."

"Yes, sir, they bend the rules when necessary. I've come equipped to handle both genders."

"Good." He finished off his coffee. "You know Reza?"

"Yes, sir, he and I have worked together before. He's a trusted ally, sir."

"Good to hear. He's going to be leading us up into these mountains to the east of us for the next month, teaching us the trail systems and pointing out new rat lines to us. In the next few weeks, we've got to get a handle on these damned raids and stop them cold in their tracks."

"What about drones, sir?"

He snorted. "The CIA has authority over all the drones and flies them out of Camp Bravo. I've been on their ass every day by radio, begging them to give us one over the valley. They keep stonewalling me."

Bay frowned. "Sir, have you contacted Chief Phillips? He's running the new SEAL platoon that just rotated into Camp Bravo. I worked with the SEALs over there last year. Different platoon, but I think if you can fly in and see the chief, he might be able to swing a drone your way." She shrugged. "It's worth a shot, sir."

He smiled, rising and rubbing the back of his neck. "I guess I can go lower myself to the SEAL Chief, get down on my knees and grovel for mercy," he grumbled.

Bay realized Anderson was teasing her. "They're good guys, sir. Kept my butt out of a sling a number of times last summer."

"Yeah, they always take the fight to the enemy. They don't blink when there's gunfire. Anyone else who has any brains is running away from it. But those guys get a gleam in their eye, grab their M-4s and they're running as fast as they can toward the damn fight."

"They wouldn't have it any other way," she said with a smile, feeling pride for them and for Gabe. "They're very brave warriors in my book, sir."

He sighed and studied the map across the planning board. "No disagreement, Doc. We might be Army and they are Navy, but we're Americans and that's what really counts. We're over here doing the same job."

"Sir?"

"Yes?"

"About a sniper? You said the Taliban are hitting the villages in this valley?"

"They are. I don't have a sniper on my team."

"Well, sir, why not ask the SEAL Chief if he's got any guys who might want a little extra hunting challenge over here? They like doing sniper work."

"Any chance your fiancé, Griffin, was one?"

She laughed. "Yes, sir, he is. I learned a lot from him."

"It's not a bad idea, Doc. I'll give the Chief my sad song, and maybe he'll feel sorry for an Army son of a bitch and lend me some SEAL help, since I can't get a drone assigned to us." He regarded her and said, "Glad you're here, Doc. Go get situated. Any one of my sergeants will be more than happy to help you adjust to your new digs here. Any problems, see me directly. Okay?"

Bay stood up. "Yes, sir."

"Dismissed, Doc."

Bay turned, set her cup on the planning board and shrugged the heavy ruck over her shoulder. She exited the stifling confines of the windowless house.

Reza stepped from between the houses, grinning like a fox. "Well, did you like Captain Anderson?"

"Very much," she said, walking with him. "Do you know where my house is?" Reza knew everything. She'd come to rely on his almost photographic mind.

His face brightened. "I do! This way!"

GABE WAS EXHAUSTED as he sat down at his computer in his condo. Bay had been gone a week, and he was worried because she hadn't checked in with him. She'd promised to try and Skype him. He knew she could only do that at Camp Bravo, not in the valley where she was located.

His fingers itched to type an email to Chief Phillips to see if Bay had gotten to Bravo yet. He'd called Phillips shortly after Bay had flown out of Lindbergh Field. Phillips had rule over the entire platoon and was the man who could make anything happen by coordinating with the three officers above him. When Gabe had told him Bay was his fiancée and that she was in the area, he promised to keep an eye on her. He slept a little better knowing that. SEALs took care of their own.

His computer beeped. His heart raced. It was a Skype call from Bay.

"Hey," Bay said, smiling happily, "how are you?"

His heart crashed in his chest, powerful emotions nearly choking off his reply. Staring hard at Bay, he noticed how her cheeks were flushed pink, her soft, curly hair pulled back in a ponytail. She wore SF cammies.

"I'm good. Good. How are you?" All calls and emails were run through SEAL HQ back in Coronado. Gabe couldn't say much and had to keep their communication bland. Hell, he wanted to reach through that screen and haul Bay into his arms and kiss her senseless. Just seeing the light dancing in her blue eyes made him feel an avalanche of relief. She looked good. And happy.

"I'm getting acclimated to my new digs over in the valley. Got a really squared-away SF captain over there. His team could care less whether I'm a woman or not."

Gabe chuckled. "Right on. You're an 18 Delta, so they don't care if you have two heads and sprout horns." He heard her laughter, husky and sweet. His euphoria deepened as he saw her wrinkle her nose, her beautiful lips pulling up into a huge smile over his comment. He loved her. His lower body ached, needed relief. Gabe couldn't think two thoughts on any given day without thinking of Bay, remembering the times they'd hotly loved one another until they were utterly exhausted.

"Did you get with Chief?" he demanded.

"Oh, yeah, I did." Bay hooked her thumb over her shoulder. "He's been wonderful, Gabe. When I can manage to get a helo hop over here, he lets me use the team computer. Really sweet of him."

Sweet had nothing to do with it, but Gabe nodded and said nothing. "You're now part of the SEAL family, Bay. He's gonna treat you right."

"He sure has. And, hey, the guys in this platoon have been really nice to me, too." And then she gave him a wicked grin. "Unlike your team who wanted to burn me at the stake."

He absorbed her laughter, drinking in the beauty of her face. "Your nose is sorta red. Been outdoors a lot? Patrols?"

"I've been working clinics outdoors. No patrols, though. The captain wants me to stay in the village where it's safer."

"Smart man. Tell him thank you." That was profound news and a relief to Gabe.

She grinned. "Well, the captain said he didn't want an angry SEAL climbing his ass, so he *really* wanted to keep you happy."

Gabe's hands were sweaty. He'd had such fear for Bay going out on patrols, his imagination going wild, having a nightmare about her being killed. "Hey, tell that captain I appreciate him watching your back. But you're right, I'd damn well climb anyone's ass if they didn't properly take care of you."

"Well," she murmured, "I think you guys in the SEALs have such a tough reputation, that it's already a done deal."

He sobered. "I love you." Gabe didn't give a damn who heard him. Bay's face softened, and so many emotions crossed her very readable face. She struggled.

"I love you, too. And I miss you so much, Gabe…."

"It's mutual, believe me." He saw longing in her expression. And sadness that they were once more separated from one another.

"It has to be hard on you, too."

Gabe snorted. "Hell, I'm stateside. What's gonna happen to me? Get bit by a pissed-off rattler because I ran too close to the manzanita bush he was resting under? Find a scorpion in my sleeping bag and get stung?"

Bay shook her head, laughing. "God, you make my day, Griffin."

How badly Gabe wanted to reach out and simply touch her flushed cheek, kiss her lips, feel Bay lean into him, her arms sliding around his neck. His throat tightened with those intense memories.

"I'm glad I do," he said. "I want to see you smiling and happy over there." He wondered if she felt him come to her at night when she slept.

"You make me feel happy," she whispered, losing her smile. "I'm busy, so it takes my head out of missing you so much."

"You're not too busy, are you?" Gabe demanded, frowning. Bay had promised him to not wear herself out like she had before.

Holding up her hands, she said, "I've been a good girl. Reza is here, and he's like my guard dog, taking your place. He meets me at my house every morning, and then we have MREs at HQ. Every morning, he sizes me up. 'Baylee, you have shadows under your eyes. Baylee, you look thinner. Baylee, aren't you eating enough?'" She smiled a little. "He's a miniature you, Gabe. Trust me on that one."

"Tell him thank you from me. That's a stroke of luck Reza is there with you. For how long?" More relief tunneled through Gabe. He'd worked with Reza before, and the man was solid gold.

"Another two weeks. He's busy showing the team new rat lines up in the hills and mountains above our village."

"He's a damned good person."

"He's someone I can confide in. I can trust him with my secrets." She gave him a teasing look.

She was such an imp, but how he loved her. "Things you should be telling me instead?"

"Ohhhh, I keep it aboveboard," she promised, her lips curving more. "But I have active dreams at night. Can't talk to anyone about them, however, and you aren't here to tell them to…."

Gabe grinned and chuckled. His spirits lifted just

hearing her voice, seeing her face and making sure she was really all right. He couldn't ask her details about anything; that was forbidden. Top secret was exactly that. "I sent you a care package. You should be getting it soon."

"Ohhh, surprises?"

"Yeah, surprises just for you. I know how much you love them."

"Listen, do me a favor? Can you go to some of the NGOs that the SEALs work with? This village is so poor, Gabe. All the kids need shoes. Could you check into this when you get a chance? I'd really like to have about seventy pairs. The children are all running around barefoot."

He nodded. "Can do," he said, thinking that Bay, as usual, was watching out for the children. She was going to be one incredible mother someday. And she would be carrying *his* child. His lower body burned with need for her.

Bay looked at the watch on her wrist. "My time's up. I got two SEALs standing in line waiting to talk to their loved ones, so I'm outta here, Shark Man."

He grinned, wanting more time with her. Wanting to capture her laughter and replay it so he could feel her near him. "Okay, next week?"

"Maybe. I'll try as often as I can." Bay smiled sweetly, touched her heart with her hand and then extended her hand toward him. "I love you…."

He sat there and returned the hand signal to her. A lump formed in his throat. "I love you, too, baby. Stay safe out there…."

The screen went blank. Gabe sat there feeling euphoric and, at the same time, horrible dread. His emotions were up and down like a roller coaster. Never before had he experienced something as intense as his love for Bay. One of the SEAL wives who found out Bay was overseas had told him the same thing. There wasn't a day that went by when she didn't feel abject terror to dizzying joy, too. It was just part of a human's emotional makeup when their loved one was overseas and in harm's way.

Rubbing his chest, Gabe scowled, hating how emotional he'd become since Bay had left. No other woman had ever affected him like that. He sighed. Well, the tables were turned, weren't they? Instead of the man going overseas into combat, the woman went instead. And he was the one left home to do the worrying and the not knowing. Getting up, he ran his fingers through his hair in frustration.

Gabe went into the kitchen and poured himself a cup of coffee. Leaning his hips against the counter, he stared through the quiet condo. When Bay had been here, the place filled him with warmth, bubbling vitality and life. Now, it was sterile, gray and damned depressing to him. He sipped the coffee, his brows knitted. Bay was in what was considered a "hot" valley, a place where frequent, ongoing clashes with the Taliban were happening all the time. It didn't help him sleep at night. Dammit, anyway. If only she'd been assigned to a SEAL team, he'd have breathed a helluva lot easier. She was in a bad place with an enemy who hated Americans with a fanatical passion.

When he'd talked with Chief Phillips a week earlier, the SEAL had been blunt about Bay's location.

"It's a damn snake pit. Mustafa Khogani, cousin to Sangar Khogani, that a SEAL sniper team just took out last year, is heading up the Hill tribe efforts to put new rat lines through that Shinwari tribe valley. Mustafa is a sick son of a bitch."

"Aren't they all?"

"This guy is real special," Phillips had snarled. "He sweeps down on a Shinwari village, kidnapping little boys and girls between six and twelve years old. He's a sex slave trader. Some of our teams have found these children dead, dropped like garbage along ratline trails a few days after they had been kidnapped. They were children who were badly injured during the kidnapping. The bastard is killing these children, not giving them medical aid to survive. We want this monster."

A cold shiver had moved up Gabe's spine as he'd heard Phillips's icy rage. "I wouldn't want to find one of those children," he'd admitted, his voice hoarse. It would be the last thing he'd want to do—discover a dead child on some trail out in the middle of nowhere.

"It's upsetting the platoon plenty. A lot of these guys are married and have children themselves. You can imagine them stumbling upon one of Khogani's victims. Mustafa is a sociopath. He doesn't care. He just discards them, keeping the healthy, uninjured children and then selling them to the highest bidder once they get them across the Pakistan border."

"Jesus," Gabe had whispered, rubbing his face. He

couldn't imagine the terror and grief of the Afghan parents. Worse, discovering their young son or daughter was found dead. Even more sorrow-compounding, finding out how the child had suffered and died. Gabe had seen the ruthless brutality in the Taliban ranks for too long, but this was new. And horrifying. "Can't you get a sniper team tracking that bastard?"

"That's what we're doing. We're coordinating a team with the SF captain over in that valley. That's the one Bay is assigned to. The captain came crawling over here last week pleading, hands out, begging us to interfere and provide him a SEAL sniper team. He also asked for our sniper platoon assets to start scouring the hills above the village to capture Khogani and his bunch, but it's a no-can-do. He's got to get the ragged-assed Army in gear to do that. We have our own areas that need our attention and protection. He asked for a drone, but my hands were tied. We can't even get one except for the Ravens our teams use out on patrol."

Gabe's mouth had thinned. "Did you tell Bay all of this?"

"No, couldn't. This is SEAL intel. She's with Army SF. I'm assuming the captain filled her in, though."

Anxiety had feathered through him as he'd considered the info. "Maybe that's why that SF captain is requiring her to stay in the village, then."

"Probably so. I'd sure as hell ground her, too. What the military doesn't need is for someone like Mustafa to get his hands on an American military woman. It's something we all live in fear of happening. It would turn into a media nightmare."

"I know…" Gabe had rasped. His mind leaped painfully to that scenario. Chief Doug Hampton had discussed his worry with him the day Bay had arrived at their platoon. So far, no woman combat soldier had ever been captured by the Taliban in Afghanistan. Jessica Lynch had been captured in Iraq and it had been SEALs that had rescued her. Hampton said it would happen sooner or later as more women were on the front lines, that one would be captured, tortured, raped and, most likely, beheaded. And it would all be videotaped and then put up on the internet for the horrified world to see. It was only a matter of time. Hampton had been adamant with him to keep Bay protected and safe. No way, on his watch, was she going to fall victim to this terrifying scenario. He wiped his mouth, fear grating through his gut.

Gabe had ended that call with the chief, more anxious than before the conversation. Worry was eating a huge hole in his stomach.

CHAPTER SEVEN

MUSTAFA KHOGANI LAY on his belly, binoculars pressed tightly against his eyes, hidden among the brush over-looking the most southern Shinwari village in the valley below. Next to him, his second-in-command, Zmarai, was studying the village through his sniper scope.

"Something new," Mustafa growled. He zeroed in on a woman in SF clothing who was holding a medical clinic for at least twenty children and women of all ages. The clinic was on the edge of the village, near a huge stand of trees that spilled out of a wadi, ravine, thousands of feet above them. The grove of trees pro-vided shade from the blistering sun overhead.

It was a good place from a medical standpoint, but from a military strategy perspective, a very poor choice. But good for what he had in mind.

Zmarai said, hesitant, "A third of the village chil-dren are lined up. "Which ones do you want tonight when we sweep down there to kidnap some of them?" They routinely kidnapped young children, and they sold them into the sex slave trade across the Pakistan border. The children would then be cleaned up, given haircuts, new, clean robes and photos taken of them.

From there, the photos were sent to prospective buyers across Asia and Europe. It brought in operating money to keep his lord's army fed and supplied.

Snorting, Khogani said, "Tonight? Look at where they are! It would be easy to ride down into the wadi, undetected. We could get so close that a mere two-minute gallop would reach all of them. We'd catch them all off guard."

"It's daylight, my lord," Zmarai rasped. They had always raided a village at dusk. He studied each young child waiting patiently beside their mother as the American military woman doctor treated them. Barely able to stand what would happen to any of them who were kidnapped, Zmarai closed his eyes for a moment, trying to get a stranglehold on his disgust. He was Muslim. And because he was one, the sale of children as sex slaves made him sick.

Pulling the binoculars away, Mustafa scratched his long, black beard. His mind seemed to consider the possibilities. Unlike Sangar, his cousin who had been murdered by SEAL snipers last year, Mustafa had more original ideas. Sangar had been too conservative and careful. Mustafa liked to keep his enemy off balance. He seemed sure that the Special Forces team in the village below them wouldn't be expecting an attack in broad daylight.

"There's a cave about two kilometers from here. We could reach it before the Americans could ever react with Apaches."

Zmarai said, "Yes, there is a cave." He worried

about a drone high above, watching the whole attack. That wouldn't be good for them.

Mustafa smiled. "And it goes back a long way, and we can come out the other side of the hill into another wadi, maintaining our cover."

Nodding, the Taliban soldier looked over at his lord. "That is so. You want to strike hard, grab some of the children and then ride for that cave?" He wished for the thousandth time that Mustafa would lose his obsession with stealing young children. It was sick and perverted and against Islam. Otherwise, he was a brilliant, tactical Taliban leader.

"Yes." Khogani sat up and crossed his legs. "But I want that woman doctor, too."

Black brows raising, Zmarai stared in disbelief at him. *"Her?"*

Shrugging, he growled. "The bulk of my forces are ten miles from here up in the mountains. We have a lot of wounded men who are desperate for a doctor. She could treat them. We could have our own, personal American doctor."

Compressing his lips, Zmarai thought long and hard. True, there were many Taliban soldiers who were wounded or in dire need of immediate treatment at their main cave right now. Although they could get bandages and drugs from the Pakistan hospitals across the border, they had no real medic among them. Their last medic had been killed when a B-52 bomber had dropped a laser-guided JDAM bomb on them during a night firefight a week ago. It had killed twenty of Mustafa's finest soldiers as well as his own personal bodyguard. And without a medic riding with them, they would lose more men to bacterial infection than any amount of American bullets. The soldiers would die a slow, painful death, blood poisoning setting in and killing them.

"She's an infidel woman. Would your men allow her to treat them? To even touch them?" Zmarai wondered out loud.

"My men will do exactly as I order them. The ones who try to quote Koran to me that a woman shouldn't touch them will be shot in the head." His full lips drew away from his yellowed teeth. "That will put a stop to that garbage. I need my men fit for duty. Pakistan is not providing us with a medic, and we need one if we're to keep the pressure on this valley. She will be useful to us."

To whom? Zmarai didn't verbalize the question. Some of his soldiers would want to kill her immediately. Military women were hated even more than the male infidels. Women should not be seen out in public without a burka covering their entire body, to hide them from the eyes of other men. The woman doctor below wore a green scarf on her head, but that wasn't enough for Zmarai.

Other soldiers would want to torture her to make an example of her to the other Americans. For them, it would simply be another way to get even with the Great Satan. And then, his mind ranged over other more political problems. The warlord in Pakistan, who directed public relations for al Qaeda, would probably be happy because he'd want video of her capture—or worse. He liked putting videos on the internet of soldiers being tortured or beheaded. To see an American military woman in a similar video would be a coup, a world event. Inwardly Zmarai saw Mustafa's plan as a potential moneymaker because his lord would sell the doctor to this Pakistani for such purposes once he was done with her services. There were many financial reasons to capture the woman, he thought, admiring his lord's intelligence.

"If you did that," Zmarai said carefully, "you would have to keep her heavily guarded. She is a soldier. She knows how to escape and evade. She may try to kill us."

"She's only a woman!" Mustafa snorted. "She's not a man! But you're right, I will have you put two trusted guards who will go everywhere with her. I need her medical skills."

"What if word gets back to Pakistan that you have captured her?"

"Perhaps the khan will hurry through my request for a Muslim medic, eh? It's his duty to provide one to us, after all. This could shame him into spending the money to get one for me. I had to stoop so low as to kidnap an American woman medic in order to save my good soldiers. That would embarrass him into action."

"Would he want to videotape her?"

"I don't care what he does with her after she's taken care of my men. We would take her across the border. He could sell her into the white slave trade for all I care."

Zmarai's conscience flared. He didn't feel good at

all about the idea of kidnapping the American woman soldier. In his early forties, Zmarai was the father of four boys, ages six through twenty. He loved them fiercely, and he fought with the Taliban to bring strict Muslim rule back to his country. He'd ridden with Khogani for a year and saw him commit untold crimes and brutally shoot any soldier who didn't instantly obey his order, no matter how despicable the order was.

"I think it's a good idea," Mustafa said in a self-congratulatory manner. "I will get value out of her in many ways." He grinned more broadly and scratched his crotch. "Who knows? I might even grow bored and turn my attentions to her, instead. The khan in Pakistan wouldn't care because she's a whore, anyway. I could then sell her after she's serviced me."

Zmarai nodded, keeping his expression neutral. He had no love of women pretending to be men. Combat was no place for them. They belonged at home, raising children. These American women had to know the price they would pay if they were captured by them. Still, that bothered him because as a devout Muslim, women were sacred and not to be defiled. Or raped. It was a heavy load he carried in his heart. Zmarai wasn't sure he could continue to be Mustafa's commander of the two hundred men who rode with him. Where was his lord's morals? His values? The Koran did not sanction the things his leader did to Afghan women and children.

"Get the men," Mustafa ordered.

Jerking out of his reverie, Zmarai nodded and stood, the sniper rifle resting beneath his arm. He quickly moved to a grove of trees down below the ridge where they'd been patiently awaiting orders.

BAY FELT THE hot Afghan sun bearing down on her between the boughs of the pine trees. The green scarf had worked its way off her head, pooling around her shoulders. She was treating a squalling baby, the mother worried as she patiently crouched nearby. After giving the baby girl a vaccine, Bay smiled over at the mother, reassuring her in Pashto that her daughter would be fine.

As she looked up, Bay noticed that the line of women and children had grown again. And it was already noon. Her stomach growled to remind her she needed to eat. But after one look at their anxious and hopeful faces, she remained sitting in that old chair that had been provided to her along with a deeply scarred wooden table in the shade of the grove.

She asked the SF sergeant, who was acting as her bodyguard, to get her an MRE for lunch from her hut. He hesitated because he was her security. Finally, after she pleaded with him, he agreed, saying he would be back shortly.

As she waited for the next child, a three-year-old little girl who limped, her tiny hand clenching her mother's hand, Bay heard an odd sound. The ground began to vibrate beneath her feet. What was it? An earthquake? Afghanistan was rife with them.

Suddenly, several women near the rear of the crowd started to scream. Bay stood up, looking in the direction they were pointing and shrieking. Her heart slammed into her chest, pounding with adrenaline as she saw twenty Taliban horsemen burst out of the nearby wadi.

The horses were galloping hard toward the group. Bay jerked her radio to her lips, calling Captain Anderson, warning him of the attack. She didn't hesitate, pulling the .45 pistol she carried, taking the fight toward the charging group of horsemen. Several fired their rifles, their shots going wild and wide. Bay threw herself on the ground, belly first, making herself a harder target to hit. Where were Anderson and his men? The only gunfire she heard was from the Taliban racing down upon the terrified group of scattering women with children.

Breathing hard, sweat running down her temples, Bay held the .45 with both hands and began to fire slowly and systematically. She saw one, two, three soldiers torn off their charging mounts by her carefully aimed bullets. Where the hell was the help?

The line of women and children moved like a writhing, startled snake. Some mothers grabbed their children, yanking them off their feet as the riders dove into them. Others fell, covering their children with their bodies as the horses' sharp hooves ran over them.

A murderous-looking man with a black beard riding a huge black horse bore down on her. She scrambled from her prone position to kneeling, holding her pistol out and steady in her hands. She saw the hate, the sneer on his lips as he galloped straight towards her.

Her world slowed down, and that was when Bay knew she was in a life-and-death moment. She realized

she could die in this daylight attack and had no time
to look around for help. Taliban soldiers were tearing
little boys and girls from the arms of their screaming
mothers. Shrieks of the frightened children filled the
air, wails from the mothers, their arms outstretched
toward the fleeing soldiers who had stolen their crying children.

Her hands bucked as she fired at the swiftly moving
black horse and rider. The bullet struck his leg, and he
cursed, kicked his horse savagely, directly aiming at
her. And then, from behind, she was thrust forward
into the dirt, her head slamming into the dust. Pain
and burning sensation radiated hotly over the right side
of her back. Stunned, unable to breathe, Bay tried to
move. She realized someone behind her had shot her
in the back, striking her Kevlar vest.

Oh, God. Oh...God...

MUSTAFA JERKED HIS black stallion to a sliding stop. He
leaped out of the saddle, his right calf bleeding, nearly
crumpling beneath him. Cursing the infidel whore for
shooting him, he jumped upon her just as she was trying to roll over and aim her pistol at him. With a snarl,
he wrenched it out of her hands. Balling his fist, he
used all his weight and strength to slam it down into
the left side of her face. He heard the crunch of bone,
and satisfaction roared through him. The woman cried
out, and then her eyes rolled back in her head. She
slumped unconscious beneath him.

Zmarai skidded his horse to a halt, the animal dancing around, tossing its head. Mustafa gestured sharply

for Zmarai to help lift the American woman, so they could throw her over the front of his saddle.

Mustafa cursed richly as he discovered the American woman was a lot heavier than he expected. Huffing, he grabbed her and hauled her over to the horse. Between the two of them, they were able to drag her across the saddle.

"Run!" Mustafa roared. He turned and recognized the large rucksack that combat medics carried. Limping over to it, he grabbed it, shrugged it over his narrow shoulders and then mounted his frantic, frightened stallion. Looking up, he saw several SF soldiers running toward them. Bullets zinged and snapped around him. He sank his heels into his stallion, and the animal leaped forward, nostrils flared red, lunging toward the wadi.

Mustafa quickly galloped into the thickly lined ravine. In seconds, the trees covered their escape, hiding them from the enemies' sights and bullets. He laughed triumphantly, watching as his men up ahead spurred their mounts, whipped them mercilessly with riding crops.

He felt a thrill of triumph. Five boys and three girls squirmed and cried beneath the arms of his soldiers. Eight! It was a good day! Even better, Zmarai rode ahead of him, the woman medic held in place while he galloped ever upward through the trees. She would pay dearly for shooting him. That, he promised her. His knuckles hurt, and he looked down to see them bruised and swelling from striking her so hard. She would get more of the same when it suited him. He'd never expected her to shoot three of his soldiers and then wound him. *Satan's whore!*

CHAPTER EIGHT

GABE JERKED AWAKE, a scream on his lips. Disoriented, breathing hard, sweat running down his temples, he felt as if he were underwater, suffocating, unable to reach the surface for air.

God...what?

His mind tumbled. He looked at the digital red letters on the clock on the bed stand. It was 12:30 a.m. As he gasped for breath, his gut was tied in knots. He lay naked in the bed, feeling a horrible rush of anxiety tunnel and twist violently through him. Another nightmare? Hell, he had them regularly. This one was different. Very different. It raised the hair on the nape of his neck.

He forced himself to sit up, swinging his legs over the bed. The moment his bare feet hit the cool bamboo flooring, it gave him something to focus on, something to ground himself with. His reaction to the nightmare was joltingly different.

What the hell?

Gabe forced himself to control his breathing; something he was very good at because he was a sniper. He could damn near control every bodily function he had, including lowering his heart rate.

Wiping the sweat off his face, he blinked several times. Why was he feeling so damned scared? What the hell was this all about? He stared at the clock, making mental calculations that it was noon for Bay in Afghanistan. Daytime was safer than nighttime over there. The Taliban struck during the dark hours.

Had he had a precognitive dream about her? One that showed him something that was going to happen to her? The SEAL chief's phone call last week had made him edgy. Tense. Maybe he was just working that out in his dream state? How the hell did he know? He was no friggin' shrink.

Standing, Gabe walked out of the bedroom, down the hall to the kitchen. He wanted water, his mouth feeling as if it had cotton balls in it. He stood at the sink, filled the glass, tipped it to his lips and slugged down the liquid. Finishing off the glass of water, he set it in the sink, turned and walked into the quiet living room.

Frowning, he felt restless, as if he had something important to do. His mind raced with questions. No answers were forthcoming. Rubbing his face with his hands, he muttered a curse. Dammit, he needed this sleep so badly. The past week, he'd been involved in the swim qualifications down at the SEAL base located on Coronado. He was in the water eight to ten hours a day. If the trained dolphins who protected the ships in the bay weren't trying to bust his ribs as he put a fake limpet mine on the side of a cruiser's hull beneath the water, then they were dealing with harbor seals whose duty it was to protect exactly that:

the harbor. SEALs trained dolphins and harbor seals to defend and protect all the ships in the San Diego Bay. Whether they were dealing with nuclear-classed submarines, cruisers, a carrier or destroyer, they had been taught to kill an enemy frogman trying to sink a ship in their bay. His ribs were bruised as hell. His partner, Hammer, had busted a couple of ribs when an aggressive dolphin had taken him head-on yesterday. Hammer had lost that round and would be benched for six weeks while the fractures healed.

Looking around the near-dark condo, Gabe couldn't shake the awful, roiling anxiety roaring through him. He felt his belly tighten, as if he were going to get hit with an unknown fist coming his way. *Damn.* Maybe a warm shower would help calm him down? It always had in the past.

Just as Gabe emerged from the bathroom, the white towel hanging low on his narrow hips, the phone rang. Looking at his Rolex, he saw it was two in the morning. An unsettled feeling avalanched him. No one called at this time of night. His mind spun with shock as he hurried to the phone sitting on the granite island in the kitchen. The only call he'd receive at this time of morning was….and he angrily shook his head, not going there. *No.* It wasn't *that* phone call. It just couldn't be….

Grabbing the phone, he growled, "Chief Griffin here."

"Gabe? This is Chief Phillips."

He felt all the air getting sucked out of his lungs, stunned to hear the SEAL's voice calling from Camp

Bravo in Afghanistan. Knees weak, Gabe suddenly sat down. "What's happened to Bay?" he asked, holding the phone so tight his knuckles whitened.

"I'm sorry to call you," he began heavily. "At noon our time, Mustafa Khogani attacked the village where she was holding a medical clinic. There were twenty Taliban riders, and they swept up through the line where she was helping the women and children."

"Dammit, is she all right?" he ground out, his breath choking in his throat. Closing his eyes, he heard the SEAL Chief draw in a deep breath as if to fortify himself.

"No, she's been kidnapped, Gabe. Reza, the terp, saw her shot from behind. Reza told Captain Anderson he recognized Mustafa Khogani on his black stallion come riding up to her. Bay fired at him, hitting him, we think, in the left leg. She was stunned by a Kevlar hit from behind. It threw her forward and to the ground. Khogani leaped off his horse and punched her in the face before she could get a second shot off at him. Reza said she went unconscious at that point. Khogani put her up on another rider's horse, who is unidentified, and they rode for the wadi and disappeared into the underbrush. Khogani then ran over and grabbed her medical rucksack and took it with him."

Gabe couldn't breathe. He couldn't speak. A knot in his throat was so painful, he couldn't pass words through or around it. Gabe's mind spun with the information. He'd snapped awake at twelve-thirty in the morning. That would have been the exact time Bay had been kidnapped.

He rubbed his face savagely. "Chief, get me ordered over there right now. I'll get my commander to let me get over there as soon as possible. I'm coming over as a strap-hanger. I'll find her…"

"I'll do it, Gabe."

"What's being done right now?"

"We had no drones in the valley," he said, his voice tight with anger. "Those CIA boys here at Bravo knew we desperately needed one over there because of all the ongoing attacks the past two months. They just laughed at us when we requested eyes on that valley. If we'd had a drone on station, we'd have seen Khogani coming. This could have all been avoided."

"I'll deal with them later. Whose mounting the rescue effort?" Gabe's heart was pounding so hard in his chest, he thought it might tear out of it. His mind whirled with shock, fear and rage. Bay was kidnapped. *Jesus.* She was in the worst kind of trouble. Could he get over there fast enough? Was there enough military assets to pull free in order to help aid the search for Bay? What was Khogani going to do with her?

God…no…no…please, protect her until I can find her…please…

"Captain Anderson is working with Reza. The Afghan interpreter is tracking Khogani and his men with two SF soldiers."

"Is that all?" Gabe barely hung on to his mounting rage. *Dammit!*

"Hell, no, Gabe, that's not all. But you know as well as I that a woman soldier being captured, the shit is hitting the fan straight up to the Pentagon and into

the White House to the president. Command was first
going to remove Anderson's people immediately out
of the country. But we were able to talk them out of
it. Besides, Captain Anderson refused to go. From our
end we're sending two four-man SEAL fire teams into
the area. They've already been airlifted over there and
are beginning the hunt."

"What about drones now?" he snapped, his fury
mounting over Bay's kidnapping.

"The CIA just got one over there an hour ago. We're
coordinating with our two teams and with Reza. Our
teams are using Ravens. As soon as they landed on
that mountain ridge by helo, they sent their drones out.
So far, they've not spotted anyone."

Wanting to cry, to scream, Gabe shut his eyes
tightly, trying to think what to do next. "Can you get
me a flight out of Anderson in Washington, D.C.?"
Chiefs could move the whole world if it pleased them.
He knew Phillips was upset and involved. He had
Bay's back in this debacle. She was one of them, and
he had no doubt that Phillips would expend every effort to locate her.

"I'm on it, but I'm not sending you through D.C. I'll
send you west out of California. I've started making
the connections already. You just get your orders cut
from your end, Gabe. I'll handle the rest."

"I've got to get over the fastest way possible, Chief.
It can't be two or three days from now. Bay won't have
that kind of time and you know it."

Because Bay could already be dead. Her tortured,
mutilated body would be thrown onto a goat path to

rot until the vultures found her. Or until a SEAL team accidentally stumbled upon her body. His stomach clenched painfully as he wildly looked around the silent condo. Breathing raggedly, he waited.

"Okay, I'll make it happen, Gabe."

"You've got my cell phone number?"

"Yes. I'll call you with steady updates as I receive them. You're in the loop."

Desperately trying to steady his breath, his heart hurting, Gabe whispered roughly, "Thanks, Chief Phillips. I owe you a whole helluva lot on this one."

"I'm sorry this happened, Gabe. I've got the entire platoon on standby. If anyone is gonna find those slimy bastards, it'll be us."

"Thanks," he choked out, all his strength deserting him as he hung up the phone. His stomach roiled. Turning, Gabe barely made it to the kitchen sink where he vomited up everything he'd eaten the night before.

"Wake her up!" Mustafa ordered his men. His leg was continuing to leak blood. The American whore had caused his wound. Not caring if the woman was still unconscious an hour after they'd arrived at the second cave on the other side of the mountain, Khogani wanted something done to stop his pain.

One of the soldiers took a bucket of water, throwing it on the woman who lay sprawled out on her back in the sand of the cave. They'd stripped her of the Kevlar vest and took her .45 pistol and holster away from her. They'd found a knife hidden within her trousers, strapped to her right ankle. As the water splashed savagely against her bloodied and swollen face, she moaned. Mustafa stood there, his arms crossed. She began choking. Smiling a little, he watched the whore's eyes open to slits, her hair soaked, her face pale.

"Get her up!" he growled, snapping his fingers.

Instantly, two of his soldiers curved their hands beneath each of her armpits and hauled her up to her feet. Her knees collapsed beneath her, and she cried out. Blood was dripping out of her nose, the red splotches hitting the front of her uniform and boots.

"Shake her! I want her awake!"

Bay felt pain in her arms as she was jerked around. Her head snapped back and forth. She tried to compensate, everything spinning around her. Gasping, her lungs heaving, she gagged and vomited.

Khogani snarled and strode forward. He wrapped his hand into her loosened hair, jerking her head up. "Look at me, whore!" he yelled into her face in Pashto.

Bay grunted, pain tearing across her scalp. Her eyesight was blurred, and she was seeing double. Her knees kept giving out. She felt the grip of men's hands on her upper arms, shaking her savagely, trying to make her stand on her own. Angry black eyes glared back at her. The man's bearded face hovered inches from her own. She smelled garlic and goat on his breath, and it made her even sicker.

Trembling, Bay tried to stand, tried to make her knees work for her. Pain increased as he viciously tightened his fingers into her hair. She gave a little grunt as he forced her head back, fully exposing her throat.

"Whore! Either you wake up or I'll slit your infidel throat here and now!"

His hot, rotten-smelling breath made her gag. Adrenaline suddenly shot into her bloodstream. Her ears were ringing, his Pashto threats distorted. Gasping, Bay made herself look into his angry, small black eyes. It was the same Taliban soldier who had ridden the black horse. Bay recognized the sneer on his lips, his yellow coated, rotten teeth.

Mustafa cursed and released her hair. Stepping back, he settled his hand on the butt of his curved scimitar blade. His eyes slitted as he watched her struggle to stand instead of continually collapsing. Her left eye was nearly swollen shut. He smiled, watching her fight into conscious awareness. He flicked his wrist, telling the two soldiers to release her.

She staggered, caught herself, and then locked her knees, swaying unsteadily. When she slowly raised her head, her wet hair framing it, she glared fearlessly at him.

"You are a doctor, are you not?" he snarled, jabbing his finger down at her rucksack sitting at his feet.

Bay blinked, fighting to remain upright. Dizziness made her want to fall to the left. She saw the murderous hate in the man's eyes and knew he was good for his word to slit her throat. Swallowing painfully, she rasped in Pashto, "...I'm a combat medic."

A pleased look came to Mustafa's face. "Very good. You're stronger than I thought. And you speak our language. You have endlessly surprised me so far." He moved toward her, his hand shooting out, his fingers wrapping strongly around her neck. "You killed three of my men, whore...."

Shocked by the unexpected attack, Bay threw up her hands to break the hold. Instantly, two soldiers grabbed at her arms and jerked them behind her. Her shoulders burned with pain, and she gave a little cry, trying to ease the pressure against them.

The man with the black beard laughed. He squeezed her throat slowly, his face inches from hers, his eyes drilling into hers. "You killed three of my men. You are going to pay for that." He squeezed her throat more tightly.

She fought, but the other two soldiers held her firm. Kicking out with her boot, she wasn't able to land a blow, as he easily dodged her feeble attempt. Watching her strain, her eyes go wide because he was slowly choking off her breath, Mustafa smiled, enjoying her agony. Her face began to turn mottle-colored, her mouth opened, gasping, gagging for breath.

Suddenly releasing her, he laughed. "You are mine, infidel! You will do exactly as I say! If you don't, I will guarantee that your life will be hell on this earth. You will die slowly. Painfully. Your American soldiers will find your naked body cut up into pieces, thrown to the vultures along a goat path. Do you understand me?"

Gagging, Bay dragged huge draughts of air into her burning lungs. She barely heard the threats, thinking she was going to die. Her knees gave way.

"Let her fall," Khogani snarled to his soldiers.

Bay collapsed to the floor, a hand around her bruised throat, gasping for air. Her head hurt, her cheek was hot and swollen, throbbing with vicious pain. She marginally tried to assess her injured state. Her ribs were sore and bruised, and she had no idea how that had happened. She remembered his fist coming down, the snapping sound cracking throughout her head and then…unconsciousness. Head hanging down, black spots dancing before her tightly shut eyes, she tried to relax and just breathe. Just breathe and get oxygen restored to her faltering systems. *Oh, God, he almost killed me…*

Her attacker sat down on a flat boulder that was one of many scattered around the large, dry cave. The afternoon sun slanted into the farther recesses. As she slowly pushed herself upright to her knees, he smiled.

"What is your name, woman?"

Bay felt the fine dust of the cave beneath her hands and fingernails as she rested them tensely on her thighs. She lifted her head, warily watching the man. He had to be a leader because the two soldiers stood tense, waiting for his next order. *Captured.* She'd been kidnapped! In broad daylight. She tried to think what to do. Geneva conventions…escape and evasion tactics. Her shorting-out mind wouldn't work, wouldn't help her. Swallowing painfully, her mouth dry, she forced out, "Thorn. Petty Officer first class Thorn. U.S. Navy."

"You're a thorn all right," Mustafa growled, jabbing his finger down at his wounded left calf. "Look at what you did to me!"

Bay said nothing, her eyesight finally beginning to clear. She wasn't seeing two of everything and was relieved. Touching her left cheek, she winced. The whole left side of her face felt like a mushy marshmallow. When he'd hit her, she was sure he'd broken her nose and cheekbone. It felt like it, the pain beginning in earnest as the adrenaline began leaving her system. Shaky, Bay knelt on the floor of the cave, trembling so damn bad she felt as if she was falling apart. Bay smelled fear. It was her fear. She feared him, whoever he was. The glittering black shards of his eyes held no light. He took great pleasure in seeing her suffer. "You must fix me up," Mustafa snapped, jabbing down at his wounded leg. "I'm bleeding. Stop it from hurting."

Bay saw her medical ruck in front of her. Could she get to her feet? If she didn't, he would have those two soldiers drag her over to him and slit her throat. Compressing her lips, she crawled forward on her hands and knees. Gasping for breath, steadying herself, she brought up one knee, trying not to sway back and forth like a drunk.

"Hurry up!"

Wincing at his sharpened command, Bay heaved herself to her feet. When she leaned over to pick up her ruck, she almost nose-dived. Her balance was off. Very off. Blood was still trickling out of the left side of her nose as she slowly put one boot in front of the other. She saw the bullet wound she'd given him, saw the dark, hate-filled look on his face. His hand rested tensely over the butt of his curved blade in a sheath on the right side of his body.

She swallowed with difficulty, her throat aching. She managed to fall to her knees in front of his wounded leg. Blinking, trying to clear her fogged mind, Bay opened her ruck with trembling fingers. Gloves...she needed gloves... Focusing on that, she managed to pull on a set of latex gloves. Now, to focus on finding a syringe and filling it with enough lidocaine so that as she examined the seeping wound, he'd feel no pain.

Bay slowly opened the top of her ruck. *Syringe. Bottle of lidocaine.* Her mind couldn't multitask. Hell, it barely held one word. One thought. One movement. Biting down on her lower lip, her fingers blindly ran into her syringes stored in another pocket.

The man watched her. When he saw her draw a certain amount of liquid out of the bottle, he gripped her wrist hard.

"Are you going to try and kill me by shooting me up with too much morphine, whore?"

Pain drifted around her wrist bones where his fingers bit deeply into it, grinding them together. Freezing, she rasped, "No. This is lidocaine. It's to numb the area where the wound is located. You'll feel less pain. You'll be more comfortable as I clean it out."

A new soldier, tall and lean, entered the cave. His light brown eyes held hers as he came over and snatched the bottle out of her hand.

"What does it say, Zmarai?"

"Lidocaine, my lord." He dropped it back into her ruck. "It's as she says. It's not morphine."

Grunting, Mustafa smiled a little at his commander. "I'm glad you have some English, Zmarai. From now on, you will remain with her as she deals with my wound, eh?"

Bowing, Zmarai murmured, "As you wish, my lord."

Bay realized he was afraid she'd kill him. She'd like nothing better, but if she did it, the other three soldiers would kill her. She wanted to live. As she worked to remove the fabric from around the gunshot wound on his leg, her heart ached with grief. *Gabe.* She loved him so much! Reality crashed down upon Bay. She wasn't going to get out of this alive....

CHAPTER NINE

How could she escape Mustafa Khogani? Bay closed her eyes, shivering as the temperature at eight thousand feet dropped below freezing. She lay in a small cave guarded by two Taliban soldiers as dawn arrived. They rode at night to avoid detection by Americans and their drones overhead. They'd ridden from the first cave beneath cover of darkness to the present one. A musty grain sack had been thrown over her head, her hands tied in front of her, riding a horse led by the commander called Zmarai. He, of all the soldiers in this unit, seemed least disposed to glare at and hate her. And he was the only one who made sure she had plenty of water to drink and a little food to eat. He'd done what he could to allow her to help her own injuries, giving her the time to do it.

Tomorrow morning, Khogani was taking her to another cave in this complex to work on twenty-five Taliban soldiers who had been wounded in an earlier attack. That was why he needed her. Zmarai had told her Pakistan medical supplies awaited her and she would not want for anything. What he didn't say and was clear to her—they didn't have a medic among them to help the injured. And that was probably the only reason she was still alive. They needed her medical skills. What would happen to her tomorrow after tending the Taliban wounded?

Thoughts of being beaten, tortured and raped crowded into Bay's mind every moment. She remembered all too clearly that, during the three-week-long advanced course SERE—Survival, Evasion, Resistance and Escape course—the instructors had made it very plain to the forty volunteer military women undergoing combat training at Camp Pendleton that, if any military woman was caught, rape was a reality. It was a tool of power and control over a woman. Females, the instructors warned them, presented a whole other perspective of what it meant to being taken prisoner in combat. Taliban and al Qaeda didn't honor the Geneva Conventions embraced by the rest of the world. And it was that international accord that would keep a woman from being tortured and raped after being captured by an enemy force. Shivering, Bay used her ruck as her pillow and balled up into a fetal position, trying to sleep.

To keep track of days, Bay took an ink pen and had placed a mark on the inside of her ruck. This was the second day. Tomorrow would be the third.

Her heart ached as she pictured Gabe's hard, warrior face before her. Surely, he was over here looking for her? Would his SEAL team allow him to do that? Bay had no idea. But she took hope that Chief Phillips at Camp Bravo was doing something to try and find her.

If only.... Oh, God, if only she could leave a trail of

bread crumbs of some kind. But Khogani and his men were wily. They rarely stayed out in the open, moving into one of thousands of caves in the Hindu Kush to avoid the rapacious eyes of the Predator drones. Twice, she'd seen Apache helicopters very near where they were hiding. The helicopters used thermal imaging to try and locate human body heat. She knew they were searching for her.

Gabe...I love you, I love you so much it hurts. I'm so sorry, my beloved...so sorry. I didn't mean this to happen...

Tears slid down her dusty cheeks, warm trails that dripped off the sides of her face. In her closed hand she held the carved jaguar. Luckily, she'd put it in her ruck, and so far, none of the Taliban had rifled through it to steal or take anything out of it. Not even her surgery scalpels. Maybe her captors didn't know what they were, but they were usable weapons. Bay would use one of them to try and escape Khogani. And there wasn't a moment that didn't go by that Bay wasn't looking for an opportunity to escape.

Since she was completely disoriented, Bay was thankful for her compass, which she kept in her ruck. The cave she lay in was small. It had connecting tunnels to it. The two Taliban soldiers stood guard at the entrance, AK-47s in hand, prepared to shoot her if she tried to leave.

Trying to sleep, Bay closed her eyes. Suddenly, she heard a child's echoing wail somewhere very far away. The echoes were faint but disturbing, floating through the tunnel system. Sitting up, she blinked, her heart starting to pound. Was she imagining that child's cry?

The cave was airless and suffocating. Was she starting to lose her mind? Why did she hear that child's shriek of utter pain? Touching her aching nose, Bay pulled two more ibuprofen out of her cammie pocket and drank them down with the glass bottle containing muddy-looking water. Zmarai had thoughtfully given it to her, telling her in very serious tones that she was lucky he'd found it for her.

Settling down once again, placing the right side of her face against the ruck because her left side was horribly swollen, Bay closed her eyes. Exhausted, in shock, she trembled inwardly. Fear ate at her. Everything was unknown. Khogani was like a cobra striking out at her unexpectedly, keeping her off balance. She feared he'd rape her and shuddered at the possibility. God, he stank like goat, his beard littered with bits of food, smelling of rotten meat and garlic. Her stomach churned.

And then, she felt Gabe nearby. She felt him come to her. Bay didn't care if it was her imagination or not. Her fingers tightened around the carving, pressing it against her heart, the only physical link she had with the man she loved with desperation. She felt his hand move gently from her shoulder, down across her torso to her hip, as if to soothe her, calm her.

The edges of sleep lapped at Bay as she sensed Gabe settling his tall, strong body against the curve of her back, hips and legs. His hand slid gently beneath her neck, curving around, drawing her even closer to his body. To him. Her lips parted, and she moaned softly because he was so real to her, his moist breath falling across her neck, reminding her just how real it really was. And when Gabe eased his hand across her waist, settling it against her belly, long fingers splayed outward, Bay felt incredible heat radiating from him to her. A ragged sigh slipped from between her swollen lips as his powerful, loving protection surrounded her. His bodily warmth seeped into her, and in minutes, Bay stopped shivering beneath the thin, torn blanket.

Gabe was with her. He was *here*.

It gave Bay such overwhelming comfort that the fear that dogged her dissolved. She fell into a deep, healing sleep for the first time since her capture.

GABE HALTED HIS black gelding as Reza brought his fist up in a signal that meant "stop." Dressed hajji, looking like an Afghan, he waited, squinting across the eleven-thousand-foot ridge, the horses standing knee-deep in summer snow. Beneath his Afghan clothes, Gabe wore his SEAL cammies. The voluminous and baggy clothing hid the fact he wore his H-gear, a harness that surrounded his waist and chest. In fifteen pockets was as much ammo as he could carry for his M-4 rifle and SIG pistol. Plus, Reza had added huge saddlebags to each of the sturdy mountain horses. They were an arsenal on four legs, and he anticipated no mercy when they found Bay.

The wind at dawn was sharp and cold. Gabe had wrapped his neck in a yellow and green shemagh, a woven cotton scarf Afghans often wore. The colors

of the shemagh denoted he was from the Shinwari
Tribe. The mighty Hindu Kush mountains at this time
of morning, just before dawn, were incredibly clear
and beautiful. Pale pink outlined the peaks to the east
of them.

Gabe knew Reza had seen something. They each
wore a radio headset, the mic close to their lips, hidden by the Shinwari shemagh over the lower half of
their faces and necks.

"What do you have?" Gabe asked quietly.

Reza stood up in the stirrups of his saddle, pointing north, a spotter scope in hand. "Look…Taliban…"

Instantly, Gabe dropped the reins on the tired
horse's neck and pulled his scope out of his side
pocket. Quickly, he moved it through the general area
where the Afghan had gestured. His heart started to
pound. Sure enough, there were at least twenty Taliban on horses. His eyes narrowed. His heart stopped
beating. The second rider's head was covered by a
sack. That was the way they treated prisoners so they
could never know where they were. It prevented the
prisoner from trying to escape.

"That's Khogani!" Reza rasped, his voice excited
as he watched them through his scope. "In the lead!"

"That could be Bay, second horse from the front?"
Gabe's mouth went dry. His whole body contracted
with tension. "What do you think, Reza?"

Reza held the scope, looking intently at the second
rider in line.

Gabe couldn't tell, the shadows were too deep. They
were a good two miles across the valley, on a ridge

west of the group. Even Night Force scopes had their maximum distance. He waited, trusting Reza because the man lived in these mountains and knew them intimately. Controlling his hope, controlling his emotions, his mouth flat and hard, Gabe continued to watch the small group of riders on a goat path at least five thousand feet below them.

"I think...I think it is. I can see her hands...they aren't a man's hands. Look closely...see what you think," Reza said, low excitement in his tone.

Gabe had the eyes of an eagle, and with a Night Force scope, it simply increased his ability to see clearly. The group moved into deep shadow and around a turn. He lost the first four riders. *Dammit!* Pulling the scope away from his eye, he muttered, "I can't see her, but your assessment is good enough for me."

Reza smiled brightly. "If it is Bay, then she's alive. They're taking her somewhere."

"But where?" Gabe demanded, looking around at the silent, pristine world. The pink along the eastern peaks deepened to rose. It reminded him of Bay's soft, natural mouth. Reza turned his horse and pulled up next to Gabe. "In the direction they are heading, there are several hospital caves the Taliban sometimes use. Not all the time," Reza said, frowning, adjusting his shemagh to stay warm, "but often enough."

Nodding, Gabe indicated he was familiar with hospital caves. He'd come across them before on patrols in these unforgiving mountains. They'd find spent IV bags, torn wrappers that had once contained battle dressings and emptied syringes littering the floors, along with emptied bottles of antibiotics in those large caves. Sometimes, they'd find dead bodies of Taliban who had perished despite medical care. Rubbing his chin, feeling the three-days' growth of beard beneath his fingertips, Gabe let his mind range over options.

"I'm calling it in."

Reza nodded. "I would. None of the other teams have found a trace of her."

Gabe pulled out his radio and changed channels. He had a direct line into Chief Phillips at Bravo, who was coordinating the SEAL search for Bay. He then used his Night Force scope which would give him the range of where the Taliban where seen. Then, he pulled out his GPS unit, firing a laser beam into the area. Armed with the intel, he called in the numbers. Phillips would direct a drone flying at twenty thousand feet, unheard and unseen, over into their area. They had to be careful. If Apaches were sent in, Khogani might smell a trap and know he'd been spotted.

And what would happen to Bay? He might slit her throat. The horror of that happening slammed through Gabe. His emotions started to unravel. Just as quickly, he jammed them back into his kill box. Emotions had no place in this hunt. Absolutely none, if he was going to find Bay and rescue her.

"I know a goat trail off this ridge into that area," Reza said, cheerful once again. He pointed back from where they'd come. "Turn around, we'll go down."

"Damn glad," Gabe muttered, shivering from the cold. His heart rose with hope as his horse slowly and carefully negotiated the snow and then the slippery rocks at lower altitude. By the time the sun had risen, sending its golden, warming rays across the peaks, Reza had located the little-used trail. They'd have to go down into a very narrow valley and then back up the other steep, rocky side in order to reach the same trail the Taliban had been on earlier.

Hang on, baby. Just hang on. I'm coming to get you. Don't you lose hope...I'm going to find you and rescue you...I love you, Bay...

BY THE TIME they hit five thousand feet, a radio call came through from Phillips. Gabe gave Reza the silent signal to stop, as he turned up the volume to listen. The messages were always terse and short. What had the drone found? It was on station somewhere above them. Phillips had given Bay's rescue the name Operation Pegasus. She was given the code name Amazon.

"Black Bird Actual, this is Black Bird Main. Over."

Gabe responded. "This is Black Bird Actual. Over."

"Amazon has been sighted. Repeat—Amazon has been sighted. Stand by for GPS. Over."

Gabe nearly came undone. Tears jammed unexpectedly in his eyes as he fumbled for and found his computer to type in the coordinates. He didn't trust his voice, his vision blurring for a moment. Clearing his throat, he keyed the mic. "Go ahead, Black Bird Main." He typed in the latitude and longitudinal coordinates, his heart soaring.

"Anything else, Black Bird Main? Over." Gabe wanted more intel. Where did the drone see Bay? Was she still on the horse? Had the drone actually photographed her face? His heart hammered in his chest, and he could hardly sit still.

"Roger. Positive ID on Amazon. Repeat—positive ID on Amazon."

Relief, sharp and searing, scored through Gabe. For a moment, he tightly shut his eyes. Tears leaked from the corners of them. His entire chest and heart trembled with fear, with fierce hope. "Roger, Black Bird Main. Actual, out." His voice was unsteady. Twice, he cleared his throat, shoving back his emotional reaction.

When he opened his eyes, he saw Reza grinning and throwing him a thumbs-up. The Afghan's eyes lit up with such joy that Gabe found himself grinning. Bay was alive! The drone had photographed her face after the sack had been taken off her head as the Taliban group had halted in front of another cave complex. The photo was grainy, but in color, blurred, but Gabe could see it was Bay. Peering at it, he saw the right side of her face, her hair messy, her face dirtied with sweat. There seemed to be blood near her nose, but he couldn't be sure. She must be feeling terror. *God, let me get to her in time.*

EXHAUSTION MADE BAY DIZZY. For twelve hours, she'd medically tended injured Taliban soldiers. If not for Commander Zmarai's quiet presence always with her, some of the soldiers would have struck her. Many spit at her, their eyes burning with hatred. Some balled their fists as she touched them for the first time. And always, Zmarai was there, giving his wounded soldiers a sharply worded command not to touch her.

Bay felt almost safe beneath Zmarai's shadow. He was patient, didn't push her to hurry, and always got whatever she needed because he had another soldier standing by to run back to the cave where all the boxes of medical supplies were kept. Every so often, he would tap her on the shoulder, giving her a bag filled with goat milk. At other times, he'd slip her scraps of food to keep her going. Bay wondered how this tall, proud Hill tribesman, who was clearly a leader in his own right, could work under Khogani.

It was near midnight, and she finished examining and stitching closed an infected wound on the last soldier's right thigh. He'd been feverish, and she'd given him as much antibiotics as his body could tolerate without outright killing him with a massive overdose. Bay wasn't sure the man would last through tonight.

"Come," Zmarai ordered, "stand and come with me."

Wearily, Bay got to her feet, pulling her ruck over her right shoulder. Her head ached. The high-potency ibuprofen tamped down the pain, but far from all of it. She could barely lift her feet as she followed him through dimly lit passages. The whole cave network had electric lightbulbs strung sporadically between them. She vaguely heard the chutter of a generator, which supplied the hospital caves with the necessary light.

Suddenly came the sound of a child wailing. She yanked to a halt, gasping, turning toward the sound. It wasn't that far away. She felt a hand on her arm.

"Come," Zmarai ordered sternly, his dark eyes holding hers.

"But…there's a child who's hurt…I hear it…." She saw his mouth turn down, his eyes holding some kind of unknown pain in them. "Can't we… I mean, can't I go help that child, too?"

Again, she heard terrible, wrenching cries of pain drifting down through the tunnels toward them. Zmarai's lean hand tightened around her arm momentarily.

"Ignore the cries," he snarled. He turned sharply on his heel, striding faster down another tunnel, away from the crying, sobbing sounds.

Bay's heart pounded with anguish. The child, whether boy or girl, she couldn't tell, was still screaming. Begging in Pashto. She couldn't make out the words, only the heart-wringing sounds of being in horrible pain. She hurried to keep up with Zmarai, his shoulders tense and hunched forward as he swiftly moved toward an unknown objective. This was the second night in a row she'd heard a child crying piteously.

The first night, she thought she was going to go mad. But now, she heard it again, and she was wide awake and conscious this time. What was going on? Bay couldn't stand to see a child cry. It broke her heart, and she often cried afterward when having to tend Afghan children who had suffered so much through the wars across their desert country.

"Here," Zmarai said abruptly, stopping. He jabbed his finger at a small cave no more than ten feet wide and long. "I'll have one of my soldiers bring you food and drink. You are to stay here for the night."

She met his anguished expression. His mouth was set in a hard line. Was he upset with her? "Thank you," she whispered softly. "I—I couldn't have done all of this without your help, Commander."

His mouth quirked, and he glared at her. "I will come and see you tomorrow morning. You must go through and check all those men once again."

"Of course…good night…"

Bay had no more than sat down, placing her ruck with her ratty, thin blanket, when another soldier stopped at the entrance to her cave. She looked up, suddenly fearful. This wasn't one of Zmarai's loyal soldiers. This was someone new.

"Lord Khogani wants to see her right now," the soldier snapped at the other man who guarded her at the cave's entrance. "Release her to me!"

Zmarai's soldier looked worried, glanced down the cave where his commander had gone earlier. "She is to stay here. The commander ordered it," the soldier told the other.

The new soldier spat out, "Enough of this!" He charged into the cave, grabbing Bay's arm and yanking her to her feet. Forcefully shoving her ahead of him, he snarled, "Move!"

Bay felt her heart beating harder. What was going to happen to her? Where was she being taken? The soldier shoved her roughly into another well-lit cave. For a moment, Bay held her hands over her eyes, the place incredibly bright compared to the other caves. As her eyes adjusted, she watched Mustafa Khogani, who was perched on his Persian rug, surrounded by bowls of steaming food, eating with his right hand. Two servants hovered nearby, waiting to serve his every whim.

"Sit," the soldier snarled, hauling her over and pushing her down on the opposite end of the rug.

Bay fell hard and tried to sit up. Mustafa grinned and returned the stare. Suddenly, she felt like a trapped animal. What was that unholy look in his eyes? He was shoving food into his mouth, bits dropping across his beard and chest. His thick black hair lay in dirty ropes around his narrow, calculating face.

"Eat," he invited. "I heard from my commander that you've done very good work on my men today. You deserve to be rewarded." With a flourish, he made a sweeping gesture toward the food sitting between them.

Instinctually, Bay felt terror and wasn't sure it was entirely her own. One of the servants handed her a small brass plate. She knew she'd better eat to keep up her strength, even though her stomach was tied in hard knots. There were goat steaks steaming on a platter with couscous, dried figs and dates in yet another. Her mouth watered. If not for Zmarai, she'd have starved the past few days. This looked like an unbelievable feast in the middle of godforsaken nowhere.

Mustafa wiped off his mouth with the back of his sleeve and had an expression of enjoyment as she ate. He smiled once again. "You need to keep your strength up," he warned. "There is hard work ahead of you."

CHAPTER TEN

Bay FELT A wave of fear so stark and present in Mustafa Khogani that she didn't taste anything she ate. He watched her like a prey, his eyes obsidian slits, following her every move. The silence was thick and taut. Her right hand shook as she choked down the food.

Her intuitive side was screaming at her to run as far and fast as she could away from this man with the dead-looking black eyes. He said nothing, eating voraciously, like a starved wolf. Refusing to meet his gaze, Bay kept her head bowed, eyes on the brass plate held in her left hand. With every passing moment, it was harder and harder to swallow, the food became a growing lump jammed in her throat. Now, Bay understood how it felt to be monitored. The hair on the back of her neck stood up, a clear warning of impending danger. She could *feel* the Taliban leader probing her with his eyes, his lurid thoughts.

"I'm tired." Khogani yawned, standing up, stretching fitfully. He pointed over to one corner. "Take that with you," he ordered, his voice lowering. "See what you can do for him. You're a medic." Then he smiled a little, taming his thick mustache across his upper lip between his thumb and index finger.

Bay quickly set the plate down and stood up. She in no way wanted to earn one of his sudden rages by being too slow to follow Khogani's orders. Peering into a dark corner at one end of the cave, she squinted, hand shielding her eyes as she slowly walked in that direction. Blankets lay piled up in a heap. Was Khogani giving her more blankets to stay warm at night? Unsure, Bay walked to the rear of the cave and into the shadowed recesses. As her eyes adjusted to the gray gloom, she leaned down over the blankets.

A sudden gasp escaped her. The black hair of a child peeked out from beneath them. Kneeling down, concerned, Bay frowned. Gently, she opened the blankets, and they revealed a six-year-old boy, naked, curled up in a fetal position. Her eyes narrowed as she saw blood on his thin brown legs, pooling in the blankets below him. The child moaned, his body clenching and spasming, his one leg jerking. He moaned again, burying his head in his spindly arms. Heart starting to hammer in her chest, Bay felt icy terror stab through her.

My God...this was the child that was crying?

She gently examined him, softly moving her hand downward toward the blood.

Oh, no...no...

Bay drew in a harsh, explosive breath, able to see the child's right leg had been broken, the white of the bone sticking up through the torn flesh. This must have been the child she'd heard screaming. Shutting her eyes, trying to stop the flood of rage tunneling through her, Bay could feel Khogani's burning gaze on her back, observing her for reaction. Watching her...

Gulping, Bay quickly covered the boy with the dirty, flea-ridden blankets. She had to get him out of here and get him medical help. Khogani was a monster. A horrible, horrible monster allowing this child to suffer without any medical care for days. Her stomach rolled violently as she carefully lifted the boy into her arms, bringing him close to her, shielding him from the bastard's gleaming eyes. The boy moaned, his eyes barely opening. Turning, Bay glared across the cave at the Taliban leader.

"See if you can save him. Unfortunately, he fell off the soldier's horse on the way here and broke his leg. He's a sweet young boy who will fetch much as a slave on the Pakistan black market. Perhaps you can fix him so he can be sold later."

Mouth set, Bay bowed her head, biting hard on her lower lip until she tasted blood. She quickly passed Khogani and exited the cave, heading back to where she had been kept earlier, a soldier leading the way and one behind her.

The child moved, a whimper slipping between his pale, thinned lips. Heart pounding with anger and helplessness, Bay felt tears burn in her eyes. She couldn't cry now. She had to think of how to save this child's life. Give him relief from the terrible pain.

Upon reaching her cave, Bay laid the child down and quickly pulled her rucksack over, rummaging through it for gloves and a flashlight. Khogani's two guards left. The guard who was under Zmarai's command turned his back on her, refusing to watch. As she quickly assembled the medical supplies she might need, Bay realized all the soldiers knew Khogani was selling the children. That was why they'd stolen so many young boys and girls in the raid on her village. Shutting her eyes, fighting off huge emotional updrafts of rage, Bay forced herself to concentrate.

A quick examination of the child's broken leg made her nauseous. The boy's leg was infected and needed to be reset with surgery. Feeling overwhelmed with the seriousness of the break, Bay gently touched his hair, murmuring softly in Pashto to him. She quickly gave him a shot of morphine, enough to render him unconscious so she could work on him. Almost instantly, the boy's taut face relaxed. His face grew ashen even as the pain was removed. Never had Bay felt so damned helpless. She bundled the child up, keeping a hand on his shoulder as she called out to the guard in Pashto.

"Please, let me see Commander Zmarai?"

The guard tensed. "He sleeps."

"This boy needs help," she demanded, her voice strong with authority. "Please, wake him! This child needs a hospital…I can't do anything more for him here."

Another guard appeared at the cave entrance, staring down at the boy and then over at her. He nodded to the man on guard and ordered him to do as she asked.

Fighting back tears and nausea, Bay waited for what seemed an eternity. Finally, a drowsy-looking Zmarai showed up. When he saw her kneeling by the boy, he became enraged.

"You dare wake me, woman?" he demanded, coming to a halt in front of her, glaring.

Gulping, Bay gestured to the boy in the blankets. "This child needs to go to the hospital right now, Commander. I can't save his life. He needs an operation immediately or he's going to die. Please…can't you do something? Help him?" she pleaded, her voice cracking with emotion.

Zmarai's eyes flickered to the child and then snapped back to her. His mouth thinned, and he gave her a hard look.

"Let it go, doctor. There's nothing to be done here for this boy. Better to fill him with morphine and let him die because he's going to, anyway. You will at least speed his death, and he will no longer suffer."

Bay cried out, "No!" She gripped the hem of his trousers. "You can't let this little boy suffer a horrible, undeserved death! You can help him. Please…God, have mercy…."

He slapped her hand away from his trousers, breathing hard, giving her a look of frustration. "Woman, shut your mouth or I'll shut it for you!" He lifted his hand threateningly toward her.

Bay sobbed. "You can't let this child die like this! You tell me you are Muslim. You tell me you believe in love and helping others." Her voice broke. "Then show your compassion for this child, dammit!" She cringed, standing firm, waiting for him to backhand her.

But then Zmarai's face hardened. Something else came into his eyes, and she pressed on. "I ask nothing for myself, Commander. I ask you to consider with your heart, to save this boy's life."

"Shut up!" he roared, leaning down, grabbing her

shoulder. "You know not what you ask, woman!" His breath came in hot spurts of fury as he shoved his face into hers. "Child slavery is a reality," he ground out. "I do not agree with it any more than you do, but I cannot stop it. Khogani is my khan! I must follow his orders, and so must you."

He released her, spinning around and disappearing down the tunnel.

Bay could barely contain the gulping sobs within her. The guards gave her an unhappy look, but they said nothing, turning their backs on her. Tears burned in her eyes. Her hands shook as she tried to comfort the child who had been torn from his mother. This was insanity! Bay knelt by the child, talking softly to him in Pashto. The morphine would keep him comfortable for now.

Bay heard heavy footsteps coming in her direction. She jerked around. A gasp tore from her.

Khogani grabbed her by the hair, hauling her backward, dragging her away from the boy. "You are Satan's whore! How dare you speak to my commander like that!"

Something snapped in Bay. She screamed and grabbed his hands, yanking them out of her hair. Leaping to her feet, she crouched, facing him. "You sick bastard! You monster!" she shrieked, and she carried the fight to him. In one swift movement, Bay kicked at his crotch.

"Whore!" Mustafa thundered, barely missing her boot by an inch as he leaped aside. He yelled for his guards. Bay watched them launch themselves at her,

three against one. She saw their hatred, the lust in
Khogani's eyes. And it was clear what he was going to
do to her. And she wasn't going down without a fight,
the son of a bitch. Gabe had taught her close quarter
defense, and she lashed out sideways with her boot,
catching a guard hurtling at her. She kicked him in the
chest. The man cried out, thrown backward. The impact threw her off her feet. Khogani snarled, leaping
upon her, sitting on her midsection, his hand lunging
for her neck.

"No, whore, you're mine," he rattled, closing his
fingers more tightly around her slender throat.

Bay gurgled. A scream jammed in her throat. She
lifted her hands to break the hold he had on her neck,
but two more guards were there, pinning her arms
above her head.

"Strip her," he roared to the other two guards behind him. "Pull down her trousers!"

Breathing raggedly, her nostrils flaring, she felt
Khogani's hatred flood through her. He kept his grip,
barely allowing her to suck a little air into her oxygen-
starved body. Bay struggled violently, grunting. His
hands jerked at her waistband, yanking the trousers
off her hips, pulling them down below her ankles and
off her feet. She sobbed and fought.

"You don't know when to quit," Mustafa snarled in
her face, watching her eyes dim, watching her mouth
contort into a soundless scream. He leaned back, feeling for her underwear. Catching the cloth, he jerked
the material, ripping it away. He grinned, watching
her eyes flare with fear and disgust.

"Yesssss," he hissed near her ear, "that's good. You're scared now, aren't you?" He gave a low laugh. "And you're mine. I'm going to make you regret you're a woman. When I'm done with you, no man will ever want you again. I intend to keep you around. You will be my personal sex slave...."

His fingers tightened more around her soft throat. Bay choked and fought, trying to jerk her hands free. Four soldiers held her arms and legs down. Khogani's face leered into hers as her vision began to gray. His yellow teeth, the garlic on his breath, his fingers tightening, tightening...

Bay watched her vision dissolving. Felt his other hand groping her, pinching her hip, her thigh, forcing her thighs farther apart. The grayness gathered, and her body convulsed from lack of oxygen. Her eyes rolled upward in her skull. Bay went unconscious from the suffocating hold he had around her throat.

PAIN...BAY'S MIND was fuzzy, lingering on pain that forced her awake. She heard herself groan. Bruising, rippling sensations floated up through her lower body. She felt dirty, a terrible sense of shame and helplessness snaking through her. Her face was jammed into the dirt, saliva leaking out of the corner of her mouth, her hair coated with the dust.

Blips of the boy with the broken leg, blips of Khogani laughing, tunneled through her fragmented mind. Closing her eyes, Bay felt her throat aching like fire. It hurt to swallow. It took another ten minutes for her to become fully conscious.

Everything was dark except for some gray light shining from the nearby tunnels. Bay slowly sat up, burning nonstop between her legs. She looked down and saw her trousers nearby. And then, it hit her like a baseball bat to her chest. Gulping unsteadily, tears coming to her eyes, Bay tried to calm herself, tried to think past what had happened. She felt as if someone had torn out her insides. Hesitantly, she tried to sit up and straighten her legs. Every movement hurt.

She looked up and saw a guard, but he was sitting down, leaning against the rocks, sleeping at the entrance. His AK-47 lay nearby as he snored deeply.

Breathing raggedly, Bay knew she had to escape. If she didn't, Khogani would do this again. And again. She had no memory of the actual rape. Nothing.

She grit her teeth, forced herself to stand up. Dizziness almost knocked her over, but she fought it because if she didn't, she was dead. Leaning down, Bay slowly, quietly pulled on her trousers, buttoning them with shaking fingers. Warm blood slowly moved down the insides of her thighs.

As she scanned the area, Bay saw that the boy was missing. Her heart cracked, and she bit back a sob. The child had been innocent. *Innocent...* She pulled on her boots and quietly walked over to her rucksack. She had to take it with her or she'd never survive escape without it. The ruck contained some protein bars she always packed away in case of emergencies. Picking up the empty glass bottle Zmarai gave her, she tucked it into her cammie pocket. She'd need it if she could escape.

Straightening and easing the straps of her ruck across her shoulders, Bay summoned all her energy and attention on stealing that AK-47 lying beside the heavily sleeping guard.

Biting her lower lip, she picked it up and moved as quietly as she could. She knew the cave complex well enough to know where the two entrances were located. At a fork in the tunnel, Bay turned right, heading for the smaller opening, praying there were no guards at the entrance. *Oh, God, give me strength to get through this...*

It was now or never. She couldn't stand to have Khogani's hands on her again. Shivering violently, she reeled through the traumatizing impact of the assault upon her.

Bay wanted to scream out in rage, but she swallowed the urge. Tears burned her eyes as she approached the entrance. It looked open and without guards. Relief, sharp and powerful, raced through her. She crouched behind a rock wall, waiting, listening and watching for any shadowed movement. Maybe the guards were outside the opening?

How she wanted to sprint out of the opening. Wanted to run so damn badly, but she remembered Gabe's words. He was a sniper. He knew patience. He knew waiting would gain him what he needed to know. She felt his words whisper through her mind, pushing away the sense of humiliation and filth inhabiting her.

Everything remained quiet. Out there, in the night, was her freedom. Her heart turned to Gabe. Oh, God, how would he react to this brutal assault? She loved him so much. Would he turn away from her, not able to touch her again? Bay closed her eyes, tears sliding into the corners of her pursed mouth. Somehow, her heart told her, he would still love her. She had to hold on to hope.

She eased unsteadily to her feet and slipped like a shadow out into the night. As she did, Bay tried to remember everything Gabe had taught her about being a sniper in a hide. His words flowed more strongly through her mind. She squinted, her eyesight adjusting to the night. Overhead, a full moon shone down, a cold and emotionless witness, showing her the goat path south of the cave complex. Relief and terror pounded through Bay as she quickly and silently continued away from the caves. Away from Khogani.

Gabe's voice, deep and low, remained her guide. His sniper tricks, his concealment skills, flowed through her pained, bruised senses. The farther she got away from the cave, the more hope tunneled through Bay's rapidly beating heart. *Home*. She had to get home!

Back home to Gabe.

More than anything, Bay knew he'd love her, hold her, no matter what had happened to her. Tears streaked silently down her drawn cheeks as she allowed herself to let his love flow through her, guide her and keep her sane.

As the grayness preceding dawn crawled upon the eastern horizon, Bay discovered a wadi off the goat path. She had no idea how long she'd run down the path heading south. She'd gotten out her compass from her rucksack at one point, knowing now the direction of the village where she'd been kidnapped. The moon made it easy to trot unsteadily for miles along the thin, rocky goat trail. The air was freezing, but it felt so damned good against her hot, sweaty flesh. Bay drew the clean oxygen deeply into her lungs, fear of being discovered spurring her to keep up the unrelenting pace.

Bay was incredibly weary, feeling the last effects of the adrenaline leave her bloodstream near dawn. She would experience adrenaline crash soon, so she chose a thick stand of brush for cover. Moving into it as quietly as possible, Bay found a small hole between all the heavy limbs. The wadi was narrow and rocky.

As she sat down, Bay heard a slight trickle of water. She shrugged painfully out of the ruck. *Water?* Was she hearing things? Her mind would flatten out for minutes at a time, and Bay had no idea of who or where she was. She'd fly into a panic, her heart fluttering with abject terror. And then, her mind would give up information and knowledge once more. Unsettled and frightened that her mind wasn't working right, she fought what felt like insanity stalking her, just as Khogani had stalked her. Bay was more afraid of losing her mind than anything else. Without it, she couldn't get home to Gabe.

Slowly lying down and rolling over, Bay flattened out on her stomach, searched for and found the water just below the rocks. Quietly pulling a number of stones aside, she created a small pool of water. The water was infested with all kinds of evil bacteria and parasites that could kill a person—that she knew for sure. Sitting up, she opened her ruck, rummaged around and found the purification tablets. She pulled the bottle out of her cammie pocket, placed it on its side in the water, listening to it burp and burble. When it was filled, she dropped two tablets into it and waited.

Her mouth was so dry. She had no idea how far she'd come. She'd need water in order to keep going. People could live weeks without food. They'd die in three to four days without water.

As she sat still, her hearing became acute. The wind was inconstant. The sky was lightening. Bay had to push on because when daylight came Khogani would discover she'd escaped and send out a search party on horseback to find her. They had expert trackers, too.

She didn't want to think what would happen to her if they caught her. A violent fear shook Bay physically, her body remembering what had been done to it. The sense of being unclean welled up through her. If only she could take a hot, hot shower and have soap so she could clean herself off. She could rid herself of his smell and his greasy hands upon her body.

Wiping her mouth, Bay shook the bottle, dissolving the tablets. She drank deeply and quickly. Four more times, Bay filled the bottle and purified the water before she was ready to get up and keep trotting as far away as she could get from Khogani and his men.

CHAPTER ELEVEN

BAY TROTTED ANOTHER three miles before she decided to find a place to lay up for the coming day. Another wadi, this one three thousand feet long down the rocky slope of the mountain, looked like a good place to hide. Gabe's words about a hide drifted through her mind. Bay couldn't control her brain. Sometimes, her mind just stopped working, and she felt a horrible sense of abandonment, suddenly confused. But she kept trotting down the trail.

She remembered this was the way home.... *Home to Gabe.* And then, her mind would return, but not always with the same information or memories. It was driving her to distraction not being able to control her memory. She knew deep shock could create this mental effect. Khogani had struck her so hard against her cheek and temple, he'd probably caused her a Grade Three concussion. That would explain her on again, off again mind antics. Her lower body ached, and she could feel a fever coming. She had to stop and take care of herself medically, or she'd never make it back to Gabe.

Weaving quietly down through the deep stands of trees and brush within the wadi, Bay discovered another spring, this one much larger, about three feet wide and on the surface. She moved at least a thousand feet farther down before feeling safe enough to stop. Shedding the ruck, Bay opened it with trembling hands, seeking and finding antibiotics in one pouch.

She always kept a bar of soap in her pack and pulled it out of the ziplock bag. And a clean washcloth. She pulled on a pair of latex gloves and cleaned herself up the best she could. The fever was taking hold in her lower body, a sign of infection. The blood had stopped leaking down her legs. Quietly as she could, she tore open a battle dressing. It was big enough to clean up the worst of the damage. Filling the water bottle, dropping purification tablets into it, she used that water to dampen the dressing.

Bay didn't know pain until she tried to take care of herself. By the time she was done, tears were leaking down her tense cheeks, her breath coming out shallow and fast. The medic in her understood that, regardless of pain, the wound area must be cleaned thoroughly or else. Taking off the gloves and dropping them inside the ruck, Bay slowly pulled up her trousers. Every movement was agony as she forced herself to kneel down over the water and wash her face and hands free of the dirt and blood with the soap and the washcloth. Her nose and cheek ached like hell, but the feeling of a cool cloth across the area felt heavenly, if only for a few seconds.

Her entire body was trembling when she finished her ministrations. At least she was cleaner now. Her hands, lower arms, face and neck were washed free of blood and dirt. She was somewhat clean. Next, she took a maximum amount of antibiotics to fight the infection. Feeling light-headed, Bay looked around the grayed area, dark shadows of branches surrounding and hiding her. Gabe's voice returned. She remembered him telling her never to hide in an obvious place like a wadi; the Taliban would look there first. How badly she wanted to lie down for just a moment and rest.

Fighting to keep her eyes open, Bay slowly pulled the ruck to her side. She groaned softly as she heaved the heavy gear across her shoulders. She had to get out of here.

Moving south of the wadi, at least four hundred feet away from it, Bay found a deep depression behind a group of rocks crowded against one another. Her memory flashed a picture of her and Gabe hiding in a rocky depression on another Afghan mountain. Yes, this was a good lay up. Her feet wouldn't listen to her, she was shivering from the cold, her body exhausted beyond its physical limits. Nearly falling into the depression which was at least ten feet deep, filled with rocks of all sizes, Bay slowly looked around.

Gabe had taught her to blend in. Her cammies appeared to be the same color as the white, tan and gray rocks surrounding her. She spent minutes of unknown time building her hide, a U-shaped hole beneath the lip, putting rocks around her so that if the Taliban came over the lip and looked in, they wouldn't see her.

Her body was shaking so damned badly, she had to stop work. After placing the ruck in the shadowed recess she'd patiently dug out in the wall of the depression, Bay pushed it to one end. She slid awkwardly into the slit below the lip of the depression and, once lodged inside it, curled into a fetal position. The natural overhang would keep her safe from any prying eyes above. Bay collapsed, her head resting heavily on the ruck. She felt more feverish. It would take the antibiotics forty-eight hours to take hold. Until then, she would battle fever on top of everything else. Fever would play with her barely functioning mind.

At least she was free of Khogani, and for that, Bay was grateful. She was a Hill woman. She knew mountains, knew how to survive in them. She could find her way back home armed with the knowledge Gabe had taught her. The challenge was dodging and avoiding Khogani, who she knew had to be looking for her by now. Before she'd gone into her hide, she'd made certain she'd created backward walking or back tracks that would confuse the bastards trailing her. She'd walked on rocks before entering the depression. No one could trace her over rocks. They'd lose her trail. And she'd be able to hide from them. Those were Bay's last thoughts as she fell into a deep, exhausted sleep.

GABE SET UP his sniper rifle, looking through the Night Force scope. They'd made it across the valley and up the other side to a goat trail that led directly into the cave complex just before the sun rose. They were a thousand yards east of the goat path.

Reza lay at his side, scanning the area north of them through a spotter scope, his sniper rifle nearby. They were a good five miles away from Khogani's complex, just below a rocky hill above the goat path.

"Looks like they're all riled up this morning," Gabe muttered under his breath as he spotted a single-file group riding their way.

"Khogani looks very angry," Reza agreed.

They watched twenty Taliban horsemen gallop out of the cave, heading south down the goat path toward their position. Sometimes they'd stop, and the lead soldier would dismount, kneel down, looking for something, and then mount up once more, and they'd gallop onward.

Gabe searched frantically among the riders for Bay. They were much closer this time, each face clear and distinct. His heart sank. They'd spent all night quietly climbing the damned narrow path for three thousand feet. They'd walked the whole way, leading the hard-breathing, laboring horses. It had been torturous, slow, dirty work. His knees were killing him. His heart was racing with dread as he once more searched each rider's face, praying he'd missed Bay among them. But he didn't find her on the second inspection.

"Bay isn't with them. I wonder where they're going in such a hurry?" Gabe asked, worry in his tone.

"I don't know."

Gabe called in the intel to Chief Phillips by radio. The drone had been off-line for twelve hours now, due to a computer malfunction. The ability to send streaming video back to the SEAL HQ had stopped, and it had left them blind. Gabe wanted to curse in frustration. A new drone would arrive shortly over-head to replace it.

They'd lain unmoving, hidden by the rocks just below the top of the hill, as the Taliban had rushed out of the cave like a disturbed hive of bees earlier. Directly across the goat path from where they hid, there was a long wadi, at least three thousand feet, sloping down to a small valley below. Gabe ran his scope up and down it, along each side of it. *Nothing.*

Where was Bay? Was she all right? What were these guys looking for? Gabe closed his eyes for a moment, ugly, terrifying emotions churning through him. He was helpless to stop them. He loved Bay, dammit. He wanted her *out* of here! *Alive.* Safe in his arms where she belonged.

His patience as a sniper warred with his anxious heart because he'd seen too much brutality by the Taliban before. He just couldn't think any further about it, too scared for Bay...for himself, to go there.

The group of riders was within a thousand yards of where they remained invisible. Gabe's eyes narrowed, watching the same man dismount, move slowly around the front of the group. Looking...looking.

"Oh, shit!" he rasped. "Bay must have escaped! They're tracking her. That's why they're stopping so often. They're looking for her boot tracks!" His entire body tensed as he watched their main tracker. He was closely studying the dirt and rock path. And looking toward the wadi, pointing at it.

Gabe's adrenaline surged. Jesus, had Bay made it this far under cover of night? He wanted to scream because that was when the drone went belly up, unable to send live video feed of Khogani's cave entrance to the SEALs at Camp Bravo. If she'd escaped, they'd not been able to see her slip out of the cave. And, God, Gabe hoped Bay had; the only way she could go was south on this path. Though frantic, he thought of what to do next.

"They're hunting for her," Reza said softly. "They're backtracking now...."

Swallowing hard, Gabe watched them intently through his sniper scope. The tracker seemed confused, following tracks that doubled back and went in the direction they'd just ridden. "Bay was born in the mountains," he told Reza softly. "Her father taught her to track. She's creating confusion with her tracks. She's trying to throw them off her trail by backtracking."

"Call in the QRF?" Reza asked, his voice hoarse.

Gabe shook his head. "No...not yet. We have no idea where she's at." Or even if she's hidden in the area somewhere nearby. His mind gyrated, recalling a night last year on another Hindu Kush mountain slope when Bay had been with him on a mission of mercy. They'd been set up in an ambush by the Taliban. He'd raced with her up a rocky mountain slope, hoping to evade and escape the enemy. She'd wanted to go hide in the tree- and brush-lined wadi, but he'd told her that would be the first place the Taliban would look. Instead, he'd taught her how to hide out in plain sight and not be seen. That was what snipers did so well.

He vividly remembered that freezing night out in

the open in that rocky depression with her. *Oh, God, let Bay have remembered that...* He watched as the riders dismounted, a few of the soldiers holding the reins of all the horses. The rest of the enemy ran quickly around the wadi. His heart started a slow, dreaded pound. Had Bay remembered not to hide in a wadi? Or was she wounded?

"They think she's in the wadi," Reza whispered, sounding anxious.

"Yeah..." Gabe focused on the soldiers not only going into the wadi, but also running like gazelles along either side of it. If Bay was in there, they'd find her. There would be no escape for her. His mind tumbled over brutal choices. Call in the QRF? Two Chinook MH-47s would be bearing thirty SEALs coming in to meet this group with maximum firepower. But where was Bay?

Gabe couldn't call in a QRF if he didn't know where Bay was located. A firefight would sure as hell ensue, and she could be killed by friendly fire, a ricochet or by a Taliban bullet. And if he called in a B-52, which was circling on a racetrack at thirty thousand feet above them right now, a five-hundred-pound, laser-guided JDAM would blow all them to hell, but it could also kill Bay, too.

He felt bile gather in the back of his throat. He so badly wanted to do something. Anything. But he couldn't. The sniper in him knew patience and waiting was the only answer to this unresolved situation.

He let out a painful, ragged sigh. "No...we wait." Those were the hardest three words he'd ever spoken. Watching the Taliban crawl around the wadi, the light revealing more and more every passing minute, searching for the woman he loved. Bay was his life....

Bay, where are you, baby? I know you escaped. Where are you?

And he ruthlessly moved his scope beyond the wadi, looking to the north side of it, studying the rocky scree. And then, he patiently began to scan the south side beyond the wadi. His gut was screaming at him. He sensed Bay hiding south of the wadi. But where?

Suddenly, Gabe heard a triumphant shout from one of the Taliban soldiers hidden by the trees and brush within the wadi. Though unable to hear what was said, Gabe watched all of the soldiers race into the wadi, AK-47s unsafed, their muzzles up and ready to fire. *Shit!* Had they found Bay? His heart hammered wildly in his chest. Gabe trembled violently, controlling his raw emotions, watching the soldiers leaping and running to one, specific area hidden beneath the trees. Holding his breath, his hand tightened against the stock of his Win-Mag .300 rifle. Sweat trickled down the sides of his face. *Watch. Wait. Just fuckin' wait...*

"They've found something," Reza whispered tensely, an ache in his lowered voice. He moved the spotter scope, trying to discern what or who it was.

Gabe held his breath, hardly able to think, his heart in utter turmoil, gripped by icy terror. He wanted to cry. Five Taliban popped out on the south side of the wadi; one of them was waving something in his hand. *What the hell?* Gabe zeroed his sights in on the one man waving something white around in his hand. More and more of the soldiers gathered around him, shouting excitedly. They were like bloodhounds on the scent of their quarry. *What the hell did they find?*

Gabe adjusted the fine hairs on his Night Force scope, breathing slowly, trying to keep his backlog of emotions savagely controlled, in his kill box. If he gave into his emotions, he couldn't do his job. He wouldn't be able to focus and protect Bay.

His heart stopped. Gabe groaned softly. The soldier was waving a battle dressing around in his hand. Gabe recognized it immediately. And then, his gut clenched so painfully he wanted to scream. The dressing was bloody. Bay's blood? *Oh, God, baby, where are you?*

"No," Reza muttered, his voice breaking as he recognized what was in the soldier's hand. Mouth tightening, Gabe watched the men dancing around, triumphantly yelling and shouting over their find. A black-bearded man emerged from the wadi, giving orders, waving his arms angrily at them. *Khogani.* His entire body tensed, and Gabe ached with dread for Bay. Had they found her?

And then, the men dispersed, running down both sides of the wadi that stretched for such a long way. Gabe felt a little of his fear recede. "They haven't found her," he rasped. "They're still searching for her…they found the battle dressing…that's all…."

Reza's voice was low with hope, with excitement. "Yes, that's right. She must have left the dressing there? A decoy to throw them off her trail, perhaps? They're going to search the rest of that wadi all the way down to the valley floor below."

It hurt to swallow. Sweat was leaking into his eyes, stinging them. Gabe blinked rapidly, trying to clear his blurred vision. Looking again, he didn't see any of the Taliban. None was in view. All of them had moved into the wadi. He felt a tiny trickle of relief, but not much. Bay was wounded. "Let's look on either side of the wadi," he roughly ordered Reza. "Bay knows better than to hide in an obvious place. You take the north side, I'll take the south."

For long minutes, the slant of sun slowly creeping toward the rocks and scree along the south side of the wadi, Gabe carefully looked at every last damned rock, discerning whether it really was one, or just Bay, blending in and looking like the surrounding area. He was a sniper. He knew what to look for; tiny telltale signs that might lead him to where Bay might be hiding was all he needed. Just *one* sign, dammit.

Just give me one clue, baby...just one...

And yet, if he couldn't locate her, the Taliban trackers might not be able to, either.

"They're coming back," Reza warned him tightly, an hour later. They had searched the entire length of the wadi and come up empty-handed.

A tight grin crossed Gabe's sweaty face, the sun now climbing higher. "Yeah, she's not in there," and he felt his heart fill with hope.

Good going, baby, you screwed them royal...

He managed a slight chuckle, watching the soldiers wearily climb up the three-thousand-foot-long slope toward where their horses stood on the goat path.

At that moment, he heard a cryptic message from Chief Phillips in his earpiece.

"Blue Dog online."

His heart raced with hope as he made one click on the radio, to let Phillips know he'd heard the transmission. The drone was now on station directly above them! Quickly, Gabe whispered their GPS coordinates, asking for the long-range, delicate video camera on the drone to scan north and south of the wadi. Maybe, just maybe, an overhead shot would reveal Bay's location *if* she was in this area at all. He looked over at Reza, who grinned widely, huge relief in his expression. Hope burned in his dark eyes, too.

Gabe watched, sweating heavily now, the sun hot at almost ten in the morning. The Taliban kept searching, kept looking, coming up with nothing. There was frustration and anger in all their faces. Bay had duped them. Khogani was yelling and waving his hand around at his weary soldiers.

Oh, baby, you've evaded them. God, I love you. Just hang on. I'm going to find you...

BAY SLOWLY AWOKE, flies buzzing around her, biting her exposed flesh. At first, she didn't know where she was at. And then, she heard angry Pashto voices floating her way. Terror shot through her, fully awakening her. Adrenaline surged through her body, her breath changing, becoming ragged and shallow. Tensing, she felt pain shoot through her lower body. What time was it?

Her mind churned, receded and then clarified. It took precious time to focus, to lock in on this one question. As she looked at her watch, the dials appeared blurred. Blinking, her vision cleared. It was ten in the morning. She'd slept a long time.

Heart pounding with fear, she heard Khogani's voice rising with shrill anger. It sent terror plunging through her veins. He was so near! Squeezing her eyes shut, Bay could barely breathe as the voices drifted closer and closer. Oh, God, was she hidden well enough? Had she dug enough dirt and rock out from below the overhang to completely disappear inside it?

Bay tried to pull the exposed toe of her boot even tighter against her tucked body. Fear sizzled through her as she thought of the Taliban discovering her. She pressed her hand hard against her trembling lips. She didn't dare make a sound. Not one.

GABE FOLLOWED THE progress of the soldiers as they fanned out across the scree slope, still searching for Bay. Where the hell had she hidden? If he couldn't find her, they wouldn't either. Maybe… He knew what to look for and although they were trackers and familiar with their own territory, they still had not located Bay. His heart squeezed with pain, with fear, as they slowly moved around, looking at rocks, looking for anything that might lead them to where she hid.

"Blue Dog bingo."

Gabe's eyes widened. His heart lurched. That meant the drone had located Bay! *Oh, Jesus…where? Where?*

He clicked the radio once. They were too close, and any speaking could alert the Taliban to the position of their hide. His mouth grew dry as Phillips gave the

GPS coordinates. He clicked acknowledgement, his hands trembling. He slowly moved his GPS unit across the goat path, watching the tiny red laser beam hum over the landscape, numbers tumbling and turning. His breath jammed in his throat. There, twenty feet away from where a Taliban soldier stood, was where Bay was hidden.

Dammit!

Gabe had studied that one spot so many times before. His gut told him it was a good spot to hide. And Bay had. Oh, God, she'd done it right! She'd remembered his lessons. A shudder of powerful emotions worked their way through him. Relief, love for Bay, love for her incredible courage and bravery under such terrible, life-and-death circumstances. She'd remembered. She'd learned. He was so damned proud of her.

Gabe quietly laid the GPS unit aside, giving Reza a hand signal to train his spotter scope on the area he indicated. Quickly, he turned his own scope on the scree. Where the hell was Bay? It was all rocks. He could find nothing to indicate her presence.

His heart thundered unrelentingly as the soldier drew closer and closer to her hide. He was looking around, being careful, being thorough. Gabe had him in his sights. His finger softly brushed against the two-pound trigger, waiting…just waiting.

Gabe knew if he discovered Bay, he'd shoot the bastard dead before he could warn the others of her hide. And then everyone would hear the bark of the Win-Mag and come running straight at them. And then, he'd have nineteen men rushing to kill him and Reza.

At least the focus would be off Bay. Gabe's mouth compressed. He settled his breathing, steadying, slowing his heartbeat.

He felt more than saw Reza draw up his own sniper rifle, ready to fire. The Afghan was a damned good shot, and between them, they might stand a chance if attacked. Gabe knew, though, if he killed the one soldier stalking Bay's hide, the entire group would instantly know where they were hidden.

Quickly, he pulled all twelve mags from his H-gear, laying them out in neat rows so he could reach for a fresh mag, slam it into his rifle and keep on firing. Nineteen Taliban against two of them. His lips drew away from his clenched teeth.

Good odds for a SEAL sniper. Bring it on…

As the soldier stopped and looked around, he scowled. Gabe watched his every expression, saw confusion in his face. Just then, he heard on his radio, "QRF on the way." Relief washed through him, but Gabe knew that as soon as they heard those Chinooks coming loaded to the teeth with SEALs ready to take the battle to them, the Taliban would instantly react. And Bay would be in the middle of it all.

Gabe sweated heavily, watching the soldier halt at a lip of a slight depression. He was right on top of Bay's hide. Would he see her? His finger moved solidly but lightly against the trigger, waiting. Just waiting…

The soldier stiffened, peering down into the depression, his mouth popping open in disbelief.

Shit!

He turned to yell a warning. Gabe caressed the trigger. The Win-Mag bucked savagely against his right shoulder. He watched as the pink mist of the bullet slammed through the soldier's head. The man crumpled, never getting to cry out Bay's location.

"Son of a bitch, Reza, get ready to fire...."

The Afghan watched through his scope. "Bring the fight to us. She's unarmed," he whispered tightly.

Gabe watched as the shattering sound of the rifle's bark echoed loudly across the area, alerting their enemy, throwing down the gauntlet at them. Every Taliban's head snapped up in their direction. That was just as well because they could fight back. Bay couldn't. He sensed she was wounded, hurting. How badly, he didn't know, but it scared him as little else ever would. Gabe wanted to leave his hide, run that thousand yards and get to Bay's side, help her. Protect her, but dammit, he couldn't.

Now the enemy was like an angry hive of disturbed wasps moving straight toward them. It would take the QRF at least half an hour to reach them. Gabe knew the odds, and they weren't good. During that half hour, they'd have to fight, kill and not get killed themselves. And they probably would not survive it, but he was going to take as many of the bastards as he could with him before that happened.

The QRF had Bay's position, and they would swoop down, find her, take her to safety. That was all Gabe cared about. He loved her. He'd felt her love in every caress of her eyes on him, in every touch of her long, beautiful healer's fingers softly skimming his body. He'd found love when he never thought he ever would.

And he was all right with dying, because Bay had entered his life, breathed her love into his badly wounded and scarred heart. Gabe's only regret was he'd never be able to tell her again how much he loved her.

"Rock it out," he growled over at Reza. Gabe keyed his radio, giving the chief the present situation. And then he settled down to start taking the fuckers out, one bullet at a time.

Reza fired first. A soldier screamed, his AK-47 flying out of his hands, yanked backwards by the .300's bullet slamming through his body.

Gabe saw Khogani shrieking at his troops, pointing to where they were hiding on the knoll across the goat path. Teeth clenched, he aimed for the bastard's head. Khogani was going…right…now…. And he fired. The rifle bucked, the harsh bark of the fired bullet surrounding him. He watched the bullet fly true in a classic head shot. One moment, Khogani was shrieking at his men, the next, half his head departed his body, dissolving in the air. The leader crumpled into a heap on the goat path. The soldiers kept moving toward them, bloodlust in their faces, their screams of fury pounding and echoing around the area.

Bullets were flying into their position. They spit up dirt into geysers, snapped past Gabe's head. None of it bothered him. He turned his cold rage and funneled it into picking off soldier after soldier with his sniper rifle. He was going to get even with every last one of these bastards for touching Bay, for hurting her. Dammit, every one of these sons of bitches was going to hell under his rifle's muzzle. He had three hundred rounds, and he intended to use every last damn one of them to take the enemy out.

CHAPTER TWELVE

BAY HEARD THE boom of a Win-Mag .300. She gasped, jerking, oblivious to her pain. And then, an AK-47 fired in answer. They each had their own distinctive sound. She heard two more booming sounds from two Win-Mags. Those were SEAL sniper rifles! *Two of them!* Gasping, her eyes widening, Bay couldn't believe her ears. They were here! SEALs! *Gabe...*

Pushing hard, Bay groaned and tumbled out of her hide, rolling into the rocks below. She landed on her back, the AK-47 gripped tightly in her hand. She panted in pain, her eyes blurred and then clearing. Two SEAL snipers against how many Taliban? Her mind cleared for a moment, and she could think. Actually think!

The blue sky above her looked so peaceful, a sharp contrast to the angry screams of Taliban. Gasping for breath, Bay turned over and dug the toes of her boots into the rocks, pushing her head carefully up and over the ledge of the depression to take a look.

Bay could see Taliban charging across the goat path toward a small hill no more than fifty feet away from it. She noticed the wink of the Win-Mags, their roar taking their bullets to the fury of the enemy attacking them. Two SEALs against so many Taliban! Breathing raggedly, Bay glanced down at the AK-47 in her hands. She knew how to use one. She'd been trained to do it. Hands shaking, she pulled out the magazine. It was full.

Lifting her chin, ignoring the excruciating pain tearing through her lower body, Bay pressed herself against the side of the hide to gain stability in order to shoot accurately. The SEALs wouldn't survive no matter how good they were as warriors. In her heart, she knew Gabe had to be one of those snipers. She knew with every sobbing breath she took, he had not abandoned her! He'd come after her. He'd found her!

A fierce, overwhelming love for him welled up through her, calming her. Lying the AK-47 down on the rocks to steady the barrel, she pointed the muzzle at the backs of the soldiers charging the hill. Bay set the selector to single shots. She only had one magazine. And she had to make every shot count. She leaned her shoulder into the metal stock, focused though the iron sights on the nearest Taliban and fired.

GABE SCOWLED, SEEING a Taliban soldier at the rear suddenly crumple and fall. *What the hell?* He and Reza were firing slowly but accurately at the Taliban closest to them, not at the rear of the group. His shoulder ached as he continued one fire, one bullet at a time. Whoever was closest was the one he sighted on. And then, after he saw a second soldier at the back of the group fall, he wondered where the bullet had come from.

He lifted his head for just a second, bullets snapping by him. His eyes narrowed to slits as he saw some-one at the edge of the depression. Bay! And she had an AK-47, aiming and firing at the rear of the group, taking them down! His throat ached with relief. She was alive!

Gabe forced himself to return to firing at the sol-diers racing and clawing up the hill to reach them. His mind worked like a deadly precision instrument. Now, with Bay in the fight, the Taliban were caught in a cross fire. None of them seemed to realize it yet, because she was killing those in the rear. His mouth thinned into a hard line, his eyes narrowing as he worked the rifle, the buck powerful, rippling through his entire body. He heard Reza's Win-Mag, felt the heat of the Taliban bullet as it passed so damned close to his neck, his flesh burned in the wake of the pass-ing speed of it.

The bloodcurdling screams of the Taliban grew closer. As fast as Gabe could fire at one, two more soldiers would pop up in his place. They were within a hundred feet of their position. He kept firing, the burning smell of cordite stinging his flared nostrils. They were going to get overrun....

BAY WATCHED THE soldiers racing up the hill toward the SEAL's position. *No! Oh, Lord, no!* They'd be overrun in less than a minute. Gabe was there! Without think-ing, Bay jammed her boots into the wall of the hide, scrambling, lifting herself up and out of it. She wove on unsteady knees, forcing herself to stand.

She yelled hoarsely in Pashto, hoping her voice would carry above the gunfire and screams. Two of the soldiers at the rear hesitated mid-hill, turned and looked her way. Bay waved the AK-47 up in the air at them, a challenge. And then, those soldiers screamed at the ones in front of them, excitedly pointing in her direction.

Satisfaction thrummed through her as half the soldiers nearing the summit turned around. Their mouths dropped open. They recognized her! She gave them a tight grin, her teeth clenched as she stood and fired a bullet into the group. One soldier fell.

For a second, the Taliban froze. And then, half of the group turned, running back down the slope toward her. The other half continued to fight their way up toward the crown of the hill. Bay felt rage and channeled it. She staggered to the depression, needing cover because the bullets were starting to snap and pop around her. She had no Kevlar, no way to protect herself. As she fell into the depression, pain ripped up though her. Relief soared through her. She'd at least crippled the attack against the SEALs and split the Taliban force. Now, maybe Gabe and his partner, whoever he was, could handle half the size of the attackers. SEALs didn't surrender. Not ever. And now, she mentally counted the bullets left in the mag against the amount of angry soldiers running toward her position.

If she fired accurately, she had just enough bullets to kill all the enemy racing in her direction. Turning, Bay leaned against the rocky wall, her head and shoulders above it, the AK-47's barrel planted on the earth to steady her aim. She saw their hatred. She tasted it. But Bay funneled her fear. One bullet, one enemy...

GABE GASPED AS he saw Bay reveal her position, shouting to get the Taliban's attention. He couldn't believe it. Instantly realizing what she was doing, he cursed richly. Bay was trying to stop them from being overrun. In that second Gabe was never so scared. No matter what she'd endured, no matter how injured she was, Bay was bravely making herself a target to save them. *Dammit!*

He kept his eye on the enemy. They were within fifty feet when Gabe yelled over to Reza, "Pistol!" And he yanked the SIG Sauer 9mm pistol out of the drop holster on his right thigh, swinging it up, firing as the first soldier came over the crest at them.

At a certain point, sniper rifles were too unwieldy to use. Especially in close-quarters fighting. Gabe watched as Reza dropped the rifle, going for the .45 at his side. Now, it was pistols against AK-47s. And his KA-BAR knife. Jerking the long blade out of the sheath strapped around his left calf, Gabe held it ready in his left hand, close to his body.

Four Taliban leaped over the crest, firing down at them. Gabe burned with hatred as he fired the SIG calmly into the shrieking group. Two fell. He felt a hit to his Kevlar, knocking him forward two paces. But he didn't fall, instead dropping to one knee, his SIG remaining deadly accurate.

Reza took on two more. The .45 bucked, large holes in the chests of the Taliban opening up, blood flying all around them. Gabe's whole world slowed down to milliseconds. Four more soldiers leaped at them. His hand bucked. The SIG barked. One soldier was left standing, and he'd thrown himself at Gabe. His hand was out, a curved blade in it, intending to stab him in the chest.

Like hell he would! Gabe sidestepped as the soldier flew by. SEALs were taught to use both their hands with equal ease. As the soldier passed by him, inches between him, Gabe jammed the KA-BAR up into the man's gut. He heard him shriek. Instantly, Gabe jerked the knife out of his soft abdomen, falling backward, avoiding the downward slice of the man's blade.

Another soldier jumped him from behind, and Reza yelled a warning. Too late! Gabe growled as he saw a knife slash downward out of the corner of his eye. The blade struck his Kevlar where his heart lay. The point snapped off. The soldier screamed, lifting his hand to try again. He wouldn't get a second chance. Gabe snarled a curse, bringing the KA-BAR blade up from the left, thrusting it savagely into the man's side. Ribs crunched and broke beneath the force of the blade's entry. The man uttered a cry, surprise in his expression.

Gabe hissed, shoving him off to one side of himself, giving his KA-BAR a powerful jerk to remove it from the man's torso.

Another soldier leaped at him. Lying on the ground, he rolled up to the left and fired straight up at the enemy with the SIG. The man screamed, dropping his

AK-47. The weapon bounced off Gabe's helmet, and he rolled to avoid being hit by the descending body.

The smell of blood, sweat and burning gunpowder surrounded them. Gabe leaped to his feet, shooting two soldiers who had jumped Reza. Breathing hard, Gabe swung around, expecting more enemy to charge them. There were none. He was confused for a moment until he suddenly heard sharp exchanges of gunfire below the hill. Staggering, his back hurting from the Kevlar bullet hit, Gabe spun forward, jumping over the ledge, moving toward the top of the hill. *Bay!*

Gabe stood for just a second, seeing five Taliban closing in on Bay's position. She was firing slowly, accurately. Bullets were raining down on her. With a curse, Gabe turned.

"Get your Win-Mag," he yelled at Reza. Leaning down, he grabbed up the weapon. His SIG would not cover the distance, but his rifle sure as hell would. He grabbed two mags, racing down the hill full speed, his eyes on Bay, automatically releasing the spent mag in the Win-Mag and slapping in a full one. In one motion, the bullet fed into the chamber.

BAY KNEW SHE was in trouble. She noticed the hatred in the men's eyes as they ran toward her, firing their AK-47s on full automatic at her. Almost simultaneously, out of the corner of her eye, she saw a SEAL running down the hill toward her, rifle in hand. Giving a cry, she recognized Gabe's form. He was firing the rifle at the men who were about to leap into the depression and kill her. The seconds slowed to a painful crawl.

Gabe was trying to save her. Bay was overwhelmed with the knowledge he had somehow found her.

One Taliban soldier jumped down at her, firing his weapon. Bay knew she was going to die. He fired directly at her head even though she raised her AK-47 and fired simultaneously up at him. Her world went dark.

GABE SCREAMED OBSCENITIES as he saw the Taliban soldier leap into the depression, firing down at Bay. He'd skidded to a halt, jamming the Win-Mag to his shoulder, pulling the trigger. Midway down, the Taliban soldier's body jerked sideways. But it was too late. *Oh, God, it's too late!*

Through his scope, Gabe watched Bay crumple and disappear into the depression. *Son of a bitch!* He roared out her name, running as hard as he could across the goat path. Behind him, Reza fired the Win-Mag twice, taking out the last two soldiers. Hitting the scree at full speed, Gabe stumbled, nearly fell, righting himself, his gaze pinned on the depression. All the Taliban were dead, bodies lying everywhere. Was Bay alive? How bad was she hit?

Breathing in explosive gasps, Gabe skidded to a halt at the lip of the depression. His gaze whipped from the soldier, who lay dead three feet away from Bay. She was unmoving, the AK-47 in her lifeless hand, lying on her side among the rocks.

Gabe cried out her name and fell to her side. Automatically, he reached into his cammie pocket for his blow-out kit, the emergency medical packet filled with

items to save another SEAL from a gunshot wound or
from bleeding out. Gently, Gabe eased Bay over on her
back, pressing his fingers against her heavily bruised
throat, trying to find a pulse, trying to find life.

There! He swallowed his emotions. His eyes teared
for a second as he felt her slight, fluttering pulse. Rapidly, he raked his gaze across her body, trying to see
where she'd been shot. And then, horrified, as he carefully moved her head, he discovered blood leaking
down the left side of her skull, across her delicate ear,
soaking into the dirty, curled strands of hair. Oh, God,
her face was horribly swollen, bruised.

Gasps tore out of his mouth. Gabe heard helicopters approaching, the puncture of rotor blades never
sounding so good to him. Two medevacs were following them in because a QRF force might need them. He
had a battle dressing and quickly pressed it to the side
of her temple and wrapped it around her head where
she'd taken the bullet. Gabe couldn't tell if the bullet
was in her brain or had just grazed her and ricocheted
off her skull. He began to pray for the first time in
his life as he slid his hands beneath her shoulders and
thighs. Lifting Bay gently against his body, her head
lolling against his chest, a sob tore out of Gabe's contorted mouth. His chest hurt so damn much, he felt
as if he was going to die from grief.

Reza appeared at the lip of the depression. His eyes
widened enormously as he saw Bay unconscious in
his arms. Without a word, he thrust out his hand and
helped Gabe scramble up and out of the hole.

"They're here!" Reza shouted, pointing to the two MH-47s landing several hundred feet away.

Gabe tried to think through his shock. "Run to them! Get me a medevac! Bay's been shot in the head. Hurry!"

The SEAL force emptied out of the rear of the Chinooks. Also a Black Hawk medevac landed hundreds of feet farther down behind the Chinook on the goat path. Shoving his legs forward, out of breath, feeling shaky with terror, Gabe pushed forward into an unsteady trot. He held Bay tightly in his arms, not wanting to injure her any more than she already had been. He caught sight of Chief Phillips racing toward him, his face set.

Gabe didn't even slow down as the Chief met him. "Head wound," he yelled over the rotors beating around them. The dust was rising on the goat trail, the SEALs were rapidly deploying, M-4s ready, moving toward each of the Taliban soldiers to make sure they were dead.

Phillips nodded, pointing behind the Chinook. "Get her and yourself onto that first medevac!"

As Gabe was halfway to the Black Hawk, two medics leaped out of the helo and raced toward him. Fear and grief riddled him. He stumbled, nearly fell, holding Bay tight against his body. Righting himself, Gabe met the two men. One was older, maybe late thirties, the other younger.

"Let us take her," the older medic yelled above the cacophony.

"No way," Gabe snarled at them, pushing past them

and into a trot. Only fifty feet to go and Bay would be on a litter. Then, they could help her.

The older man turned, gripped Gabe's arm, steadying him as he ran. "This way," he yelled as they hit the rotor wash pummeling them with eighty-mile-an-hour blasts as they drew near the medevac.

Gabe bowed his head, protecting Bay. Brush, dirt and dust kicked and swirled violently around them. He was grateful for the older medic's guiding hand on his arm, pulling him toward the lip of the helo.

There, Gabe climbed in, gently depositing Bay on the litter strapped to the bulkhead of the bird. And then he shoved himself quickly to the rear, allowing the two medics to instantly hop on board. Gabe grabbed a helmet and pulled it on. Plugging the connection into the ICS panel, he'd be able to communicate directly with the two pilots and medics.

The older medic's last name on his flight suit read Taft. Gabe gasped for air, sucking it deep into his burning lungs, his eyes never leaving Bay's white, unmoving face. Taft pulled on a helmet and put the mic to his lips.

"Head wound," Gabe told him, his voice unsteady. "Left side, temple."

"Roger that, sir." Taft lifted his head after a swift examination of Bay. "Casevac," he told the pilots. "Bagram. It's a nine-line. Redline this bird. She's critical."

Closing his eyes for a moment, Gabe felt the Black Hawk break earth, the gravity pushing down upon him. He opened his eyes, breathing raggedly, watching the two medics quickly cutting away the sleeves on

Bay's cammies, exposing both her pale arms. Feeling
as if he were in some kind of unending nightmare, he
watched Taft push an IV into each of her arms. The
younger medic named Marbury followed the older's
directions quickly and efficiently. Sobbing for breath,
his back throbbing painfully from the Kevlar hit, Gabe
bowed his head, his hand across his face, tears falling.

Critical. Bay was critical. He couldn't lose her!
He just couldn't! No matter what Gabe tried to do,
he couldn't stop the tears from flowing. The roar of
the helicopter covered his sobs that wrenched unwill-
ingly out of his chest. He simply couldn't conceive of
life without Bay in it. Her soft, shining eyes, her full
lips, her husky laughter riffled across his heart and
memory. Bay had always lifted him and made him
feel happy for the first time in his sorry-assed life.

He heard Taft's voice tense as he snapped orders
to Marbury. Gabe lifted his wet face and watched as
the medic placed a blood pressure cuff on her upper
right arm. Taft leaned over her, listening to her heart
through his stethoscope.

Only now was Gabe beginning to realize the terrible damage done to Bay. The entire left side of her
face was swollen, nothing but purple-and-red bruises,
her left eye swollen shut. What kind of hell had she
endured? Gabe knotted his fist, wanting to kill whoever had done this to her. He was racked with murderous rage.

His life focused only on Bay. Taft took the dressing
off her head, peering intently at the head wound. Gabe
couldn't read his taut expression. The medic quickly

cleaned the area, replacing it with a dressing, wrapping gauze around her head. Her light brown curls looked stark against the white bandage.

Gabe's gaze moved down across her limp body. It was then he saw dark blood staining her trousers on the insides of her thighs. A groan tore out of him. Gabe felt a new kind of terror ripping through him. And Taft found it in his examination of her. Bile rose in Gabe's throat as he watched the medic quickly cut her trousers from ankle all the way up to her waist. The other medic did the same on her other leg. Old dried blood along with bright red blood coated the insides of both her thighs all the way down to her calves.

Gabe turned away, unable to watch as Taft went to examine the source of her bleeding. *Why?* Why had they done this to her? A wrenching scream worked its way up through him. Gabe's cry was drowned out by the thundering sounds of the helicopter. He turned away, head pressed against the cold metal of the bulkhead, his eyes jammed shut. Hot tears fell down his tense face.

Gabe felt like a coward by turning away when Bay had bravely faced her captors head-on and he had not. When he turned back, he could see that several warm blankets had been placed across her lower body, tucked in around her waist. Taft's face was filled with fury. Their gazes briefly met. Gabe felt his whole life slipping, tumbling into free fall. The medic didn't have to say anything. The look on his face said it all. He knew Bay had been raped....

AT BAGRAM HOSPITAL, Gabe followed the gurney bearing Bay into the emergency room. He wasn't going to leave her side. Taft quickly gave the stats to a young woman doctor with red hair and green eyes. The name embroidered on her white coat said Captain S. Guardian. Gabe wondered if it was some kind of sick joke being played on him as he stood, gripping Bay's cold hand. Waiting. Waiting again. *God, hurry. Do something for her! What the fuck is taking so long? Get your asses in gear!*

Dr. Guardian glanced over at him, then gave orders to her nurses, turned and thanked Taft.

Taft nodded and then went over to Gabe.

"Sir, she's got a chance of making it. Okay? Do you hear me?" His eyes burrowed into Gabe's.

Those were the sweetest words Gabe had ever heard. Turning, he looked over at the lean medic. "Th-thanks…I appreciate everything you did for her…." He choked up, his eyes burning with unshed tears, unable to speak.

The medic gripped his shoulder. "Hang in there, sir. She's got you fighting for her. Never surrender."

CHAPTER THIRTEEN

GABE SAT TENSELY in the surgery lobby of Bagram hospital. It had been four hours since Bay had been wheeled into surgery. Four of the longest, most torturous hours of his life. Dr. Guardian was a neurologist, and he hoped against hope her name really meant every word of it. Right now, Bay needed a guardian, someone who could pull her out of death's embrace and bring her back to him.

He was so immersed in his grief over Bay that he failed to even hear Dr. Guardian approach until she touched his shoulder. Gabe jerked, his head snapping up, automatically going into a defensive posture.

"Whoa, Chief, take it easy, I'm not the enemy," she said, stepping away, holding up her hands.

Gabe's heart pounded with adrenaline as he regarded the red-haired doctor with suspicion. When he sensed her fear, he instantly forced himself to relax.

"Sorry," he muttered. "How is Bay? Is she going to make it?" He tried to read the woman's large, compassionate green eyes. She wore light blue scrubs, the cap still over her head, the white mask hanging around her neck. Her hair was in a ponytail and contained within a fine, white netting.

Dr. Guardian pulled up a chair opposite him and sat down. Her face was somber as she regarded Gabe. "I understand you and Baylee Thorn are engaged?"

He swallowed, a jerky nod of his head. Gabe was afraid to try and speak, feeling his throat close off, afraid of what she was going to tell him. He tried to prepare himself. He could face a damned firefight, his heart slow and steady. He could kill in close-quarters combat without remorse. But this was worse. Much worse. Gabe had no training for it. No experience on how to cope. He was a mass of unraveling emotions.

Reaching out, Dr. Guardian placed her long, graceful hand over his dirty forearm. "She's going to live, Chief. The problem is she had a bullet graze her left temple. Her skull is fractured. The good news is, it didn't tear the sac surrounding her brain, but she's still got swelling in that area."

"That's good. Right?" He held her gaze, wanting her to say yes.

"Very good, Chief. I've placed Bay into a medical coma, and we're aggressively treating her with drugs to lower the swelling. If the brain swells too much, it can cause even more brain damage or kill her. We would have to go in long before that happened and remove part of the skull plate to allow it to swell and not cause damage and kill her." She seemed to notice his shock and quickly added, "But that's not going to happen. I'm keeping Bay here at Bagram until I'm convinced we have that swelling under control. Then, I'll cut orders for her to be flown into Landstuhl Medical Center in Germany. They've got some of the finest neurosurgeons in the world there. Bay is going to need very close monitoring. But more from the drug side, not the surgery side. She will be monitored and then, slowly, brought out of her induced coma when they're positive her brain isn't swelling any longer."

Her fingers tightened a little around his arm. Her touch was steadying when he felt as if he was internally flying apart. "That's all good news, too?" he managed to croak.

Dr. Guardian frowned. "It is, but, Chief, your fiancée is in for a long, rough recovery. Any time the brain is traumatized, it has to have time to recover."

"What does that mean?" Gabe growled, hating not hearing what the bottom line meant.

"Probably amnesia. Either some or a lot. We just don't know which yet." Her eyes turned sad, her voice lowering. "Right now, Dr. Jeffrey Hartly, one of our finest surgeons, is repairing her other injury. He's the best." Sarah looked down, as if bracing herself for the next bit of news. But there was no way to soften the blow that was coming. "Bay was raped. Dr. Hartly is repairing a two-inch tear to her vagina. In time, Bay will heal up and be fine. The worst is the trauma due to the rape, Chief. That's not something we can fix because that involves her emotions and mind. She's going to need time, therapy and an awful lot of love, understanding and support from you."

Gabe's insides turned into jelly. He wanted to vomit but instead swallowed convulsively, several times, fighting back the reaction. Dr. Guardian's eyes were warm with understanding, and it helped him to try to think instead of just howling like the hurt animal he was. "They beat the hell out of her," he rasped between tight lips. "Her face…"

Dr. Guardian released his arm and sat up. "Yes, Bay has a broken nose and a closed fracture located on her left cheekbone. She went through a hell I can't even begin to imagine, Chief. Bay has some damage to her larynx, too." Her voice lowered in regret. "I think they tried choking her to death, or at least close to it. Probably torture…"

Gabe's eyes glittered. "Yeah, if you want to hold a woman down, you grab her by the throat, shut off most of her air and she's not going to fight you as you rape her." His voice shook with rage. As a SEAL, he had been taught how to control another person. Holding them by the throat, nearly shutting off their oxygen until they were close to losing unconsciousness, stopped them from fighting back. He wanted to hit something. Anything. His hand curved into a fist and never had Gabe wanted to punch out something so badly as right now.

"Bay's bruises are going to disappear in another two weeks," Dr. Guardian told him soothingly, holding his shattered, angry gaze. "Her bones will knit in probably five weeks. The swelling on Bay's face will recede in the next three weeks. The surgery to her vagina will heal in six weeks." Her voice turned gentle. "What Bay is going to need from you is to be there for her. Bay's whole world got destroyed. You love her, Chief, and I've no question that she loves you equally as much. You're going to have to be the strong one here. Don't overreact to how she looks when we bring her out of that coma at Landstuhl. See her as she *was,* not as she is now. And just understand she'll return to how she looked before this happened. Let your love for Bay guide your heart with her, support her and give her hope. Don't make her feel ugly. She'll feel enough of that anyway because of the rape."

Shutting his eyes tightly, Gabe trembled inwardly, and he couldn't stop it. He could control everything, but since Bay had been injured, his emotions ruled him. He felt the doctor stand, lifted his head and stared up in her direction. There were tears in her eyes, and it shook him deeply.

"Listen, Chief, you need to go get cleaned up. I was told by my medic Taft that you took a hit to your Kevlar. You need to be examined, too." Her voice grew husky. "Bay will be transferred to a private room in about two hours. You can stay with her. We'll have a chair brought in so you can sleep in the room and remain at her side. It's a funny thing, people in a coma or who are unconscious will tell me after they wake up that they knew who came into their room, and it always gave them comfort. They need a gentle touch, a soft voice…" Dr. Guardian smiled a little, her voice strained. "Just know that your presence, your touch, your voice, is healing for Bay. It will give her hope. And if you have any questions or need anything, ask the nurse on duty or have me paged. I'll be there."

As Gabe listened to the surgeon, he found himself believing she had Bay's best interests in mind. His mouth flexed, and he swallowed. "Yeah, I hear you, Doc. Thank you," he managed, his voice low and hoarse. "Bay is lucky to have you right now...."

Moving to his side, Dr. Guardian rested her hand briefly on his slumped shoulder. "Keep your faith, Chief. Prayers are good. We've got a small chapel here if you'd like to use it. I'll be seeing Bay on my morning rounds."

Gabe sat there, feeling gut shot. His stomach churned with rage so hot and burning, it felt as if it was eating a hole straight through him. He wanted to hunt down the bastards who had done this to Bay. And it wouldn't be a clean or quick death, either. His hands curved into fists, and he closed his eyes, never having experienced rage and love so intensely as right now. Gabe suddenly stood up, hurrying across the hall to the men's restroom. Barely making it, he grabbed the sides of the nearest wash basin, leaning over and heaving his guts out.

LATER, GABE FELT clean but exhausted. He'd gotten a set of new SEAL cammies from the SEAL HQ at Bagram. They had heard through Chief Phillips that he was here on base with his wounded fiancée. There wasn't anything they wouldn't do for him, a brother. And Bay was treated as family, as well. Best of all, one of his oldest friends, Mike Tarik, who had gone through BUD/S with him, was there with his platoon. Mike was more than a classmate. He was someone Gabe could let down and talk to. Mike had taken him to the locker room, which would be private. There, Gabe had babbled on like a frightened ten-year-old boy, the fear and anguish in his voice as he told his friend the short version of what had happened.

Mike had gripped his shoulder afterward and told him he was there for Gabe and for Bay. If either of them needed anything, he'd come at a moment's notice. That was how the SEAL family operated, and for the first time in his life, Gabe was now on the receiving end of it. Before, he'd helped other SEALs, their wives and children. Now, it was his turn to be helped.

He promised Mike he'd ask for help, though SEALs weren't very good at asking for anything. Mike grinned and swore he'd haunt him if he didn't and promised to drop over to the hospital and relieve him when he needed to take a break from sitting at Bay's bedside. Gabe told him that wasn't necessary because he didn't want to be anywhere else other than with her. For a split second, he thought he'd seen tears in Mike's eyes. And just as quickly, they were gone. It left Gabe rattled, hurting and struggling to keep his emotions in his kill box.

After connecting with the SEAL unit, Gabe made a call from their HQ to Poppy, Bay's mother. She'd already been notified her daughter was missing in action. Poppy cried with relief to hear Bay had not only been found, but was alive. Gabe told her about her head wound, but not the rape. It was just too much to hit a person with all at once. Besides, he couldn't talk about it himself; he was too emotional right now to deal with it. He'd break down sobbing on the phone and that was not what Poppy needed.

He called his own mother, Grace, to fill her in. She

had cried, too—for him—because she knew how much he loved Bay. Gabe avoided the rape issue with her. And he didn't tell his mother any details about Bay. It was top secret, and he couldn't breathe a word of it to anyone, not even Poppy or her.

Gabe felt ripped open again after making those two phone calls. Mike grabbed him by the arm, powered him through HQ and outside to a Humvee. He drove him back over to the hospital, deep concern in his face for his best friend. Gabe didn't want to leave Bay alone. She'd been alone all those days when she was a prisoner, and his heart told him to be with her as much as possible. He knew Bay would feel his presence, knew she would sense him nearby, the intense protection and love he so desperately wanted to give to her.

His sweat, blood and dirt had been washed away beneath a hot shower. The clean SEAL uniform, clean hair and a shave gave Gabe a look of normalcy to those who saw him walking the halls of the hospital. But looks were deceiving, and Gabe had put on his game face, that SEAL mask, betraying no emotion to anyone. Inside, he felt as if there was a fucking war going on, his guts twisting and writhing until he felt so much pain that he wanted to double over and scream. It was a combination of grief, rage, loss, fear and confusion all balled together. But no one would ever know. When people saw a SEAL coming, they gave him room. They were accorded damn near rock god star status in the military world. And, hell, yes, they'd earned that status in giving their blood and, sometimes, their lives.

Gabe halted outside Bay's room, getting ahold of

himself as never before because he knew she would feel him nearby. Taking several deep breaths, returning to his sniper mode of operating, Gabe calmed all his emotions. He wanted Bay to feel only his love for her. His whole life, every miserable cell of his being, was focused on her, nothing else.

Nurse Trudy Turner, a pert blond Army lieutenant, smiled brightly as Gabe quietly entered Bay's room.

"We just transferred her over here, Chief Griffin. You have great timing," she told him, keeping her voice low as she checked Bay's IV one last time. Trudy pointed to a black leather recliner chair sitting next to her bed. "And that's for you." She smiled a little and came around the end of the bed. "There's a buzzer attached to the side of Bay's pillow. Press it for anything you might need."

Gabe nodded brusquely. "I appreciate it," he managed in a gruff tone, his gaze never leaving Bay's pale face.

"Me or one of the other nurses on duty will be checking on Bay every three hours for the first twenty-four hours, Chief." She quietly closed the door behind her.

Gabe rubbed his face, exhaustion beginning to pound him into the ground. There was no more adrenaline to keep him clear, alert and functioning. His body was shutting down. Mike had asked him earlier when was the last time he ate. Gabe couldn't honestly remember. Mike had tried to get him to eat, but, hell, he couldn't keep anything down. It didn't matter anyway. Gabe haltingly walked over to Bay's bedside, his gaze clinging to her.

Bay's face was so translucent. He could see fine veins beneath her closed eyes, those soft, long lashes unmoving against the paleness of her flesh. The bruising scared the hell out of Gabe. Without the dirt and blood encrusted across her features, she presented the brutality of her capture vividly, for the first time. Knees weakening in reaction, he sat down in the chair, slipping his hand into her limp one. Unable to speak, feeling tears prick his eyes, he compressed his lips, swearing not to cry. He'd cried more in the past twenty-four hours than he had in his entire previous life.

As he stared at her hand, Gabe marveled again how long and beautiful Bay's fingers were. *Healing hands.* Anyone she touched always felt better for it. He knew he did. Closing his eyes, he pictured her sweet, soft smile, her blue eyes shining with gold highlights in their depths. He swore he could hear her husky, lilting laughter tumbling through the halls of his mind and heart.

Opening his eyes, Gabe lifted his other hand, closing it over her cold fingers, trying to warm her up. Bay was so still, like a corpse. He watched the blue gown she wore barely move up and down with each shallow, slow breath she took. It hurt to see the entire left side of her face swollen. He wanted to kill the bastard who'd done this to her. His emotions got loose, howling through him. Instantly, Gabe jerked in a breath, capturing it, wrestling it to the ground, shoving it viciously back into his kill box. He worried Bay would have felt it, but her face was slack, her beautiful lips he knew so well, parted.

Soon, her fingers were warmer, and, wanting to do something—anything, Gabe moved to the other side of her bed and held her left hand. The bruise marks around her neck were prominent and served to tell him she had nearly died beneath the hands of her torturers. Or perhaps her rapist and torturer. He leaned down, his lips a bare inch from hers. Gabe needed to kiss her. God, he needed to let Bay know he loved her. Kissing her would be healing for both of them.

Ever so gently, he touched her lips. He was alarmed at how cold they felt. He raised his head, worried. Was Bay really all right? Panic started to unwind deep in him as he lifted his hand and felt her smooth brow. Her flesh felt like cold marble. What the hell was going on? He eased his hand from hers and stalked quietly out of the room and strode down to the nurses' station at the end of the hall.

Nurse Trudy looked up from the computer. "Chief?" she asked as she approached. "Is anything wrong?"

"Why the hell is Bay so cold? She shouldn't be that cold," he snarled.

"Oh." Trudy rose. "It's okay, Chief. She's in an induced medical coma. All her body functions are lowered. That's normal, there's nothing wrong."

"If she feels that cold, she's cold. Why the hell aren't there more blankets on her?"

"I'll get the orderly to bring them to you right away, Chief. She's in a coma. She doesn't feel anything."

His lips lifted from his teeth. "How the hell would

you know that?" He jabbed a finger toward her. "You get those damn blankets now. I won't have her cold. You hear me?"

A male orderly came hurrying in with four wool blankets within five minutes. Gabe grabbed them out of his arms and growled at him to leave. The orderly practically ran out of the room.

Gabe gently placed all the blankets across Bay. He'd feel her hands, her brow every five minutes. She still felt cold. Dead. *Dammit!* He was frantic to warm her. He remembered the night they had to spend out on a mountain in the Hindu Kush. Bay had been so cold then. She'd shivered violently at his side, her teeth chattering because she'd had no winter gear to protect her from the freezing nighttime temperature. Gabe had hauled her against him, giving her his body's warmth. He'd held her all night, warmed her, kept her safe and protected.

To hell with those nurses. Gabe was going to warm her up or else....

Lowering the side of her bed, Gabe removed his boots and then positioned himself beside Bay. He carefully slid his one arm beneath her slender neck and then he lay down, drawing her blanketed body against him. For the first time, Gabe felt relaxation flow through his turmoil as Bay's right cheek came to rest against his shoulder, her warm, moist breath flowing across his neck. Gabe held her gently, his hand against the small of her back. Closing his eyes, he felt his insides tremble as he felt her curves against his hard, angular body. The anxiety started to ebb.

Gabe caressed Bay's recently cleaned hair, the soft brown curls sliding through his fingers as he tenderly let his touch communicate with her. He prayed she didn't have nightmares, that she'd not remember her pain. Bay had suffered enough.

"You're safe now, baby," he whispered against her hair. "I've got you. You're going to be okay. I love you so damn much, Bay.…"

CHAPTER FOURTEEN

"CAPTAIN TURNER!" NURSE Cindy Long said across the nurse's desk.

Trudy Turner frowned, trying to finish entering her notes on a patient's chart into the computer. "What is it now, Cindy?"

"Room 101. I—I started to go in there to check Thorn's IV, but—"

"Oh, give it a rest!" Trudy stared up at the young Army shavetail lieutenant. Long had just been assigned to Bagram a month ago, straight out of officer candidate school. She was a neophyte to the military and had a lot to learn. "You leave those two alone!"

Cindy's face scrunched up. "But, they're breaking the rules!"

Giving a snort, Trudy muttered, "Dammit, Long, healing comes in many forms. Let the guy sleep with his lady, will you?"

Cindy sputtered, "But—"

"Did you realize he's a Navy SEAL?"

Blanching, Cindy shook her head, her brown eyes growing huge. "Uhhh, no…"

"Better believe it, kiddo. You don't mess with SEALs. I told you that when you first came here.

They don't take kindly to anyone being around their wounded brothers or, in this case, his fiancée." She frowned. "Are we clear on this? He'll sleep better, and she'll feel comforted even though she's in a medically induced coma. There's everything right about that. It's part of healing in case you hadn't figure it out yet. And screw the rules."

Cindy touched the collar of her white uniform, gulping. "I forgot he was a SEAL...."

"Damn good thing he's so exhausted or he'd have snapped awake and probably decked you before you could blink twice. You never wake up a SEAL. Otherwise, you're asking for a broken nose or arm. When I was based at Landstuhl, a new nurse went in to wake up a wounded SEAL. She'd been warned, too. She touched his shoulder, and he threw her across the room and broke her nose and collarbone. Helluva way to learn you tread carefully around a SEAL, huh?"

Mike Tarik knocked lightly on Room 101. He waited patiently for a response. The head nurse, Trudy Turner, had told him at the main desk the next morning that Chief Griffin was sleeping soundly in bed with his fiancée. Mike just grinned and thanked her, making his confident, cocky way down the long hall to the room at the end.

The door opened. Mike saw Gabe's drowsy features. "Man, you look like hell warmed over. How's Bay doin'?"

If it had been anyone else other than Mike, Gabe

would have decked them. Rubbing his face, he muttered, "She's okay... Come in..."

His best friend was half Saudi and half American,
born in the U.S.A. Mike's black hair was longish, just
above his shoulders, his light brown-gold eyes large
and intelligent. Gabe had seen him pose undercover
as a Taliban operative many times in the past. Mike
was an unsung hero in the war against al Qaeda and
the Taliban. He'd been a spy amidst the enemy and
had given perishable intel to the SEALs to capture or
disrupt the enemy's planned missions. In Gabe's book,
the man had the biggest set of balls he'd ever seen.
Not many men would worm their way into a Taliban
army and not be found out. Mike spoke Pashto, Arabic, English and French. He was a stand-out SEAL.

Mike quietly closed the door behind him. The room
was almost dark, the venetian blinds drawn across the
small window. His gaze moved to Gabe's fiancée. She
looked like a broken porcelain doll to him. This pained
him since he could see the effect it had on Gabe. Mike
watched him struggle to wake up.

"Hey, man, I came to relieve you. Let me stay with
Bay for a while. You need a shower, coffee and a hot
breakfast down in the cafeteria."

Gabe knew he was right. "Yeah...okay..." He
moved stiffly, having stayed in the same position all
night holding Bay. He walked over to her bedside,
looking down at her. Was he seeing things? There was
a slight flush across her right cheek. Was she responding to him holding her all night? His heart squeezed

with hope. Gabe touched her hand, her fingers, and they felt warmer.

Mike stood near the door, concern across his square face. Nodding, Gabe leaned down and picked up his boots. He shoved them on and opened the door.

"Can you get Nurse Turner to come and get me in the cafeteria in case something happens to Bay?" he asked his friend.

"Yeah, I'll do that. But Bay will be fine, bro. Go on, get some food, take a shower, shave and get right with yourself, man." Mike slapped him on the back. Gabe winced, his mouth drawing in. "Hey," Mike asked, "what gives?"

"It's nothing. Took a bullet to the Kevlar in the back. I'm good."

"You sure?"

"I'm good. I'll be back in less than an hour."

"Roger that."

As Gabe stiffly leaned against the wall of the shower, he waited as the scalding hot water loosened up his locked-up back and knee joints. Old injuries reared their ugly head at times like this. After putting on a fresh set of cammies and rolling his shoulders as he straightened, Gabe headed toward the bank of elevators opposite the nurses' desk.

As he passed the station, a young nurse stared open-mouthed him, her eyes wide. What the hell? He was in no mood for a starstruck little girl.

By the time he returned to Bay's room, Gabe felt a hundred percent better. Taking a shower in the men's locker room had worked minor miracles on his bruised, battered body. He'd bought a mocha latte for Mike from the cafeteria. With his left hand, he pushed the door open to Bay's room. His SEAL brother was in the recliner, watching Bay. Grateful for Mike's support, Gabe quietly went over and handed his friend the latte.

"I know you'd die without at least three of these a day," Gabe said gruffly. Mike loved his coffee. The guy ran on a caffeine high all the time. He even packed coffee in his ruck when out on patrol, completely addicted to the stuff.

"Hey, man, thanks." Mike got up and moved aside. "She's fine. Sleeping like a baby."

Gabe moved to Bay's side, sliding his hand down hers. She was still warm, and the flush remained on her cheek. "Did she move?"

"Well," Mike said in a low voice, sipping the latte, "she moved her lips."

Gabe's heart thudded once. "Did Bay say anything?"

Shaking his head, Mike said apologetically, "She was whispering something, but I couldn't hear what it was. By the time I got up and went over to try and hear what she was saying, it was too late. Sorry."

Worried, Gabe wondered if Bay was already being stalked by virulent, gutting nightmares. He knew what they were like. "I'm going to go down the hall and talk to Nurse Turner about it. Can you stay here for just a moment more—"

"Yeah, go ahead. I'm due out on a night patrol at 2100 tonight, so no sweat."

Nurse Turner listened attentively to the SEAL. Cindy, the other nurse, was nearby, eavesdropping.

"Sometimes, Chief Griffin, a patient will mutter or talk while they're in an induced coma. It's not unusual," she said, patting his hand. "No worries. She's fine. And by the way, Bay is scheduled out of here tomorrow morning. She's already been assigned a berth on a C-5 heading for Germany. You'll be going with her. Landstuhl now has her records, and she's already been assigned a neurosurgeon, a Major Cory Torrance. That's great news because she'll oversee Bay's coming out of the coma."

Heartened, Gabe nodded. "That's good to know. Thank you…" He forced a smile he didn't feel, but the nurse had gone out of her way for Bay, and he was grateful.

"Dr. Torrance is a very kind person, Chief. She's someone you can ask anything of regarding your fiancée's condition. If I were you, I'd take advantage of that because no one knows where Bay will be when she awakens. Ask the doctor plenty of questions. Okay? Let her educate and prepare you."

Gabe felt his gut tighten with fear. What did Turner mean, prepare him? He thinned his lips and gave her a curt nod of thanks.

"You okay with any other SEAL visitors who might drop by today, Chief?"

He halted and turned. "Any time."

"Thought so."

GABE WAS DOZING in the chair late that afternoon when a light knock came at the door. Instantly, he sat up, sleep torn from him. He glanced first at Bay, who appeared fine, and then he rose. Opening the door, Gabe stared in the face of a female Army general in a light green short-sleeved blouse and dark green gabardine slacks. Her bucket hat was tucked beneath her left arm.

"Chief Griffin? I'm General Maya Stevenson. Would you like to step outside with me for a moment, please?"

A general? *WTF?* Gabe stared. He was momentarily stunned and then abruptly nodded. "Yes, ma'am," he murmured, closing the door behind him.

The woman's gaze rapidly assessed him. Her black hair lay around the shoulders of her Army green uniform. He saw the gold wings on her left side of the blouse, denoting she was an Apache combat helicopter pilot. Who the hell *was* she?

"Chief, let's take those two chairs over there near the wall?" She pointed to them across the way from Bay's room.

Gabe brought the chair out for her, and she thanked him and sat down. He sat down stiffly, his body tightening back up on him. "What's this all about, ma'am? I don't know who you are."

Maya smiled a little. "As it should be, Chief." She nodded toward Bay's room. "Bay is one of my forty women volunteers who make up Operation Shadow Warriors. I know you know about it because Bay was in your SEAL platoon last year."

Rubbing his face, his mind not functioning well,

Gabe uttered, "Yes, ma'am, I remember that. We signed papers swearing we'd never talk about it."

"Yes, that's correct." Maya's voice lowered. "I've been reading the medical reports and updates on Bay. How is she doing from your perspective?"

"Okay, I guess," Gabe said wearily, seeing the care burning in the general's eyes.

"And how are you doing, Chief?"

"I'm good, ma'am."

She gave him a measuring smile. "Damn, you SEALs are good at lying through your teeth. You take it to an art form."

"SEALs don't complain about pain, ma'am. We're always in some kind of pain one way or another."

Shaking her head, Maya said, "I read the report you filed on that op to rescue Bay." Her voice dropped with feeling. "Chief, you're one damn brave man, and so was your Afghan partner, Reza. I want to personally thank you." She held out her hand toward him.

Gabe couldn't look her in the eyes because he suspected she had tears in them. He took her hand and shook it. "I didn't do anything any other SEAL wouldn't have done for Bay, ma'am."

"You SEALs are so damned humble." She gave him a softened look. "I'm here for two reasons, Chief. First, you need to know I personally talked to your SEAL Team 3 commander. You are officially on medical leave and won't be required to rejoin your platoon when Bay is transferred home to the States."

His eyes widened. "Ma'am?" How the hell could she finagle that? His heart pounded with relief because

Gabe had been worried the Team would order him to duty soon. His days with Bay were numbered, and the last thing he wanted to do was be torn from her side. Bay would need him.

"Secondly," Maya went on, holding his startled gaze, "I've talked to a number of professionals about Bay's condition. Providing there arc no complications, to a person, they've all recommended she go home as soon as possible to continue her recovery. The psychiatrists I've discussed her condition with feel that she'll respond more positively to a safe, nonthreatening home environment." She grimaced, looking beyond him toward the nurses' desk. "And I think both of us can agree, she'll want to recover at home."

"No question about that, ma'am," Gabe said, frowning.

"Chief, you're on medical leave for as long as Bay needs you at her side. Now, I know you have less than a year left on your present contract before you re-up. Correct?"

"Yes, ma'am."

"I need to know one thing from you, Chief. Are you reenlisting?" She watched him carefully.

Gabe swallowed against his tightening throat, looking toward Bay's room. He turned and stared at the general. "No, ma'am, I want to be with Bay. She's going to need me, and I want to be there for her when she does. I don't want to be dragged off to thirty days of rattle battle when she's in the middle of a crisis. The neurosurgeon has already told me she might have partial or full amnesia. I'm not letting anyone help her but me and her family. I'm a known quantity in her life, like her mother and sister, ma'am."

Maya smiled. "You're a damned good SEAL, Chief. Your heart's in the right place." She stood and patted him on his shoulder. "You can expect your medical leave to be the length of the rest of your military service, then. I'll make it happen. Okay?"

Stunned, Gabe stared up at her, not quite believing what she was telling him. He'd get his pay, and yet, he'd be able to remain with Bay, no matter where she was sent. "More than okay. Thank you, ma'am."

"Good. Now, give me five minutes alone with Bay?"

"Of course," Gabe said. He started to stand, but she pushed him back down in the chair. "At ease, Chief. You need some rest, too. You look like hell warmed over."

CHAPTER FIFTEEN

GABE HELD HIS BREATH. Dr. Cory Torrance stood on the opposite side of Bay's bed. Since arriving at Landstuhl five days ago, Gabe had felt relief more than worry. The black-haired fortysomething-year-old neurosurgeon had been more like a mother hen to him and Bay than the brilliant doctor she was. She'd patiently led Gabe through the harrowing medical process of looking at CAT scans, MRIs and the multitude of test results, carefully explaining them to him in understandable terms. And now that Bay's brain was no longer swelling, she had reversed the induced medical coma.

Swallowing, Gabe continued to stand and hold Bay's warm fingers within his hand. Over the past twelve hours, Bay had slowly started to become conscious. Watching her eyelids move, her lashes quivering, Gabe felt fear mixed with hope.

Dr. Torrance took time to school him in brain injury and the many possibilities. Bay might wake up and recognize him immediately. Or not recognize him at all. That scared the shit out of Gabe as nothing else. He could handle everything, but not that. How could he forge a connection with Bay if she didn't recognize him? Didn't remember what they'd shared? Remember their love? He'd gone stir-crazy over those possibilities, and it was all he could do to stand relaxed, as if he were fine. But he was far from it, his gut clenched into a painful fist.

"She's coming up again," Dr. Torrance told him quietly, catching his worried gaze. "I want you to imprint her, Chief. I'm going to step out. Bay needs to see your face first. Your voice. Her brain will automatically connect with you on every level. Keep your tone low. Keep holding her hand. If she asks questions, remember what I said?"

It hurt to swallow, the lump growing in Gabe's throat along with his fear amping up. "Yes, ma'am, I do. I'll make it happen."

Dr. Torrance smiled gently. "You press that button when you want some help in here. Otherwise, we're not going to bother you. Bay needs focus right now, not a gaggle of doctors and nurses flying around her room, creating disruption."

Grateful beyond words, Gabe watched the tall doctor leave, the door quietly hiss closed behind her. He rubbed his eyes, forcing his fears aside. Forcing back his anxiety. He gently moved his fingers down Bay's left lower arm, wanting her to know he was here. Wanting her to know she wasn't alone. Or abandoned. His mind raced with the ton of information. Jesus, he felt as if he'd been to medical school since landing at Landstuhl.

The psychologist assigned to Bay's case had educated him as well about rape. He had no idea what to expect, completely ignorant of how the rape might affect Bay in the short and long term. The shrink had been compassionate but didn't waste her words. Both she and Dr. Torrance were afraid if Bay's memories of both her capture and rape came together, it would create a major emotional crisis for her. How to handle it?

Right now, Gabe felt out of his league. Completely. All he knew was he loved Bay, and he needed to trust his heart and gut. It had kept him alive on some very bad missions. It would have to be his internal compass in knowing how to support Bay, no matter where she was emotionally. No matter how much information the docs threw at him.

Gabe drew in a sharp breath as her eyes slowly opened. Seeing the blue irises set around huge black pupils made his heart race. He held Bay's fingers a little more tightly, leaning over, trying to get her wandering attention.

"Bay? It's Gabe. You're all right, baby. You're here in a hospital." Dr. Torrance had warned him to keep his sentences short and speak slowly. Bay would feel overwhelmed with too much information at once. He watched her eyes widen slightly over his huskily spoken words. Did that mean she remembered him?

Oh, God, let it be so...

BAY FELT MIDWAY between floating and feeling how heavy her body had become. She was warm, and she heard a man's voice, but she couldn't understand all that he'd said, the words garbled. Her mind wandered. And so did her gaze. She saw a light blue wall in front of her. At first, things were blurred, but then they'd come back into focus. What caught most of her attention was someone holding her hand. She felt the roughness of his fingers, sensing it was a man's hand. Oddly, it gave her comfort. And when he touched her hair, Bay closed her eyes, hungrily absorbing the feeling, how it made her feel safe.

So many emotions percolated through her as she became more conscious. Some were good. Others, well, appeared like a black hole. Fear skittered through her as she teetered on an imaginary edge of an abyss, looking down into it. Bay knew if she fell into it, she'd be lost forever. She wasn't sure what would be lost, only that it would swallow her up and she'd die.

"Bay? Baby, look at me?"

His voice sounded so familiar. Bay was weak. It took all her energy to move her eyes to the left and look up. Blinking slowly, she studied his ruggedly handsome face. It was his green eyes, so alive and yet filled with wariness, that affected her the most. As her heart took off at a gallop, Bay felt incredible joy filtering through all the other roiling emotions coming alive within her.

She opened her mouth. It felt so dry. She was thirsty. Though she wanted to speak, her throat began to close up on her, pain filtering down through it. Her brows turned down as she struggled.

"Baby, don't fight so hard. Take it easy…easy…"

His voice was balm blanketing her fear, her anxiety now nipping like a rat terrier at her consciousness. His eyes grew warm and anxious for her. His face was close to hers, but not too close. As her vision cleared, she realized he was standing next to a bed. Her bed. Bay sensed anguish around him. Why? She felt safe with him. *Safe...*

Gabe tried to force all his emotions down into his kill box as Bay's blue eyes became clearer. It took another half hour before he saw her becoming more aware of him. Her fingers curled weakly into his palm. Damn, that felt so good. His spirits surged with hope. Bay kept trying to speak, her voice rough and barely a whisper. Leaning close to her lips, he heard her rasp, "Water..."

Pouring water into a glass, Gabe eased his arm beneath her shoulders. Bay was incredibly weak, her head lolling against him, unable to hold it up. Frightened, Gabe gently maneuvered her around, and he pressed the edge of the glass to her lower, chapped lip. He was heartened as she began to drink and swallow the liquid. It made him want to cry. Bay was awake. She was in his arms. She was drinking water. How the little things in life became suddenly so critically important. *Milestones.*

Dragging in a deep, slow breath, Gabe watched Bay drink the entire glass of water. That had to be a good sign, right? Now, he wished Dr. Torrance was here to walk him through it, tell him it was a step in the right direction.

"More?" Gabe asked quietly, holding her upturned gaze. Bay was looking at him, and for the first time, he could see her trying to identify him. Her brows moved up and then down, confusion coming to her blue eyes. Her lips glistened from the water she'd drunk. Lips he'd worshipped as he'd made love with her. Damn, he ached for her in every possible way.

"Bay? Do you want some more water?" Short sentences. To the point.

It took all of Bay's efforts to move her head to one side just slightly, a "no" to his question. She felt warm and cared for as he held her easily beneath his supporting arm. Nostrils flaring, she inhaled his familiar male scent. Just his unique fragrance chased away a darkness she felt stalking her. Her name was Bay. Yes, she knew that now that he'd mentioned it. Her mind was doing slow cartwheels. She closed her eyes, suddenly exhausted, brow falling against his jaw.

Gabe set the emptied glass on the tray and watched her eyelids droop closed. There was a flush to Bay's cheeks, although the green-and-yellow bruises on the left side of her face hid it. Her face was half as swollen as before, and she was able to fully open her left eye. Damn, Gabe was euphoric. He wanted to scream with joy. Bay was alert! Her eyes followed his movements. Dr. Torrance had told him to watch to see if her eyes tracked him. If it didn't happen, they were in deep shit.

His heart pounded with hope as he gently laid Bay down. Feeling shaky and needy, Gabe sat in the chair, holding her hand and waiting. Dr. Torrance warned him she would be very, very tired and most likely sleep a lot, wake up for five minutes and then crash again.

THE NEXT TIME Bay awoke, she felt heavier, more "here" than "there." She slowly moved her hand across the nubby texture of a blanket across her stomach, luxuriating in the sensitive awareness in her fingertips. She heard or felt movement near her, and this time, it was much easier for her to open her eyes. She stared up into a set of green eyes, focused like an eagle upon her. Oddly, Bay didn't feel threatened by the man. Instead, a warmth flowed through her, chasing away the cold she felt in her extremities.

She slowly licked her lips and was mesmerized by his hard, expressionless face. But his eyes…yes…she could see a fierce glint in them, and she suddenly felt surrounded by an incredible feeling of love. She absorbed it. Thirsted for it without reason.

For long minutes Bay was simply a sponge, his roughened fingers upon her own, grounding her. He fed her energy. It was a feeling. A fierce, quiet, intense feeling that made her become a starving beggar, absorbing everything he would infuse her with. The continued flow of warmth curled gently through her, easing the anxiety that hovered in the wings of her mind.

Gabe watched her, breath suspended. Did Bay recognize him? He swore she did. He felt it, dammit. He saw it in her eyes, as if she knew him. Nothing was more important to Gabe. He stood there, icy fear bolting through him. His mind twisted with the possibility Bay didn't recognize him. *What then?*

Dr. Torrance had slowly gone over what he should say. Not what he wanted to say. His mouth felt dry. His heart continued to hammer in his chest. Just being able to hold Bay's hand in his meant the world to him. At least she hadn't pulled her hand out of his. But maybe she was so damned weak, she couldn't?

Gabe saw her struggling, her brow wrinkling, her eyes growing dark. She had to be trying to place him, and he sensed her panic. "It's okay, Bay. You're safe. You're here with me…." Instantly, he saw her struggles cease. How desperately Gabe wanted to smooth those wrinkles away on her forehead.

Dr. Torrance had warned him not to take for granted that she wanted to be touched. Rape played out differently in the survivor, and she told him until he knew for sure that she was not threatened by his presence as a man, he had to keep his hands to himself. That meant not kissing her, either. He'd have to communicate with Bay, watch her body language, listen to her voice and facial expressions in order to make her feel safe. Not threatened.

"Bay?" he asked, his voice low. "Do you know me?" Adrenaline leaked into his bloodstream as Gabe watched her closely. He ached with fear over her response until her eyes went soft. Bay slowly licked her lower lip, and he could see her thinking. He could feel it. His hand tightened imperceptibly around her fingers.

"I— You seem so familiar to me…."

Shock struck him. Gabe forced himself not to respond, the ache in his chest turning bitter and helpless. "My name is Gabe Griffin." He choked back his terror and did what Dr. Torrance had told him to do. "I'm a good friend of yours. I'm here to take care of you."

"Th-thank you," she whispered, suddenly looking tired. Her eyes kept closing, and she slurred her words. "Thank you for being with me…."

DR. TORRANCE SAT with Gabe outside of Bay's room. She'd listened to everything he told her. He'd kept his voice low. He'd brutally shoved his feelings into his kill box. After giving the doctor the lengthy report, he raised his head, staring into her gray eyes. He wanted to scream in frustration. In fear. Bay did not recognize him.

Reaching out, Dr. Torrance gripped his slumped shoulder. "This isn't a bad beginning, Chief. Give Bay a few days. A coma puts the brain in park. It's got to fire back up, get back online. From my perspective, she's coming out of it fast. She's strong and she's tough. All that works for her, not against her."

Gabe was numb with grief. His hope was destroyed, and not even Dr. Torrance, who was very nurturing and kind, could dig him out of the pit he found himself in. "What now?" he asked hollowly.

"I'm keeping her here until I'm convinced she's got her full brain function back."

"And then?"

She smiled a little, patting his arm. "You can take her home, Chief. General Stevenson has been working with me behind the scenes to ensure she'll have a rape counseling therapist, a neurosurgeon who will help her continue to thrive. Bay has a good team, but most importantly, she has you."

Closing his eyes, Gabe rasped, "I don't know about that."

"Take it a day at a time, Chief. Expect nothing, receive everything. Her brain has to heal first. And then, memories will come, both good and bad. You've forged a strong emotional connection with Bay. You were the first person she saw when she became conscious. That imprint will work for you, not against you. I'm sure with time, the good memories will surface. She'll remember you, remember your love and that she is going to marry you." Torrance frowned. "The brain's memory is another question. If the trauma is so powerful and the brain feels Bay will become unstable and be unable to cope, it won't give up the details of the trauma."

"What will it do then?"

"Sit there like a toxic waste dump." Dr. Torrance sighed. "The body never forgets the trauma it experienced. The cells remember it. The spirit remembers it. Her brain will withhold the nature of the trauma until or if it feels Bay can survive the impact of those memories and emotions. If the brain feels Bay can't cope, those memories will never download consciously to her. It's a primitive knee-jerk system built into the brain to allow the person to survive. So, the brain becomes the keeper of toxic secrets, but the toxicity will leak out anyway, sooner or later, on an unconscious level. Bay may feel anxious. For example, strange men, sounds or smells may trigger and scare her. We don't know yet what will spiral Bay into a defensive posture of feeling unsafe. You'll have to watch her closely for reaction and learn what those triggers are."

"But—" Gabe opened his hands, feeling desperate "—can't you *force* the mind to dump this shit? Get rid of it?"

"I wish it were that easy, Chief, but only counseling, maybe hypnotherapy, can help pry open that door to that vat of worms. The other problem is if Bay remembers her trauma too soon, it can spin her out emotionally, and she'll become unstable. There's a lot of razor edges the brain is considering. We're not privy to its reasoning or decisions it makes on Bay's behalf. The brain will always make a decision to keep her stable and able to survive."

"How can we know which will happen?" Gabe demanded hoarsely, never wanting Bay to remember what happened to her. It would break her. It would destroy her. He knew it would. Could he love her enough? Hold her close enough? Protect her enough so that she could survive those memories if they did come back? Gabe didn't know, his anger mounting because he felt pinned down by the bastard who had done this to her. Gabe dragged in a ragged breath, miserable.

"There are so many unknowns here, Chief. I know you're frustrated. There are no easy answers. You also need to work with the rape crisis counselor yourself. You're a man. Bay was injured badly by a man. The counselor can give you tools to help Bay trust you, not see you through the filter lens of her rapist. It's vital she trust you. If Bay can, it's a bridge, a doorway, to her healing. If she can separate out you from her rapist, she stands a chance of recovery.... And so many rape survivors cannot do that. It's a long, harrowing process then. We just have to wait and see."

Leaning his elbows on his thighs, Gabe savagely scrubbed his face. How the hell was he going to do this? He was a trained SEAL who could go up against the meanest sons of bitches the world could throw at him, and he could deal with it. But this? *Jesus!* He felt absolutely incapable of handling it.

"Listen," Dr. Torrance whispered, gripping his shoulder as she rose. "You're overwhelmed, Chief. Don't get caught up in details. Just monitor Bay. Be there at her side. Let her begin to tell you what she wants. What she needs. I think when you get her home to West Virginia, back to her mother and sister, she'll settle in and her brain will start opening up to the past. To you."

Gabe lifted his face from his hands, numb. The doctor smiled patiently at him and released his shoulder. Though he wanted so badly to vent his emotions, he turned and stared at Bay's door. The Navy had taught him how to kill, how to survive. No one else had taught him how to do this. Bay was broken into a hundred pieces, emotionally speaking. Her body had been broken. And her spirit was fractured. And Dr. Torrance was asking him to pick up the pieces and glue her back together again. How the hell was he going to do that?

Gabe dragged in a deep, serrating breath. He was so damned tense, he felt he might snap in two. Maybe Dr. Torrance was right: get Bay home, to the safety of her cabin, the love of her mother and sister. Then, maybe she could begin to heal.

He wiped his face harshly. There were so many fine lines to walk. Oh, God, if he made a mistake… Gabe lived in terror of doing just that. Looking up at the ceiling, he felt his entire life slowly rotating in a completely new direction. It wasn't Bay's fault that she'd been injured and traumatized. Somehow, he was going to have his love for her guide him because he sure as hell wasn't a shrink or a rape crisis counselor.

As Gabe stood there, he recalled Bay's reaction when they'd walked the sand dunes in a small cove near La Jolla, California. She'd spotted a California gold poppy, dropped to her knees, gently cradling the bloom between her hands. Gabe had knelt beside Bay, sponging in the joy radiating from her beautiful face, watching her long hands gently cup the flower. She'd leaned down, nose in the bloom, inhaling its fragrance. It was such a simple act, but it had profoundly affected Gabe.

His mind clicked over so many powerful, emotional moments he'd shared with Bay. At home, she could begin to cobble her torn life back together again, one small step at a time. Holding one flower at a time within her cupped hands. Focusing her heart and soul on that one bloom, appreciating it, being one with it because he'd seen her do it before. *Baby steps,* Gabe warned himself. *Baby steps and don't screw this up, Griffin, because you won't get a second chance…*

CHAPTER SIXTEEN

GABE REMAINED NEAR the SUV as he watched Poppy Thorn come running to greet her daughter, who was making her way toward the cabin where she'd been born. His heart burst open as Poppy, who wore a beat-up straw hat on her head, threw her arms around Bay. Even better, Bay had instantly recognized her mother at the hospital. He'd shown her photos of Poppy and of her sister, Eva-Jo, whom she recalled immediately.

Both women sobbed against one another. Gabe felt guilty, wishing Bay would throw her arms around him like that. It was a selfish thing to think about under the circumstances. At least Bay recognized someone. That was good news, progress. Gabe tried not to feel jealous under the circumstances. Above all, he wanted Bay to have connection with those she loved.

The July summer heat was high and humid, but the tall trees surrounding the huge two-story log cabin shaded it and brought the temperature down a little. Gabe was sweating freely, glad he was wearing a black T-shirt, olive green cargo pants and boots. There was a bit of a sluggish breeze.

He studied the cabin that sat on top of the small hill. Bay had known she was coming home. The two weeks spent at Landstuhl had strengthened her on every level, thanks to Dr. Torrance and her team. He felt grateful for all the military nurses and doctors who had made Bay's entrance back into the world a soft landing, not a hard, jolting reentry.

Bay wiped her eyes as she eased from her mother's strong, loving arms. Tears continued to spill down her cheeks as she held Poppy's warm blue gaze. At forty-nine, she was deeply tanned, healthy and vibrant. "It's so good to see you, Mama, so good," she quavered. Bay looked around. "Where's Eva-Jo?"

Sniffing, Poppy gave her a wobbly smile and wiped her eyes with an embroidered handkerchief. "She's in the lowlands being schooled in Dunmore. Eva-Jo will be back by three today, honey." Poppy lifted her work-worn hand, gently touching the left side of her daughter's face. "You look so thin and tired, Baylee. What you need is some good home cooking to put some meat back on your bones."

Bay looked down at herself. She'd chosen a dark orange tee, jeans and some comfortable sandals to wear. It was true, she had lost weight. "I can hardly *wait* for some home-cooked meals, Mama."

"Well, I'm gonna feed both of you. Come and introduce me to Gabe, your friend?"

Turning, Bay smiled over at Gabe. He waited, looking ill at ease near the SUV he'd rented at the airport. "Mama, he's helped me so much. I know him, and it's driving me crazy, but I can't remember why I know him."

"Tut-tut," Poppy said, gripping her hand and leading her forward. "He's your best friend, honey. Those memories will come back in time. He's a good man."

Gabe stood and watched the two women walk toward him. Poppy was just as tall as her daughter. She wore a short-sleeved simple white blouse, a dark blue skirt that fell to her ankles. He saw she was barefoot, and he managed a slight smile, liking her independent nature. Anxious, he looked over at Bay. Her cheeks glistened with spent tears, but for the first time, he saw real happiness shining in her blue eyes. His heart lifted with hope. Bay was smiling again. For the first time since…and Gabe shoved those thoughts into his kill box. All he wanted to do was see her smile, see life return and chase the shadows he always saw lurking in the depths of her eyes.

Bay was already having nightmares. Dr. Torrance had given her sleep medication, so she could continue to heal and stop the sleep interruptions. No sleep, poor recovery, she'd told Gabe.

"Gabe Griffin!" Poppy said, breaking into a warm smile. "Finally, I get to meet you in person!"

Gabe offered his hand to the woman with the elfin smile. She pushed his proffered hand aside, threw her arms around his broad shoulders and hugged him. Surprised, he took a step back. And then, Gabe awkwardly put his arms around her. Poppy didn't go much for social protocols, he realized. He glanced up and saw Bay watching him, her face radiant. God, the warmth of her smile shed light into his black soul, lifting him once more, making him feel a tentative thread of hope.

"Well," Poppy said, releasing him, "you're home,

too, Gabe, whether you know it or not." She grinned wickedly and stepped back, seeking and finding her daughter's hand.

"Yes, ma'am," he managed. He'd talked to Poppy about Bay and her rape issues before bringing her home. She knew not to refer to Gabe as anything except Bay's close friend. Not her fiancé. Never speak of them loving one another. It had torn him up on that phone call, and Poppy had cried. She'd cried for him, understanding the untenable position he had been trapped within. "Pshaw. You call me Poppy or Mama. I don't care which. Now, come along. I have your and Bay's bedrooms ready for you in that smaller log cabin you see on the side of the hill."

Gabe lifted his chin and saw a one-story log cabin about a hundred feet away from the main house. He frowned, not understanding why Poppy was putting them up there instead of in the main house. He glanced at Poppy and she gave him a sharpened look that said: *keep quiet, I'll talk to you later.* Gabe nodded, sticking his hands into the pockets of his jeans, following the two women who walked hand in hand.

"Is Bay sleeping now?" Poppy asked, pouring Gabe a cup of hot coffee in the kitchen of the main house.

"Yeah, she's pretty tuckered out. She usually goes down for a nap in the afternoon, and then she'll sleep until early evening, wake up and not be hungry." Gabe grimaced. Food seemed to repel her. *Why?* Bay had to eat to regain her strength.

Poppy sat down at the old wooden table opposite

him. She pushed several strands of hair off her wrinkled brow. "When a person has a piece ripped out of 'em, they lose their appetite. How are you doing, son?"

He shrugged, his large hands wrapped around the red ceramic mug. "I've been better, Mrs.… I mean, Poppy."

"You're looking pretty thinned out to me. You've been through a lot with Bay. And she's leanin' on you pretty hard from what I can see."

Amazed at her insight, Gabe stared at Poppy. He'd told her nothing about the top secret mission. All she knew was Bay was an 18 Delta combat medic and nothing about Operation Shadow Warriors.

"Yes, ma'am…I mean, yes, I want her to lean on me. Bay trusts me."

There was such strength in the woman's deeply tanned features. She had Bay's oval face and high cheekbones. In fact, he saw a lot of Poppy in Bay's features. And that Hill grit was there, too. He sensed it, felt it.

"The reason I put you two over in the other cabin is because Dr. Torrance called me three days ago. She gave me a lot of information and said that Bay is progressing very quickly. Maybe too fast. What she's worried about is her memory coming back too soon. I guess my daughter is having nightmares? And they sedated her so she could sleep at night?"

"Yes. But why not keep Bay here at your home where she's close to you?"

"I only have three bedrooms in this house, son. Eva-

Jo, me and a guest bedroom. I don't think Bay and you are sleeping together yet?"

God, how he wished they were. "No...she sees me as a friend, a confidant, is all. Nothing more." It hurt like hell to admit it.

"That's what I thought. Well, there's two bedrooms with a door between them over there in that smaller cabin. Floyd, my husband, built it years ago. He'd built that cabin for Bay. She wanted to get her degree to become an R.N. and then come back home to help serve the people of our mountain. The cabin was to eventually become her home." Poppy grimaced. "It didn't quite work out like we thought. But Bay knows that cabin. She used it as a teen and had her drawin' supplies, her canvases and paints over there. Eva-Jo used to pester the daylights out of Bay, and she found the cabin a place of solace and was able to be alone for a while. My daughter needs time alone. It recharges her batteries."

"Bay needs quiet," Gabe agreed, sipping the coffee.

"More than ever right now. I'll keep Eva-Jo plenty occupied. Right now, Bay doesn't need the shadow of her little sister following her around like a lovesick puppy. My second daughter has the mentality of a ten-year-old. She's improved with schooling, but once she sees Bay is home, I intend to keep her focused on other things. Dr. Torrance said Bay needs to do the things that appeal to her. And babysitting Eva-Jo ain't one of 'em."

Relieved, Gabe said, "Maybe I can help babysit Eva-Jo, then?"

Chuckling, Poppy said, "Eva-Jo will probably dote
on you." She peered at Gabe. "I can see why my daughter fell in love with you. You have a kind face. A quiet
way about you. There's no drama, no arrogance in
your bones."

Unexpectedly, heat rushed up his neck and into his
face. He avoided her sharpened look, staring down
at his coffee cup. His voice went hoarse. "I love her,
Poppy."

"I can see you do, son." She reached out and patted his hand. "And I can see how much you're suffering, too. Everything's landed in your lap. You have
a broad set of shoulders, but you're bearing a heavy
load. It will wear a good person down and out. I know
because my husband Floyd contracted Black Lung
for nearly ten years before he died. There were days
when I felt lower than a snake's belly in a wheel rut.
I had two daughters to raise, a very sick and failing
husband. Lordy, I know what it's like carrying a loved
one who's sick, Gabe." She wagged her finger in his
face. "You come to me, you hear? You're gonna need
someone to talk to. To share your tears with. You're a
caregiver at this point in my daughter's life. You need
support, too, and I can help you out." Poppy patted
her shoulder. "My shoulders aren't as large and wide
as yours, but I've held hundreds of men and women
as a Hill doctor and let them cry right here…." She
patted her shoulder again. I'm good at holdin' people
together when they're breakin' apart during a long-
haul crisis. Okay?"

Gabe managed a pained smile, or as much of one as

he could muster. Poppy was fierce. Strong. Wise. All attributes that Bay had, too. "Yes, ma'am…I mean… sorry, I'm used to the military. We need to stay in close contact with one another. Dr. Torrance said that."

"You cry much, son?"

Startled, Gabe stared at her. "Pardon?"

"Cry? You know? As in tears?"

Gabe saw that determined look snapping in her narrowed blue eyes, her lips pursed. Damn, she was like a laser-guided JDAM, just blowing the hell out of his cover. How did Poppy see beneath his game face? Feeling naked in front of her, Gabe managed, "Not if I can help it. I stopped crying when I was a young boy."

Snorting, Poppy muttered, "Well, ya better get in touch with your emotions again because I can sure feel that nest of snakes writhing inside you, Gabe. It don't do anyone any good to pretend you don't feel. You love my daughter, I can see that plain as day. But you're hurting her and yourself if you don't cry. Tears heal. Did you know that?"

Gabe eyed her wryly. "Yeah, your daughter said the same thing to me more times than I can count."

"Oh, I betcha Bay's said it more than a few times to you. You're a tough one, you are. But love has a funny way of making even the strongest man drop to his knees. You're human, Gabe, and I know loving Bay and getting her well is going to be an unadulterated, living hell on you. So, keep your hankies ready!"

GABE WAS RESTLESS. On edge. It was midnight, and he lay in his bed, the moonlight streaming through the curtains at the window. It was plenty light enough to see the open door that led into Bay's bedroom. He ached to be with her, holding her, giving her that sense of safety she needed.

Bay's first day at home had energized her, but it also tired her out. She'd gone to bed shortly after dinner, not wanting to take the sleeping pill. Gabe didn't feel good about it. Would a nightmare stalk Bay tonight because she hadn't taken her medication?

He was tired to his soul but completely alert and waiting. For what, he didn't know. His mind refused to turn off, as it did on most nights. He felt utterly useless. Bay had treated him like a much-loved and trusted brother at the hospital. Sometimes, Gabe would briefly touch her hand, but not often. Or hug her, like a brother, not a lover. She'd always been glad to see him when he returned to her room. He lived to see happiness coming back to Bay's eyes when her gaze rested upon him.

Damn, there was such unrelieved tension in him. Gabe felt torn. Poppy's admonishment about crying damn near undid his massive control over his feelings. She was scary! And Bay had that same, homed-in radar, that same kind of clairvoyance. Poppy saw straight through him, warts and all, too. He was in big trouble with Poppy, but simultaneously, Gabe felt her love and care shower him, as well. She seemed to understand what he was going through.

Bay's scream shattered his roiling thoughts.

Instinctively, Gabe leaped out of his bed and raced through the open door. He went to her room and found her huddled against the headboard, her voice growing hoarse with whimpering cries.

Gabe advanced to the bed, sitting down, facing her. Gently, he placed his hands on her shaking shoulders. "Bay…baby, it's all right. You're safe..safe…."

She lifted her head, breathing hard, her chest sharply rising and falling beneath her lavender nightgown. Dammit, he should have insisted on her taking the sleep med. It was too late now.

Gabe's heart twisted in his chest as he saw that blank look in her eyes. That scared him even more. Her hair had partially fallen across her face, tears splattering down her cheeks. Groaning, Gabe said to hell with it and pulled Bay into his arms. He was supposed to talk her down, but he couldn't handle her cries.

Bay moaned as Gabe dragged her into his embrace. He stroked her hair, whispering to her, trying desperately to pull her out of the clutches of the nightmare that still held her prisoner. Gabe wasn't sure if she'd scream and push him away or not. This was the first time he'd held her like this. Tears burned in his eyes, his mouth thinning as he absorbed Bay's sobs, her warm tears running down across his chest. He hurt so damned much for her.

Gabe rocked her gently, as he would rock a hurt child, whispering softly to Bay, his voice trembling with barely held emotions in check.

Slowly, Bay's sobs stopped. She began to hiccup. Gabe felt her burrow deeper, pressing her face against his shoulder and neck, literally trying to hide in his arms. Relief soared through him because Bay hadn't pushed him away. And she could have. Closing his eyes, Gabe continued to rock her and move his hand across her unruly hair. Her trembling began to recede, and Bay's breathing slowed down. Her hands were clasped between them.

"That's right, baby, just lay here in my arms. You're going to be okay. The nightmare's gone, it won't come back tonight. I'm here…I'll hold you…."

Bay felt Gabe's warm, hard arms around her dampened nightgowned body. She desperately clung to his rasping words. She fought against the things she'd seen and felt in the nightmare. Her lower body ached. What had happened to her? What was wrong? Flailing between raw fear and anxiety, Bay found solace in the gentle rocking motion in Gabe's arms. His warm, moist breath whispered across her cheek. He felt safe. Oh, God, she needed to feel safe!

A black, bearded face leered out at her. Bay choked on a sob and winced. Gabe's arms tightened in response. Those black eyes…oh, God, he was dangerous to her! Her heart started to speed up as his face hung there, an apparition from her unknown past, haunting her. Scaring her until she almost became paralyzed with fear.

"It's okay, baby. I'm here…." Gabe reassured her. He could feel how damp Bay's nightgown had become. She was sweating profusely, shaking, a frightened rabbit in his arms. What the hell should he do? What would help her? His mind spun, his emotions twisting violently within him.

Trying to still himself, Gabe homed in on his heart.

It was the only voice he could trust right now. What did Bay need? What could he do to help her stop sweating and trembling like this? Her sobs began again, soft and halting at first. Her fingers dug into the flesh of his chest. What the hell kind of nightmare had this kind of hold on her? Frustration ripped through him. He felt as if he were going to die if he couldn't fix this.

And then, Gabe said to hell with all of it, following his heart. "Come on, baby, lay down here beside me. I'll hold you. Whatever you're seeing, it can't hurt you anymore. I'll keep it away from you…."

Gabe eased Bay down onto the bed. She was still caught up in the nightmare, her eyes wild-looking and unseeing. The moment he got up to move to her side, she cried out, tucking herself once more into a fetal position of protection. Patiently, he lay down beside her and pulled the sheet over them.

As soon as Gabe gathered Bay into his arms, she calmed down. He brought Bay firmly against his body, and she nestled her face against his shoulder, her brow against his jaw. She was burrowing against him, as if to try and hide once again. From something. From someone…

Soon, Bay stopped shaking and finally breathed with a slow, even cadence. Her fingers, once curled tightly against his chest, relaxed and eased open. Every once in a while, Bay would hiccup, her body spasming. And then, she'd quiet once more. He'd do anything to get those nightmares out of her head. *Anything.*

Gabe let her fall asleep. Holding her was such an incredible gift to him. He'd unexpectedly gotten to hold Bay for three nights at the Bagram hospital. That time with her had fed his starving heart and soul. And now, he got to hold Bay once more. God, he needed this intimacy with her so damned badly.

Gabe closed his eyes, a shudder moving through him, his heart aching for Bay. Her scream…Jesus… he'd never forget that ear-shattering scream. Exhausted, Gabe didn't want his mind going to that dark place within him. He didn't want to try and imagine why she'd screamed like that. Shutting his eyes tightly, he nuzzled his face into Bay's silky, curled hair. He inhaled her natural fragrance, and it fed his broken soul in every way. Gabe continued to hold the woman he loved more than his own life. Sleep stole in, and all his demons dissolved. For one night, Bay was here, beside him and in his arms, where she belonged.

CHAPTER SEVENTEEN

BAY AWOKE SLOWLY, sunlight streaming in through the white, lacy curtains. The window was open, and she could hear a robin singing outside. Had she been dreaming? As she opened her eyes fully, she tried to remember. Had Gabe held her last night? Or was that just a wish fulfillment?

She sighed brokenly, rolling over on her side. Gabe was more than a friend. She knew it but couldn't remember. Since she'd become conscious at Landstuhl, she ached to be touched by him. Held.

Once she dragged herself out of bed, she pulled on her purple robe over her nightgown that was stiff and smelled of sweat. Bay needed some coffee and shuffled out of the room and down the hall, barefoot.

Bay halted when she saw Gabe at the sink, his back to her, looking out the large window. An incredible feeling of love washed over her. He was dressed in a tan T-shirt that showed off his powerful upper body, olive green cargo pants and hiking boots. Just knowing Gabe was close steadied her. And then, he turned, meeting her eyes, as if somehow sensing she was standing there.

"How are you doing?" Gabe asked quietly, warily

searching her drowsy features. "How about a cup of coffee?" he asked, pulling out a wooden chair at the table for her.

"Yes, that sounds good," Bay managed in a whisper. Drawing the robe tightly around her, she walked up him. Bay wanted to swim in those dark green eyes. "Gabe, I feel like I'm imagining things...."

"Like what?"

She sat down. "Did I—I mean, did you hold me last night or was I dreaming it?" Feeling suddenly shy, Bay dipped her head, staring at her clasped hands in her lap.

Gabe crouched down, one hand on the arm of the chair, his other falling over her tightly clasped hands. "You're not going crazy, Bay. You had a nightmare last night and screamed. I heard it and came in to try and help." His voice lowered, holding her startled gaze. "You wouldn't stop crying. I slid into bed and held you until you finally stopped sobbing, and then, you went to sleep. I held you the rest of the night."

Biting her lower lip, his voice like a balm to her shattered confidence, Bay gave a jerky nod. "Okay... then I wasn't imagining it." She pulled her hands free of his and covered her face. "I hate the night!"

Her muffled words tore at Gabe. All he could do was stroke her hair, as if soothing a wild, crazed animal. She drew in deep breaths, as if struggling to calm down. "I know you do. I wish I could take those nightmares away from you Bay...."

Bay lifted her head. "Y-you did. I stopped seeing his face when you lay with me. I—I could feel your warmth, your protection, Gabe. He stopped coming after me." She lowered her gaze, never feeling as weak as she did right now.

Grazing her temple, moving a few tendrils behind her ear, Gabe asked, "Who was coming for you?" He watched the fear enter her eyes, and it ripped his heart apart. His Bay, who had been so confident before the rape, was little more than a shattered mirror of her original self. But he could tell that his touch eased some of the fear, and he moved his hand across her tense shoulder.

"I'm not sure," Bay whispered, fighting not to cry. "He hated me. He was coming at me. I saw him reach out toward me...I guess that's when I started screaming?" She clung to Gabe's searching, turbulent gaze.

"I don't know, baby, I don't know. I wish I did." Gabe unwound and stood up. He gently laid his hand on her shoulder. "Do you want that coffee?" Gabe didn't know what else to say. Or do. The question seemed so damned inane. Unimportant.

"Y-yes, please."

It gave him something to do. Anything rather than stand there, his guts in twisting knots, casting around, trying to say the right thing. Whatever the hell was the right thing to say? Gabe handed her the mug of coffee and sat down next to her with his cup. She took several grateful sips. At 0600, the sun was just cresting the tops of the trees outside the cabin. It was peaceful. No people, just the soothing, comforting sounds of nature.

As she felt more stable, Bay realized it was because Gabe was near her. He fed her strength. Stability. Hands wrapping around the cup, she looked at him. "I need you to tell me more, Gabe. I—I know I'm an 18 Delta combat corpsman. I know you, but I can't remember from where." Tears gathered in Bay's eyes, and she reached out, gripping his hand on the table. "Please, tell me what I don't know? I'm dying inside because my heart goes crazy every time you touch me. Last night," she breathed softly, "I felt safe when you held me, Gabe. You have no idea how much solace and peace it brought me from this constant anxiety that just keeps bubbling up through me in the background."

Her pleading gaze tore at him. God, how much to tell her? What was enough? Too much? Dr. Torrance had warned him about this. Gabe was scared of overwhelming Bay. Or triggering an avalanche of memories that could tear her apart. As her tears fell silently down her cheeks, he gripped her hand and shut his eyes. *Crying...no, please, don't cry, baby... God, anything but that...*

"Gabe?"

Her trembling voice tore through him, and Gabe opened his eyes and held hers. "We're good, close friends," he told her, his voice unsteady. He told her how they'd met last year when she was assigned to his SEAL team in Afghanistan. Gabe feared saying much more than covering their four months of working together. He left out the soul-stealing kiss they'd shared the morning he was to leave for the States. He'd never forget that one, searing kiss with Bay. Their first kiss. A forever kiss indelibly branded on his heart and soul.

Frowning, Bay listened, absorbing everything. She

began to relax, the sound of his voice dampening her anxiety. She stared at their hands. "There's more," she whispered, holding his gaze. "I know there is…"

Moistening his lips, he rasped, "Bay, you've been through so much. We have time, and we can talk about this more as you start getting those memories back." He instantly saw anguish in her eyes. He felt terrible.

"You held me," Bay said, her voice stronger. "You made my nightmare go away…."

Trapped. Gabe flexed his mouth, holding her haunted gaze. "What do you want, Bay? Just tell me and I'll go through hell to get it for you."

Gabe had no idea what to do now. The damned doctors said to let her memories come back on their own and then talk about them, not the other way around.

Bay managed a shy look and whispered, "Will you hold me tonight? When I go to bed? I hate taking those sleeping pills. I wake up in the morning, and I feel like I'm split into pieces. It takes me half a day to feel somewhat whole again."

Given Bay's trauma, he thought about the repercussions of sleeping next to her. What if she woke up thinking he was going to rape her?

"I don't know, Bay," he said, running his fingers through his hair.

She hadn't been told about the rape—yet. The medical people had told her that she'd injured herself, but hadn't said how. Would Bay figure it out on her own? It was coming sooner than later. The man she saw in her nightmare was either her torturer or her rapist. Or both. Gabe wanted to curse, to get up and run to hell away because he felt inept at handling all of this. He didn't know what the right answer was for her anymore.

Bay's hand tightened over his. "In my heart, it feels right, Gabe. I mean…if you don't want to, I know it's a silly request. Friends don't usually sleep together." Her expression was filled with confusion, uncertainty.

Ah, hell. Gabe turned her hand over, gently holding her long, spare fingers. "We'll try it, okay? And it's entirely up to you, Bay. You're in control here. All I want to do is help you, baby, not scare the hell out of you. Or hurt you."

Instant relief came to Bay's eyes. A flush flowed across her cheeks, and she suddenly appeared shy, the way she was before they'd ever kissed the first time.

"Thank you…"

Eva-Jo joined Bay in their mother's five-acre garden that afternoon. Bay crawled down the rows of beans on her hands and knees. The beans were almost ready to pick, and she was pulling weeds alongside her enthusiastic, nonstop-talking sister.

Gabe hated weeding but grudgingly worked at it, a couple of rows away from the women. He heard Eva-Jo prattling away, her hands gesturing everywhere. Even from where he knelt, weeds in hand, Gabe could see Bay was getting tired of her sister clinging to her and the endless, ongoing chatter.

It was nearly three in the afternoon. Pushing to his feet, Gabe walked between the rows over to Bay.

Eva-Jo looked up, smiling gaily. "Look, Gabe! Look at all the weeds I've pulled!"

He forced a warm smile. "You're good at weeding, Eva-Jo." Gabe turned his attention to Bay. She had stopped and rested back on her heels. There were tiny beads of perspiration along her hairline. She looked exhausted. Holding out his hand, he murmured, "How about a nap?"

Bay lifted her hand and took Gabe's. "Definitely." She smiled gently over at Eva-Jo. "You beat me, Squirt. You got twice the amount I did."

Preening, Eva-Jo yelled, "Yipppeeee!"

Gabe pulled Bay to her feet, and she dropped her last handful of weeds into her sister's huge pile. "Let's go," Gabe urged Bay, guiding her toward the gate half an acre away.

At the cabin, Bay went straight to her bedroom. Gabe hung out in the kitchen, washing his dirty hands. Exhaustion lapped at her, and she pushed off her shoes and lay down. As soon as her head nestled into the pillow, she fell asleep.

Gabe was out in the kitchen making dinner for them when Bay emerged two hours later. He heard her coming down the hall and twisted a look over his shoulder. She seemed confused, scrubbing her eyes as she made her way to the kitchen table and sat down.

"How was your nap?" he asked, rinsing his hands and drying them on a towel.

"Interesting," she mumbled.

That got his attention. Gabe turned and poured her a cup of coffee he'd just made. "Want to talk about it?" He slid the cup in front of her.

She gratefully took the coffee. "Thank you."

Bay was always thoughtful of others, always aware of other people's contribution to her. It was one of the many reasons Gabe loved her so damned much. Searching her blue gaze, he saw something new in her eyes. What was it? He stilled his impatience, waiting for her to speak.

"Gabe, I remember more things about Camp Bravo...."

His heart skidded. He put the towel on the table and sat down opposite her. "What do you recall?"

"Hammer. I remember the faces of all the SEALs in your platoon now." She managed a bit of a triumphant look. "It's as if you mentioned it, and then the rest of it just downloaded as I woke up a few minutes ago."

"You mean, it acted like a trigger?" He was thinking in sniper terms.

Nodding, Bay sipped the coffee, thoughtful. "I think I remember everything about those four months now." She launched into specific experiences.

Gabe sat there, wondering if her memories included their relationship. He hoped so. Bay's eyes were lighter, her voice stronger as she recounted everything in the next hour about those four months she'd spent with his SEAL team. Gabe was shaken by the amount of memory dumped. And scared. It was only a matter of time before she remembered her assault. Dr. Torrance had said one memory might come back, and it might be months before another returned to the survivor.

"Well? Is that right? Am I remembering correctly?"

"You're on the money, Bay." But she remembered nothing about them. Gabe swallowed his disappointment and smiled because he could see how excited and hopeful Bay was. "That's great."

Her face became radiant beneath his praise. Heat sheeted through his chest, wrapping around his strongly beating heart. It was the light in Bay's eyes that lifted him, smothered him with hope. Real hope. At that moment, Gabe wanted to reach out, gently cup Bay's cheek and kiss her. But the fear of her other memories stopped him cold. Instead, he took a drink of his coffee, burning his tongue.

GABE SAT SHELLING peas and dropping them into an aluminum bowl sitting in his lap. It was early August, and the dog days of summer were upon them. The family of women was all busily canning in the kitchen. Large mason jars of the bright orange, sliced carrots and green beans were on the table in front of him. A sense of peace pervaded Gabe. Though Bay had regained some of her memory in early July, her mind seemed to have stopped giving her any more information.

Gabe lived in hope of her remembering them, their engagement. He'd been able to lay with her on some nights when she asked him to. He fought himself not to touch her in any intimate way. God only knew how badly Gabe wanted to make love to her, but he knew it couldn't happen. The rape hung over him like a damned Sword of Damocles, a threat in both their lives.

He heard the women's collective laughter, a slight smile pulling at his mouth. Poppy was a tour de force, there was no question. And her daughters were just as happy as she was. Gabe compared his own childhood to Bay's. He remembered her fondly telling him about the cabin, about her parents. Being here, he felt a special appreciation because Bay had had an almost idyllic childhood. Maybe that was what gave her the backbone, the confidence and clarity for what she wanted out of her life.

Bay was going weekly for counseling sessions in the nearest town south of them, in Dunmore. She had no clue the woman was a rape crisis counselor, only that counseling was part of her recovery. Progress was being made, though.

Sometimes, he'd silently walk in on Bay, and she'd whirl around and gasp, her face going white with terror. The counselor told him it was a PTSD reaction. Now, he made noise to make sure Bay heard him coming, so he didn't scare her to death.

Gabe finished the bowl of peas and took them over to the counter. Tonight, the four of them would share a family meal at Poppy's home. She'd asked him to gather enough peas for the meal, and he had. Moving out the kitchen door, Gabe ambled to the screened-in porch. He sat down in the old, red wooden rocking swing at one end of it, tipped his head back and closed his eyes.

"Gabe?"

Bay's soft voice was close. He opened his eyes. She was standing before him, holding out a glass of ice-cold lemonade toward him. "Mama said you'd earned this." And she smiled.

Their fingers met and touched, the glass frosty and wet. "Thanks."

Bay sat down next to him. "This has been the most fun I've had since getting home," she admitted. "I love to can fruit and vegetables."

He tasted the tart and sweet lemonade that Eva-Jo had made earlier. "You're happy." It was said simply, but it was the truth. They locked eyes, and Gabe died a thousand deaths, wanting to love her when she gave him that tremulous smile of hers. It was getting tougher to lie at her side. She was completely unaware of the strain on him. And Gabe wasn't about to tell her.

When he held her, she slept deeply. Bay was regaining her weight, eating well, and her eyes were far clearer than they'd been in July. He'd sell his damn soul to see her healed. He'd sleep with her and never touch her if that would get her back to being herself. Gabe never thought of himself as a monk, but now, he was one. Life held so many damned torturous twists and turns.

A dark green Chevy truck filled with cut wood chugged noisily up the dirt road to the main cabin. Gabe remembered that Poppy had wood being delivered today. She had a woodstove, not electric baseboard or natural gas or propane to heat the two cabins. Gabe had never met the man she'd hired to deliver it.

Bay frowned and looked toward the truck. She was jumpy about anything she didn't recognize. Always on guard. Alert. Tense. He reached out and briefly touched her shoulder.

"I think that's the guy who cuts the wood for your mother."

Frowning, Bay said, "I've never seen this truck before."

"He usually comes in the late afternoon when you're napping, that's why."

The truck stopped. The man climbed out and walked around the front of the vehicle.

Bay choked. The glass dropped out of her hand as she leaped to her feet. It felt as if someone had hit her in the chest with a fist. The man had black hair and a black beard. When he lifted his hand in hello and looked up at them, she gave a guttural cry.

Gabe sprang to his feet as her glass of iced tea shattered on the porch. Her choking cry was like that of an animal knowing it was going to die. The shrieking sound seared through him as he reached out to grip Bay's arm. And then, just as suddenly, her knees buckled. *Jesus!*

Making a lunge, Gabe caught Bay before she collapsed onto the deck. He heard Poppy yelling at the wood man. Eva-Jo raced out on the porch, shaken and panicked. The wood man halted, his brows shooting up in surprise, his expression confused. Breathing hard, Gabe managed to gather Bay into his arms. She'd fainted. He turned, seeing Poppy race out the door, her eyes wide.

"Something happened," he growled. "Let me get her to your bedroom."

"Yes, hurry!" Poppy looked fearful. Her glance went from Bay to the wood man standing at the bottom of the porch, nonplussed by the sudden flurry of unexpected excitement.

Gabe cursed under his breath. That man had somehow accidentally triggered something for Bay. *Dammit!* He pushed the door to Poppy's bedroom open with the toe of his boot and quickly laid Bay down on the quilt covering the full bed.

Poppy ran in, panting. She went over to her wan daughter. "I'll get a cold cloth."

Gabe made sure Bay was breathing all right, tipping her head back to open her airway. He sat down facing her, picking up her limp, cold fingers. Jesus, what the hell had just happened out there? He anxiously watched her face as he opened the collar around her neck. Bay was waxen, her lips slack, her breathing shallow.

Poppy ran back in, thrusting the cloth into his outstretched hand. "I'm calling Dr. Evans," she said, her voice off-key.

"Do that," Gabe called, gently bathing Bay's forehead with the damp cloth.

Eva-Jo ran in, sobbing. "I-is Baylee okay? Is she hurt?"

Gabe turned, seeing her anxiety. "She's going to be all right, Eva-Jo. Can you get me some water for Bay?" He had to get her out of here, her sobs loud and upsetting even to him. He felt badly for Eva-Jo, who leaned so heavily on Bay for emotional support.

Feeling Bay's pulse with his two fingers, Gabe felt it bounding and leaping. What had scared her so badly that she fainted? Bay wasn't the kind of person to faint.

Hell, she'd faced life-and-death combat with him and was as steady and cool under fire as he was. Her fright told him something about the extreme trauma that had triggered it.

The wood man pounded on the screen door, the sound reverberating through the house.

"Hey, Miss Poppy? What's goin' on in there? Can I help ya'll?"

Irritated, Gabe wanted to tell him to shut the hell up. His voice made Bay tense again, even in unconsciousness. Gabe had never seen a reaction like this in his life. Should he be doing something else for her medically? He pressed the cloth against Bay's face and neck.

Bay moaned. Her lashes fluttered. She felt a cold cloth on her brow, felt someone's warm hand gripping hers. Feeling as if she were spinning out of control, she opened her eyes. Gabe was staring down at her, fear reflected in his eyes. Fear for her. Heart pounding, she heard another man's voice. *Oh, God! It was his voice!* Weakly, she pushed herself up on her elbow, jerking her attention toward the open bedroom door.

"Hey, Miss Poppy?" the wood man called.

Gabe turned as the man in the black beard peered around the corner of the door. He opened his mouth, but his words were cut short.

Bay gasped, scrambled up against the headboard, shrieking and throwing her arms over her head to protect herself.

"Get out of here," Gabe roared, leaping to his feet and moving toward him, his fist curled.

The man blanched. His eyes went huge, and he quickly left.

Bay sobbed, moving into a fetal position. It was then the whole memory of her capture, tending Taliban injured soldiers and Khogani raping her, occurred. Bay slid down on the bed, crying wildly.

Gabe stood helplessly, unsure what to do. He dropped the cloth, and he pulled Bay into his arms. She shrieked, fighting him, lashing out.

Staggering back, shocked, Gabe blinked. She must have remembered *everything*. The horror showed on her face. He couldn't stand to watch her curled up, trembling violently, whimpering like a hurt animal, her hands over her head, trying to hide.

Wiping his mouth, Gabe cursed softly. He walked to the other side of the bed, crawled across it and, in one motion, slid his hand beneath Bay's neck and beneath her thighs. It took all of his strength to lift and turn her directly into his arms. He didn't care if she fought him or not—Bay had to feel safe.

Poppy raced into the room, her eyes filled with tears. She halted. "What can I do?" she demanded.

"I don't know," Gabe growled, holding Bay against him, her weeping tearing him apart. "She saw that man. It triggered... God, I don't know what the hell it triggered. A flashback, probably."

Poppy stared at her daughter curled up against him, her face pressed against his neck, her hands covering her face, weeping as if her soul was being torn apart. "I've got Doc Evans coming. He'll be here in about thirty minutes."

Nostrils flaring, Gabe rasped, "Okay. Keep that guy with the beard the hell out of here. And don't let Eva-Jo in."

Nodding jerkily, Poppy said, "I'll make sure. Just holler if you need anything? Anything else I can do, Gabe?"

His mouth drew into a tight line. "No."

The door closed. Thank God, Gabe thought, focusing fully on Bay. She hadn't fought him. Once he got ahold of her, she collapsed against him, weeping ceaselessly. He closed his eyes, leaning back against the headboard, one leg on the floor, one on the bed. All Gabe could do was croon softly to Bay, slip his fingers gently though her hair and hold her.

CHAPTER EIGHTEEN

BAY SLOWLY OPENED her eyes. It was dark. And she was warm in her own bed. But her throat was raw, and she felt beaten up inside. The bedroom door quietly opened. She turned over on her back, looking toward it. Recognizing Gabe's silhouetted form, she relaxed.

"I'm awake," she croaked. Her head ached. Her whole body felt dismantled, torn up and then hastily cobbled back together again. The light from the hallway was just enough for her to see Gabe walk around the bed. His eyes glittered with unknown emotion. She could feel his worry. As he sat down on the bed, his hip resting against hers, Gabe reached out and barely touched her cheek.

"What happened out there this afternoon, baby? What set you off?"

Struggling, Bay pushed herself up into a sitting position with Gabe's help. She leaned against the headboard, drawing the blanket up around her waist, suddenly cold. His hand came to rest next to hers, and she slipped her fingers in his grasp.

"The black beard," she whispered tiredly. "The man bringing in the load of wood. I saw the beard and...and—" her voice broke and she fought to speak.

"Gabe, it was Mustafa Khogani. He raped me." She lifted her hands, pressing them in shame against her face.

"Ah, baby, come here...." Gabe moved closer, pulling her gently into his arms so she could lay her head on his shoulder. Taking the blanket, he drew it up around her shoulders, trying to keep her warm. "I'm sorry, so sorry," Gabe whispered, his voice cracking. He rested his cheek against her hair, moving his hand gently up and down her back.

Bay shut her eyes tightly, trying to speak. Her throat tightened. She forced the words out, her voice hoarse, stumbling over the memories in the cave. Her voice shook with grief as she told him of the child Khogani had not helped. She spoke in rapid-fire sentences, as if she couldn't get words out fast enough, or it would eat her up alive. And all the while Gabe's arms surrounded her, holding her strong, holding her safe. Bay was engulfed in anxiety and paralyzing fear as she recounted her captivity to him. She'd feel Gabe tense. Feel him tremble. Or, he'd murmur soothing words to her and hold her closer, as if trying to sponge away some of her terror, her grief and pain.

It hurt to talk after she finished. Drained, Bay dragged in a broken breath.

"It's over, baby. The worst is over. You remembered it. Dr. Torrance said better out than in." Gabe pressed a chaste kiss to her hair. "I'm so damn proud of you, Bay. It took a helluva lot of courage to tell me." Gabe stroked her dampened back, feeling her beginning to lose the tension she'd held so long.

"Oh, God, I feel so...so dirty and—and..." Bay's voice trailed off and she turned her face into his shoulder. Humiliation flooded her. No amount of soap and water would wash away this feeling of being unclean. "Who would ever want me now?" She collapsed against him, a sob tearing out of her.

"Shhh," Gabe rasped unsteadily, his eyes filling with tears. "Let's take this one minute, one hour at a time, baby." Struggling to contain his violent grief over how badly injured she really was, Gabe whispered against her ear, "Listen to me, Bay. I won't ever leave you. You got that? I'm here. I won't walk away and leave you, so stop thinking that way. A rape can't define who you are. Don't let it...."

Gabe's low, broken words were a balm. It stunned her that Gabe wasn't repulsed. He was a friend. But what an incredibly strong and steady friend even in the worst hours of her life. Bay reached out and gripped his upper arm, feeling his corded muscles leap beneath her fingertips. "Just let me get my feet under me, Gabe. I know you can't stay here forever. You have to get back to being a SEAL." Bay closed her eyes, nestling her brow against his neck. "I'll get better. I promise...."

Her words tore Gabe apart in ways he could never have prepared himself to handle. Bay's memories of them still hadn't resurfaced. He was a friend. Not her lover. Not her fiancé. Now, she had the rape to contend with.

He held Bay tenderly and never wanted to let her

go. Never... Gabe sensed the worst wasn't over. The worst was just beginning....

THE COOL FALL breeze blew more leaves from the surrounding trees. Gold, red and orange leaves tumbled and sailed through the air around the cabins. Gabe was out with a rake and plastic garbage can, gathering them up. From the kitchen window, Bay watched him work. His face was sweaty and hard-looking, focused on the task at hand. The sink felt cool and calming beneath her fingertips. The clouds above the mountain were fluffy, the sky a deep blue.

She couldn't help watching Gabe. He was athletic, in top shape. Every morning, he ran five miles. When Gabe returned, he was soaked with sweat and then showered. Afterwards, she'd make breakfast for them. It was something Bay looked forward to, sitting with Gabe, losing herself in his burning green gaze, hungry for any touch he'd give her.

Sorrow moved through her. Ever since she'd told him about the rape, she'd felt Gabe retreat from her. Oh, it was nothing obvious. Just that she no longer felt his protectiveness around her. Maybe because she'd been violated. And yet, Gabe remained her friend. They had long talks at night in front of the fireplace in the living room. He cared for her, tried his best to always make her feel comfortable.

A frustrated sigh slipped from between Bay's lips. Since that day she'd seen the wood man with the black beard, everything had subtly shifted between them. Gabe no longer slept at her side. He slept in the next bedroom. It was still a comfort to her that he left the door open between the rooms. For that, Bay was grateful. Her nights remained tortured. She refused to take sleep medication. The meds drugged her, suppressed her symptoms, and she hated what it did to her the next day. Bay would rather take the risk of being awakened by nightmares, instead. It was the lesser of two evils.

Sometimes, she would awake screaming. When that happened, she'd always find Gabe at her side, soothing her, whispering words of comfort, holding her until she could get her bearings. Bay felt like a useless weakling. Depression hung around her, dragging her down, making her feel even more exhausted, if that was possible. She finally was told that her counselor had been a rape crisis counselor all along. Bay didn't hold it against her. She now had a solid understanding of what her brain was doing. It was withholding certain memories and then releasing them at some unknown point in the future. As the counselor said, the worst was over because she remembered her trauma. And by remembering, she could move forward and slowly continue to piece together her broken life.

Bay sensed she didn't know all the trauma. She remembered the kidnapping by Khogani, the terrible days in the cave, but that was all. There was more, she knew it, but her brain refused to give it up yet. All Bay felt was overwhelming sadness and endless tears that came out of nowhere. Her heart ached. She wanted Gabe. Every time he came near her, she felt such a sweet rush of emotions toward him. Her heart pounded, but it wasn't with fear. It was with need of him, his touch, his eyes warming as he met her gaze. She was starved for something more with him and was utterly frustrated as to what it was.

Poppy knocked on the door and called, "Helllooooo. Bay? Are you in there?"

Turning, Bay called, "Come in, Mama."

Poppy smiled a hello as she walked into the kitchen. "Do you have time for a cup of coffee, honey? Or are you fixing dinner?"

"No, coffee sounds good, Mama. I've pretty much got everything ready to put in the oven for our supper." Gabe had worked hard outside every day the past week, rarely coming in except for meals. He was avoiding her. Bay set to work fixing a fresh pot, her hands trembling as she did so.

Poppy sat down at the table, watching her. "Gabe told me what happened to you," she said quietly, holding Bay's blue gaze.

"I'm glad he did." Bay grimaced. "I was going to, Mama, but I just found myself unable to speak of it again, to anyone. I'm sorry...." Bay took the cup and sipped the coffee, watching her mother's reaction. Poppy nodded and reached over and patted her hand.

"Sometimes, life throws us curves, honey." She peered into her daughter's shadowed eyes. "I know you didn't volunteer for that top secret operation and expect this to happen to you."

"No, I didn't." Bay gave a one-shouldered shrug. "Does anyone?"

"No, but war is a terrible thing."

"I know it, up front and close in ways I'll never be able to forget, Mama."

"Have any of your women friends from this operation group contacted you? Called you?"

Bay nodded. "Several have. It's good to hear from them." She moved her fingertip around on the table, tracing the horizontal grain of the wood in front of her. "They don't know what happened, only that I took a hit." Bay frowned. "I just can't talk about it yet. I really hate going to the rape counselor right now. It hurts me too much. I need a time-out, some breathing space to try and heal."

"Then tell your counselor that. I'm sure she'll agree with you," Poppy gruffly concurred. She saw grief in Bay's eyes. "Why the sadness, honey?"

Mouth quirking, Bay sighed heavily. "It's Gabe."

Poppy's brows flew up. "Oh?" Slowly turning the cup between her hands, Bay whispered unsteadily, "Mama, I'm falling in love with him." She gave her a pained look. "I—I don't know when it started." Bay rubbed her aching brow and whispered, "He's a friend. I remember him as a friend. He was kind to me when I was assigned to his SEAL team. He was my mentor." She smiled a little, feeling anguish stir in her heart. "Gabe was so protective of me over there, Mama. Oh, he knew I could take care of myself, and I did. But he was always there. I knew I could count on him. I could trust him with my back. And he made me laugh."

Bay smiled fondly. "Gabe is so incredibly funny. When I had to go get SEAL gear to wear at Bagram air base, he flew in with me." Her mouth drew into a real smile. "You should have heard me squawking like an upset hen who had just laid a walloping egg when he wanted me to get a knife to wear. Have you ever seen one of those blades?"

"Yep, in fact, there's one in your pa's military trunk out in the shed. It's a KA-BAR in a leather sheath," Poppy said. "They issued one to every Marine. He kept his when he got out."

"I didn't know that...." Bay looked toward the ceiling for a moment, reining in her quixotic emotions. "Wait until Gabe hears this. He'll howl," she chuckled, shaking her head. "I was giving him *such* grief over at supply. I didn't want to wear that hog. It was damn near as long as my lower leg, Mama."

Poppy's mouth stretched into a grin. "So, how'd he take it?"

"Oh, you've seen Gabe put on his game face, that tough, hard unreadable mask that silently tells you that it's his way or the highway?"

"Yep."

"That's the look he gave me when I threw a tizzy about having to wear that gawdawful sword on my leg."

Poppy grinned. "I'll bet your pa is up in heaven right now laughing his socks off."

Warmth moved through Bay. She deeply loved her mother because she could talk about any subject and not be afraid of her reaction to it. "I'll bet he is, too."

"Now, what about this falling in love with this young man? Can we talk more about that?"

Bay chewed on her lower lip. "Mama, I swear, I

don't know how it happened. I—I think it's because I'm so screwed up. My emotions run like an elevator. One minute I'm up, the next, I'm down. I'll cry over nothing. I'll just start sobbing. I can't control it." Bay twisted her mouth and said in a strained tone, "Gabe has been there for me from the beginning. He's been my rock, Mama. I honestly don't know what I'd have done if he hadn't been there at both hospitals with me. In my heart—" and she touched her chest "—I've been slowly falling in love with him."

"And is this a two-way street?"

"No…"

Poppy grimaced. "Honey, you know when a person gets really hurt, it takes them a while to sort everything out. Right now, you're in the middle of a thunderstorm, and it's pouring rain so hard you can't see a foot in front of your eyes, no matter which direction you turn and look. I think if this love is genuine, it will prove itself out over time."

"Gabe's hurting, too." Bay rolled her eyes. "I mean, how would you like to be around a crybaby like me all the time? I wake up half the nights screaming, caught up in a nightmare. The rest of the time, I'm moody as hell. Sometimes I snap at Gabe. And I get angry, and I take it out on him." Bay opened her hands, her voice breaking. "Mama, he doesn't need this. Gabe doesn't deserve it. He's like a whipping post, and he just stoically absorbs whatever I dish out. He's able to sort me out from what's happened to me, if that makes any sense?"

Poppy nodded. "It does. But, honey, don't you think

if Gabe didn't want to be here, he'd already have gone? He's been at your side for almost three months straight now since you left the hospital. There has to be some underlying connection between the two of you. Don't you think?"

Feeling weepy, Bay swallowed the tears. "I don't know, Mama. Like you said, I'm an emotional thunderstorm. I never know from one minute to the next what my damned emotions will do. Sometimes, they whipsaw, and I've got to appear to be the most unbalanced, super-emotional woman Gabe has ever seen in his life, bar none."

Poppy patted her daughter's hand. "You're doing the best you can, honey. Give Gabe some credit. He's older and he's mature. He's seen a lot in his life. He does care for you. Certainly you know that?"

"I thought he did, Mama. But since last week…" Bay placed her hands over her face, afraid to say the words. Taking several deep breaths, Bay fought away the tears.

"What?" Poppy demanded.

"We had this connection…I've always felt his protection, Mama." Bay lifted her face, her voice hushed with pain. "It's gone since he knew I was raped."

"What happened to you is enough to make a grown man cry. Don't you think he's going through his own hell knowing how much you're hurting? You have to give him some space and time to adjust to it all. I know Gabe thinks he's above being a mere human being because he's a SEAL, but I think last week, he found out just how vulnerable he is to your trauma."

Bay nodded. "That makes sense to me. I never looked at it that way. I've been so selfish, Mama."

Poppy finished off her coffee and stood up. "Be patient with yourself and with Gabe, honey. You're both hurting…and over time, you'll both sort it all out. Just be patient."

GABE FINISHED RAKING out the fallen leaves in Poppy's garden. The sun had already set, and the chill was setting in for the night. Poppy was walking toward him through the deep shadows. Placing the plastic can to one side of the shed, Gabe hung the rake between two nails on the side of the building. He nodded hello to her.

"Your garden's clean for a while, Poppy." And then he managed a one-cornered smile. "At least until the wind knocks the next bunch of leaves off the trees around it."

"It looks great, Gabe. Thanks so much." Poppy's concerned expression humbled him. "I just wanted to see how you were doing," she said gently. "It's been very hard on you these last few weeks with Bay. And it fell on your shoulders to come and tell me the next morning. How are you feeling, son?" Poppy reached out, squeezing his lower arm.

Poppy's nurturing touch felt good on his arm. Or maybe she was holding him in place so he wouldn't run away. Which is what he wanted to do right now. Her blue eyes narrowed on him, and Gabe knew he'd have to say something or she was going to haunt the hell out of him until he did. Sighing, he admitted, "I'm whipped, Poppy. I'm tired to my soul. I'm bled out."

"Yep, those are all signs of caregiver burnout." She waved her finger in his face. "Young man, I told you early on to pace yourself with Bay. But you haven't done that. You're trying to help her every step of the way and, son, sometimes, it's better that you're not there to always catch her when she stumbles."

Gabe looked at her, stunned. "What?" Had he heard right? Poppy's face went stubborn. He'd seen that very look on Bay's face before. Gabe girded himself, knowing there was more to come.

"Caregiving is not a well-known science, Gabe. My daughter is traumatized, and she does need help. By supporting her, you're helpin' her move through the pain. In my experience, needing another person comes and goes, sort of like a tide. Bay needs to start getting a sense of herself. There are times she doesn't need you there, Gabe. And if you can learn to pick up on those times, she'll get stronger instead of always leanin' on you. That's how she's going to get strong again, through her own trials and errors. Every time she falls down, you don't have to be there to pick her up. Bay will always feel like a victim if she isn't allowed to stand on her own two feet."

Scowling, Gabe felt anger burn in him. "She needs me."

"I'm not disputin' that. I am pointing out that you need some time alone, too. You need some rest, Gabe. You're as sleep deprived as Bay is. Maybe more so."

Confused, Gabe shook his head. "I love her. You

don't quit on someone when the going gets tough, Poppy. Am I sleep deprived? Hell, yes. Am I sickened by what's happened to her?" His voice cracked, and he looked away. "I wrestle with that every night, Poppy. I lay in my bed and I want to scream. I want to cry. And I want to kill Khogani all over again with my bare fists. I fall asleep dreaming of making him hurt ten times as much as he hurt Bay. I'm sorry. I'm not in the best of moods. You're catching me when I'm really down."

"I understand," Poppy said softly, walking over and sliding her arm around his waist and giving him a good, strong hug. "Up until this happened to Bay, you were going to be my son-in-law. I still consider you that. Nothing's changed."

"I'm not so sure I am now, Poppy," he said wearily. "It's a one-way street. I love Bay. I know our history. Bay doesn't remember any of it...." He felt his heart twist with anguish, the pain so deep he went numb.

"Perk up. I've got some good news for you."

Gabe warily looked over at her as she released him from her hug. Her blue eyes were bright. "What news?"

"Bay and I just had coffee. I was just goin' and checkin' up on her. I asked why she was so sad-looking, figuring it was due to the big emotional blow of remembering what had happened to her."

Gabe shook his head. "Where's this going?"

"Bay was sad," Poppy said in a gentle tone, "because she said she's falling in love with you, even though she realizes you're 'just a friend' to her." She threw her hands on her hips. "Well? Does that compute? Do you get it now? She's falling in love with you all over again, Gabe."

Gabe's mouth fell open. He quickly shut it, his mind spinning, his heart doing funny flip-flops in his chest. "Are you sure Bay said that?" My God, could it really be true? Could she fall in love with him again? It blew away every thought he'd had in his reeling mind.

Chuckling, Poppy said, "Bet your last bottom dollar on it, son. Now…" And she got tough with him. "You figure out a different plan between you and Bay. Give her some time by herself. Why don't you spend some time carving? I'll send you on all-day errands around the county. I've got a lot of things I gotta buy before winter sets in. Both of you need to just have alone time. You can be gone eight hours a day and then you can come back, have dinner together and talk. You'll give her the space she needs to start strengthening herself, Gabe. It's like exercise, only it's on an emotional and mental level. I'll be here for Bay if she needs someone while you're conveniently away." She grinned a little. "Besides, being gone a few days every week out on my fall errands will make her heart grow fonder toward you. Don't you think?"

In utter disbelief, Gabe stared at Poppy. Emotions rose swiftly, tightening his chest, filling him with renewed hope. There was so much to think about. To feel his way through. "I don't know how to handle this, Poppy. Bay remembers the rape. I remember Dr. Torrance warning me big-time about not trying to get intimate with her after the memories came back. It could pressure her, or scare her…break the trust I've built with her."

"Listen, you've always loved her! You know Bay, and unconsciously, she knows you. She's always trusted you. Just be gentle, patient and slow with her is all. She's like a horse that's been beaten half to death. They're always wary at first, but love and patience always wins them back over. Think about ways to do that, to give her a chance to show you she loves you. It isn't always about the man taking the helm. Sometimes, you gotta let the woman set the pace and let her make the first steps forward. Okay?"

A slow grin worked its way across Gabe's face, fierce hope tunneling through his heart. "I hear you, Poppy. I'll take your words and ideas and make them work."

She sighed dramatically and nodded. "Good, then. Come with me back to the house. I just made two fresh apple pies this afternoon. And that's a favorite of Bay's. Come over and pick one up and take it home as dessert for the two of you after your dinner tonight."

"Yes, ma'am."

CHAPTER NINETEEN

BAY LOVED OCTOBER. It was her favorite month of the
year. She saw Gabe splitting wood on the knoll above
the cabin, near the blue Ford pickup truck. He'd been
cutting wood all day long and bringing it back to each
of the cabins for the winter supply. For now, her mother
wouldn't allow the black-bearded wood man anywhere
near the place. The sun was overhead, feeling warm
on the slightly chilly day. Dried leaves crunched beneath her feet as she walked from their cabin up the
knoll where the wood stack was growing.

Gabe had taken off his T-shirt, his upper body
gleaming in the sunlight. Bay had always appreciated his lean, taut muscling. He wasn't bulked up like
a body builder, rather more like a honed, champion
boxer. She watched his muscles flex and tighten as he
brought the long-handled axe down on a quarter piece
of wood. The sound of it splitting cracked through
the air.

"Time for a break?" she called, approaching him.
She placed a glass of iced tea on a post nearby. Gabe
turned toward her, his face gleaming with sweat. His
chest was covered with dark hair, a thin line down the
middle of his flat, hard belly, disappearing into his

jeans. It was his green eyes that narrowed instantly upon her that made Bay's heart speed up.

Over a month had gone by since she'd remembered the rape. In that time, Gabe had changed a number of his habits. On most days, he was gone or out chopping wood. He came in for daily meals she cooked, but then left shortly after eating. In a way, Bay missed his constant presence, but in another way, it worked for both of them. Like her Mama remarked one day, about three weeks ago, she didn't need Gabe fused to her hip 24/7. And they'd both laughed and agreed.

"Hey," Gabe murmured, wiping the sweat off his brow with the back of his arm, "that looks good. Thank you." He brought the head of the axe down, and it stuck in a larger tree stump he used to split the wood on. As he reached for the cold glass of iced tea, Gabe felt his entire body tighten with need for Bay. She stood unsurely before him, her hands clasped in front of her. The breeze gently moved her light brown hair around her cheeks. As he looked at her, he could see how she was finally starting to regain her lost weight. She filled out her jeans and pink sweater rather nicely.

Tipping the glass to his lips, Gabe drank thirstily, a hint of lemon and honey in the tea. The sour taste reminded Gabe of their awkwardness around one another in the last couple months. Poppy sent him on errands nearly every day. Or, he'd buy a load of wood and split it for hours each day. Poppy needed to have enough to carry the two cabins over the coming winter. Bay was content to stay on the mountain, not ready for crowds and strangers yet.

Poppy had been right: seeing less of Bay was strengthening her. He'd seen incredible changes, good ones in her, as a result. After finishing the glass of iced tea, he grinned. "Thanks," he said before handing the empty glass to her.

Their fingers met and held.

"Dinner's at six," she said, glancing quickly at the sky. It would be dark about that time. "I made your favorite. Beef roast, potatoes and carrots."

Gabe wanted to stare at Bay like a lovesick puppy. Her cheeks were flushed, and he was moved by her sudden shyness, not quite holding his gaze for very long. She'd been like that with him when she'd been with his SEAL team in Afghanistan. Gabe wanted to reach out and slide his hand along the clean line of her jaw, tilt her head and kiss her. How many times had he entertained that thought? *A hundred times a day.* "Gravy, by any chance?"

Bay laughed. "It's easy to see what you want."

There it was again, that invisible protection surrounding her like arms embracing her. How she had missed that sensation, along with that heat in his gaze. In the past few months, it had returned, and never had she felt such utter relief. It was as if they were once more invisibly connected to one another.

As Gabe stood casually with his large, spare hands resting on his hips, Bay wanted to blurt out her growing love for him. How would he take her admission? What man wanted a woman who had been defiled as she had been? Bay was afraid of his answers and couldn't get up the courage to speak to him about it.

Wiping his brow with his long fingers, Gabe gave her a wry look and said, "Men are simple to read in comparison to women, believe me."

"Oh, you're so prejudiced, Griffin," she said, chuckling, and turned away, walking down the knoll toward the cabin.

He grinned and watched the soft sway of her hips. Her legs…God, her legs were a mile long, shapely beneath those loose-fitting jeans she wore. He'd entertained running his hands up and down them way too many times. Every day it was getting tougher for Gabe to stop his physical reactions toward Bay.

He turned, grabbing the axe. When to touch Bay? Where to touch her? Would his hand in the wrong place trigger her again? Send her into crumpling pain and panic once more? Gabe couldn't stand seeing Bay suffer. She was looking him in the eye again, instead of always looking off to one side. He couldn't jeopardize what she'd rebuilt in herself.

The coolness of the breeze hit his sweaty body. It felt good. Now he needed a truckload of ice cubes to put his hungry body into permanent deep freeze.

BAY SAT ON the couch, Gabe sitting on the floor, leaning against it, inches separating them. They'd had dinner earlier and gone to the living room to have dessert. It was becoming a nightly ritual Gabe looked forward to. They listened to classical music on a radio. This was their quality time. A time to share what each had done during the day.

Gabe held a plate with a huge piece of apple pie

slathered with whipped cream in his hand. A sense of
tranquility settled around him as they ate in silence,
the clink of the fork against the plate one of the few
sounds. Flames cracked and popped in the fireplace,
sending heat radiating throughout the cabin. The soft
snap and crackle of the wood burning provided a sense
of peace to the cabin.

"I finished my canvas today," Bay told him, setting
her empty plate on the side of the lamp table. Poppy
had pushed her into getting back to her painting. So
had Gabe.

"Can I see it?" Gabe finished his pie and set his
plate to one side. He tipped his head to the right, catching her expression. He saw some worry in Bay's eyes
as she rose. "Hey," he called softly, catching her hand
and gently tugging on her fingers. "Come down here
for a second? You've got some whipped cream on your
nose."

Bay colored fiercely, absorbing his strong, warm
hand around hers. "Oh, jeez," she murmured, embarrassed. She lifted her hand to wipe it off.

"Uh-uh," Gabe murmured, smiling as he coaxed
her to come and kneel next to him. "Now, if you sit
real still, I'll get it...." He caught the tiny white stuff
on her nose with his index finger. Gabe popped it into
his mouth and gave her a wicked grin.

Bay sat back on her heels, feeling lighter. Happier.
She loved these moments when he was intimate with
her. Gabe had showered earlier and wore a cream-
colored long-sleeved corduroy shirt. His dark hair was
still damp, and stubble emphasized the lean planes of

his smiling face. Bay drowned in his green eyes and sighed. She sat down, wanting to get closer to him. She caught the scent of the pine soap he'd used, the sunlight on his flesh and Gabe's special male scent that was only him. Her gaze focused on his strong, well-shaped mouth. How many times a day did she think of getting up enough courage to kiss this man? Fear had stopped Bay because she was afraid of Gabe's reaction. Friends didn't kiss one another.

"Uh-oh," Gabe teased, "I see a second spot of whipped cream. You're in trouble."

"Oh, you're kidding me." Bay's eyes widened with distress. "Where?"

Gabe eased his hands around her shoulders. "Come here, I'll show you…." He pulled her across his lap, hoping like hell she wouldn't react negatively to his action. Gabe couldn't help himself any longer. He had to touch her. He craved intimacy with Bay so damn badly, he was barely sleeping anymore at night. He felt her thighs meet and slide across his. Looking up into her face, he saw surprise, not fear. Not yet…

Keeping his tone light, Gabe brought Bay against his body, her arm easing around his shoulders. "Now…" He slowly brought his hand up, not wanting to startle her with too swift a movement. Gabe keenly monitored her reaction, feeling how her body was responding against his. If, at any moment, he felt her freeze up, he'd instantly stop, knowing it was triggering something bad inside her.

"It's right here," he rasped, moving his thumb across her pouty lower lip.

Bay's eyes widened momentarily and then grew deliciously drowsy, telling him she liked his touch. Gabe slid his fingers along her left cheek, gently turning her a bit more and angling her such that he could lean up and capture that soft, waiting mouth of hers. His body thrummed with scalding lust. He felt himself growing hard, hoping like hell Bay wasn't aware of it. This wasn't where this was going. At least, not yet.

Gabe looked deeply into her confused blue eyes, gently trapping her chin. "I have a confession to make."

"What?" she whispered, barely able to get the word out, entranced with his eyes burning with heat. He was going to kiss her, she just knew it. Her whole body trembled with excitement over that sudden realization.

He grinned and said, "I lied. There's no more whipped cream on you." Gabe's smile faded, and he held her warm gaze. "I want to kiss you, Bay. May I?"

She blinked once, caught in a scorching daze of hunger. His hand was on the center of her back, his other roughened palm cupping her cheek. She opened her lips to speak, and her mind disappeared. The serious look in Gabe's eyes brought her back to earth. He was patiently waiting. Watching her. Watching for reaction. Gulping, she managed hoarsely, "Yes…I'd like that…."

"But, listen, baby, we need to get some ground rules set here first. Okay?"

Bay nodded, resting her hand against his chest. Beneath her palm, she felt the slow thud of his heart. "What rules, Gabe?" And then she shook her head. "Yes…I'm sorry…I forgot for a moment…." *About the rape.* About what triggered her pain. Gabe's eyes darkened for just a moment, his male mouth tightened imperceptibly.

"You're in the driver's seat, Bay. You have to be, after what's happened to you." Gabe caressed her flushed cheek with his thumb, feeling the velvet softness of her flesh. "I don't know where that line is with you. I can't read your mind, baby. You have to tell me if I scare you or…God forbid, hurt you. I live in a special hell worrying I'll accidentally harm you. If something frightens you, doesn't feel good to you, stop me. Okay?" Gabe's gaze dug into her sad blue eyes. She tucked her lower lip between her teeth, and he watched her confidence dissolve. Dammit, this had to be talked about. Gabe couldn't do anything without Bay's help. She had to speak up. *Patience…* He gave her a tender smile and saw her respond gamely to it.

"You're right," Bay replied in a hushed tone. "I'm not afraid of you, Gabe. I know you won't hurt me." And her voice broke as she looked helplessly down at him.

His heart shattered. Bay was struggling, the flush disappearing from her cheeks. She *was* scared, and he sensed it, saw it.

"Baby," he cajoled, sliding his fingers through her hair, "we'll be patient with one another. Okay?"

She swallowed hard and in strangled voice asked, "How did you know, Gabe?"

"Know what?" he asked, searching her eyes.

"Th-that I wanted you more than just as a friend." The words rushed out of her, fearful-sounding yet filled with yearning. For him. Afraid to meet his eyes, Bay sat very still, so afraid of Gabe's reaction to her whispered admission. Had her silly heart led her wrong? It had told her he loved her, too. He drew her against his chest, her head coming to rest against his. "You have no idea, baby, how long I've been waiting to hear you say that." His voice shook with emotion, and Bay lifted her head away from his, shock registering in her expression. Good shock, not bad. The corners of Gabe's mouth slowly pulled upward. Her lips parted, amazement registering in her blue eyes. And then, the look he'd been waiting so damn long for: yearning for him alone.

Time slowly ebbed to a halt as Gabe lifted his hand once again and slid it against Bay's jaw, guiding her down, guiding her lips toward his. A burning ache built rapidly within his tense body. Never had he wanted anything more in this moment than Bay's lips settled against his own. God, he'd waited months for this one, exquisite moment....

His warm, moist breath caressed her nose, mouth and cheek. She closed her eyes, wanting Gabe so badly, her lips parting, pleading silently with him to kiss her. His mouth skimmed her lips as softy as a butterfly's wings. Her heart skittered. Her breath hitched as she leaned more surely toward him, wanting his mouth firmly upon hers. His lips molded against hers, giving her his heat. All Bay's fear and anxiety melted beneath Gabe's slow, deliberate exploration of her. She felt cherished as he parted her lips, deepening their kiss. She moaned, but it was a moan of pleasure and need, not fear or pain.

Her world turned hot and needy as Gabe caressed her lips. A shudder worked through her as her body reawakened. Their breathing became uneven, and she gripped his shoulder, wanting more. He hesitated, as if silently asking her if this is what she really wanted.

Bay felt so damned greedy, wanting his mouth on hers, infusing her with life. Somewhere in the halls of her memory, Bay knew Gabe's mouth intimately, had kissed him until her soul sang with joy. He smiled beneath her lips, a smile of a man who liked his woman's audacity. Did Gabe love her?

Bay couldn't help but get caught up in the fever of his mouth, his tongue sliding against hers, their hearts thundering against one another. Inhaling his male scent, she suddenly felt free in a way she hadn't felt before. His hands ranged from her shoulders down her lower arms. His tongue moved teasingly against hers. Stroking her slowly and then moving boldly to meet her shy challenge. Bay gave a soft cry, her fingers sinking into his taut shoulders. She wanted the kiss to go on forever.

Reluctantly, Gabe eased from her swollen, wet lips, his breath ragged. Bay's eyes were filled with arousal. It made him feel good. Feel whole, when he hadn't felt that way in a damned long time. Gabe smiled into her blue eyes. "That was a good first step we just took." His brows moved down as she didn't respond. "Are you all right, Bay?"

"I'm fine...just fine...."

Gabe wanted to get up, carry Bay into his bedroom and make love with her all night long. His body ached, the pain nearly unbearable. He framed her face, watching the arousal in her eyes. Yeah, this was a good first step. No land mines. No terror. No screams. It wasn't Bay's fault, and Gabe knew that. But one wrong move could destroy her fragile state. And destroy her trust in him.

Bay lifted her hand, trailing her fingertips along his cheek. She tried to smile, but seemed so shy still. Had they gone too far, too fast?

How could he tell her how much he loved her? Gabe's heart lurched, ached and cried out in protest. She may have responded to him, but how did she really feel about the kiss, about him? He could still taste her on his lips. It would have to be enough for now.

CHAPTER TWENTY

GABE WORRIEDLY WATCHED Bay as she helped take a tray of Halloween cookies to Poppy's burgundy Toyota minivan. The three women had baked half a day, getting ready to bring caramel-coated apples and dozens of frosted cookies to Eva-Jo's school in the town of Dunmore.

Eva-Jo was decked out in a fairy costume wearing a glittery white skirt and bright pink blouse, along with a crown and a wand with multicolored ribbons attached to it. Poppy had created the fairy dress with Bay's help. Gabe tried to settle his anxiety. This was the first time Bay was going to step out into a social function since returning home.

Eva-Jo was singing and dancing around the burgundy minivan as Poppy and Bay carefully stowed the food into the rear of it. Gabe was the driver, and he carried two gallons of apple cider, one in each hand, to the van. Eva-Jo was singing at the top of her lungs, caught up in her own inner world. Gabe would have appreciated her infectious joy more if he wasn't so damned concerned about Bay. He'd tried to talk Bay out of going. Her therapist was actively urging her to begin to flow into mainstream society. Bay wasn't ready, and Gabe knew it in his gut, but he couldn't stop her. She chose to listen to her counselor over his advice.

Everyone settled into the van, midafternoon sunlight slanting through the woods, leaving beams of light shooting through the naked tree branches. Bay sat in the seat behind Gabe. Poppy sat up front in the passenger seat. She turned to make sure singing Eva-Jo was strapped in, too. Bay had already done the duty.

"Okay, off to Eva-Jo's school," Poppy said, smiling.

Bay sat quietly. Eva-Jo stopped singing and was waving her fairy wand around, entranced by the ribbons floating on the air. By accident, she hit Bay in the throat with the wand.

Instantly, Bay jerked away, gasping. Her neck was particularly sensitive. She'd gotten used to wearing a mock turtleneck sweater but nothing tighter around her neck. She couldn't stand anyone to touch it. She pressed her hand over the affected area while Eva-Jo kept playing with her wand, oblivious.

Bay looked up in the rearview mirror and saw Gabe's gaze on her for a moment. She hoped he hadn't seen her jump like a scalded cat in the backseat. Her heart was pounding, and no matter what she did, it wouldn't calm down. She tried to concentrate on the winding dirt road they took down the side of the mountain.

Gabe was a good driver, and Bay tried to force her mind off her smarting neck. The memories of Khogani nearly strangling her overwhelmed her. When she pulled her hand away, there was a small amount of blood on two of her fingers. Grimacing, Bay took a tissue out of her small purse and placed it against the minor wound.

As Gabe turned left on Black Mountain Road, he again checked his rearview mirror. Bay seemed upset. What the hell had happened? Frustrated, he couldn't stop the car and go ask her. They had to arrive at Eva-Jo's school by a certain time. There would be two hundred children and adults, along with their guardians and parents, celebrating their annual Halloween party. It was one of the most important days in Eva-Jo's life.

Mouth tightening, Gabe paid attention to the two-lane asphalt road. Dunmore sat in the Allegheny Mountains of West Virginia. It was where Bay went for her weekly appointment with the therapist, Jolene Carter. He knew the road almost blindfolded because he was the one who drove her to and from her appointments. Seneca State Forest surrounded them, thousands of acres of woodlands on small, lumpy hills.

As they pulled up at the two-story brick school, Eva-Jo was singing again and whirling her wand around. Gabe's nerves were wearing thin. He opened the sliding door so Eva-Jo could climb out. He glanced over at Bay, who was unbuckling. What the hell? She was frowning, and he noticed the blood and a small bruise forming on her neck. *Damn.* It was obvious where she got this. He waited until Bay turned toward him to scoot off the seat.

"Did she nail you with that damned wand?" Gabe asked under his breath, picking up her hand and helping her out. Bay's eyes were shadowed. He could feel the tension in her body.

"She didn't mean it," Bay murmured. "It's nothing, Gabe. Really." Would he believe her lie? Bay hurried to the back of the van to meet Poppy. Together, they carried the covered cookie trays into the gymnasium. Gabe brought up the rear with the apple cider in each hand.

Bay wasn't prepared for the high level of noise, laughter and music echoing around the huge gym. She followed her mother to one end of the crowded hall where children energetically milled with adults. Many of them were decked out in costumes. Eva-Jo went running merrily into the crowd, waving her fairy wand around, showing it off to everyone. Bay found herself wishing she could be so carefree.

Gabe kept an eye on Bay as he helped the two women distribute the sheets of cookies across six long tables. He peeled off the foil and set them down. People began crowding forward, wanting to grab some goodies before they disappeared. He felt children pushing in around his legs, jostling and stretching their arms forward toward the food on the table. They were smiling, laughing and playful. Gabe felt anything but. He looked left and noticed a bunch of teen boys crowding in around Bay. She looked ill at ease as she tried to take foil off the last batch of cookies on the table.

Gabe extracted himself from the children. Other anxious kids immediately flowed into the vacant spot. A half dozen mentally challenged boys, some nearly six feet tall, jostled around Bay, trying to get to the cookies, stretching their arms around her to reach them. She suddenly lost her balance as two boys pushed too hard.

Instantly, Gabe was there, sliding his hand around Bay's arm, stopping her from falling.

"I've got you," he said, shielding her with his body as the teens surged forward and past them. Gabe guided Bay away from the crowd of over a hundred people swamping the food tables. He placed his arm around her shoulders and led her out toward an empty area in the center of the gym.

Bay steadied her breathing. The music tore holes into her sensitized nervous system. The unrelenting screaming and shrieking of the children made her ears ring. She knew that Gabe was talking to her, but she couldn't hear him. In seconds, Bay felt herself leaving her body again, floating, seeing herself below. Anxiety, mixed with a huge fist of grief, exploded up through her. She felt Gabe's arm tighten around her waist, and she leaned against him, her hands over her ears, her eyes tightly shut.

When Bay closed her eyes, to her horror, she once more saw the six-year-old little boy lying semiconscious in a pile of blankets, his leg broken. She heard Khogani laughing, pointing at the child, telling her to fix him. Bay tried to stop the movie flowing through her head, but she couldn't.

No...oh, no... I don't want to see him again...please, God, I don't...please, no...

Gabe cursed softly, hearing mewling cries whisper brokenly between Bay's contorted lips.

Son of a bitch!

Gabe knew she shouldn't have come. This was just too much for her to handle all at once! Bay leaned heavily against him, her hands pressed against her ears. Her cries were drowned out by the noise, music and continued laughter. Gabe led her toward the closest exit. Bay was stumbling, as if drunk, beneath his arm. Breathing hard, angered at the therapist, he shoved the door open. He ushered her into a deserted school hall.

"It's okay, Bay," Gabe breathed, hauling her against him. He leaned back into the row of lockers, wrapping his arms around her. She buried her head against his shoulder. He could feel her trembling.

Dammit! Desperately, Gabe looked around. The music and noise were fairly well blunted by the hall of lockers. He could feel Bay working to control her breathing, felt her struggling to stop shaking. Gently stroking her hair, Gabe choked on a lump growing in his throat. Frustration curdled in him, and he closed his eyes for a moment, trying to get a handle on his mounting anger.

Gabe had taught Bay that old diver's trick of bringing down her heart rate. If she opened her eyes, she stopped seeing the child and Khogani. But the raw and terrified feelings of what Bay saw, what she was feeling, writhed through her. She pulled out of his arms. "I need some air," she rasped, searching desperately to find a door to escape through, panic nearly overwhelming her.

Gabe gripped her hand. "This way, baby. Just hang on. I'll get you out of here…."

As Gabe pushed open the outer door, Bay lunged

past him to escape outside. She staggered and then righted herself, holding her face up to the sky, dragging in draughts of fresh air through her opened mouth. Her stomach was roiling, and she pressed her hand against herself. She felt Gabe come to her side. Knowing what she had to do, she leaned over, hands on her knees, concentrating on slowing the panic attack. Gabe kept his hand on her back, as if to let her know she wasn't alone. When Bay closed her eyes this time, the scene in the cave was gone. *Thank God.*

This time, she wasn't going to cry even though the tears stung the backs of her tightly shut eyes. If she was going to get well, she had to work through the anxiety and panic by herself.

Gabe stood tensely. He watched Bay lean over, gasping for air, fighting the raw terror that wanted to control her. Anger reared up through him, and he wanted to punch his fist through anything he could find. The terrible sense of helplessness, the frustration of knowing that Bay wasn't ready for socialization, tore him apart. Adrenaline was leaking into his bloodstream as well as hers. They'd both seen combat. It had changed their reactions forever. Wiping his mouth, Gabe looked around. They were in a parking lot, and he saw no one. Right now, he didn't want to talk to a soul.

Finally, Bay slowly straightened up. She pushed her curly hair away from her face. The sun had set, the sky a lighter color now. The wind was picking up, and she put her arms around herself. When she looked over at Gabe's angry features, Bay's stomach clenched. His eyes were so flat and dangerous-looking. It scared her for a moment because her own emotions were running loose within her. She could see he was fighting not to say anything.

"Let's walk," she suggested in a strained tone.

Giving a jerk of his head, Gabe followed her lead. Bay gave him a silent look of thanks as he settled the coat around her shoulders. Right now, Gabe was a big, bad guard dog. His game face was in place, his eyes hard and unreadable. She kept walking around the black asphalt parking lot. Walking helped her come down. The more she moved, the better, more stable she felt. Gabe hadn't touched her, hadn't tried to put his arm around her waist or shoulders. She could feel rage radiating off him.

She frowned. "You were right. I wasn't ready for this. I'm sorry, Gabe."

He cut a look in her direction. Bay's eyes were sad-looking, and he felt her apology. But he was angry. Damned angry at the therapist. Gabe had held his opinion concerning her. In his one and only meeting with Jolene, she informed him that she preferred to hear the background directly from the patient, not him. Gabe had angrily walked away from their meeting, knowing that if Jolene knew nothing about Bay, she was bound to make assumptions and errors. And Bay would suffer because of it. The counselor didn't know Bay had gone through capture, rape, killing the enemy, escape and injury.

Nostrils flaring, Gabe growled, "That therapist of

yours is full of shit! There's no way you were ready for this, Bay. You trusted her, you didn't trust me."

Bay slowed to a stop. She stood a few feet from Gabe. Deeply affected, she managed in a hoarse voice, "I know you're upset. You have a right to be...."

His hands curled into fists, and then Gabe forced himself to relax. "Did you feel she was right, Bay? Did you seriously feel up to this?" He jabbed his finger at the building behind them.

His anger felt like barbs being shot into her body. Bay wrapped her arms a little tighter around herself. "Look, I was wrong. Okay? I made a mistake and I've paid for it." Her voice lowered with apology. "And so have you...."

Gabe was breathing harder, his eyes slits. "What about next time, Bay? You can't trust your own sense of self, yet. That's why I'm here." Gabe jabbed his thumb at his chest. "Dammit, you can't do this to yourself!" His voice cracked. "Why didn't you listen to me instead of that therapist?"

His rage struck her full force. Desperately, Bay tried to separate out Gabe's reaction from the man she loved. She lifted her lashes, meeting his anguished gaze. He was hurting so damn much. "I—I wanted to get better, Gabe. You're right, I didn't feel up to it, but I thought I could do it anyway. I wanted—" and Bay's voice grew resigned "—I wanted to show you I was getting stronger. That I didn't need to be babysat day in and day out." Gabe snapped his chin up, his eyes flaring with rage. "Dammit, that came out wrong," she said quickly, holding up her hand. "What I meant to say—"

"Your therapist called me a babysitter?" Gabe ground out. "Those are her words, Bay. They're not yours."

Grimacing, Bay nodded. "Yeah, those are her words. She was just wanting me to get out on my own more because, sooner or later, I'd have to anyway."

"I suppose she called me a crutch? An enabler?"

The dark warning in his voice shook her. She felt physically slapped by his cold rage and icy stare.

"Yes, she used the word enabler," she quietly admitted.

"That's ridiculous!"

Bay cringed. She saw the anguished look Gabe gave her. "I told her you weren't, Gabe," she offered, her voice trembling. "I didn't believe you were…."

"Given the amount of hell you've gone through," Gabe rattled out angrily, "that woman doesn't get it! She hasn't a clue, Bay, as to how you managed to survive! Dammit, I do!" His voice cracked, and he yelled, "I was there! I saw it all!"

Stunned, Bay gasped. "You were?"

Aw, hell, he'd blown it!

Breathing harshly, Gabe scrambled. He hadn't meant to tell Bay anything before her memory had given it back to her first. He saw confusion in her eyes, her lips parting in agony.

"I'm not saying anything else," Gabe rasped. "Let's get to the van. It's damned cold out here."

Bay stood, paralyzed by his hoarse cry that plunged straight through her heart. Gabe had been there! Wherever "there" was. Her only memory was of the cave, of

Khogani, ministering to the wounded Taliban soldiers and the rape. Her mind hadn't given up anything else. She had no idea how she'd gotten out of the cave or how she'd managed to survive captivity. Her memory was a blank, and it wasn't yielding anything. The look on Gabe's tortured features gripped Bay, scared her, and she felt anxiety explode within her again.

With a croak, Bay suddenly turned away from him. She bent over, hands pressed against her stomach and throat, heaving, the sounds terrible and embarrassing. Tears stung her eyes, her mouth watered, and bile burned the back of her throat. She tried to wipe her tears away when it finally was over. Her hand trembled so badly that she couldn't even wipe the saliva away from her mouth.

Gabe ruthlessly jammed everything into his kill box the moment Bay started to get sick. He walked to her side, sliding his arm around her hip, allowing her to lean against him as Bay retched her guts out. He felt as if someone had twisted and torn him in half. Reaching into his back pocket, he pulled out a white handkerchief. He pressed it into Bay's hand. He was a damn failure. He'd gotten angry and let fly with something Bay hadn't recalled yet. He'd seen the gut-shot look on her drawn features. And he'd witnessed the result of his actions.

Son of a bitch.

Bay wiped her mouth and forced herself to stand up. Tears matted her lashes, and she rubbed them away with her shaking fingers. "Gabe, take me home, please?" She needed to get out of here, to get away from him. Bay desperately needed to be alone, to figure it all out. She saw his eyes filled with misery. With defeat.

"Come on," Gabe muttered, "I'll drive you back to the cabin."

CHAPTER TWENTY-ONE

"WHERE'S BAY?" POPPY asked Gabe. It was the morning after the Halloween party.

Gabe scowled. "I guess she's still sleeping. Why?" Last night after he'd driven Poppy and Eva-Jo home, he'd found Bay's bedroom door closed when he'd finally got to the cabin around nine. And the inner door between the bedrooms had been shut, as well. Bay had needed some space, even though he'd wanted desperately to apologize for his words and actions out in the parking lot earlier.

"My old blue Ford truck's gone. It was there last night when we came in."

He froze. Moving across the kitchen, Gabe quickly went to the door of Bay's bedroom. Pushing it open, he saw the bed was made. Panic started to eat at him as he saw a note lying in the center of the bed. He grabbed it. His gut began to crumble as he read it.

Dear Gabe,
I have to leave. This isn't your fault. It's mine.
I have to go away. I have to try and figure out
what's wrong with me and figure out how to fix
it. I'm so sorry I hurt you so badly. You were al-

ways loyal and you never gave up on me. Please tell Mama that I've taken her truck. Tell her I'll call her and she's not to worry about me. I wish I could repay you, Gabe. You deserve so much more than I could ever give you. Love, Bay

Reeling, Gabe took the note out of the room and handed it to Poppy. His mind moved at light speed, calculating when Bay had left. How the hell had he not heard her get up and leave? He'd been utterly exhausted by their argument last night, and he remembered falling into bed and immediately dropping off to sleep.

"Oh, Lordy," Poppy cried softly, pressing her hand to her mouth. Her eyes filled with tears. She looked up at Gabe, a sob tearing from her. "What are we going to do?" she cried.

Raking his hand through his hair, Gabe sat down. He had to or his knees would buckle. "Sit down for a minute, Poppy. Let me think...."

She sniffed and blotted her eyes as she sat opposite him at the table. "Should I call the police?"

"No," Gabe muttered. "Not yet. They won't go after a missing person for at least forty-eight hours after they've turned up missing." His heart felt so damned heavy in his chest, he could barely breathe. *Think!* He had to think! He jerked a look up at Poppy. "Where did Bay go when she was hurting? She must have had some kind of favorite place."

"Wh-what?"

"Kids always have a favorite hiding place. Where was hers?"

Rubbing her brow, Poppy looked stunned. Her face had gone white.

Gabe held on to his deteriorating patience. What if Bay stopped for gas somewhere and some asshole made a pass at her? Gabe couldn't shut off other horrifying possibilities.

"Oh, Lordy," Poppy muttered. "She and her pa went fishing at Stony Bottom on the Greenbrier River. It's a nice area on the river, and it was her favorite place to be with him. They went almost every month during the summer. She didn't fish, but she loved being with Floyd and did a lot of hiking in the area. They were so close," Poppy whispered. "I know Bay misses him terribly."

"Where's Stony Bottom?" Gabe asked, trying to sound calm. His stomach burned. His heart felt as if someone was slowly ripping it in half. Getting up, he grabbed a pen and paper from the telephone stand near the couch. He placed them in front of Poppy. "Can you draw me a map? Is it nearby?"

"It's only about five miles southwest of us," Poppy whispered, drawing the map on the paper. "Bay would hike along the Greenbrier River Trail. She particularly liked the area where a small bridge crosses it. There's a nice grassy meadow on the other side with a hill that's about twenty-eight hundred feet high behind it. She'd take her watercolors along with her and paint over there. It parallels the Greenbrier River, Gabe. It's deep backcountry. Hikers during the day, but black bear, deer and smaller animals most other times. It's all national or state forest land. That's where Floyd would go to take down bucks for the poor people on our mountain. He and Bay would go down there every fall and hunt. It's rich, beautiful woodlands. Real Hill country."

"I'll get a map of it up on my iPhone," he muttered, taking the piece of paper.

Gabe's gut told him that was where she went. Bay wanted to be alone. To think. To cry. She had no one to hold her or help her now. He felt so damned miserable he couldn't even cry. "Did you find anything else missing? Anything she might have taken with her? That could give us a clue as to what she was thinking."

"I don't know." Poppy rose to her feet. "Let's go out to the shed. All of Floyd's tent and hunting gear are stored in there."

The door to the shed stood open as they approached it. He figured Bay had come and taken camping gear, maybe a sleeping bag, and grabbed some food from their refrigerator before she left.

Poppy peered in the door, turned the light switch on and looked around.

"You're right, she took the tent, two sleeping bags, the Coleman stove, a fishing rod and Floyd's tackle box." Poppy stepped inside and walked over to an old, battered military trunk that her husband had gotten when he joined the Marine Corps. Lifting the lid, she whispered, "Oh, Lordy. Floyd's KA-BAR knife is gone!" She whirled toward Gabe. "She wouldn't cut herself, would she?" Poppy blanched, her voice quaking with terror.

"Bay isn't someone who gives up. I don't think she took it for that reason." Gabe scowled. "Your husband had a Win-Mag .300 rifle. Where is it?" He wasn't going into deep woodlands without a weapon. God only knew who or what was out there. Bay could have taken the knife for protection purposes, maybe to cut bait or gut fish she caught, not with the idea of slicing her wrists and bleeding out. She was too damn strong to do that.

"It's in the house. Come on!" Poppy practically ran back to the main cabin. Inside, she led Gabe to the rifle on the wall. Gabe brought it down. It was a beautiful piece, well cared for, the stock a rich honey oak color. "Do you have his rifle cleaning kit? Any shells?"

"Yes, everything's in that drawer." She pointed to the cabinet below where the rifle was displayed.

Crouching down, Gabe found what he needed. There was a box of shells for the Win-Mag. He also found two .45 pistols in holsters and a cleaning kit for them, as well. He took the pistols along with the ammo. Feeling a little better, Gabe put everything in an old canvas duffel bag and hauled it out to the newer pickup, a dark green Ford F-100. Poppy followed him.

"What are you going to do?"

"Try and find her."

"Lordy, Gabe, that's thick backcountry. You can get lost easily. Turned around."

He gave her a patient smile. "I won't get lost, Poppy. If I could find my way around with a compass and map in the Hindu Kush mountains of Afghanistan, I won't have any problems here with these hills."

"Oh…of course. I forgot, the military taught you that kind of stuff." She touched her brow, rattled by Bay's disappearance.

"Can you pack me a sack of food, Poppy? I'm going to get my military gear from the other cabin, and I'll meet you here at the truck."

"Yes, yes I can!" she said before turning and hurrying back to her cabin.

Gabe felt better now, having a focus, a plan and, most important, an objective. *Stony Bottom.* Well, hell, that about summed it all up regarding their relationship, didn't it? Bay was hitting rock bottom. Mouth pursed, he trotted back to change into his cammies and get out his military gear packed in a large duffel bag.

BAY SANK INTO the warmth of the two sleeping bags she'd combined in order to stay comfortable in her tent. She'd spent the morning hiking to her favorite spot not far from the bridge across the Greenbrier River. The sky was cloudy, a gunmetal gray, the wind cold from the north. She wasn't sure if it was going to rain or snow.

Earlier, she'd called her mother, who was relieved to hear she was all right. Bay didn't want to cause her mother any more stress than necessary. She kept the call short and told her she was safe. That she was going to be alone for at least two or three weeks. She didn't ask about Gabe, feeling too guilty for running out on him after their argument.

The tent breathed around her, night falling, the wind picking up. Emotionally, Bay felt numb. Outside, she could hear the nearby gurgle of the river, the sound soothing away her anxiety. Closing her eyes, she saw Gabe's face hovering gently before her. A ragged sigh tore from her lips, and Bay felt tears well up in her eyes. She loved him, and she'd taken advantage of his good nature and kindness. She should have sent him back to the SEALs, back to his platoon a few weeks after she returned home. Bay didn't know who felt more helpless: her or Gabe. There was a desolate look in his eyes, raw agony for her reflected in them. And she didn't have the emotional strength to support him at all. That had torn her up.

"I'm a mess," she muttered into the jacket that she'd rolled up to become her pillow. Bay refused to allow Gabe to continue being tortured by her PTSD symptoms. He deserved better than that. All he got out of this raw deal was to take care of an emotional invalid. That wasn't what she wanted from him. Gabe had stood loyally by her, asking nothing for himself. He'd given her everything. And now she'd broken his trust. Her heart bled for him. She loved him so much. But he'd never know. Not now…

She heard the first splatters of rain on the canvas tent. She loved rain because it always soothed her, calmed her busy-bee mind. Soon, Bay drifted off to sleep.

GABE IGNORED HIS discomfort, the rain pelting down around his newly constructed hide on the thickly wooded hillside. He'd located Bay near midafternoon. He was relieved to see her and called Poppy immediately to let her know. It was then that Poppy had told him Bay had phoned minutes earlier so she wouldn't worry. Bay hadn't told her mother where she was, but that she was safe. Poppy could now rest and not worry. He promised to give her daily updates. Poppy had cried, grateful for his care and thoughtfulness.

Gabe had created a hide about a thousand yards from where she'd put up her tent on the other side of the bridge in a yellowed grass meadow located three hundred feet away from the bridge over the river. Gabe watched Bay through the Night Force scope, clearly able to see her face. Seeing the anguish in it. Damn, he hurt for her.

Twice, he'd almost gotten up and left his hide made of brush, branches and dried leaves sprinkled over it like roofing, and gone down to talk to her. But what would that have accomplished? *Nothing.* Instinctively, Gabe knew Bay had to have this time alone to think and figure things out. Her life was in shambles, just so many puzzle pieces lying around her. And God knew, he wanted to help her pick them up and help her put them back together. But Poppy's words months earlier echoed in his memory, that he had to sometimes let her stumble, fall and pick herself up. This was one of those times.

He kept the Win-Mag pointed in the direction of the tent. He'd covered it with some light gray netting so the barrel wouldn't shine and accidentally be seen by others. The scope gave him what he really wanted;

clear access to the location around Bay's tent. He'd noticed as he'd created his hide, there were plenty of hikers crossing the bridge to get to the main trail, people riding horses, tons of bicyclers along the trail, as well. Just before sundown he spotted six men, all but one Latino, carrying very heavy packs on their backs. The leader was a tall, powerfully built bald white man. They looked focused, as if they had an objective, hurrying across the bridge, oblivious to the beauty surrounding Stony Bottom. They didn't stop, take photos or simply stand and breathe in the natural beauty around them. That made them stand out, and Gabe was suspicious.

Bay hadn't exactly chosen a quiet spot, Gabe thought. But this was her childhood haunt. And he understood it probably gave her a sense of continuity and nurturing that she was so desperately seeking. His mouth pursed. Something he hadn't been able to give her. Wincing inwardly, Gabe thought he would never stop loving her. If anything, he loved her more. Right now, Bay couldn't even love herself.

He'd taken some blankets off the beds in the smaller cabin and made a comfortable, dry nest inside his hide. It was a good six feet wide and ten feet in length. No one would find him on the slope of the woodlands-coated hill. The trail was down below him, and he seriously doubted anyone would wander up the hill toward him. He didn't realize until he consulted Google, how popular the seventy-six-mile Greenbrier Trail was. He did now, watching the trail clear of hikers as night fell.

Gabe was thirsty. Water was the one thing he'd for-

gotten. His SEAL buddies would never allow him to
live this one down. Water was a first-line gear. Even
rookie BUD/S graduates wouldn't ever forget to bring
water. He had. Once he'd located Bay, he'd hiked down
the trail after dark with his night vision goggles in
place. Gabe had taken along his ruck, driven into a
nearby small town and bought ten gallons of water
and some more food and batteries for his radio and
NVGs. Packing his supplies in, Gabe settled in for the
long haul, whatever that meant. He kept watch until
one in the morning, the rain softly falling around his
hide. No one was walking the bridge and the trail at
this hour. It was clear. Everything was quiet.

Gabe spotted a small band of whitetail deer as they
emerged from the wooded slopes of the hill right behind Bay's tent. They were spooked by the tent and
walked warily around it, heading for the river to drink.
There was something peaceful about rain falling and
watching the deer drink and then go back into the
meadow and start munching on the yellowed grass.

Gabe dozed off at the Win-Mag. His head fell forward, and it immediately jerked him awake. Automatically, he scanned with the scope, making sure Bay
was safe down there across the river. Glancing at his
Oyster Rolex on his wrist, it was 0130. He crossed his
arms on the dirt embankment and laid his head down
next to the rifle, closing his eyes. Very shortly, Gabe
fell into an exhausted sleep.

GABE WAS AWAKE long before Bay emerged from her
tent. The air was crisp, hanging in the forty-degree

Fahrenheit range. Low, foglike clouds hung above the smooth surface of the river. He watched with his binoculars, sitting in front of his hide after having a cup of hot instant coffee.

Gabe saw as she stretched fitfully, dressed in a pair of baggy gray sweatpants and a heavy red sweater and a green nylon jacket. She looked rested, and he heaved a sigh of relief. The sky was clear, dawn lightening the shadowed meadow area.

She crawled back into the tent and carried out a small Coleman stove. She proceeded to make herself a hefty breakfast of three eggs and a lot of bacon. His girl had her appetite back, and that made him feel good.

BAY FELT EYES on her. She looked up across the river toward the wooded hill. Usually, she'd have trusted her feelings of being watched. Now…well, she couldn't trust herself at all. She went to the bank of the river, crouched down and washed her plate and flatware, scrubbing them with sand to cleanse them. The sun was up, the rays shooting across to the crown of the hill in front of her. The peace was exquisite, and she felt her spirit respond to the pristine surroundings.

GABE HISSED A curse, quickly jerking the binos away from his eyes. Snipers knew if they watched their target too long through a scope, the targets would become peripherally aware they were being watched. And stalked. He tensed when Bay stood up, frowned and looked up in his direction. Gabe waited, slowing his breath, feeling himself become part of the thick vegetation surrounding the hide. At a thousand yards, he couldn't pick up her facial expression without the scope or binos. Still, it warned him that Bay's all-terrain radar was working just fine. He couldn't afford to get caught watching her for too long again.

As Bay moved back to her Coleman stove, to fold it up and set it inside her tent, Gabe moved quietly back into his hide. He leaned his belly against the wall of dirt, his right hand near the trigger of the Win-Mag, his left arm folded across and in front of him.

He spotted movement from behind the meadow on a smaller trail. Scowling, he zeroed in with his Night Force scope on ten men walking very hurriedly toward the bridge. They, too, had heavy packs on their backs. And they all had that same determined look on their faces as the other group had the night before. Who the hell were these dudes?

This time, Gabe looked more closely. The leader was a tall white guy, with a shaved head and a perpetual scowl on his meaty face. Moving the scope downward across his torso, Gabe spotted the tip of a pistol muzzle an inch below the heavy coat he wore.

Moving farther down, he studied his pants. Yes, there was probably a knife or a small pistol on the outside left leg, hidden within the folds of his cammo pants.

He tensed as the leader looked into the meadow, halted and intently studied Bay's small tent. Then, they moved on. The hair on the back of Gabe's neck stood up. It was a warning. *Dammit.* All the men were wearing camouflage Army gear.

Was this some kind of Army gig? A forced march to get them in shape? Gabe had no idea, but he put it on his list of things to do today. He grabbed his computer, a modernized wheel book snipers always carried on them, and took a page for the commandos, as he referred to them. He marked down last night's group and how many were in it, as well as intel on this latest group. *Something* was going on. But what?

CHAPTER TWENTY-TWO

AFTER THE SECOND WEEK, Gabe moved his hide. Those Army dudes, or whoever they were, stepped up their activity by running through the meadow twice a day where Bay had her tent located. They were smart, doing it at dawn and late dusk, when she was asleep or inside her tent for the night.

Gabe used his camera with its long-range lens, continuing to take photos of every man's face and gear. He had a bad feeling about them. This morning, the men quietly moved through the foggy meadow, heading for the Greenbrier River bridge. He was within a hundred feet behind Bay's tent. His new hide took advantage of a fifty-ton boulder surrounded on all sides by trees and brush. No one, not even Bay, would ever know he was there. And that was the way Gabe wanted it for now.

Although he had the Win-Mag set up, it was much easier and less cumbersome to use his binos as he lay against the wall of dirt and rock. As always, Gabe felt the hair on his neck rise just before he'd get eyes on the group of men coming around the hill and heading toward the bridge. Sure enough, through the ground fog creeping silently across the meadow, he saw the bald leader once more.

Usually he led a group every three or four days. This time, six men walking like overburdened pack mules trudged wearily behind him. And always, Baldy would stop, glare toward the tent in the meadow, work his mouth and then move toward the bridge. Gabe could see the distrust and worry in his eyes. Maybe Baldy was concerned as to why the tent was always there. Thinking it was a spy watching his movements.

Gabe typed the intel in his wheel book computer after the group had crossed the bridge and were down on the Greenbrier Trail, heading north.

For a moment, he simply enjoyed the cold forty-degree temperature, the fingers of opaque fog stealing in slow, graceful twists and turns across the area. Gabe longed to be in that tent, holding Bay. Kissing her, loving her. God knew, he had a lot of time to fantasize about their stalled relationship as he watched her sitting outside her tent to paint or sketch. He often wondered what she was drawing. What beauty did Bay see that touched her heart?

He set the binos aside and made his breakfast of hot coffee thanks to a chemical pack that heated the water. He'd put a couple of slices of turkey between two pieces of bread and slowly chewed on it, his gaze always moving, noting and watching the surrounding area as the day grew lighter.

Suddenly, he heard Bay scream. It was that wild, scared scream he'd heard so many times before at the cabin. Dropping the sandwich, Gabe bolted out of the hide, his heart lurching in his chest. And then, he skidded to a halt fifty feet down the hill. What the hell was he doing? Breathing hard, Gabe paused, torn. He stared hard at the tent, and from this distance, he could hear Bay sobbing like a frightened child. Gabe's eyes grew dark, and he wanted to run that short distance and go to her. *Hold her.* Bile rose in his throat as he continued to listen to her sobs until they lessened and eventually stopped.

Angrily, he turned on his heel and climbed quietly up the hill to the promontory of the massive rock. His heart was tormented. He grieved for Bay. Slipping back inside his hide was the last thing he wanted to do right now. As he slid into his observation position, Gabe rubbed his bristly growth of beard beneath his fingers. Every cell in his body screamed he should protect Bay. Hold her against the torture he knew she was reexperiencing. Closing his eyes, Gabe forced himself to slow his breathing, to get ahold of himself, even though adrenaline was racing through his bloodstream, pushing him to act.

From his other position on the opposite side of the river, he wouldn't have heard her screams because he'd been too far away. Now, with his new hide directly behind her tent, a quarter of the way up a hill, he could. Gabe's mind twisted in devastation. Did Bay have nightmares every night? Or not? She had at first when coming home, but eventually, it reduced to one or two a week. *Dammit!*

His heart convulsed in agony. He loved her so damn much he could barely tolerate the pain ripping through him. Yet, Gabe knew if he'd go running down there to announce his presence, he couldn't predict what Bay's reaction would be. His heart was utterly vulnerable where Bay was concerned.

Gabe pulled out of his misery as he heard the tent open up. Bay emerged. She had on a pair of dark red flannel trousers, her red cable-knit sweater on and her green jacket. He saw the back of her head, her hair tangled and uncombed. She headed through the swirling mists toward the riverbank. Swallowing hard, his throat tight with emotion, all Gabe could do was watch and hurt for her. And for himself.

BAY LIFTED HER face to the sun, feeling the warmth penetrate her coldness. She sat by the river after lunch, her sketch pad in hand and her pastel chalks sitting beside her on an old, rotted log. The remnants of the nightmare from this morning still haunted her. Shivering even though the day had warmed up to nearly sixty degrees, she concentrated on sketching a great blue heron that was on the opposite riverbank, looking for fish to cat.

Drawing helped ground Bay. It allowed her to focus on something beautiful and creative instead of being held a constant prisoner in her own internal, tortured darkness. Her sketch pad had at least twenty sketches contained in it now, some in pencil, ink or in pastel chalk colors. Each one was better than the last. As a child, she had always carried a sketch pad and colored pencils when she came here with her pa. He would fish, and she would go find a quiet spot and draw or paint something that caught her attention. Something that was beautiful.

Gabe quietly whispered through her mind, grazing her heart. God, she missed him so much. It had been two weeks since she'd run away from the cabin. She'd call Poppy every third day to let her know she was all right. A little while ago, Bay had finally gotten up the courage to ask her mother about him

"How is Gabe?"

"He's gone," Poppy said.

Bay had stood very still, gripping the cell phone until her fingers hurt as the pronouncement worked its way through her.

"What do you mean he's gone?" she'd asked, her voice unsteady.

"He's gone, honey."

"Where? Back to Coronado? Back to his SEAL platoon?" She'd heard Poppy give a heavy sigh.

"I don't know, Baylee."

Something so beautiful and so fragile that she'd clung to since becoming conscious at Landstuhl, that fed her hope to keep fighting, shattered into a million glittering fragments within Bay. Her heart had bled, and she'd sworn she'd felt it shrivel and die within her chest.

"Oh…" was all she'd managed to choke out. She'd pressed her hand against her eyes, feeling tears gather. She'd just lost her best friend. Her love. When she'd ended the call, Bay stood there staring out at the smooth surface of the quiet river.

A new kind of agony riddled through her. Somehow, Bay had thought Gabe would always be there for her, as he had in the past. The corners of her mouth pulled inward. She had no one to blame but herself for him leaving. She was the one who ran away from him. Gabe had been loyal. Faithful.

Tormented, Bay turned and trudged toward her tent, head bowed. Her entire life was turned inside out. She felt like an aircraft spinning out of control. The rape had taken so much from her soul, permanently stained her life, destroyed who she was. Her mind refused to give up anything else about those huge unknown gaps that were driving her crazy with wanting to know what else had happened to her.

Judging from the look in Gabe's anguished eyes that afternoon they'd argued, something traumatic had occurred. She couldn't take any more.

Touching her wrinkled brow, Bay reached her tent, knelt down and crawled inside. She put the cell phone near her jacket that doubled as her pillow. The canvas tarps surrounding her made Bay feel a little safer. They weren't Gabe's arms, but it served to help her feel secure. She sat there, knees drawn up, her arms around them, her head resting on top of them. Rocking herself a little, Bay closed her eyes. Warm tears drifted down her drawn cheeks. For the first time in a week, she cried. This time, it was for Gabe. And she cried for him, knowing how much he'd suffered, too. For a love that he'd offered her, and she'd run away from. Now all that remained was an empty shell of herself. No longer did Bay feel anything at all except for how agonizing it was to draw in her next breath. How much more could she bear?

GABE WAS RESTLESS. As a sniper, he'd learned to crush that feeling and wait. Patience was their hallmark. He could wait until hell froze over, if that was what was demanded of him during a mission. It didn't matter the weather, the temperature, how much he physically suffered, he'd learn to wait. His gaze remained on the green canvas tent. The November weather had turned, becoming colder and rainy for a few days. Now, the sun was back out, the sky a deep cobalt-blue as he looked up at it.

Near noon, Bay was sitting near the river like she always did at this time of day. The past week, Gabe had seen her go downhill. He could see it in her drawn features. The hollows of her cheeks were more pronounced. She no longer brought her Coleman out each morning to make herself breakfast as she had in the past few weeks. Worried, he couldn't figure out why her sudden decline. What had happened?

Gabe remembered Dr. Torrance warning him at Landstuhl that Bay would hit an emotional "wall." A place where it smacked her down, gutted her emotionally, left her depressed and giving up. Every PTSD patient would hit that wall sooner or later, she warned him. And it was then that someone who loved her would have to step in and help her fight back, symbolically be her hope until she internalized it once again and was able to move forward by herself once more.

He watched Bay stop drawing. Her profile was clean and beautiful but he sensed her profound anguish, as if…as if she'd given up. Frightened of that discovery, Gabe wondered if he was making it up because he wanted any excuse to leave his hide, walk down there and let her know he was nearby. But he stayed where he was.

A WEEK LATER, at dawn, Bay crawled out of her tent. She felt numb and empty. Why did she continue to struggle when she felt no hope? And then, Bay froze. There, sitting in the tufts of damp yellowed grass just a foot away from the tent opening was a carved jaguar. It was no more than two inches long, delicately rendered. Beautiful.

Entranced, Bay knelt down. The carving looked familiar. Reaching out, she curved her fingers around it. The moment Bay touched it, felt the smooth golden wood resting in the palm of her hand, she closed her eyes. This carving meant something important to her. Something so profound, so quintessential to her soul and heart, even if she couldn't remember why. Pressing it to her wildly beating heart, Bay moaned and tipped her head toward her chest. She could feel the warmth of it seeping into the cold abyss that inhabited her mutilated soul. It infused her with hope, something she'd lost a week ago.

It was then, eyes closed, that her brain gave up more memories. She saw Gabe smiling as he invited her over to a rock he was sitting on near the bay at sunset. His eyes burning with love for her. She sat down on his thigh and placed her arm around his broad shoulders. Gabe then handed the carving to her. Bay gasped, felt intense love for Gabe as she turned and threw her arms around him, thanking him for the utterly beautiful gift

he'd created for her. He'd carved the jaguar he said
to be her protective guardian spirit, because she'd be
leaving shortly for her next rotation into Afghanistan.

For the next half hour, Bay knelt there, the carving
against her vulnerable heart, finally understanding
the breadth of their original relationship. She understood how consummate their love had been for one
another, the memories of so many happy times they'd
shared. Some were at his condo, many at a beach near
La Jolla, scuba diving with Gabe in the kelp beds as
he searched for abalone to make steaks later that night
for them. She saw them making slow, delicious love.
And then, the last memory was of Gabe standing there
at Lindbergh International Airport, near the security
line, kissing her goodbye as she left for Afghanistan.
This time, she was going alone, ordered to a Special
Forces team in an Afghan village in a valley. She saw
the searing grief on his face as he reluctantly released
his fingers. She had to leave.

Bay loved Gabe so damned much she could barely
breathe. Soft cries of utter loss, of finally understanding what she had done by running away from him,
overwhelmed her.

She had no idea of time as she knelt just outside her
tent, gripping the carving against her aching heart.
When she finally managed to struggle above the powerful memories now alive and a part of her once more,
Bay slowly sat up. She scrubbed her damp face dry,
looking toward the river. Her mind wasn't working
well, and she wasn't thinking clearly at all, prisoner to
a new avalanche of emotions and memories now cir-

culating through her heart and body. Was she making all of this up? Was the carving merely a figment of her distorted imagination? She believed in magic, she always had. That part of her was strong and unaltered.

Slowly, Bay opened her palm and gazed at the jaguar, almost afraid it would no longer be there. That it would mysteriously dematerialize. But it was there. And it felt so physical, so rock solid in her palm that it infused her with hope. She saw the tiny stippling holes pressed into the wood's gleaming surface across its gold coat, denoting the cat's many black spots. The fierce snarl on the cat's broad face told her he was guarding her, always watching over her. Gabe would be this close to her while she was gone to Afghanistan, he'd promised her.

The sun felt good on Bay's chilled body. The fog moved in soundless fingers through the meadow, hiding the river not far from her tent. There were a few birdcalls, and she eagerly absorbed them. Everything was so still, as if Nature was holding its breath and waiting. For what?

Bay moved slowly to ease the stiffness of being in one position for so long. She sat down and crossed her legs, holding her palm open, just staring at the carving. Her mind was spongy, but in her heart, this was a lifeline, a gentle nudge to her brain about happier times. And God knew how she needed to see and feel something good, clean and positive about her life after her unrelenting hell. It had dragged her to a place of such darkness, Bay didn't have the strength to struggle out of it on her own anymore.

The sun continued to climb into the sky, warming her more. There were white, puffy clouds here and there, telling her a new front was going to come through the area. This time, snow would probably fall instead of rain. It was late November, and that was when over seventy inches of snow would begin to cover the Allegheny Mountains, making everything look new and clean. Clean instead of dirty. Light instead of soul-devouring darkness. Just holding the carving gave Bay something to cling to. It fed her, as if Gabe were here, with her. His unswerving love for her had helped her get this far. But her mind simply refused to work, as if stuck in neutral. Bay wasn't sure of anything anymore.

GABE WARILY WATCHED BAY. He'd taken the biggest risk of his life by carving the jaguar again and then, in the middle of the night, laying it close to her tent. His stomach hurt, afraid of what it might or might not do for Bay. He hoped it would bring her memories back of happier times. Of them being together. Their incredible, undying love for one another. He had no idea what her reaction was because, from his position, Gabe couldn't see the front of her tent. He lived in a special hell of not knowing.

Only much later, when he saw Bay stand up, her hand pressed to her heart, did he know for sure, she'd found the carving. The look on her face shook him as little else ever would. She'd turned, looking to her left, and he'd gotten a quick glance at her profile. Her cheek glistened with tears; her lower lip trembled. Gabe had

no idea what it meant, only that his arms ached to hold
Bay, his heart screaming at him to reveal himself to
her now because she needed him. His intuition, which
had saved his life countless times in the past, warned
him to wait it out. *Again. Patience.* It wasn't what he
wanted to do, dammit, but Gabe wasn't going to go
up against his gut instinct.

BAY SAT ON a fallen log on the bank of the river. It was
the place where she sketched and drew every day. Near
midafternoon, more memories fell into place for her.
This time, her eyes tightly shut, she saw herself in
the cave where she'd been beaten and raped. She escaped, running away from Khogani. She now understood what Gabe had yelled out in desperation to her
in the parking lot. He had been there! He and Reza
had tracked and found her! And Gabe had saved her
life after she'd been shot in the head.

Bay was numb as she saw the entire firefight on
the scree slope of the mountain. She had stood up to
try and stop the enemy from overrunning Gabe and
Reza's position on that small knoll across the goat
path. She'd crawled out of her hide to try and help.
Bay saw it all, felt all the powerful, wrenching feelings, her fear, her love for Gabe and nearly losing him.
Bay had used herself as a target in order to save them.
That was why she had stood up, screaming at the Taliban to get their attention.

The satisfaction of knowing she'd helped save their
lives, as half of the enemy force turned and charged
her, felt healing to her fragmented soul. She'd willingly

have given up her life because she loved Gabe. And
Reza was a dear friend, a loyal friend, she'd worked
with before. She didn't want to see either man killed
by the Taliban. And as she had turned to leap back
into the hide in the depression of rocks, she'd glanced
over and seen Khogani not more than fifty feet away
from her. Half his head had been missing. Somehow,
Bay knew in that instant, Gabe had killed him. And
it had given her hope that she could survive this firefight where they were hopelessly outnumbered. Confidence to somehow survive it and not die as she fired
repeatedly at the charging, screaming soldiers who
wanted her dead.

Drawing in a ragged breath, Bay's gaze clung to
the slow-moving water. The river was so deep, with
strong currents beneath it, just as she had strong currents of love emerging and quietly flowing through her
once more. Those feelings of love, of being cherished
by Gabe, began to dissolve the grip of darkness that
had slowly been strangling the life out of her. Closing her eyes, the carving clenched in her hand, Bay
bowed her head, completely overwhelmed by so many
memories, good and bad.

At dusk, she finally moved from the log, trying to
push her feet in front of her to get back to her tent.
She'd not eaten or drunk anything all day. The sky was
red and gold, beautiful, and it filled her. She could feel
the first tendrils of fragile desire awakening within
her. Just when she had given up, the carved jaguar had
miraculously appeared and fed her heart, whispering
for her to hold on, to not give up. Had it magically re-

appeared to help her in her worst moment of need? It must have. She remembered Gabe telling her one time SEALs had a saying: Never surrender.

Bay was exhausted. Listening to her need for rest, she knelt down and slipped inside the tent that had been her home for the past three weeks. She placed the carving beside her, picked up a bottle of water and drank the contents.

Bay slipped beneath the warm sleeping bag, nestling her head into her jacket and closing her eyes. She pressed the carving against her heart, as if Gabe were that close. Loving her. Holding her. Watching over her and keeping her safe....

CHAPTER TWENTY-THREE

SOMETHING SNAPPED GABE AWAKE. He'd dozed inter-
mittently every night, like he always did. Blinking,
he saw dawn crawling across the hills, a fragile pink
color chasing away the darkness. He felt danger. What
kind? Instantly, he moved to the Win-Mag, looking
through the Night Force scope. Panning, he moved
past Bay's tent toward the meadow to his right. There,
just coming around the hill, was Baldy and ten men
following him obediently with heavy packs on each
of their backs.

The sky lightened, and Gabe could see the lead
man's face clearly. His senses instantly went on high
alert. Heart starting a slow pound, Gabe could feel
adrenaline leaking warnings into his bloodstream.
Years of combat had honed his senses to a fine bladed
point. Baldy was looking intently toward Bay's tent
where she slept. She was unaware of what was going
on around her. Baldy's focus never left the tent.

Gabe quietly stood up, shoved the .45 in his drop
holster on his right leg. Grabbing the other .45, he
jammed it into the waistband at his back. Impending
danger screamed at him as he shrugged into his heavy
Kevlar vest and swiftly Velcroed it into place.

Gabe didn't need his helmet, instead settling a black baseball cap on his head. He leaped silently out of the hide and moved like a noiseless shadow down through the trees, aimed at the intruder who had just changed direction. Baldy was heading straight for Bay's tent where she slept.

Nostrils flaring, Gabe halted near the last tree, hiding behind it. He saw Baldy give a hand signal to the mules, telling them to stop. They did, confused looks on their collective faces. Cold ice flowed through Gabe's veins as he saw Baldy pull out a KA-BAR from a sheath he carried beneath his heavy jacket.

The son of a bitch.

Gabe stepped out of the shadows, his palm brushing the butt of the .45 in his drop holster.

Baldy jerked to a halt as a man dressed in camo gear appeared like a ghost out of the tree line and stopped in front of him. He scowled, anchoring to a halt. His feral gaze quickly assessed the unknown intruder, his upper lip lifting away from his teeth. Whoever he was, there was a flat, hard look in his narrowed eyes. The bill of the cap he wore hid the upper portion of his face, but there was no mistaking the man's intent. His mouth was tight. Determined. Baldy's gaze dropped to his right hand resting almost casually over the butt of the pistol he had in the holster.

"Get outta my way," Baldy snarled softly. "This ain't any of your business."

"It's my business," Gabe rasped. "If you're smart, you'll turn around and leave right now."

Snorting, Baldy relaxed a little. "Who the hell are you?"

"Your worst nightmare, asshole."

"You ATF?" he growled.

"Doesn't matter." Gabe watched the man, felt his rage, felt him wanting Bay. Anger exploded through him. Baldy was a hulk of a man, maybe two hundred and thirty pounds and six and a half feet tall. Gabe sensed he'd been in the military. He was carrying a KA-BAR. Anyone who really knew how to handle a knife always kept it close to their side like he did.

Rubbing his chin, Baldy squinted through the gray dawn light. "What's your business here?" Baldy hurled back, pissed.

"She's mine."

Baldy stared belligerently at him. There was ten feet between them. The tent was to his right. And then, he must have noticed Gabe's embroidered symbol above the left pocket of his shirt. "What the hell is a SEAL doing out here?" he rasped, moving his fingers open and closed around the handle of his KA-BAR. He wasn't going to get any backup from those mules.

Gabe smiled a little. A cold, unnerving smile. "I told you, she's mine." He saw Baldy's eyes flash with anger. There was no way the guy was going to reach him quick enough to stick a blade into him.

Gabe only worried about Bay. Did she hear them talking? He prayed she was still asleep because if she came out of that tent right now, she could easily become a pawn to Baldy. He was close enough to grab her, and Gabe wasn't going to let that happen one way or another. His heart beat slow and steady. He was poised. Ready for whatever this bastard wanted to hand out.

Rock it out...

With a hiss, Baldy jerked the knife upward.

Instantly, Gabe's hand blurred as he slapped the butt of the .45 with his palm and lifted it out of the drop holster in one smooth, unbroken motion. He squeezed the trigger. The blast was tremendous, the kick hard against his hand, wanting to jerk his entire arm upward and backward as the bullet fired. The noise echoed around the meadow like thunder rumbling through it.

Baldy screamed, the bullet striking his hand. The KA-BAR flew upward as he crumpled to the ground. He held his bleeding hand-cursing and sobbing.

While moving forward, Gabe holstered the .45 and jerked a pair of plastic flex-cuffs from the pocket of his H-gear. The man was rolling around, screaming repeatedly. Gabe jerked him up by his meaty shoulder, straddled him and shoved him down hard. He smashed his face into the grass, momentarily stunning him. In seconds, he'd hauled both his thick arms behind him. He'd cuffed so many prisoners over the years it took seconds for him to tighten the unbreakable plastic bands around his thick, hairy wrists. At no point did Gabe lose sight of the men frozen on the path beside the meadow.

Baldy was squalling as Gabe moved away. At that instant, he saw Bay emerge from the tent, her sleepy eyes suddenly wide with confusion.

"Stay there," Gabe ordered her, drawing his .45 and walking toward the group of men.

Gasping, Bay looked into Gabe's hard, flat-looking eyes. Her mind reeled with shock. For a split second, his face softened.

"Stay right where you are, Bay," he said. "Please?"

Nodding jerkily, Bay watched Gabe's face resume that unreadable SEAL mask as he turned on his heel, pistol in hand as he strode across the meadow toward the men wearing large packs. Bay stared at the man cursing and rolling around on the ground. Fear shot through her as she looked at the blood on his body and face. What had just happened?

Gabe barked at the men in Spanish to shed their rucks, lie down on their bellies and put their hands behind their backs. They obeyed immediately, real fear in their faces. They'd just seen him take down Baldy, and they didn't want to be next.

Breathing harshly, Gabe went from one man to another, swiftly flex-cuffing every one of them. When he was finished, the meadow was lighter, and he could see Bay standing unsurely at the front of the tent. Baldy was still shrieking in rage. Served the son of a bitch right. Gabe ordered the men to sit up and not move. Instantly, they complied with his order.

Jogging toward Bay, Gabe pulled out his cell phone and hit the number for the county sheriff's department. He slowed as he approached, his eyes never leaving hers. He gave the GPS location of the meadow and told the dispatcher what happened. He suggested she bring at least four deputies and an ambulance. Flipping the cell phone closed, he dropped it into his pocket.

Bay felt her heart explode with hope. Gabe walked toward her with that lethal, boneless grace, his narrowed, glittering eyes holding hers. He flicked a glance toward the bald man. And then he shifted his full attention to her. She felt an overwhelming sense of protection enveloping her, warming her, easing her fear.

"Gabe…" she whispered, automatically stepping forward. He opened his arms to her, his face allowing her to see the love he held for her alone.

"Come here," he said thickly. In seconds, Gabe swept the woman he loved into his arms, holding her, holding her tight. He groaned and pressed his face into her hair, felt her tremble as she slid her arms around his waist.

"You're safe now," Gabe growled near her ear. He inhaled Bay's sweet scent, felt her warmth, her soft cheek brush against his. Easing her back just enough to stare down into her eyes, Gabe said, "I don't know who these guys are, but this one was coming toward your tent." His voice lowered. "I wasn't going to let that happen, Bay."

Shaken, Bay felt his hands holding her firmly. She looked again toward the angry, cuffed man. "I— My God…"

He nodded. "It's okay, baby. You're safe. No one's ever laying a hand on you again…."

THE SHERIFF'S DEPUTIES arrived ten minutes later. Bay stood by the tent, arms wrapped around herself as she watched Gabe talk with the head deputy, a redhead about forty-five years old. The meadow was flooded with sunlight. The sky was a light blue.

She shivered because it was barely above freezing. The paramedics from the fire department were taking care of the bald man with the hand wound. His murderous small eyes made her shiver, and she turned away. They starkly reminded her of Khogani's black, lifeless glare.

Biting her lower lip, Bay had so many questions for Gabe. How did he get here? She watched him in the distance, her heart opening fiercely with joy. He'd saved her. *Again.* Gabe had protected her. A crazy bunch of emotions rolled through her. Every once in a while she saw him turn to look at her, as if to check and make sure she was all right. And every time she felt Gabe's heated gaze upon her, an incredible flood of love flowed through her.

The bald man walked away with the help of the two paramedics, his right hand wrapped in white gauze. A sheriff's deputy came over with his camera, taking a photo of the KA-BAR lying in the grass near her tent. He picked it up with gloves on and placed it into a brown evidence bag. Then, he turned to her, notebook in hand, wanting to interview her. What could she tell him? Not much.

Gabe hung on to his thinning patience. He'd just wrapped up interviews with the head deputy and turned, walking quickly back to where Bay stood. She looked alone, and he could see the stark, worried expression on her face. And then she gifted him with an unsteady but soft smile of welcome.

"How are you doing?" he asked, placing his hands across her shoulders. Gabe had to touch her.

"I'm okay. More confused than anything else. That gun blast ripped me out of my sleep." She saw his mouth quirk with apology.

"I knew it would. I was hoping it wouldn't come to that, but the guy went for a knife." Gabe's voice softened. "I'm sorry, Bay. This isn't the way I wanted to come back to you."

He so desperately wanted to kiss her. "The deputy told me this dude I wounded is wanted by the FBI and ATF. He's a major drug runner. Those guys with him carrying the rucks are mules. The deputies found cocaine in bags in their rucks."

"Oh, my God."

He gently squeezed her arms. "They were coming through here at dusk and dawn every day since you've been here."

Stunned, she blinked. "This meadow…it was where I grew up…it was so peaceful…."

Gabe nodded. "I know that, baby. Everything changes. I'm sorry."

Her mind worked furiously over his statement. She lifted her hands, resting them on Gabe's arms. "How do you know that? I mean—"

Gabe smiled wearily. "Baby, it's a long story. What do you say we get your gear wrapped up and we'll go home?" He touched her cheek with his fingers. "I know your mother is worried sick about you. We can talk after she knows you're safe?"

For a moment, Bay swayed in his arms. *Home.* The word had such power over her. She still couldn't believe Gabe was here. Holding her. Giving her a tender look of love that said so much without anything being said at all. "Yes," she whispered.

"Why don't you give your mother a call and let her know we're coming in? Don't say anything about what happened, just that you're coming back home with me. We can fill her in on the details once we get there." Gabe glanced at his Rolex. "It's only 0800. I'll get things packed up here."

Nodding, Bay hungrily absorbed his embrace. His hands were strong without being hurtful. She stepped away, dizzied by the sudden turn of events. With her cell phone, she made a call to her mother.

"CAN WE TALK NOW?" Bay asked Gabe as they entered their small cabin. They'd spent an hour with Poppy and Eva-Jo. Everyone was glad she was home again. And so was she. Bay shut the door quietly behind her and watched as Gabe set the tent and duffel bag that belonged to her father, Floyd, behind the couch. He took off his cap, running his fingers through his short hair.

"Come on over." Gabe motioned to the couch where they'd spent many happy nights with one another.

A flicker of fear moved through Bay as she sat down next to him. She curled up, one leg beneath her, facing Gabe. He looked incredibly exhausted, and she reached out as he eased back and slid her fingers across his hand. "It was you who put that jaguar carving there for me to find, wasn't it?"

He rubbed his face. "Yeah, it was." The look in her half-closed eyes touched him deeply. Gabe felt Bay searching, trying to put all the pieces together. "When you left here," he began, his voice husky with emotion, "I asked Poppy where your favorite hideout was as a kid. She told me Stony Bottom. I grabbed my gear and took off after you. Luckily, you were there."

Bay dragged in a ragged breath. "Gabe…I'm so sorry. I hurt you so much, and I didn't mean—"

"Baby, it's okay. I understand why." Gabe tipped his head toward her, soul-deep tiredness in his tone. "I was a jerk that night out in the parking lot. I shouldn't have yelled at you, shouldn't have… Hell, I was in the wrong all the way. I let my anger at the therapist blow up, and I took it out on you. That's not acceptable." He managed a slight, pained grimace. "It's me who should apologize, Bay. Not you. Okay?"

Her heart fluttered and she absorbed his fatigued smile. They were both run into the ground in different ways. Gabe had fought so hard to help her. "I didn't mean to break your trust, Gabe." Bay touched her brow. "I'm trying to learn about my emotions, but damn, they whipsaw on me, out of the blue. The music and noise, the crowds at the gym got to me that afternoon. I felt like a piece of raw meat."

"I know," he murmured softly. "It took me two weeks of watching over you from my hide to get it. Dr. Torrance said you'd eventually hit the wall, and you did. I had a lot of time on my hands, Bay, while

I kept you company up on that hill. You were trying to stand on your own two feet. You're not the kind of person to lean on others. You've always been strong and independent."

"But I wasn't strong." Bay studied him through her lashes, her voice tight with regret. "You needed a break from me, Gabe. You were trying to do everything for me all the time. I saw you hurting, and it hurt me." She pressed her hand against her heart. "I wanted to get well as fast as I could. I didn't want you having to be standing strong for me at every turn."

"Poppy gave me an ass-chewing about that," Gabe admitted wryly, moving his fingers across hers. "She said I was burned out, and I needed to give you some space. I didn't listen to her, and she ended up being right. I was wrong." Tears glistened in her eyes, and Gabe would have given anything to see the pain in them dissolve. "Baby, I was stretched too thin. My emotions caught up to me, and when you had that panic attack in the gym, I nearly lost it. I'd tried so damned hard to protect you, and when you listened to that therapist instead of me, something broke inside me."

"Oh, Gabe—"

"Stop saying you're sorry, Bay." He grimaced. "You shouldn't apologize because you're battling one hell of a trauma. I should have let you try your wings. I shouldn't have blamed you for trusting your therapist. Sitting up on that hill for two weeks gave me a new perspective on myself, you…and us…."

"I know what you mean," Bay admitted, leaning

her brow against his shoulder, feeling so very, very ancient and old. "When I held the jaguar carving in my hand," she whispered, "everything else came back to me." Bay lifted her head as she felt him tense. Gabe turned toward her, startled.

"What do you mean?"

"I remember us, Gabe." Bay touched his bearded face, giving him a searching look. "I remember everything. You carved a jaguar for me before I left and went on my last deployment to Afghanistan without you."

The hardness in his eyes melted and as she saw his lips part, a powerful sense of protection overwhelmed her. The sensation erased Bay's anxiety and fear. "I remember how I escaped out of that cave now." She told him because he had no idea of how she'd evaded Khogani, either.

Gabe sat quietly, listening to Bay's memories, holding her hand. He released her fingers when she was finished. "You're the most incredibly brave woman I know," he whispered unsteadily, sliding his arm around her shoulders, drawing her against him. Something old and fearful dissolved within Gabe as he realized Bay finally knew all about them. About their love. As she eased beneath his arm, nestling her head against his shoulder, he allowed a gutted sigh of relief to flow out of him.

Bay wrapped her arm around his waist, holding him with her incredible woman's strength. Gabe felt his entire world alter and shift. Shift back to where it had before all this had happened to Bay. He knew things were different, however. They'd taken a step forward, but, God, there were so many other steps ahead of them. Still, Bay remembered....

"I never stopped loving you, baby. Not for a second," Gabe whispered against her ear, kissing her temple.

"I know...." Bay choked, simply allowing herself to love Gabe with every cell of her being. "That's why you followed me when I ran away."

"You didn't know what we had, Bay," he said wearily. "I did. I figured I'd just hang around and make sure you were going to be safe, that's all. I know you needed downtime. You had to have it. I hadn't backed off or given you the space you needed, either. In a sense, I was smothering you." His mouth turned down. "That's really why you ran. I forced you to run."

With the strength of his arm around her, she surrendered to Gabe. "I wish my reactions would just go away."

"They will in time, baby. You just have to be patient with yourself. I have to give you your space, too." Gabe managed a strangled laugh. "Love is supposed to set us free, not suffocate us to death."

She nodded, absorbing his quiet strength, his rock solidness that was now an important anchor in her life. "I was falling in love with you all over again, Gabe." Bay lifted her head, her face inches from his. His eyes darkened and flared with hunger. For her.

"Even not knowing about our past together, I still fell in love with you all over again." Bay stretched forward, her lips barely touching his. Never had she wanted anything more than Gabe's mouth upon hers, his male stamp, his strength and caring that she knew he could give her so well.

Groaning her name, Gabe dragged Bay into his arms, lost in the fragrance of her as a woman, her soft lips yielding against his. Her arm wrapped strongly around his shoulder, her other hand framing his face, clinging to his lips. He felt her smile beneath his mouth, boldly move her tongue teasingly against his. Oh, God, he wanted Bay so damned badly the explosiveness of need nearly edged out his steel control over himself. Her mouth was wet, cajoling, gently biting his lower lip and then moving her tongue sweetly across it. A deep shudder worked through Gabe. She was hungry, assertive, and this was his woman he knew so well.

The uncertainty of the wounded Bay was gone. In its place, to his surprise and pleasure, was the very brave woman he'd met in Afghanistan last year. Her fingers moved up into his hair, massaging his tight scalp, sending wave after wave of electrical jolts down through his body. Her breath was hot, moist and flowed across his cheek and nose. She was as eager and hungry as he was. Another shudder worked through Gabe as her hand moved beneath his shirt, her fingers spreading fire across his chest.

With a growl, Gabe tore his mouth from hers. They stared at one another, breathing hard like two animals warily circling one another. Bay gave him that heated smile that made his body grow so damned hard he wanted to double over in pain. The look of her drowsy blue eyes glinting with gold was all he needed. In one swift movement, he stood up, turned and slipped her into his arms.

Bay sighed, her entire body quivering with need for Gabe. "Where are we going?" she asked breathlessly, clinging to him, her head resting against his shoulder.

"To bed," he growled, holding her gently, "to love you…"

CHAPTER TWENTY-FOUR

IN HIS LIFE, Gabe had met and known many kinds of fear. But the one at his doorstep with Bay appeared insurmountable. He had no experience with a woman who had been raped. As he laid her gently on the bed, her hair fanning out in soft brown curls around her flushed face, he tasted fear. Always, as a SEAL, he'd push through fear, ignored it and not allowed it to control or distract him. This time, it was completely different.

Moving up beside Bay, his arm beneath her neck, her body next to his, Gabe leaned over, moving his mouth tenderly against hers. When he eased away, holding her gaze, he had never been more scared.

"Listen, baby, we've got to talk before we go any further." He moved several curls from her right cheek, holding her blue and gold gaze. He wanted her so damn badly he could barely think, much less talk. With the way her eyes grew shadowed, Gabe knew Bay sensed where this conversation was going.

She slid her hand along his shoulder. "I don't know how I'll react, Gabe."

He pursed his lips, hearing the uncertainty in her husky voice. Bay looked normal, healthy, eager to make love with him. Everything looked so damned right and perfect.

Nervous, Gabe cupped her cheek. "I'm not going to lie to you. I need you so damn much I don't know which end is up anymore. But things have changed."

His chest tightened as he saw her eyes grow moist. "I'm afraid if I touch you in the wrong place, do something wrong, I'll send you into a panic attack." *Or worse.* He felt trapped with no exfil point. Leaning over, Gabe brushed a kiss to her brow. "You've got to help me, Bay. You have to let me know what you want, the way you want it, okay?"

She nodded, finding her voice. It came out low and rattled. "I'm scared, too, Gabe. I don't know how I'll react. I just want to love you." Her voice cracked. "I've asked my therapist about this, and she just gives me vague answers. She tells me every rape survivor is different. Some don't want a man touching them at all." She moved her hand restlessly across his tense shoulder. "I want *your* touch, Gabe. I can't tell you how often I've craved your hands loving me. And when you do touch me, I feel whole…I feel hope." Bay swallowed, her gaze clinging to his.

"What else did she say?" he asked quietly, wanting to always touch Bay and see her eyes turn soft as he stroked her, as he made her skin tighten or flush with pleasure.

Shrugging, Bay sighed and said, "That some survivors can enjoy sex. Others can't. Or they're okay with specific kinds of sex, but not all types of sex. That touching the wrong part of their body turns them off or triggers them into a panic. She said it's so individualized. I have to experiment and find out."

"Great," he said, and they shared a wry look. Her leg lay across his, and it felt good. She had long, beautiful legs, and Gabe wanted to explore them slowly and thoroughly. More than anything, he wanted to please Bay, let her know that she was a woman, no matter what had happened to her. He was damned if he was going to let her trauma define him or her.

Wrinkling her nose, Bay said, "Maybe the best way for us is just try, Gabe." Her brows fell, her voice nervous. "I want to please you. Having sex is part of loving you. And I know you've loved me well in the past. We're good together. I remember now...."

Her voice turned dusky with longing. It riffled over every sensitized nerve in his body. Gabe recognized that dulcet sound, and it fed his heart, his body and inflamed his soul.

"We'll get that back sooner or later, baby. I promise you. But for right now, I just want to welcome you home, back to me, to what we had before that was so damned sweet and good...."

His roughly spoken words sizzled through her entire body like an awakening song. "We'll go as far as we can," she whispered against the hard line of his mouth. "I'm yours, Gabe. I've always been yours, and I want to love you so much it hurts...."

Groaning, he moved his hand to the top button of the soft purple velour top she wore. "We're both hurting," Gabe agreed, and as he eased the button free, moving his hand gently beneath the soft fabric, slowly exploring her collarbone, he whispered against her mouth, "Over time we will heal one another, baby. Love never gives up, love never surrenders...."

Bay wanted to become completely lost in Gabe's touch, his kisses, and feel him move her into dizzied heights of euphoria. She was nervous and wanted to please him, but he shushed her, asking her to lay back and let him undress her. She watched his mask dissolve and saw the man beneath, his vulnerability as he eased the velour top open, revealing a silky pink camisole beneath it. His eyes changed and darkened as he drank in her breasts swelling beneath the material, her nipples tight and peaked.

He met her half-closed eyes and whispered unsteadily, "You are so damned beautiful, Bay," and he feathered light, wispy kisses from one collarbone to the other.

Bay closed her eyes, focused on his moist breath flowing across her upper chest and neck. Her flesh tingled wildly in the wake of his mouth. She moaned as Gabe's roughened hands slowly outlined the outer contour of her breasts, the coolness of the silk contrasting with the tightening heat radiating from them. An ache began to fill her; her lower body was coming alive even though he hadn't touched her there at all.

As Gabe brushed her nipples with his thumbs, a moan tremored through her, and she instinctively arched her hips against him. Her breathing was becoming faster, more shallow, as he teased them. Bay wanted to keep her eyes closed, focus on Gabe's hand, his breath, his mouth. It kept her mind from engaging with the trauma, and she sank farther into a cauldron of heat simmering beneath his hands.

The moment his lips captured the first nipple, Bay cried out, gripping his arms, feeling the scalding shock bolt down to her womb. It felt so good, dissolving her nervousness. His mouth caressed the other peak as his calloused hand slid beneath the material, easing it upward. She longed for his lips upon her nipple once again. Anxious for his heated touch again, Bay breathed raggedly and gave a shuddering sigh of pleasure.

She stared up into Gabe's stormy green gaze, which made her lower body react powerfully. His mouth curved, and he gently took her lips, as if to tell her how much he loved her. He opened her, moved his tongue slowly inside her mouth, teasing her. Every move was unrushed, nothing hard, sharp or jolting. And as Gabe kissed her, he unbuttoned her jeans. He moved his hand down to the waistband, slipping his fingers beneath the material and sliding his fingers slowly across her abdomen. He found the soft mound of her curls. Her breathing changed drastically as the heat of his palm excited her body, wetness collecting swiftly between her thighs. Moaning, Bay arched up into his hand, wanting more, wanting him.

Gabe felt tension in himself, felt the dogged worry hounding him as he opened her jeans even more. Bay's face was flushed, breathing shallow, clutching at his arms, her hips insistent against him. Was he being too conservative with her? Too slow? The wrong step in any direction would cause an explosion. Gabe eased the jeans off her hips, down her legs, and he dropped them by the bed. She wore a set of silky boxer shorts and he skimmed his hand from the outside of her thigh, curving it inward. Bay called his name, and it made him grow harder, if that was possible. He was still dressed and wanted to wait before he got naked beside her.

Gabe gently eased her thighs open. She was incredibly slick against his fingers as he moved beneath the silk, testing her, seeing if she would react negatively to him.

As Gabe cupped his hand against her hot, silky core, his arm went beneath her neck, drawing her up into his lap. She drowsily opened her eyes, her brows drawing down, as if not understanding what he was asking of her.

"Trust me, baby," he rasped, kissing her nose, cheek and finally her mouth. "This time is for you. Take all you want...."

Bay found herself settled between his legs, his back resting against the headboard, and she was held in the crook of Gabe's arm. She whispered his name, feeling weak with need, the fire licking up through her lower body, her womb spasming as his fingers slowly explored her. Bay closed her eyes, a soft cry erupting from her lips as he drew a slow circle around her wet opening. Breathing faster, she pressed her cheek against his jaw, whimpering, wanting more of him.

Gabe smiled against her parted lips, taking her, inhaling her breath, sharing it. As he moved his fingers inside her, she arched tautly against him, her cry reverberating into his mouth. He breathed her in, feeling her writhe in his arms, her hips grinding against his hand, begging for more. Gabe could feel her building toward orgasm, some part of himself feeling relief. He stroked her, teased her, and her little cries of pleasure fed him confidence.

Loving her fiercely, Gabe eased Bay into the curve of his right arm, capturing the tip of her nipple, suckling her. In seconds, she came loose in his arms, a mass of heat and rippling muscles clenching around his fingers, her hoarse cries of ongoing pleasure the sweetest sounds he'd heard in a damn long time. They'd taken their first step together.

"HAPPY THANKSGIVING!" POPPY cried as Gabe and Bay stepped into her warm cabin. Outside, snowflakes were falling thick and fat, covering the area in a blanket of clean white snow. Poppy kissed Bay and then Gabe. They gave her a bottle of champagne and some flowers they'd bought in Dunmore earlier in the day before the blizzard arrived.

"It all smells wonderful, Mama," Bay whispered, hugging her again. "How big is the goose?"

Poppy smiled and gestured for Gabe to take their coats and hang them on the pegs along the wall. "He's a twenty pounder this time."

Eva-Jo was busy at her desk in the corner of the living room. She loved coloring and coloring books. Walking over, Bay hugged her younger sister, who looked up and smiled.

"Look, Baylee, look! I drew this and colored it."
She proudly held it up to her. "Do you see what it is?"

Gabe came over and slid his arm around Bay's
shoulders. He saw Bay frown and put her finger to
her lips in thought. She looked beautiful, her hair soft
and recently washed, her cheeks flushed and blue eyes
shining. In the week she'd been home, he'd never been
happier. Nor had she.

"Ummm, is it a turtle, Eva-Jo?"

"Noooo, Baylee." She shook the paper at her. "Don't
you see it?"

Gabe saw nothing but colorful abstract lines on it.
What was Bay going to do? It looked like a dreaded
Rorschach test to him.

"Well, is it fish, bird or four-legged?" Bay looked
over at Gabe. He was smiling, and her heart swooned
over his rugged good looks. The past week had been a
special kind of hell on them, but they'd gotten through
it together. Like he said one night in bed after they'd
made love, no land mines so far.

"You don't know," Eva-Jo said with a pout.

"You're right, I don't," Bay admitted, kissing her
forehead. "But you look beautiful in your new red
dress. Mama did a nice job of putting those ribbons
on it." Ever since Halloween, Eva-Jo had fallen madly
in love with colorful ribbons of all kinds. Poppy had
sewn four half-inch grosgrain ribbons around the waist
in red, white, green and yellow, all favorite colors of
her sister's.

Eva-Jo smiled and touched them delicately with her
fingers. "Baylee, aren't I pretty with them?"

Bay leaned over and whispered, "You're the most beautiful girl here, Eva-Jo."

Gabe felt his heart open wider, if that was possible. He saw Bay's giving nature in the tender look she gave her sister. Eva-Jo was twenty-five, tall and had a woman's body. The red velvet dress Poppy had made for her was tasteful, an empire waistline, the material falling to her ankles. Gabe gave Poppy a lot of credit, having continued to raise her daughter. Because of challenges, Eva-Jo could never live on her own. Looking over at Bay, he saw the same compassion in her expression. That was why she was such a good combat medic. Her touch, her voice, could calm anyone wounded on the battlefield. Hell, she'd tamed him, and he wasn't exactly a softy, although she claimed he really was. Gabe couldn't buy that. He was a SEAL, after all.

"Time to eat," Poppy sang out.

Bay turned and hurried to help her mother with all the food that was to be brought from the kitchen into the dining room. Gabe opened the bottle of champagne. Eva-Jo took her latest artistic drawing and set it next to her plate at the table. Classical music played softly in the background. The fireplace crackled with roaring flames, a black grate around the outside of it. After the early evening dinner of goose, as a family, they would trim the Christmas tree that Gabe had chopped down two days ago with Bay's direction and help.

BAY SAT WITH Eva-Jo at the cleared table later, each of them cutting construction-paper circles, stars and trees. Eva-Jo was excited about putting all kinds of different

colors of glitter on them. Gabe helped her mother string
the lights on the tree first. The blue spruce was six feet
tall and looked stately and beautiful in the corner of
the living room. As Eva-Jo completed the glittering of
each decoration with gusto, Bay would punch a hole in
it and slide a bright, thin red ribbon through it. She'd
then tie a knot in it so it could be hung later. Her heart
felt close to bursting as she looked around the happy
room. Though she missed her pa terribly, Gabe's presence brought a man back into their family, giving it a
special energy that uplifted everyone.

When the tree was fully decorated, Bay stood back
and admired it with Gabe, proud of their handiwork.
Poppy had poured them a glass of red wine, giving
Eva-Jo a glass of apple cider. Gabe caught Bay's fingers and tugged on them, leading her over to the old
leather couch. Poppy flopped down on the chair next
to it, giving them a tired but happy smile. She picked
up her glass of wine and said, "Cheers."

Bay smiled softly, lifting her glass. She knew Gabe
preferred beer over wine, but he had the good grace
to take a glass anyway. He was that kind of man. She
slid her hand across his broad shoulders, content to
curl her feet beneath her and lean into the shelter of
his body. He was solid, strong and warm. And his
laughter over a joke Poppy told made her heart swell
fiercely with love for him.

"THAT WAS SO wonderful tonight." Bay sighed, snug-
gling up against Gabe's naked body. She decided the
only way to desensitize herself, to work through her

rape, was to not run from it. Thank God she had the memories of their loving one another before it had happened. That was her compass. Gabe's arm moved around her shoulder and drew her up against the hard length of his body.

"It was good." For the first time in his life, Gabe felt genuinely wanted within a family. Her family.

"I'm just sorry your mom couldn't make it down," Bay said, placing a small kiss on his warm flesh. Inhaling his scent, she felt her entire body respond to him.

"Grace said she'd fly down for Christmas," Gabe promised, closing his eyes, feeling a contentment he hadn't felt in a long time. That sense only happened when Bay was at his side. Love was a powerful drug; and she was the only woman he ever wanted to be addicted to for the rest of his life.

Sighing softly, Bay moved her fingertips through his dark chest hair, allowing it to curl around them. "I love you."

The words touched him as nothing else ever would. Turning on his side, Gabe stared into her half-closed eyes, her lips soft, her expression one of pleasant tiredness. Caressing her cheek, he leaned over and slid his mouth across hers. A soft moan filled her throat, and she moved her hips against his, feeling his erection. Since coming home, he'd not tried to enter her. She knew why. Gabe was afraid of hurting her. Bay felt frustration thrum through her, wanting him. She could feel Gabe place tight control over himself as he caught her hand as she slid it up across his hip to touch him. Breaking the kiss, she whispered, "I'm not afraid, Gabe."

He brought her hand to his chest, his eyes intense and narrowed. "You've never been afraid, baby. But I am." Gabe placed his hand over hers. "Maybe I need some time to adjust?"

"Love will never hurt me," Bay said softly, searching his dark eyes. "My mind and heart know the difference, Gabe." He needed to trust her, perhaps? She said nothing more, respecting his need to move deliberately. After all, he was a sniper, and by personality, he was a man of infinite patience, waiting for however long it took to meet his objective.

His mouth quirked. "Neither of us knows that yet, Bay. We're not alike in some ways. You jump into the fire, and I sit and look at it and figure out how to jump into it without getting burned."

Resting her brow against his, Bay said, "I think we're doing okay?" He'd easily brought her to orgasm with his hands and his mouth. There was such trust between them, a clear path in that minefield he referred to. And she'd been able to satisfy him the same way, but now, she wanted him in her, like it should be. There was a keening ache deep within her that craved being one with Gabe. Bay luxuriated in the memories, all incredibly sweet and hot. Fused with one another, the fierce love lingering between them made her want to re-create that once more. She saw the hesitation and uncertainty in his eyes.

"I talked to my therapist about us the last session," she murmured.

"Oh?" The word came out flat, his expression suddenly wary.

"I told her, so far, so good."

He grunted, lying on his back, throwing his arm across his eyes.

Well, she got his body language. Shaking her head, Bay propped herself up on her elbow, running her fingers across his powerful chest. "She asked me where I was sensitive in my body."

"Hell, I could have told you that. For free…"

Holding back her laughter, Bay absorbed his growl of frustration. When Gabe didn't like someone, he didn't bother to withhold his feelings. "Look at me."

Grudgingly, Gabe pulled his arm away from his eyes and stared up at her. He saw humor and warmth in Bay's gaze, her mouth sweetly innocent. "What?"

"You're such a badass, Griffin, when you want to be."

He snorted. "I'm a SEAL. What did you expect? Mr. Nice?"

The corners of his mouth twitched, laughter softening the hard glint in his eyes. "You're my badass. You will always be." Bay gave him a quick, hot kiss. "And you need to not turn off just because I want to tell you something my therapist shared with me."

His mouth thinned. "Okay, what did she say?"

Feeling his ire, Bay waited him out until he lost the chip on his shoulder. "In the last session she asked me where I didn't want to be touched." She motioned to her neck. "I told her here. I can't even stand anything tight around my neck anymore. Mock turtlenecks are all I can handle in the clothing department."

Gabe lost his humor. He vividly remembered those deep, purple bruises around Bay's throat, the damage done to her larynx that had finally healed up. "Where are we going with this, baby?" He really didn't want to drag up her beating tonight. It made him angry and wanting to kill Khogani all over again for what she'd endured.

"Patience, okay?"

"You pout beautifully, you know that?" Gabe looked at her full lower lip, wanting to kiss her, but he knew she wanted to talk.

"Don't get off the topic, Griffin."

"Guilty, but I can't help it if you're a red-hot babe and all I think about is hauling you into my arms."

She laughed softly. "Thank you, but can we revolve back around to our earlier discussion?"

Gabe placed his hand beneath his head, watching the shadows play softly across her face. "What else did she say?" His heart pounded with love for Bay. She was beguiling, teasing and so damned idealistic and honest.

"Well, I'd think you'd be a little more enthusiastic about what she said."

One eyebrow rose. "Go on, you have my full, undivided attention."

She grinned. "You're infuriating at times."

"And you love me anyway, don't you, baby?"

Sighing, Bay whispered, "Yes, with my life."

Holding her glistening gaze, Gabe sobered and

reached out and caressed her cheek. "I'm really listening."

Bay curled herself against his left side, resting her head on his chest, his heart beneath her ear. He shifted, his arms going around her, gently stroking her shoulder. The tingles felt warm and comforting to her. "She thought we should continue to explore one another when it felt right. I told her I was ready for intercourse. I'm healed up, and I'm fine."

"And so she gave you permission to do so?"

She laughed against his hairy chest. "God, Griffin, sarcasm drips from your lips."

He sighed in frustration. "I don't need that therapist to tell me anything about you and me, baby."

"I understand why you don't like her, but she's really nice, Gabe. She learned a lesson out of this, and she's trying to change, also."

"I'm happy for her."

Rolling her eyes, Bay pressed a kiss to his chest. "I learned my lesson, too. I've learned to listen to you first, not her."

"Now we're getting somewhere," Gabe growled darkly, moving his fingers through her silky hair, pulling some tendrils away from her cheek so he could absorb her beautiful, peaceful-looking features.

Bay said, "She suggested I listen to you, to go at the pace that's comfortable for you. She felt you had a better pulse on our situation than she did." Bay lifted her head, smiling into his glinting eyes. "Now, do you like her a little bit more?"

Gabe smiled and lightly touched her nose. "Finally, she's getting some sense. I should send her *my* bill."

Pouting, Bay murmured in exasperation, "You're such a pain, Griffin."

He slipped his arm around her hip and back, drawing her tightly against him. "You're going to be marrying a SEAL, baby. We're all badasses."

CHAPTER TWENTY-FIVE

BAY'S LAUGHTER MADE Gabe love her even more fiercely, if that was possible. They'd just finished a snowball fight in the yard after going and feeding Poppy's milk cow and chickens in the barn. The late morning December sky was a turbulent gray, and snowflakes twirled lazily across the mountain, the silence deep and muffled.

Gabe grabbed Bay as she tried to run from him after plastering him with a direct hit to his chest. Her shriek of delight echoed around the barnyard as she slipped in the two feet of snow.

The dancing light in her eyes grew as Gabe caught her. He pulled her to him as they fell. He protected her by taking the brunt of the fall. Her hair was damp on the ends, soaking up the snow melt as she flopped down upon him, and they hit the white stuff. Bay laughed, her breath coming out in white jets because it was below freezing.

"I surrender, I surrender," Bay pleaded, holding up her hand as he settled her across his body.

Gabe absorbed her joy, her cheeks flushed a deep pink, the tip of her nose red, her laughter sweet honey pouring through his heart. She wore a dark blue jacket, red yarn muffler her mother had knitted for her, red mittens and red cap.

Gabe relaxed into the snow, absorbing Bay's tall, firm body against his. He smiled up at her, amazed at what two weeks had done for her. Bay was relaxing more every day, more like her old self. It was only two more weeks until Christmas and he knew Bay loved this holiday more than any other. She had worked daily with her mother and sister, decorating, baking cookies, singing carols at the top of their lungs, and they had made Gabe feel a part of this spontaneous, happy family.

Gabe rolled Bay on to her side, her face close to his, her breath uneven, the corners of her mouth pulled into a devilish grin. "I accept your surrender," he growled, leaning down, capturing her mouth beneath his.

Bay sighed and drowned as his lips took hers, his arms hauling her tightly against him. There were too many winter clothes between them. She broke their kiss, laughing and tugging at his jacket. "Come on, let's finish this inside?"

He lost some of his happiness, knowing what was coming. Bay wanted *him*. She'd been stalking him, teasing him and trying to get him to stop worrying about what might happen. There were times when he'd have a flashback of sitting on the deck of the medevac, Bay lying unconscious on the litter, the medics working frantically over her broken, bloody body. *That* was what stopped him. Gabe couldn't get it out of his mind as he stared uncomprehendingly at the dark red blood staining her trousers between her thighs. Yes, he was scared. For Bay. For them. What if things went wrong?

When Gabe held her sapphire gaze, he melted. How could he keep saying no to Bay? His body wanted her. His heart pined for her. Hell, he'd never been in such agony for so damn long without a release. It wasn't Bay's fault, and Gabe kept his needs to himself, not wanting her to feel guilty because he knew she would. *Damn the rape. Damn that son of a bitch, Khogani.* He had dreams of finding the bastard and killing him slowly, making him suffer like Bay had suffered. He'd always jerked awake after one of those revenge dreams, rage tunneling through him, his fist clenched, drenched in sweat.

Only Bay sleeping at his side, her breath even and shallow, would bring Gabe down from that visceral dream. She reminded him of the kindness and sweetness of life. All Gabe knew was killing, and he was very good at it. He was dark. Bay was light. And, hell, he wanted to remove the darkness Khogani had imprisoned her within more than anything else in his life.

"Okay," he murmured.

"Really?" Bay breathed, not quite believing him.

Easing her off him, he got to his feet and held out his hand to her. "Really. Come on." Gabe gripped her damp, mittened hand. He couldn't stand in her way any longer. Bay felt she was ready. He'd never be ready, but this wasn't about him. Gabe loved her, and he wanted to make her happy. The dazzling smile Bay gave him burned through him like sunlight touching those dark, wounded places inside himself.

"Oh!" she cried, throwing her arms around his shoulders. "Thank you!"

Gabe grinned, tugging her beneath his arm, hauling her close as they walked like two awkward penguins through the knee-deep snow. "I can never tell you no," he growled, catching her radiant gaze. *God, her mouth.* Gabe could stare at it forever. He knew her lips, hungered for them against his and wanted to feel Bay breathe her life into him.

She infused his shadowed soul with shining light, lifting him, making him feel good about himself and her. Gabe looked forward to the dreams they'd talk about every night before they went to sleep. Bay was a veritable idea person with so many visions, desires, and he absorbed her excitement and idealism like a greedy, undeserving thief. She was a catalyst, a person who changed lives. And she was changing his, for the better.

"Hurry!" Bay called, shimmying out of her heavy parka, hat, mittens and muffler. She threw them on the couch, laughing as she hopped around on one foot to quickly get out of the first boot and then the other one.

Gabe sat on the sofa, ruefully shaking his head. She had the capacity to be pure child, and God help him, he loved Bay for it. He was always the adult. Gabe didn't know how to be like her, throwing caution to the wind, being spontaneous and living fully in the moment. Judging from how swiftly Bay was pulling her red long-sleeved flannel shirt off and then wriggling out of her damp, wet jeans, she was on a mission.

He'd barely gotten out of his boots and jacket before she was slimmed down to a pink camisole and feminine-looking pink silk boxer shorts. Instantly, as he stood, Gabe felt himself turn hard with longing. She was continuing to gain back so much of her lost weight, her slender legs tempting him.

"Last person to the bedroom is a rotten egg," Bay called, running down the hall.

Shaking his head, Gabe grinned and pulled off his green flannel shirt and dropped it on the couch. "No fair," he shouted. Her laughter pealed out of their bedroom. Gabe removed his jeans and dropped them on the couch beside his shirt. Wanting to love her so badly warred with his carefully closeted terror that something could go wrong. Dragging in a deep breath, he padded nearly naked down the hall, turning into their bedroom.

Bay smiled as he entered. Gabe had stripped down to his boxer shorts, a magnificent specimen of a man. She knelt on the bed, giving him a sultry smile. "You are so good-looking, it's a sin," she teased, rising up into his arms as he settled down on the bed beside her. Sliding her hands around Gabe's powerful shoulders, she luxuriated in the feel of his chest hair against her sensitive breasts beneath the camisole.

"You're such a wench," he rasped, smiling down into her glistening eyes, feeling his heart burst open.

"But," Bay whispered against his mouth, "I'm no tease…." She licked his lower lip, instantly feeling his arms tighten around her, drawing her hard against him as they fell onto the bed together. She laughed breathlessly as Gabe settled her next to him, his hand

sliding down her hip, following the long curve of her
thigh. Her flesh prickled with tiny flames. Every cell
in her body vibrated, wanting his hands moving lovingly across her body.

"No," Gabe rasped against her smiling mouth, "you
always deliver, baby."

A burst of bubbling laughter rose in her throat as his
mouth skimmed her cheek and nose, his hand moving
teasingly across the silk, following the curve of her
breast. "Oh," Bay sighed beneath his mouth, "and so
do you…" She felt the power of Gabe's mouth beguiling her lips, drowning in his masculine tenderness that
made her go hot and achy with longing.

How could Gabe ever not love her the way she
wanted? He trailed his kisses across her shoulder,
avoiding her neck. As she turned into him, her breasts
pressing insistently against his chest, she felt assertive.
She wanted to make it clear she wanted him. Bay slid
her fingers into the waistband of his boxers, and he
growled in warning, capturing her hand. She pouted,
not wanting to be halted in her exploration of him.

Gabe gave her a feral look and then rose and threw
his leg over her midsection, sliding his hands up her
arms, pulling them up above her head.

Bay gave a startled cry. She froze, suddenly transported back to the cave, Khogani sitting on her midsection, his men grabbing her arms, pinning her down.

Gabe's heart wrenched, feeling her entire body
freeze beneath him. *Oh, hell!* Instantly, he got off her,
releasing her wrists.

"Baby?" Gabe hesitantly touched her shoulder, her

breath coming out in small cries and gasps. Her eyes tormented him. Bay wasn't seeing him. She was seeing the past, a glaze over them. Gently, he touched her pale cheek. "It's all right, Bay. It's all right. Come back, baby. Come back to me." Anxiety swept through him as she trembled violently, her body almost convulsing, caught in the past. Trapped. What should he do?

Gabe framed her face, pulling her gaze toward his, forcing her to try and see him. "Bay, it's Gabe. Listen to me," he pleaded, panic ripping through him. Bay heard Gabe's voice calling her. Calling her back. His low, thick voice sounded so far away. She felt Khogani straddle her, his weight heavy against her belly. He smelled sour, and it repulsed her, his black eyes digging into hers, his mouth drawing into what looked like the snarl of a wolf ready to bite her. And then, she felt his large, dirty hand slide up her chest, his strong fingers slowly sinking into the soft tissue of her throat. She was going to die!

Her breathing became explosive as she tried to escape, bucking against him, trying to throw him off her. The hands of the soldiers gripped her wrists, pain shooting up into her arms, holding her still so she couldn't fight back. Whimpering, Bay shut her eyes, not wanting to see it anymore. It was then she felt herself leaving her body. Black dots danced in back of her eyelids as she felt his hand tightening around her throat, shutting off her air.

Gabe's urgent voice shattered her terror. Slowly, Bay fought to listen to it and pull herself out of the clutches of the flashback that held her prisoner. She felt herself being lifted, tucked against Gabe's strong, warm body, felt his arms going around her, holding her, not hurting her. It took forever to escape the terror of her rape. The slow rocking motion soothed her fractious, anxious state.

Bay was hyperventilating, gasping for breath, her hands pressed frantically against her aching throat. And then, she heard Gabe's trembling, coaxing voice against her ear. She felt safe. The power of the flashback left her reeling. Slowly, Bay opened her eyes, finding herself lying across Gabe's lap, leaning against him, her head tucked beneath his chin. He was holding her, rocking her, whispering brokenly that she was safe, that she was with him, not back there.

Little by little, she warmed up. Though her mind was still caught up in the horror from her past, Bay forced herself to relax. Her throat felt tight, as if it had been gripped for real, but she knew it was her body's reaction, her memory of nearly being choked to death. "I—I'm okay, Gabe...." Her words came out raspy and strained.

He pressed his hand against her hair, gently letting her know he'd heard her hoarse words. "What do you need, baby?" he asked, his voice unsteady.

She sighed and nuzzled against his jaw. "You. Just you..."

It hasn't been enough. The words almost came out of his mouth, but Gabe remained silent. "Water, maybe?"

Bay slowly shook her head, sliding her one arm

around his torso. "No…not right now. I just need you…. Don't leave me…."

His mouth quirked, and he tipped his head back against the headboard. "You've got me. I'm going nowhere." And Gabe didn't care if he had to hold Bay the rest of the night and into eternity, he'd do it. He could feel how fragile she'd become. Grief welled up through him. "I'm sorry, baby. I'm sorry for doing this to you." His mouth thinned, and he held back his twisting, writhing emotions.

A sigh trembled from her lips. "You didn't do anything, Gabe. You didn't do this to me." Bay ached for him, hearing the strain in his low, tortured voice. "This wasn't your fault. It's mine."

"No way," Gabe said, anger flaring in his tone. He held her a little tighter, agony scoring his heart. "This wasn't your fault. None of it was."

Bay's therapist had warned her flashbacks could hit her out of the blue. She had no idea how powerful they could be. And here she was, worried about Gabe, how much she obviously hurt him. Bay felt his tension, heard it in his tight, controlled voice. Lifting her head, she pulled away just enough to stare into his dark, anguished-looking eyes. Lifting her hand, she tenderly touched his cheek. It was damp with spent tears.

"I'm so sorry," Bay whispered unsteadily, tears crowding into her eyes. She knew how much Gabe hated tears. "So sorry…" Bay struggled to smile, to try and show him she was going to be all right. How badly Bay wanted to hold Gabe, to comfort him instead. He had no one to hold him on a bad day. His look scored her as nothing else ever would. It was a resigned expression, and Gabe realized he couldn't fix what was broken within her.

"Listen to me, Bay." Gabe caressed her hair and then cupped her chin, forcing her to hold his gaze. "We're going to work through this together. You and I." His voice grew deep with conviction. "Rape will not define you, baby. And it's not going to define me, either. We love one another, and that's what's going to support us." He gave her a tender look, grazing her cheek.

"You're not going to apologize for anything. This was done to you, Bay. It was beyond your control. But now, you have the control back. We'll talk, we'll figure out what happened to trigger this flashback, and we'll create a work-around." His hand grew firm on her cheek as her warm tears slid silently beneath his fingers. "Does that sound like a plan to you?" Gabe asked, his voice choked with emotion.

Bay barely nodded, resting against his large, opened palm. The calluses told Bay of his hard work ethic, that Gabe was a consummate warrior who was used to fighting back and defending others. Whether he knew it or not, he was infusing her with hope, erasing the helplessness she felt during the flashback. Gabe was fighting for both of them. And right now, that's what she needed, a warrior at her side to help her through her toxic experience and not allow it to continue to stain her present or future life.

"It sounds like a plan," she whispered.

CHAPTER TWENTY-SIX

THEY SAT TOGETHER at the table the next morning, snow falling quietly outside the kitchen window. Gabe was at Bay's elbow, listening to her quiet, strained voice. She'd gotten up early, and he'd automatically snapped awake. After making them coffee, she'd slid her hand into his and led him to the table, telling him she had to talk with him in detail about the rape.

Gabe tried to keep his face without expression, holding her hesitant gaze, listening to her give details of the rape that made him want to vomit. Bay's face was tight with tension, her gaze sometimes veering away from his as she recounted her capture in the cave, shame in her voice.

Gabe held Bay's hand in his, feeling the cool dampness of her fingers. The flashback had shaken her to her soul. He could see it in the skittishness in her eyes. Her voice was hoarse and sometimes broke. He knew in his heart how terrifying this was for her to recount it to him. Her courage was blinding, and all Gabe could do was sit and listen, to be a witness. Interrupting Bay would have done her a disservice as the words tumbled out of her mouth.

Finally, Bay closed her eyes and hung her head.

Drawing in a broken breath, she forced herself to look up and lock on Gabe's dark eyes that held so many unspoken emotions in them. There was no judgment in them, and for that, she was relieved.

"That's all there is, Gabe." Bay sat up, rolling her shoulders beneath the blue silk robe, unconsciously wanting to get rid of the heaviness that invaded her being.

"Let's take a break," Gabe suggested, his voice gruff. He gave her a warm look. "Maybe a bath? I can draw one for you."

She seemed to perk up a little at the suggestion. Bay had said she felt dirty, that she couldn't get clean. That is what rape did to a woman, made her feel filthy inside, and there was no way to make the feeling go away.

"Yes, I'd like that." Bay drowned in his tender smile, his fingers wrapping more firmly around hers, squeezing them to reassure her.

Gabe stood up. "Come here, baby." He held his hands out toward her. His heart ached with love for her as Bay placed her cold hands within his. Gently pulling her up to her feet, he brought her against him. She was exhausted. Bay slid her arms around his waist, resting her head against his shoulder.

"You know, there's an old SEAL saying," Gabe rasped against her ear, kissing her hair. "You never surrender. It's not in SEAL DNA to do that. We don't defend. We take the fight to the enemy." He felt her relax in his arms, and he was grateful for her trust. "Baby, you're a SEAL by proxy. You have the heart and soul of one. You're not a quitter, you're a fighter. And I've watched you since coming home fight to get well." His voice lowered, and Gabe placed his finger beneath her chin, lifting her gaze to meet his. "You're so courageous, Bay. You're like a thoroughbred born to run. That's all you know how to do, and now, you're running toward the wound that was given to you, and you're doing everything in your power to heal from it."

Her mouth quirked. "Some days are sure better than others," she managed.

"SEALs have bad days, too. We always say the only easy day was yesterday." Gabe smiled tenderly at her, seeing hope flare in her eyes. *Hope*. He understood as never before what his job was in her ordeal. It was to pick her up when she fell down. Dust her off and surround her with his love so she could gather her internal resources once more and soldier on. Then, Bay could take her fight to the internal enemy who had wounded her.

Giving a jerky nod of her head, Bay whispered, "Thank you for being here for me. I—I just am not used to these flashbacks. This one had a life of its own with me, Gabe. It scared the hell out of me."

Kissing her brow, Gabe whispered, "You've been home for months and never had one, baby. That tells you something. You're strong and you're getting stronger. And the next time I make love with you, I'll know what not to do to trigger it again." Gabe cupped her face, looking deep into her shadowed eyes. "We'll learn together. You're a woman who loves so completely. You heal others with your smile, your touch and your voice. That's who you are, Bay, and who you'll always be. I fell in love with that woman. The rape changes nothing for how I feel about you. I think you need to hear that."

Her chest tightened. "Yes," she admitted, drowning in the brilliant green of his eyes. There was such depth and understanding in Gabe. Bay was never so grateful as now for his words, for his love he was giving to her. "I love you so much, Gabe, so much."

His mouth softened, his eyes grew lambent as he leaned down and caressed her lips, balm for her shaken spirit.

"Come on, let me draw that bath for you. A long, hot soak with jasmine bath bubbles will do you good."

GABE PULLED ON his coat, ignoring his gloves as he stepped out the kitchen door and into the cold and snow. Another six inches had fallen last night. His breath made jets of white vapor as he walked toward the barn to feed the cow and chickens. He stuffed his hands into the pockets of his leather bomber jacket to keep them warm as he bowed his head to avoid snow-flakes in his eyes. The world was quiet in the morning, the gray bare-branched trees standing around the property like silent guardians. There was an undeniable sense of safety to this place, Gabe admitted, opening the door and swinging it wide.

He was greeted by a moo of hello from Elizabeth, the family Holstein cow. The chickens clucked excitedly in a huge indoor cage filled with a dozen boxes for them to lay their eggs in. Gabe inhaled the sweet fragrance of the dried bales of alfalfa stacked at the other end. The barn felt nurturing, and he broke a flake of hay off from a bale and carried it over to Elizabeth, tossing it into her manger.

As he did his morning chores, Gabe felt a building nausea grow within him. He kept replaying Bay's words about her rape. He couldn't erase her pain-filled descriptions, and he found himself angry and wanting to scream. An utter sense of helplessness flooded Gabe. He hadn't been able to protect Bay, and she had paid the terrible price of war. It would have been easier being shot dead with a bullet than to have been raped and have it wound the person repeatedly with violent flashbacks afterward.

A rape survivor would relive that humiliation and torture over and over again, depending upon what triggered it in her. It was a special ongoing hell that Gabe just couldn't wrap his mind around.

After feeding the chickens, Gabe felt as if he was going to tear in two with rage and grief. Sitting down on a bale of hay, he bowed his head into his hands, trying to breathe and control his writhing emotions. Desperate, he willed everything into his kill box. None of it would go there.

Tears burned in his eyes. He tried to drag in a breath to stop them from forming. It was impossible. A fist of anguish so powerful shook his whole body. Gabe couldn't stop the grief from being released in sobs. The sounds coming out of him were like those from an animal that had been trapped and was now in howling agony. He didn't even recognize himself anymore, imprisoned by a backlog of months of suppressing his feelings. The barn absorbed his cries.

Later, silence settled around him. Gabe raised his head, his eyes red-rimmed, his cheeks wet with tears. Elizabeth was calmly chewing the hay, watching him with her big, kind brown eyes. The chickens were making contented clucking sounds, scratching in the dirt for the mash he'd scattered in their pen earlier. A sense of peace stole through Gabe as he rested his elbows on his opened thighs.

Oddly, he felt better. Maybe cleaned out would be a more suitable phrase. Slowly wiping his face that needed to be shaved, Gabe drew in a deep, shaky breath. Scrubbing his eyes free of the last of the tears, he looked out the window above Elizabeth's stall and saw that it had stopped snowing. He could hear the wind picking up a bit.

Glancing down at his Rolex, Gabe realized he'd been out here for nearly thirty minutes. Where had the time gone? Maybe Bay was right: grief had its own way with a person, that time didn't matter, but getting it out by crying was the only way to release it in order to start the healing process.

Standing, Gabe brushed off the seat of his pants and moved toward the door. A new, powerful determination flowed through him as he opened it and stepped outside. The world was white and clean around him. As Gabe gazed around, he thought of Bay in those terms. She was like a female white knight fighting for those who had so much less than she did. A courageous warrior.

Moving his fingers through the damp strands of his hair, he felt more centered. Hope filtered into his heart, dissolving the leftover remnants of his grief and rage. Every day, Gabe told himself, was a step in the right direction. Every day. And he'd be there to walk each one with Bay.

"Here, I want you to open this before we go over to open gifts with Poppy and my mom," Gabe coaxed.

Bay was sitting on the couch, listening to her beloved Christmas music, dressed in a soft emerald-green sweater and slacks. Her hair was long and thick, softly curled around her face. She smiled as he bent over the couch and handed her the small white box wrapped in a red ribbon.

"For me?" she asked, meeting his shadowed eyes. She shared a trembling smile of thank-you with him.

"Just for you."

"Come, sit." Bay patted the cushion next to her.

Gabe came around and sat about a foot away from her, watching her. "I wanted to give this to you in private, Bay." He motioned toward it. "I think you'll understand why once you open it." His heart beat a little harder as he saw the curiosity come to her clear blue eyes. It had taken Bay a week to recover from the flashback. Him, too, understanding if one partner was deeply affected, the other would be, as well. They were learning to live through the blows but not be destroyed by them.

She gently touched the bow with gold thread among

the red of the ribbon. "What is it?" she asked, giving him a teasing look.

"Something you lost, baby. But now, it's returning to you."

Intrigued, she slowly pulled at the ribbon, the bow falling aside. With her fingers, she pried the lid open. Her eyes widened. Bay gave a small cry, jerking her head up and staring openmouthed at Gabe. He had a serious expression on his face, eyes burning with warmth, the corners of his mouth moving upward.

"My engagement ring!" She took out the delicate gold ring with the four channel-cut blue sapphires in it. "Oh, Gabe…" The Taliban had taken the ring from her Kevlar vest. And the jaguar that he'd carved, the heart he'd carved for her their first Christmas together, had been lost, as well.

"It's something good from our past coming back to you, baby. I had a jeweler in San Diego remake it for you. Do you like it?"

Her mouth curved into a sweet smile filled with joy. His heart mushroomed, and he felt intense love for his brave woman warrior. Gabe wanted to haul her into his arms and love her until she melted in his embrace.

"Like it?" Bay held out the ring toward him. "I love it, Gabe. Will you put it on my finger?" She smiled into his eyes.

Picking up her long, slender hand, he eased the ring back on to her finger where it belonged. "There," Gabe murmured, meeting her luminous look. "Now you're a woman who's engaged to a badass SEAL." He grinned.

Bay threw her arms around Gabe, hugging him,

kissing his chin, nose, mouth and cheek, anything she could find on him to kiss. Bay felt him begin to laugh, his arms sliding around her. He lay down on the couch with her resting on top of him. She kissed him some more. Gabe tunneled his fingers through her silky hair, capturing her and bringing her down hotly against his mouth. She moaned, capitulating to his superior strength, content to simply be in his arms. "Thank you," she quavered against his mouth. "You inspire me..."

Gabe settled Bay across his lap, her arm going around his shoulders. "I'm inspired, too," he said, holding her left hand and watching the sapphires gleam in the light. "How about tomorrow?" He looked up at her. "Marry me tomorrow at the courthouse in Dunmore?"

Startled, Bay gasped. "Tomorrow?"

He shrugged. "Both mothers are here. They both wanted to be able to attend our wedding. Why not now?"

"You're serious, aren't you, Griffin?"

"Never more, baby."

Her heart tripled in time. "Yes, I'd love that, Gabe. There's no need to wait, and I know Grace and my mama really wanted us to get married at a time they could both be here."

He patted her hip. "Good, because it's time."

"I can wear my grandma's gown," she said, wistful. "And I'm sure Mama will call everyone on the mountain and invite them to come to our home for a party afterward."

Nodding, Gabe said, "Sounds like a plan to me."

"Are you really ready to do this?"

"Why wouldn't I be?"

Bay shrugged. "I don't know…it just seems out of the blue."

"SEALs always have a plan, baby. You should know that by now." Gabe smiled wickedly.

She dropped a kiss on his mouth. "We're going to give them the best Christmas present they've ever had. I can hardly wait!"

A GOOD KIND of tiredness lapped at Bay. She lay in bed with Gabe, her head nestled against his shoulder. Barely opening her eyes, she whispered, "This has been the best Christmas, ever."

Gabe kept his eyes closed, absorbing her warmth, her womanly curves against him. "Best one I've ever had, too, baby."

Nodding, Bay knew from stories of his youth, he'd had no Christmases to speak of with Grace a single working mother. She spread her fingers across his chest, through his silky hair, his powerful heart beating slowly beneath her palm. He was a hero in her eyes and heart.

Something primal moved through her. She wanted to love Gabe, give back to him. No matter how battered she had become emotionally, Bay was willing to risk everything to love this scarred warrior who continued to love her with a fierceness that took her breath away. She could give him her touch, her kisses, her breath and her love in adoration of his loyalty, his steadfastness and fearlessness in the face of the over-whelming odds they'd faced together.

He'd saved her life in so many ways. Now, she wanted to heal his wounded heart, draw the toxic memories of his terrible childhood out of him. She knew she could do it; her healer side was strong and never wavered because Bay knew love underwrote her desire. And nothing in this world or any other emotion would ever destroy her love for him.

"Bay—"

Gabe felt her move slowly on top of him, her breasts gliding against his chest, her hips molding to his. He was caught off guard. As Bay pressed her hips against him, he hardened almost instantly, feeling the soft-ness of her belly giving way to his erection. Leaning up, he caught her shoulders. Moonlight sifted though the curtains, catching a gleam in her drowsy eyes. "Shhh," she whispered against his mouth, sliding her tongue across his lower lip and then moving her lips against his. "Let me love you, Gabe. I ache so much to love you."

Her trembling words shattered him, wrested his control away from him. When she twisted her hips, teasing his thick flesh, he groaned, gripping her shoul-ders. He sucked air between his clenched teeth, feeling her mouth against his jaw and corded neck, licking, kissing and feathering her lips downward.

She rose, her breasts barely skimming his chest. This was the Bay from before, and he relished her strength and taking what she wanted from him. It was such a damned turn-on as her hands traveled down the sides of his chest, her lips moving here and there, touching and kissing each scar he'd gotten over the years of combat.

Struggling, his mind melting into primal heat, his body thinking for him, Gabe couldn't stop the sweet assault of her wet core sliding provocatively up and down his length. A groan ripped through him as she placed her hips so that he could easily enter her in one thrust. Fear raced up against the fire she'd created within him. Each stroke of her sleek, liquid core along his thickness made him shudder, wanting her so damn badly he couldn't think anymore, only feel and want.

"Yes," she whispered, her lips near his ear, "take me, Gabe. I'm ready. I'm yours…"

Ah, hell, he was lost.

Her throbbing core contracted as she glided along the smooth hard length of him. It felt so good to lavish herself against him. It was like coming home. She knew his body well and reveled in the strength of Gabe. When she opened her eyes, held his glittering gaze, she saw fear mingled with need of her.

Not tonight. She'd given a great deal of thought to what triggered her psyche and body, what it would tolerate and what it would not. By mounting him, she had absolute control over her body and his. Bay was risking everything, betting that this change of position would not trigger another flashback. Her heart filled with a fierce, undying love for this man who fearlessly held her challenging stare.

No, tonight belonged to them. Not to another time or place.

"Enter me," Bay pleaded, her voice husky as she moved against him, feeling his strength at the door of her aching core.

"Slowly," he gritted out. "Take me in slowly, baby…"

Oh, yes, she would, and she adjusted her hips just so, closed her eyes and felt him lift his hips just enough to move within her. The moment he did, she shuddered with pleasure, sitting up, her fingers moving restlessly across his chest. Tipping her head back as she felt his calloused hands grip her hips and hold her as he rocked into her, she cried out softly. But it wasn't a cry of pain, it was a cry of welcoming him home within her hungry, burning body. She felt Gabe tense as she drew him more deeply within her. No longer did she worry about a flashback; the feelings of heat, wetness and rippling pleasure outran the past. Closing her eyes, her lips parted, and a moan of appreciation slid up her throat.

It was so easy, Bay thought, surrendering to his maleness, to his guiding hands on her hips. She wanted more of Gabe. Much more. Leaning toward him, she shifted, pulling him deeper within her. Both of them froze for a moment, locked in burgeoning ecstasy as his length stroked the scorching pressure building rapidly within her. Gabe rocked her slowly, fanning the hungry fire burning so brightly within her. She heard his breath turn ragged like hers.

And then, Gabe began to move his hips, his fear dissolving. In its place, keen, edgy pleasure rippled around him. He felt himself melt in the heat and tightness of Bay surrounding him. Her fingers dug convulsively into his taut chest muscles as he ground deeply into her, hearing her moan with mounting need. He felt her body spasm, like a glove tightening almost painfully around him. When she cried out, the sensation sent him over the edge. Her spine curved, her head was thrown back, a cry of utter pleasure tore out of her mouth. Gabe continued to thrust deeply into her, feeling her orgasm convulsing and constricting around him again and again.

Gritting his teeth, he tried to hold off, tried to give Bay all the pleasure she could handle and then some. Finally, as he felt her begin to relax, Gabe thrust hard and allowed himself to spill into her cauldron depths, fire racing through his body, purging his thoughts, whipping him into a place where all he could see were stars exploding behind his tightly shut eyes. His world came apart, and he groaned, clenching her hips, lost in a world of heat and timelessness.

Bay whimpered with satisfaction and sank weakly against Gabe, her head coming to rest upon his damp shoulder. He trembled violently, his release powerful, the aftereffects still vibrating throughout his taut, spent body. All she could do was move against him, prolong his release, his hands across her hips, holding her against him. A tremulous smile touched Bay's mouth, lashes sweeping downward as the glowing, undulating effects of her orgasms still whispered throughout her sated body. She felt Gabe's hands release her, his fingers moving reverently up across her back, shoulders as he sank back against the bed, drained.

Moving her legs slowly so that they lay between his, Bay smiled distantly, lost in the lusty haze of his scent, his sweaty body, his puncturing breath against her neck and shoulder. This is what she'd waited for. This is what fulfilled her, made her feel whole, cherished and one with Gabe. Nothing else would ever do. Not ever, and Bay ranged her hand across his chest, to his jaw, cupping his stubbled cheek, looking sleepily into his half-closed eyes that burned with fierce love for her.

Wordlessly, she stretched those few inches, capturing his chiseled mouth, so strong and caring, beneath her wet, pouty lips. And then she gently moved her hips, feeling him tense, his groan rolling up through his chest, music to her ears and wildly pounding heart. Cherishing his mouth, feeling his surrender in every possible way to her, Bay understood her strength as a woman. It was matchless. And his male strength complemented her, supported her and had filled her. She smiled against his mouth, pressing a small kiss to each corner of it.

"We did it," she whispered against him. Bay sensed his very male smile beneath her lips. Gabe's hands ranged over her shoulders, cupping them as he opened his eyes, drinking in her wild, tousled beauty.

"We did," Gabe agreed, his voice barely above a growl. "You're one brave warrior woman. You know that?"

Bay held his gleaming eyes and saw her reflected in their depths. "A warrior like you deserves a woman of equal strength. Don't you think?"

As he trailed his fingers down her long, curved spine, her flesh damp and velvety feeling, a corner of his mouth hitched upward. Gabe was so damn weak, so sated and satisfied that he could barely think or move. "Baby, you're incredible. You take my body, you take my heart and I'm just clay in your beautiful, healing hands."

"Mmm," Bay murmured, her brow resting against his sandpapery jaw. "You took me to places I've never been before, Gabe. I'm floating. I'm happy…thank you…." She grazed his broad shoulder, feeling the muscles leap and respond beneath her lips.

"Merry Christmas," he rasped.

Bay closed her eyes, smiling with him. "You're the only gift I'll ever need, Gabe." And that was true.

CHAPTER TWENTY-SEVEN

Six months later

"CAN YOU FEEL them moving?" Bay asked softly, lying down on the couch, her feet propped up. She watched as Gabe knelt down beside her, gently placing his large hand across her swollen belly. His hard face melted as he felt the first baby kicking on the left side of her belly.

"Gotta be the boy," he murmured with a grin, catching her shining blue eyes.

"Very good," she praised, picking up his hand and sliding it to the right side. "Feel her?"

He nodded, completely mesmerized that two little souls were being carried in the belly of the woman he loved. It was a miracle. Gabe held her moist eyes. Six months pregnant with twins, as Bay had told him, had turned her into a total hormonal sop. He leaned over, brushing the tears from her cheeks. "Happy tears, baby?"

"Very happy." Bay sniffed, catching his hand, turning it over and placing a kiss in his calloused palm.

"You're feeling okay, though?" Gabe asked, unwinding from his crouched position and sitting on the end of the couch. He took off her tennis shoes, removed her socks and gently began to knead her foot he rested across his thigh.

Bay moaned and relaxed against the pillow. "That feels so wonderful, Gabe. You spoil me rotten." Her mouth tipped into a tender smile. "And yes, I'm fine, considering I feel like a two-ton elephant."

"Your ankles are swollen," he said, frowning. Dr. Sarah Johnson, Bay's baby doctor from Dunmore, had sat down with both of them many months ago to get their heads around having twins. Swollen ankles were always expected.

He looked up, seeing the pleasure spread across Bay's radiant face as he moved his fingers upward to include her slender ankles. She'd told him two months after they were married that she was pregnant. Both agreed it had happened Christmas night when they'd made love for the first time. The luminosity in Bay's face simply made her that much more beautiful in Gabe's eyes. A madonna.

"It's okay. Swollen ankles are normal," Bay said, enjoying his knowing fingers wreaking magic across her tired, aching feet. June was a month of weeding the garden that she and her mama had planted in May. Bay discovered getting down on her hands and knees between rows to weed was becoming an acrobatic act and feat in itself. Her once strong, lean body was now awkward, and her center of gravity had markedly shifted. Bay opened her eyes, watching Gabe concentrate on her other foot.

"Is Mike Tarik arriving today? Noon, right?" He

was Gabe's best friend who was a SEAL. In some ways, Bay guessed from what Gabe had shared with her, Mike was like the brother he never had while growing up. And she didn't know until recently, it had been Mike who had watched over her like a guard dog, relieving Gabe when she was unconscious at the Bagram hospital. She wanted to thank him in person for what he'd done for them.

Gabe glanced down at his Rolex. "Yeah, he should be arriving soon."

"I don't know. This is a hard place to find."

"He's a SEAL, baby. He'll find us, guaranteed." Gabe chuckled.

He talked at least once a week to Mike by cell phone. She was anxious to meet him because Gabe thought so highly of him. Bay moved her hand lovingly across her swollen belly.

"We need names for our babies, Gabe." They'd both avoided naming them at first, for fear if anything happened. Dr. Sarah had given her a clean bill of health, much to her relief.

Gabe's hands stilled over her feet.

Bay gave him a frustrated look. "No, really. We have to have names, Gabe. I'm six months along."

"I guess it's time?" He slid his hand across the curve of her soft sole and heard Bay groan with appreciation. "Do you have names?"

"I think I do, but I want your input."

Gabe moved his fingers, massaging the area between each of her small, perfect toes. Bay sighed, closed her eyes and said, "I was thinking about our boy." He looked up and studied Bay.

"Yes?"

"I was thinking, I want him to have my Pa's name, Floyd. I don't care if it's his middle name or first name."

Gabe knew how close she'd been to her father. He shrugged his shoulders. "That sounds fine to me."

"Usually, we try and name our children after a family member, Gabe. Is there someone in your family you'd like our son to carry his name?"

Gabe frowned and became pensive. "No, no one." Gabe didn't want the stain of his family on his children. Floyd Thorn had been a fine man, a good father to Bay and Eva-Jo, and a responsible husband to Poppy. He wanted his son to have good, strong, honorable men's names to carry. To aspire to becoming himself. He halted his massaging of her foot, his hands still. "Would you consider giving our son the first name of Michael?"

She heard his hesitancy, his expression unsure. Moistening her lips, she asked softly, "After Mike Tarik? Your SEAL brother?"

"Yes. I want our son to carry good men's names, Bay. I want to be able to tell my son about these men, how heroic they are or were, that they stood for honesty, courage and honor."

Hearing his deeply hidden emotions in his tone, she whispered, "Michael Floyd Griffin. Do you like the sound of it?" Gabe's face colored, and she saw him become suddenly emotional.

"Yes, I like the sound of it. Are you okay with it? You're the one who's going to be calling him Floyd when he's in trouble and Michael when he's our sweet little warrior angel."

Bay laughed and rolled her eyes. "I see you have this all figured out, Griffin."

Giving her a shrug, Gabe's mouth pulled into a teasing grin. "Hey, you'll be seeing a lot more of them than I will during the day."

Well, that was the truth. "You'll get your turn when you come home at night," she warned him with a chuckle. Gabe had opened up a small wood shop in Dunmore, creating beautiful carvings with those large hands of his. Already, his name was spreading in the arts and crafts community. Dunmore was a tourist town, one of the gateways into the Allegheny Mountains. He'd already sold four of his five sculptures. And they hadn't been cheaply priced, either. Gabe valued his work. They were both surprised but grateful for the inflow of money. The condo building he owned in Coronado was the mainstay of their income and allowed him to build his carving business.

"I'm looking forward to it, baby." And he was. Gabe wanted to be a loving father to his son and daughter. And he especially wanted to teach his son to respect women, not use or abuse them as his father had his mother Grace. Or himself. "Okay, one down, and one to go. Any thoughts on little girl names?" He saw her face brighten. Just as Gabe thought, Bay already had some names in mind.

"Well," Bay hedged, "I was thinking of Dawn Camille. My mother's middle name is Camille." Her voice grew emotional. "And my Grandma Dawn was so important to me, Gabe. We lost her a year after Pa died, and I felt so lost."

Nodding, Gabe gently slid his hand over her ankle and foot, leaning down and picking up the socks. "I like them. Those are beautiful names," he murmured, rolling the first sock over the toes of her right foot. Moving it around so it fit just right over her toes and heel, he picked up the other sock. "You think Poppy will like the names?"

Bay laughed softly. "Oh, I think she'll be over the moon about it. She'll probably cry buckets when we tell her our daughter's middle name will be Camille."

"Yeah, you women cry a lot," Gabe muttered, teasing her as he pulled on the other sock. Patting her foot gently, he leaned down and slipped the sneakers back on each of her feet.

"Crying is always a good thing, Griffin, so just don't go there. Okay?" Bay wagged her finger at him.

His smile increased, and he winked at her. "Your eyes are like sparkling sapphires when you cry."

Touched, Bay shook her head. "You're turning into a poet, Gabe."

There was a knock at the screen door in the kitchen.

Gabe looked up, seeing his SEAL friend standing there. "Mike's here," he murmured. He got up, gave Bay a swift kiss on the lips and said, "Stay where you are. You need your rest. I'll bring Mike in, introduce him and then we'll grab a couple of beers and go out on the front porch and talk."

"Okay," she whispered, seeing the eagerness in Gabe's face. Bay had to meet Mike Tarik. Gabe had told her his father was a world-class heart surgeon from Saudi Arabia. His mother was American. It would give her another answer to the puzzle about her husband. She knew he'd suffered badly as a child, and she was curious what kind of man Gabe considered the brother he'd always wanted but never had.

"Hey, man!" Mike called, breaking out into a huge grin of hello as Gabe opened the door to let him in. "Long time, bro," he said, giving him a big hug and several hearty slaps on the back.

"Great to see you, too," Gabe said, gesturing for him to come in. Like most SEALs, Mike appeared to be someone who blended in, and didn't stand out. He wore a tan T-shirt across his heavily developed chest and broad set of shoulders, and a pair of Levi's and Nike sneakers. Mike took off his black baseball cap as he entered the cabin.

"Any problems finding us?" Gabe asked drily, leading him over to the couch to introduce him to Bay.

Snorting, Mike growled, "Ah, come on, bro. That's a low blow. Of course not."

Chuckling indulgently, Gabe led him to the end of the couch so he could see Bay. "Just jerking your chain. Mike, I want you to meet my wife, Bay. And as you can see, she's carrying two." He smiled warmly down at her.

Mike immediately lost his smile and became formal. "Nice to meet you, ma'am. I'm Mike Tarik. I want to thank you for allowing me to come for a visit."

Bay smiled, always touched by SEAL behavior with civilians. They were always the height of respect, always saying yes, sir, no, sir and ma'am. "Hi, Mike, it's lovely to meet you. Gabe always talks about you."

Mike rolled his eyes and glanced over at Gabe. He was two inches taller and weighed about twenty pounds more than his friend. "I'll bet you did," he murmured accusingly at Gabe.

Mike's cheeks turned a dull red, his eyes looking at the black baseball cap he held between his large hands. "Thank you, Mike," she said, her voice soft. "I didn't know all you'd done for Gabe and me. I was out like a light at Bagram hospital."

Tarik shrugged shyly, meeting he gaze. "It wasn't anything, ma'am. SEALs stick together. Our women are always taken care of by one of us if they need help."

Warmth pooled in Bay's heart. Mike was excruciatingly shy, his gold-brown eyes so serious-looking as he meant every word he spoke. She especially liked the warmth in his eyes and that chiseled smile of his. He was clearly an extrovert while Gabe was an introvert. Mike was just what her husband needed.

"Well, I just want you to know, I'm grateful for you being there, Mike. Gabe needed your presence. We'll never forget what you did for us."

Mike made an embarrassed sound in his throat. "It wasn't anything, ma'am. SEALs care for their own. It's just a given."

Bay smiled gently. Mike stood in a military "at ease" position, his hands clasping the cap in front of his body. He was darkly tanned, short black hair, straight black brows across what she would term "doe eyes." The man had the most gorgeous eyes, a cinnamon-brown color with gold sparkling in their depths, that she'd ever seen. He had a square face, high cheekbones and seemed almost to look as if he were from a foreign country. Indeed, he was half Saudi. His father had met his American wife in Riyadh at the hospital because she was a nurse. He'd married her, and Mike was the result. He had dual citizenship with both countries. Bay was sure Mike could easily pass undercover as a Middle East operative.

Gabe had said Mike had often gone undercover in Afghanistan, working his way into the Taliban groups. He spoke Pashto, Arabic, French and English. Mike was responsible for destroying many major Taliban operations before they could be launched against Americans. He was a real hero.

"Relax," Bay urged, "you're with friends. And just call me Bay, all right?"

"Er…yes, ma'… I mean, Mrs. Griffin."

Bay smiled to herself. Mike was so solemn and respectful toward her. She noticed he kept looking at her swollen belly. "Three more months, Mike," she said, catching his startled gaze and gently patting her twins.

"Ma'am? I mean, shoot, pardon me, Mrs. Griffin. You said three months?"

She watched his cheeks grow a ruddy color again. Bay had found out even SEALs blushed every once in a while, and it was an endearing discovery to her. Gabe was grinning and enjoyed watching Mike twist in the wind. SEALs had playful but downright rough-and-tumble relationships with one another. Her husband was positively enjoying Mike's floundering discomfort. Feeling sorry for the SEAL, she said, "Please, Gabe, can you get Mike a beer? Maybe you two would like to chat out on the front porch?"

Utter relief came to Mike's face. He flashed her a big smile. "A beer sounds real good, Mrs. Griffin. Thanks."

Gabe shook his head and growled, "Come on, before you get into more trouble. You got a real case of foot-in-mouth disease today, Tarik."

Bay put her hand over her mouth to stop from laughing. She didn't want to embarrass the SEAL any more than he was already.

Bay was fixing dinner for the three of them much later when the two SEALs ambled inside at dusk. The warm June weather made it perfect to open the screened-in windows within the cabin, the sweet smell of roses in bloom wafting through the home. Both men went to the bathroom to wash up. All afternoon as Bay rested and then got up later to work on dinner, she'd heard the two men talking nonstop, laughing and unmercifully teasing one another. She couldn't hear what they said, but they were happy, and that made her smile. She knew Gabe missed being a SEAL. His enlistment had expired and so had hers. They were now officially civilians. But nothing would ever take the SEAL out of Gabe. Not ever.

"Man, that smells good!" Mike murmured, coming over to the counter where Bay was taking a leg of lamb out of the pan. "Home cooking is the best."

She grinned. "And I'm a good cook," Bay assured him, transferring the dripping roast to a huge orange platter.

"Here," Gabe murmured, "let me help you."

"Okay," Bay said, glad for his offer.

"What can I do, Mrs. Griffin?"

"Call me Bay." She smiled up at Mike. "Mrs. Griffin is Gabe's mother, Grace."

"Yes ma'— Bay?"

She pointed to the silverware drawer to his left. "Mike? Get knives, forks and spoons out of that drawer and put them with the plates I just placed on the table?"

Mike set to work with intense focus. Bay smiled and turned away. He was probably a sniper. She'd ask Gabe later, but she knew she was right by his sudden focused intensity.

After dinner and dessert, Gabe poured everyone coffee. Mike cleared the table, carefully rinsed off every utensil and plate and dutifully placed them into the dishwasher. Bay felt like a queen with two terribly good-looking male servants who fulfilled her every wish.

When they returned to the table, Gabe put his hand on Mike's broad shoulder. "You okay with us naming our son after you?"

Mike's face went blank. And then realization hit him. And then the shock set in. His mouth dropped open as he understood the gravity of the request. "Are you serious?" he demanded, looking first at Gabe and then over at Bay.

Gabe nodded. He lost his teasing demeanor and

said, "We've been close since we went through BUD/S class together. You're like the brother I never had, Mike." He shared a look with Bay, whose eyes grew soft. "I want our son to know he was named after one of the finest SEALs I've ever known. I want to tell him about the man he was named after. It will give our son something to live up to, to strive to become." Gabe grinned. "And don't worry, I'll only tell our son the good stuff about you."

Mike chuckled. "Good thing." And then he grew serious and gazed at Bay. He wanted her input. "Are you okay with this, Bay?"

"We'd love to have your blessing, Mike," she said.

He rubbed his furrowed brow. "This is a helluva… er…I mean, a heck of a compliment," he muttered.

"Do you have any brothers or sisters?" Bay wondered.

"No, I don't. I'm an only child." And then Mike grinned suddenly and hooked his thumb toward Gabe. "Like this badass." And then he gulped. "I'm sorry, ma'am. I didn't mean—"

Bay chuckled. "Mike, I was in the service, too. It's okay. I know you SEALs speak your own language. I'm fine with it." She reached out and patted his hand.

"Well?" Gabe demanded, not giving Mike any quarter. "You okay with this?"

Mike shook his head in utter disbelief over the honor. "Man, I did not expect this, bro. I really didn't." He looked toward Bay's belly. "Yes, I'd be very honored for your son have my name. Thank you."

Gabe lay on his back, Bay cuddled next to him as much as her belly would allow. He could feel one of the babies kicking against his ribs. "They're active tonight," he muttered with a smile, moving his fingers lightly across her shoulder.

Bay groaned. "Tell me about it. And it's your son, Michael Floyd, who's kicking the livin' daylight out of me. I wish he'd go to sleep so I could."

Gabe knew better than to chuckle. "Want to lie on your back? A pillow under your knees?" Bay was getting very uncomfortable carrying twins, and he knew she was losing a lot of sleep she really needed.

Sighing, Bay said, "That would be so nice, yes. Thank you…"

Gabe retrieved the extra pillows and eased them beneath her knees. He could see her face lose some of its strain. "Better?"

"Oh, much."

Gabe sat down and faced her, gently moving his hand across her belly. "Maybe my son needs my touch?"

His hand was so large, his fingers long and square. Gabe touched her so gently, as if afraid to hurt her. "You go ahead and try. Anything to settle that rambunctious son of yours down. Dawn is already asleep over here." She pointed to the other side of her belly. "Smart girl."

"I was a hellion when I was young, too," Gabe admitted, easing his hand slowly around the swollen curve of her belly beneath the nightgown.

"What, ADD? ADHD?" she groaned.

"No, just a real action-oriented kid." He met her half-closed eyes. "Guess that's why I joined the SEALs. I like all the physical challenges, the competition and being on the move all the time."

"Great." Bay sighed. "I think your son is getting a head start. He's probably going to be born equipped with a pair of Nikes on his feet."

Gabe chuckled. "When my mother was carrying me, she told me a few years ago that I was kicking her until she was black and blue."

Rubbing her face, Bay griped, "Griffin, I swear, this is all your fault!" Her mouth twisted in frustration. "And now I got a baby SEAL on my hands? And I have three months more of this to go?"

Gabe leaned down, pressing a soft kiss to her belly. "Hey, he's settling down. Feel it?"

Bay waited a moment. Sure enough, Michael Floyd wasn't kicking anymore. She snorted. "I'll bet Michael recognizes you're his daddy. And he likes your touch. That's why he's settling down now, thank God."

Chuckling, Gabe moved up to where Bay was lying and placed one hand beneath her shoulders. He saw the translucence of her radiant skin in the pale wash of moonlight. Soft, mussed curls framed her face. Leaning down, he placed a tender kiss across her mouth. "You just call me when Michael Floyd is misbehaving. I'll come and rock him to sleep. Fair enough?" Gabe eased back, smiling down at her.

Lifting her hand, Bay stroked his cheek. "You're such a softy, Griffin. Thank you, and you can bet I'll be calling you often. I really need my sleep."

"Sweet baby, I'll be here every step of the way," he promised, kissing her, lingering across her wet, smiling lips. Bay caught his hand and pressed a kiss to it.

"I love you, Gabe. We've come so far...so far..."

He lost his smile, moving some curls away from her cheek. "We've come that distance together, baby. You never surrendered."

And she hadn't. The trauma was still there, but it usually remained in the background, no longer center stage and trying to control her life as it had earlier. The pregnancy had been healing for her, Gabe realized. Bay was going to have the twins delivered at home with Poppy as her midwife and Dr. Sarah accompanying her. Bay had been born in the other cabin, and she wanted her children born there, too. Gabe agreed, understanding how the deep roots of her Hill family had been a quiet strength to Bay throughout her trauma.

"Mmm," Bay whispered, closing her eyes. "Can you lie up against me? That would feel good, and then I can go to sleep."

Gabe saw the need in her dark, glistening eyes. Standing, he brought the sheet over her so she wouldn't have to sit up and do it herself. Easing down beside her, Gabe watched Bay relax. A faint smile crossed her soft lips.

He slid his arm beneath her slender neck and moved against her warm body. Closing his eyes, Gabe inhaled the jasmine scent of her hair that tickled his nose and brow.

For the past five months, Bay no longer had weekly nightmares, maybe one a month instead. And no more

flashbacks, for which they were both infinitely grateful. Her focus was on the babies she carried within her
body and on him. Bay had regained all her lost weight,
and he rarely saw the haunted look in her eyes anymore. She was still actively working out the trauma,
but life had been good to them, and she was like a
blossoming flower, unfolding to the sweetness of the
happiness that surrounded them.

Squeezing her fingers gently, Gabe felt intense love
flowing through his heart for her alone. Baylee-Ann
Thorn had proven to be a radiant light in the darkness of his wounded heart. She'd healed him with her
love. And Gabe silently promised her he would spend
the rest of his life returning that love to her and their
children. Forever.

* * * * *

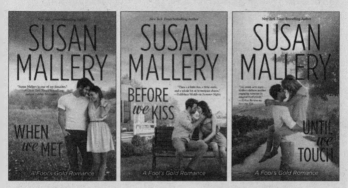

New York Times bestselling author
RaeAnne Thayne

Lucy Drake and Brendan Caine have only one thing in common...

And it's likely to tear them apart. Because it was Brendan's late wife, Jessie—and Lucy's best friend—who'd brought them together in the first place. And since Jessie's passing, Brendan's been distracted by his two little ones…and the memory of an explosive kiss with Lucy years before his marriage. Still, he'll steer clear of her. She's always been trouble with a capital *T*.

Lucy couldn't wait to shed her small-town roots for the big city. But now that she's back in Hope's Crossing to take care of the Queen Anne home her late aunt has left her, she figures seeing Brendan Caine again is no big deal. After all, she'd managed to resist the handsome fire chief once before, but clearly the embers of their attraction are still smoldering….

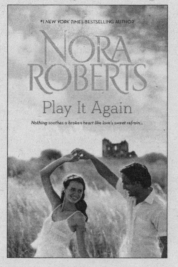

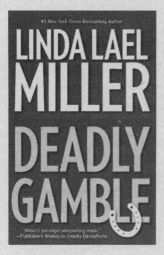

LINDSAY McKENNA

77867 BREAKING POINT	___ $7.99 U.S.	___ $8.99 CAN.
77851 HIGH COUNTRY REBEL	___ $7.99 U.S.	___ $8.99 CAN.
77821 DOWN RANGE	___ $7.99 U.S.	___ $8.99 CAN.
77772 THE LONER	___ $7.99 U.S.	___ $9.99 CAN.
77710 THE DEFENDER	___ $7.99 U.S.	___ $9.99 CAN.
77689 THE WRANGLER	___ $7.99 U.S.	___ $9.99 CAN.
77616 THE LAST COWBOY	___ $7.99 U.S.	___ $9.99 CAN.

(limited quantities available)

TOTAL AMOUNT	$ _____
POSTAGE & HANDLING	$ _____
($1.00 FOR 1 BOOK, 50¢ for each additional)	
APPLICABLE TAXES*	$ _____
TOTAL PAYABLE	$ _____

(check or money order—please do not send cash)

To order, complete this form and send it, along with a check or money order for the total above, payable to Harlequin HQN, to: **In the U.S.:** 3010 Walden Avenue, P.O. Box 9077, Buffalo, NY 14269-9077; **In Canada:** P.O. Box 636, Fort Erie, Ontario, L2A 5X3.

Name: _____
Address: _____ City: _____
State/Prov.: _____ Zip/Postal Code: _____
Account Number (if applicable): _____

075 CSAS

*New York residents remit applicable sales taxes.
*Canadian residents remit applicable GST and provincial taxes.

HARLEQUIN® HQN™
www.Harlequin.com

PHLM0714BL